FORCE

BRUTE
FORCE

MARC
CAMERON

PINNACLE BOOKS
Kensington Publishing Corp.
www.kensingtonbooks.com

PINNACLE BOOKS are published by

Kensington Publishing Corp.
119 West 40th Street
New York, NY 10018

All Kensington titles, imprints, and distributed lines are available at special quantity discounts for bulk purchases for sales promotions, premiums, fund-raising, educational, or institutional use. Special book excerpts or customized printings can also be created to fit specific needs. For details, write or phone the office of the Kensington special sales manager: Kensington Publishing Corp., 119 West 40th Street, New York, NY 10018, attn: Special Sales Department; phone 1-800-221-2647.

ISBN-13: 978-0-7860-3529-8
ISBN-10: 0-7860-3529-3

First printing: January 2016

10 9 8 7 6 5 4 3 2 1

Printed in the United States of America

First electronic edition: January 2016

ISBN-13: 978-0-7860-3530-4
ISBN-10: 0-7860-3530-7

For Al,

whose stories are some
of my earliest memories

Asia is not going to be civilized after the methods of the West. There is too much Asia and she is too old.

—RUDYARD KIPLING

Prologue

China, Pinggu District
88 kilometers east of central Beijing

The cloying odor of too much makeup and not enough soap rose from the two ragged prostitutes outside the fence, assaulting the first peach-blossom breezes of spring. Two rows of chain link, the inner one alive with high-voltage current, did nothing to stop the smell from drifting into the guard shack just inside the fortified gate. A plywood sign hung from the wrought-iron arch across the narrow road, reading MUDAN ENGINEER-ING in large block letters with the Mudan logo, a blood-red peony blossom, painted ornately on either side.

Liang, the younger of the two guards working the shack, had heard the whispered brags from the soldiers stationed inside the warehouse, out of sight of the general public. The soldiers were young—Liang's age—and enjoyed boasting about the importance and secrecy of their mission. Mudan's official stance was that they manufactured crescent wrenches of beryllium alloy. But soldiers didn't guard wrenches, no matter what they were made of. Soldiers guarded weapons.

Young Liang knew little about tools and nothing of women, least of all prostitutes who worked for no more than food and smelled like overripe lychee fruit. A head taller than his partner, Liang was bony and gaunt with thick, round glasses and a shaggy head that seemed much too large for his spindly body. The green guard uniform made him look like a praying mantis with a pistol.

A bright pool of light from the halogen bulbs atop the electrified fence chased the night back to the peach orchards across the narrow two-lane road. Fluttering moths circled in the glow above the women like flies drawn to their stench. It seemed that the prostitutes had materialized out of the darkness—a fact that only added to the uneasiness in Liang's gut.

Inside the shack, Po, the older guard, raised a wild eyebrow when he heard the girls' plaintive cries. Breathing deeply, he stood when he saw the girls, slicking back what was left of his thinning black hair and giving a gold-toothed grin. The prostitutes, noting his interest, pressed their faces against the outer fence, pushing painted lips through the links like feeding carp. Po was thirty years Liang's senior. To hear him talk, he had a depth of experience with prostitutes.

"Let us in," the girls keened, sounding like hatchlings demanding to be fed. "The night has a chill to it. We could keep you warm."

"This has to be a test," Liang whispered, his youthful voice tightly wound. His eyes flicked back and forth behind thick glasses, adding to his buglike appearance as he searched for any sign of the People's Liberation Army colonel who he was certain had come to conduct a surprise inspection.

"It is no test," Po chided. The proximity of willing women turned his voice into a hoarse whisper. He rifled through his paper lunch sack, looking for something to trade the women. He held up two boiled eggs and a glass jar of noodle soup, his eyelids drooping, heavy with lust. "This should be enough," he said. "I know that one there with the ragged cloak.

"She is talented, that one. She has a scar in the shape of a lotus blossom on her buttock. You can take her if you want to take a look at it."

"She's old enough to be my mother." Liang felt like he might throw up. "I do not care to see such a thing."

"Suit yourself." Po shrugged, pressing the button to open the gate. "You take the other one then. It makes no difference to me." He elbowed his young protégé in the ribs and gave him a wink. "They said they are cold. Maybe we can just trade the eggs and keep the soup." The older guard sauntered through the gap and began to talk terms.

A series of hollow *woofs* punctuated the squeak of gears and clanking chain as the electrified gate rumbled open. Liang watched in dismay as the two prostitutes pitched headlong against the outer fence, faces slack as they slid to the ground in lifeless heaps. He sprang for the red button that would close the gate as a barrage of suppressed gunfire cut down Po. A half breath later and the young guard felt the slap of bullets as they tore into his belly.

Liang was surprised that he felt no pain. He swayed in place, hand not quite on the red button, before slumping to the concrete floor. A dozen men, all dressed in black from head to toe, ran from the darkness of the peach orchard and filed in through the gate. Meticulous in their movements, two peeled off to form a rear guard beside the shack. Another reached in for the ring of keys on the wall inside the door. This one looked down at a gasping Liang with detached eyes.

He had the face of a professional, someone who was accustomed to killing prostitutes and gate guards. Shot in the spine, Liang was no longer a threat—not worth the bullet it would take to put him out of his misery.

The young guard watched helplessly as the dark men moved to the main door of the warehouse. They formed two lines, weapons ready, while one of them used the stolen keys to turn the lock on the door. Absent a warning call from the gate guards, the soldiers inside would have no idea what was about to happen. Liang heard more muffled shots as the attackers flowed into the warehouse like an unstoppable force, methodically killing the soldiers inside.

He was suddenly thirstier than he'd ever been in his life. His vision narrowed with each labored breath, like someone drawing a set of curtains. Soon, he could no longer see the warehouse, or the dark men when they trotted past him on their way out of the compound. He could not see what they carried with them. It didn't matter. Liang had heard the stories. There was only one thing of worth in the warehouse.

These men had come for the Black Dragon.

Three months later
Pakistan, Dera Ismail Khan Prison, 7:14 PM

The Uyghur stood with his back to the rough, unpainted stone. Youthful eyes locked on a shadow as it crept up the chipped concrete, fifteen feet across the crowded cell. Beads of sweat ran down his face, cutting trails through the grit and grime of captivity. Fifty-six other men squatted and slumped at his feet in a sea of hacking coughs and desperate groans on the filthy stone floor, all of them crammed into the fifteen-by-thirty-foot cell. The place was meant to house no more than a dozen prisoners, so the space along the wall was prime real estate, worth fighting for. The Uyghur did not have to watch his back when he stood at the wall—which made it a tiny bit easier to stay alive.

His name was Yaqub Feng, after his mother's brother who had died as a martyr fighting the Chinese devils for a free East Turkestan. His brother, Ehmet, stood to his right along the same wall. At twenty-four, he was three years Yaqub's junior. Shorter by six inches and more finely boned, Ehmet had the physical aspects of their father, a Hui Chinese Muslim. Though Yaqub had inherited their uncle's name, Ehmet possessed a double share of the warrior's fierceness as well as his indifference toward death.

Their cousin Mamoud, who'd been held with them by the American infidels at Guantanamo Bay, had died just hours after arriving in Pakistan. Cuba had been hot, but temperatures in the Punjab were unbearable, loitering over a hundred degrees, often throughout the night, cooking the minds and bodies of the men inside the prison degree by agonizing degree.

The sour stench of infection and human waste twisted up through the evening light, twining long shafts like a cancer on something beautiful—and adding to the captives' misery.

"Yaqub Feng!" a fat Pakistani known as Afaz the Biter grunted from the far end of the room, where he straddled one of the three toilet holes cut into the concrete. "I will be finished here very soon. Come and spend time with your new friend Afaz." Shirtless and glistening with sweat, the Pakistani prisoner's distended belly rested on bent knees. He listed heavily to one side, the effect of some opiate smuggled in and sold by the guards. One of his ever-present stooges steadied him from the side, a hand on the slope of a hairy shoulder.

Yaqub ignored Afaz's slurred summons and rubbed the stinging sweat from his eyes. Beyond the bars of the southwest wall, the evening sun wallowed toward the horizon in shimmering waves of heat. Crisscross shadows inched across the scarred backs and pitiful faces of the other prisoners before climbing up the stone on the far side of the room.

Afaz the Biter began to shout again.

"My men tell me you are Uyghur." His jowly face was red from his efforts at the toilet. "I tasted the flesh of a Uyghur once." He batted his eyes as if drawing on a pleasant memory. "It was much like good chicken. But . . . Feng . . . that is a Chinese name . . . and you look Chinese. . . . Chinese taste like dog." The big man roared in a huge belly laugh, showing yellow teeth. "Lucky for me, I find dog to be delicious."

Yaqub tried to ignore the Pakistani and kept his eyes on the shadow as it crept upward toward the tiny scratch he'd made in the stone the day before, minutes after his visitor had bribed the guards to see him. Together, the shadow and the scratch made a crude but reliable clock in a world where every minute seemed much like the last.

Ehmet leaned forward, glaring at the fat Pakistani. He turned to wink at Yaqub and spoke under his breath. "I will not let him eat you, big brother. I promise." There was a feral quality in his brother, a certain lust for blood that frightened Yaqub, even as he offered his protection.

Yaqub tipped his head toward the scratch on the wall. "We are almost there."

"Afaz has many men," a skinny Chinese smuggler named Jiàn Zǒu said, leaning around Ehmet. Narrow eyes flicked back and forth from Yaqub to Afaz, glowing with something that was not quite fear. "You look like people with a plan. . . ."

Neither Yaqub nor Ehmet answered.

Jiàn Zǒu swallowed hard. "But what if your plan does not work in time? We should put our heads together."

"What if?" Yaqub whispered. According to Jiàn Zǒu, he had been what the Chinese called a "snakehead"—a smuggler who was an expert at moving people across borders and evading authorities—until the day he was caught.

"I may as well fight alongside you," Jiàn Zǒu said. He had a narrow face and a wispy black mustache, which, along with his darting eyes and twitchy movements, reminded Yaqub of a rat. "Your father was Chinese," he reasoned. "That makes us cousins. We should take care of each other."

The only other Chinese prisoner in the cell, Jiàn Zǒu had aligned himself with the Feng brothers from the moment they'd arrived from Islamabad two days before. If he was to be believed, he had contacts with Chinese triads and other organized crime groups all around the world. He'd been arrested when some of his underlings decided to begin trafficking in drugs along with their human cargo.

Ehmet looked the jumpy snakehead up and down. "If we get out of here, you say you have contacts in China?"

Nose twitching, Jiàn Zǒu seemed to sense that that something big was about to occur. "I have contacts everywhere, cousin." He leaned in close. "My friends will make sure we are taken care of wherever you want to go—as long as we stay alive long enough to get to them."

Afaz growled from the other end of the room. "You should come to me on your own, Yaqub Feng! My men will not be as gentle as I will be."

Ehmet laughed out loud at that. "I will enjoy watching this one die," he said.

Jiàn Zŏu swallowed hard, but Yaqub saw him reach into the waist of his filthy trousers and bring out a sharpened metal spike. The little snakehead might tremble at the thought of death, but he was willing to run trembling toward it. Maybe they should bring him along.

"If the stories are true," Jiàn Zŏu whispered, "Afaz chewed his wife to death."

"I can see you laugh," the fat Pakistani roared. "You will not be laughing for long." His stooge brought him a bowl of water to clean himself. He pushed it away and stood to pull his pants up around his waist. They were stained and torn, forming more of an apron than actual pants. Sweat bathed the mahogany rolls of fat that folded over his upper body.

Yaqub took a half step away from the wall. At six feet tall to Ehmet's five and a half, the elder brother should have been the protector. That was not the case. Ehmet put out a hand and moved in front, placing himself between Yaqub and Afaz the Biter.

The Pakistani lumbered through the crowded room, shoving and kicking aside prisoners who didn't move out of his way fast enough. Ten feet away, he stopped. Even listing to one side, he was a formidable man with powerful arms and a low, sloping brow over piggish eyes.

He pointed at Yaqub, clicking his teeth together.

On the wall, the shadow reached the scratch.

A half a breath later a horrific explosion rattled the prison, sending a cascade of dust down the ancient brick. All eyes turned toward the outer wall trying to make sense of the noise. Earthquakes were not unheard of in Pakistan—and could prove deadly to men trapped in a dilapidated pile of stone like Dera Ismail Khan Prison.

Ehmet looked at Yaqub and smiled. This was no earthquake.

A second blast roared directly outside the bars, sending a percussive fist into Yaqub's chest. The pressure wave knocked him backwards, slamming both him and Ehmet against the stone. They'd dropped to their bellies as a third explosion tore the bars off the cell.

Prisoners coughed and choked as smoke and dust rolled into the room. It was difficult to breathe, and impossible to see. Panicked shouts and pitiful cries rose up with the dust throughout the prison complex. The rattle-can of submachine gunfire followed fast on the heels of the explosions. Outside the wall, a guard screamed for mercy—and then screamed again as he was shot. Ehmet pressed his face up from the concrete floor and grinned at his brother. Surrounded by death, he looked happier than he'd been in a very long while.

Three minutes after the first explosion, the gunfire outside had dwindled to sporadic spurts and volleys. A dark man with a flowing black beard that reached the middle of his chest stepped through the cavernous breach in the outside wall. He wore the green uniform of a prison guard and carried a short Kalashnikov rifle at low-ready. He cast dark eyes around the room until he saw the two Uyghur men. Prisoners who had not known to get away from the outside wall prior to the explosion were scattered around the room in various stage of dismemberment.

"I am Ali Kadir," the man with the beard said, grabbing Yaqub by the arm and hauling him to his feet. "We have come to set you free."

Yaqub nodded, blinking. It was one of Kadir's men who had come to see him the day before.

"We must hurry," Kadir said. "There is a vehicle waiting outside. There are three of you."

Ehmet shook his head. "Our cousin is dead."

Jiàn Zŏu scuttled up in the cloud of dust. "Take me with you," he said. "My contacts will be of use, I swear it. I assume you wish to get out of Pakistan. I am an expert at moving people from one country to another."

Ali Kadir opened his mouth to speak as a prison guard stepped through the hole in the wall, spraying the room with bullets. One of the shots hit him in the back of the neck. Kadir fell instantly, a look of bemused surprise on his lips, and was dead before he hit the ground. Jiàn Zŏu snatched up the Kalashnikov as he fell and dispatched the guard with a short burst.

"See," he said, licking his lips. "I told you I could be of some use."

Yaqub looked at Ehmet, who shrugged. "I don't care," the younger brother said, before pushing his way through the rubble to a stunned Afaz, who now lay sprawled on his back. Ehmet bent over the Pakistani, kneeling close to his face. Without warning, he ripped into the flesh of the screaming man's cheeks as if he were feeding. Blood covered the young Uyghur's lips and chin when he finally looked up. It dripped from the corners of his mouth and ran down the front of his tattered prison shirt.

Surviving prisoners, guards complicit in the escape, and Jiàn Zŏu watched in disgusted horror as Ehmet Feng spat a grisly chunk of meat on the floor. He had torn the face off Afaz the Biter. Even Yaqub, who admitted to a mild disposition, felt a surge of pride at his brother's ferocity. The story of the young Uyghur would be passed on for generations.

Ehmet turned to give Jiàn Zǒu a hard glare.

"You fought with us, you will come with us," he said through bloodstained teeth.

Yaqub shot a glance toward Ehmet, nodding. People always looked to him because he was older and taller—but everyone now knew which brother was truly in charge.

"Kadir was our transportation out of here," Yaqub said, looking at Jiàn Zǒu. "His men will give us a ride, but without him, we may need your contacts more than ever."

The snakehead's wispy mustache twitched under a pointed nose.

"You may be of some use after all." Ehmet pointed a bloody hand toward the demolished wall. "Come. We have an appointment with a dragon."

1,100 kilometers northeast of Dera Ismail Khan
K2 Base Camp, Godwin-Austen Glacier, 5:13 AM

Alberto Moretti would die on the Savage Mountain. He'd known it for years—since he was sixteen. Sitting at the wobbly table in the glow of the command tent, he leaned a whiskered face against an open palm. Weary eyes squinted under the glaring hiss of lantern light. The chapped tip of his bandaged finger traced the route his team would take to the summit. He could envision each step—the different camps, the exact spots they would set ropes, the famous Bottleneck where climbers would traverse the face under a deadly serac—tons of hanging ice—before making their final push to the summit.

As an Italian, Moretti felt a special kinship with the naked chunk of rock and ice that loomed at the head of the valley. It was, after all, a team made up of his country-men who had reached the summit first in 1954. Moretti had already climbed Everest—twice, the last time two years before, summiting on his thirty-fifth birthday. But all three of his bids to conquer K2 had ended in failure. The second highest and, arguably, the most deadly of the 8,000-meter peaks simply refused to admit him.

And Moretti was not alone. For every four climbers to reach the top, the Savage Mountain took a life. If you wanted the respect of the world, you climbed Ever-est. If you wanted the respect of other mountaineers, you climbed K2.

And climbing it was just what Moretti intended to do—if the rest of his group would ever arrive.

It had taken him the better part of a year to recruit a multinational team. Klaus Becke, a longtime climbing partner and friend, would be his second in command. The big German had radioed that he'd brought along a girlfriend. Moretti shrugged away any ill feelings over adding someone to the expedition this late in the game. Klaus was a showoff, but the most competent climber the Italian had ever seen. If he needed a pretty girl to cheer for him while he worked, Moretti didn't care—so long as they made their weather window. July was going by awfully fast and K2 always seemed to grow angrier in August.

The porters had already made the five-day trek back down the trail to Askole, promising to return at the ap-pointed time to help the expedition off the mountain. So far, eight members of the actual team had arrived in base camp—two Chinese climbers, two brothers from Wyoming, one Ukrainian, and the lone climber from Alberta, Canada. DuPont, the hulking Belgian, had wandered off again, doing whatever security profes-sionals did in the wee hours of the morning. Considering the political climate in Pakistan, Moretti had not argued with the American brothers on the team when they suggested he hire someone to take care of security. Emile DuPont, a former legionnaire, if his story was to be believed, smiled more than Moretti would have thought for someone who was paid to have a fearsome look. Still, the Belgian was a huge man with a powerful military bearing and a sly smile that said he considered lesser men as food if the need ever arose.

And then there was Issam, the cook. He was a gaunt thing, stooped, with a dragging limp and a copper tint to his skin only slightly lighter than the Balti porters. Black eyes and a full beard made it difficult to pinpoint the man's ethnicity. In broken English, Issam had introduced himself as a Moroccan. He generally kept to himself, but there was an air about the cook that put Moretti on edge, as if he was standing in the path of an avalanche. In truth, this dark man was much more frightening than their Belgian security guard.

Issam was, however, a dependable cook. Even now, when the Godwin-Austen valley was still cloaked in the indigo shadows of dawn, metal pots clanged and rattled in the adjacent cook tent where the Moroccan prepared breakfast tea and chipati, the thin, unleavened bread of the Karakoram.

The noise made Moretti hungry. He stood and stretched his back with the long groan of a man who'd spent half his life sleeping on the ice, then poked his head out the tent flap. The imposing pyramid of K2 dominated the northern landscape. The tip of its eastern summit was a brilliant orange with the rising sun.

A distant cry drew his attention back to the south, toward the Baltoro and the lower camps at Concordia. At first he thought it was an eagle, but the sound grew louder as someone in a bright yellow parka half ran, half staggered from the valley shadows toward the camp. Moretti realized it was a woman screaming for help.

And she was not alone.

Less than two hundred meters down the valley, nine men trailed her through the shadowed boulders like persistent ants. Green military uniforms stood out against gray rock and dirty snow. The men moved methodically, not wasting their breath. Soon, their quarry would reach the base camp—and run out of places to go.

Moretti nearly jumped out of his skin when the Moroccan cook began to bang on a tin plate with a metal spoon, rousing the rest of the camp.

The Italian turned in a complete circle, hand on top of his head, scanning the barren ice and rocky crags that surrounded him.

"Where the hell is DuPont with his gun?" His whisper escaped on a terrified gasp.

The woman in the yellow parka was surely Klaus Becke's type. As she drew nearer, he could see that she was tall with long brunette hair and the gaunt features the German liked so much. Even in the high-altitude base camp, she increased her speed when she neared the tents and stumbled up to Moretti five minutes after her first screams carried into camp. She slumped forward, hands against her knees, speaking between wheezing gulps of thin air.

Other climbers in camp began to emerge from their tents.

"They . . . killed everyone," the woman panted. "I've . . . never seen any . . . thing . . . like . . ." She cast her eyes around the camp. "Klaus said . . . you have . . . gun. . . ."

"Klaus?" Moretti rolled his lips, fearing her answer.

"Dead." The woman looked from tent to tent, then

over her shoulder at her pursuers. Her voice was shredded, hoarse from her ordeal. "They . . . cut off his head. Please . . . tell me you have a gun."

"DuPont, our security specialist, has one." The Italian nodded. His eyes were glued to the uniformed men picking their way across the rock-strewn glacier toward camp.

Hands still on her knees, the woman looked up. Her eyes were bloodshot, her voice pleading. "Where is he?"

"I wish I knew," Moretti said.

The woman sank to the ground. Moretti reached down and helped her back to her feet as nine frowning men strode into camp. Three of them were swathed in blood—the beheaders. The Italian sighed. He would indeed die on K2, but it would not be the mountain that killed him.

The apparent leader of the group, a man with a Fidel Castro cap, ordered all the climbers to form a line in front of the cook tent. A thick man with a fearsome black beard that was long enough to be shoved sideways in the morning breeze, he introduced himself simply as Khan. As if bragging about his intentions, he explained that his men were members of *Junood ul-Hifsa,* the jihadists who'd claimed responsibility for the cleansing at Nanga Parbat and the recent beheadings of two infidels posted online. The Taliban, al Qaeda, ISIS—to intelligence officials these were all different and unique terrorist groups, but from the viewpoint of a neck with a knife to it, one militant Islamist was the same as any other.

The Ukrainian climber vomited when he heard the news. A murmured hush ran through the line. Moretti couldn't help but think how much they all looked like the receiving end of a firing squad.

Khan seemed particularly interested in the woman

they'd chased into camp, running her name together as "Lucyjarrett" when he spoke to her. It was only then that Moretti recognized her as a reporter he often saw on the American news. A media luminary, Jarrett would make a fine trophy head for a bunch of attention-seeking terrorists to display on an Internet video.

"How fortunate to find you here, Lucyjarrett," Khan said. He reached to stroke the trembling brunette's hair where it was pasted with sweat and tears to her pallid cheek. The action bordered on tender, but the cruel edge in the man's voice made Moretti sick to his stomach.

"The US media speaks much evil of sacred things!" Khan drew back his hand as if he'd touched something filthy. "It is a blasphemy, worse than murder or fornication!"

Eyes clenched shut and trembling to the point that she looked as if she would collapse, Jarrett gave a frantic shake of her head. "You've never heard that talk from me."

"Shut your mouth!" Khan spat. He threw a glance over his shoulder. A bony man to his right let a Kalashnikov rifle fall against the sling around his neck and took a small camcorder from his military jacket. He spread his legs as if to brace himself while he powered up the camera, then nodded when he was ready.

Khan's lips curled into a half grin. "Perhaps you have not uttered the words, but you will pay for the sin."

Two of the militants moved along the line, securing everyone's hands in front of them with plastic zip ties. Moretti considered struggling, but thought better of it when one of them seemed to read his mind and prodded him in the ribs with the barrel of his gun.

Stepping forward, Khan grabbed Jarrett by the hair and yanked her head backwards, exposing her neck. Moretti gathered himself to lunge. He couldn't let them murder her without doing something. They were all dead anyway.

But before he moved, the Moroccan cook wagged his head in blatant disgust at the far end of the line. He said a few words in Arabic, and then began to speak in perfect English, absent the affected pidgin he'd always used to communicate with Moretti.

"This is cowardice!" the Moroccan said, speaking clearly and loud enough to cause Khan to pause. "She is unarmed and a guest in this country. As such she is subject to your hospitality."

Khan's chest heaved at the insult. His face darkened behind the beard. "I had thought to let you live if you were a good Sunni," he said through clenched teeth. "But you will die alongside the American whore and her friends." He smiled at the ashen woman as he drew a curved blade from his belt. "Your death will be slow and painful, so that others may—"

Moretti watched as the Moroccan cook ignored Khan's diatribe and gave a slow and exaggerated nod.

The Italian flinched as the militant leader's head snapped back from some unseen force, breaking like a melon struck with a hammer. With little left to hold it in place, the Castro cap fell to the ground. Something moist sprayed Moretti in the face. A moment later, the crack of a distant rifle echoed off the glaciers.

Chapter 1

Pericula ludus
(Danger is my pleasure)

—Motto of the Mayotte Detachment,
French Foreign Legion

Jericho Quinn began to move an instant before the 150-grain bullet thumped into Khan's head. Standing at the far end of the line of prisoners, he knew Thibodaux would pull the trigger at his signal. Quinn also knew the round from the big Marine's FN SCAR 17 would travel fast enough that there would be no apparent gap between Khan's death and the death of the young jihadist who stood across from him.

Quinn was a dark man. He'd never been one to carry extra pounds, but months of living as a fugitive had left him with deep hollows in his cheeks and a hungry look. At thirty-six, the first flecks of gray had invaded a full black beard and the temples of his shaggy hair. The copper complexion of his Apache grandmother and his fluency in Arabic made it easy for him to pass himself off as a Moroccan. In reality, he was an agent

with the United States Air Force Office of Special Investigations or OSI. At least he had been before he'd
become a fugitive.

The young jihadist across from Quinn flinched at
the sudden thud of the bullet that plowed through his
commander's skull.

Hands bound, Quinn stepped forward, sweeping his
foot inside the kid's left knee and grafting downward.
This sudden pressure bent the leg and forced the jihadist into the beginnings of a spin. Hands together,
Quinn grabbed the rifle, trapping the young militant's
fingers and snaking his own thumb into the trigger
guard as he twisted the weapon in a tight arc. The hapless kid continued to spin until his back was to his
compatriots, making him a convenient human shield.

Quinn stepped in as the jihadist fell, bringing the
short Kalashnikov up, firing as the muzzle moved across
his opponent's chest, stitching him with at least three
rounds. Flinching from the impact and the concussion
of the muzzle blast just inches from his ear, the young
man abandoned his grip on the rifle and tried to push
away. Quinn let him fall, engaging the line of remaining terrorists with short bursts from the Kalashnikov.

Jacques Thibodaux, the United States Marine Corps
gunnery sergeant posing as a Belgian security specialist,
worked methodically from a hide in the rocks above
camp. Issued to Marines in the Special Operations Command, the FN SCAR was a Belgian design, so it made
sense that a Belgian soldier of fortune would have such
a rifle. Thibodaux took out the leader and two others
while Quinn saw to the rest. Roughly four seconds
after Thibodaux's first round had entered Khan's head
just beneath his nose, seven other terrorists lay dead on
the glacier. The last surviving attacker, a twentysome-
thing youth with a great swath of blood on his chest

from the recent beheading, abandoned his weapon and fled, careening down the boulder-strewn glacier as fast as his legs could carry him. He was not much older than the boy bleeding to death at Quinn's feet, but with a much fuller beard. Quinn recognized the fleeing man as Abu Khalifa, a Pakistani Taliban wanted in connection with the murder of thirty-three primary school children during a school massacre the month before. The young militant zigzagged on the loose gravel in an effort to keep from getting shot. It was a useless effort. If Marines were anything, they were expert riflemen. Had Thibodaux wanted to take him, Khalifa would have only died with sore ankles.

Lucy Jarrett sank to her knees, her shoulders wracked with sobs. The brothers from Wyoming worked to free themselves from the restraints while other climbers fell back to the gravel, blinking in amazement that they'd survived. Alberto Moretti rubbed a trembling hand across the stubble on his face. His mouth hung open as he stared at Quinn.

"You are not from Morocco, *signore*," he whispered.

Quinn pulled his hands loose from the zip tie. "Yes," he said. "I am not."

Jacques Thibodaux trotted into camp a moment later. The massive Marine carried the desert-tan FN SCAR rifle in one hand and a small black satellite phone in the other. He looked sideways at Quinn. "Are you whole, Chair Force?" he asked, his Cajun accent palpable in even a few words.

Quinn tossed the zip tie on the ground and rubbed his wrists to get back the circulation. "I'm good."

Thibodaux whistled under his breath, looking at the body count. "I'd have sore feet if I kicked as much ass as you."

Quinn ducked into the cook tent to retrieve a small

backpack, which he slung over his shoulders. He eyed the diminishing dot that was Abu Khalifa.

Thibodaux fished a black patch from the pocket of his pants. "Glad that's over," he said. "I was gettin' tired of pretending to see out of my bad eye." Broad shoulders and muscular arms filled a navy-blue commando sweater. Close-cropped hair and an impossibly square jaw gave no doubt that he was a military man. The black patch only added to the intensity of the gaze from his good eye.

"*Miiiitzica!*" Moretti gasped in the Sicilian equivalent of *pleeease*. All this new information, fresh on the heels of nearly being murdered, had knocked the man for a loop. "And you are not from Belgium?"

Thibodaux gave the astonished Italian a shrug. "I ain't never even been there, *cher*," he said. "Shit!" The Cajun gave a sheepish grin and passed the satellite phone to Quinn. "I about forgot. The boss wants to talk to you."

Quinn took the phone, looking at the screen while he adjusted the tilt of the antenna to get a better signal. A cold wind from the glacier blew against his face.

"Hello?"

"News?" Winfield Palmer asked. The national security advisor to the former president was not the sort of man to exchange pleasantries. Driven to find those responsible for the assassination of his friend and former boss, he had no time for anything but information that moved the investigation forward. The fact that he was in hiding from the current administration—and harboring the director of the CIA, who was also a fugitive— only added to his curt demeanor. The simple stress of knowing that you only had a few moments, even on a secure line, before the NSA or some other government agency unraveled the code on your call, was enough to give lesser men a heart attack. The satellite phone func-

tioned as a portable version of an STE or Secure Terminal
Equipment, scrambling the signal with a morphing code
that had to be keyed into each separate handset in order
to decipher it. Speakers could use plain talk for a time,
but at the end of the day it was still government en-
cryption. Some NSA nerd would eventually find a way
to hack the program if they stayed on the line too long.

Quinn's eyes flicked from the bodies of the dead terrorists and down the valley to the fleeing survivor.
"Things got a little wild here for a few minutes. We do
have one Abu Khalifa in our sights, so that's something.
I'm hoping he should lead us to something more solid."

"Let the Pakistanis worry about Khalifa," Palmer
said. "There's been a development."

Quinn was normally unflappable, but he perked up
at that particular word, especially since it made Palmer
blow off a high-value target like Abu Khalifa. *Developments* were never a good thing where Win Palmer was
concerned. Good things didn't develop. They fell off
the radar. Situations that were likely to get Quinn killed
qualified as developments.

"The boys we transferred from Gitmo are in the wind,"
Palmer said, referring to the Fengs, Uyghur prisoners the
new US President had turned over to Pakistan. It was just
one more way the POTUS found to try to stir up a war
with China, who insisted they had the moral right to try
the Uyghur prisoners as terrorists for bombing a passenger train in Xinjiang Province. President Hartman
Drake had been beating the war drum for months—and
the escape of these terrorists was likely to push the
Chinese President over the ledge.

"All three escaped?" Quinn asked.

"Just the brothers," Palmer said. "Evidently the cousin
died shortly after they arrived in Pakistan. But two of
them are bad enough."

"When was the escape?"

"Last night," Palmer said. "From Dera Ismail Khan."

"You'd think they'd learn," Quinn mused, remembering the Taliban attack on the same prison in 2013. "Any idea which way they're heading?"

"Mariposa is working on that problem for us," Palmer said, sniffing like he had a cold. "She'll come up with something soon."

Quinn couldn't help but smile at Palmer's code name for Emiko Miyagi—*Mariposa*, the Spanish word for butterfly. Thibodaux had scoffed when he heard it, saying she was more like "One of those Japanese hornets-of-the-terrible-stinging-death."

Not much over five feet tall, every inch of her was what Thibodaux called badassery and bitchitude, but Quinn respected her as the warrior that she was. Both men had learned the hard way that fighting Miyagi was like doing battle against a chainsaw.

"Roger that," Quinn said. If there was something to be found, he knew Emiko would find it.

"Listen." Palmer's voice was distant, as if he were mulling over some bit of news and deciding whether or not to share it with Quinn on the phone. "There's a good chance these guys are heading back to China. I don't have to tell you how important it is that you find them before they wreak enough havoc to convince the Middle Kingdom it's time to have a go at World War III. . . ." Palmer broke into what sounded like a ragged tubercular cough.

"Are you doing okay, sir?" Quinn said. He'd never considered the idea that Winfield Palmer was subject to the ravages of disease that plagued normal human beings.

"I'm fine," Palmer snapped, a little too quickly and sounding far from it. "Call me back when you know something. It wouldn't hurt my feelings if you found these guys before they get out of Pakistan."

He ended the call without another word.

Quinn folded the antenna and stood for a long moment, staring at the looming black pyramid of rock at the head of the valley.

"What?" Thibodaux shrugged, palms up, waiting to hear Palmer's news.

"Grab your pack," Quinn said. "I'll fill you in on the way."

Moretti stared down the glacier, still wearing his hand on top of his head like a hat. "I must call the authorities . . . let them know what has happened," he muttered. "There are dead to tend at Concordia camp."

Quinn touched the Italian's arm. "I need you to wait a few hours before you call anyone," he said.

"Wait?" Moretti turned to look at him, incredulous. "That murderer has a head start. If I wait, he will slip away."

Quinn nodded down the trail, then looked back at Moretti. "We need to talk to him. To try and find out who's behind this attack." He shot a glance at Thibodaux. "Once the Pakistanis have him, he's gone."

Lucy Jarrett looked up from where she sat slumped on the ground with her head between her knees. Tears plastered her hair against swollen cheeks. She shook her head, in a deepening daze, her eyes narrow and accusing.

"It doesn't make sense," she said with the clogged nose of someone who'd been crying for half a day. "If you knew they were going to attack, why weren't you waiting at Concordia? You could have saved Klaus . . . and the others."

Jacques gave a shake of his head, kneeling down in the rocks to lay a wide hand on the woman's shoulder.

It was nothing short of amazing that a man as large and intimidating as Jacques Thibodaux could somehow muffle the dangerous aspects of his nature and turn himself into a giant teddy bear. Quinn supposed having seven young sons had given the Marine plenty of training.

"I wish we would have, *cheri*," Thibodaux said in a quiet voice Quinn knew was capable of uprooting trees. "But the information we had said these guys would attack when everyone had formed up here at base camp. We thought they had access to a helicopter, so we assumed they'd come directly here."

Jarrett stared into the morning air, her breath forming a vapor cloud around her blank face. She said nothing, because there was nothing more to say. Death, especially the death of a friend, was impossible to process quickly. Quinn knew that all too well.

"I will give you two hours, *signore*," Moretti said, hand on top of his head again. Hatred began to chase the stunned look from his eyes as he stared down the valley. "But that one killed my friends. He must not get away."

"Oh," Quinn whispered, his eyes falling to a sobbing Lucy Jarrett. "He won't get away."

He gave a quiet nod toward Thibodaux, letting him know it was time to move. Neither man would say it in front of anyone in the climbing party, but the massacre at Concordia was the least of their worries. No matter how much he wanted to follow Abu Khalifa all the way back to Jalalabad, Quinn's first priority was find the Feng brothers, and with any luck avert a war with China.

Stepping away from the others, he opened the antenna on the secure satellite phone. To locate the Feng brothers, he'd need transport, and the quickest way to get that was to call a particular wing commander in the Pakistan Defense Force. The last time they'd seen each other, Quinn had knocked out the other man's tooth.

Chapter 2

Yaqub Feng lay on his stomach in the cramped belly of the swaying jingle bus, crammed between his brother and Jiàn Zǒu, the ratlike Chinese snakehead. Ehmet had taken the spot along the outside edge where he could press his face to the metal grating where he could see out and get some semblance of breathable air. Jiàn Zǒu had a similar position and view, but wedged in the middle, Yaqub could see only shadows and choked on the dust that sifted up through the cracks in the wooden floor.

A riot of sound and color on the outside, the brightly decorated bus looked like something out of a gypsy caravan. Lengths of dragging chain and countless tinkling bells hung along the bumpers and painted trim of the gaudy monstrosity that had a permit to take tourists across the border with China and up the Karakoram Highway as far as Karakul Lake. It was the perfect vehicle in which to hide in order to get out of Pakistan—for who in his right mind would hide in something that already drew so much attention?

"It would be much easier if we went out through Afghanistan," Jiàn Zǒu said, sounding hollow, as if he'd been kicked in the groin.

"My business is in Kashgar," Ehmet muttered, still studying the situation outside the truck through tiny holes in the metal flashing. "I already told you that. It will not take long."

"In Pakistan," Jiàn Zǒu said, "you are merely fugitives. In China you are human targets. Forgive me, but it seems foolish to walk straight into the mouth of the dragon when the Afghan border is as porous as a rusted bucket."

Yaqub felt Ehmet's body tense. He lifted his head enough to turn and face the center of the truck. The sight of dried blood caking the corners of his mouth was terrifying, even to Yaqub.

"Tell me, Jiàn Zǒu," Ehmet whispered. "Did we accompany you out of Dera Ismail Khan prison, or did you accompany us?"

"I am with you," the Chinese man said. "And happy to be so. But it would make it much easier to do my job if you told me your final destination."

Ehmet's face remained neutral, as if he was passing judgment. "You should concern yourself with our immediate destination—and that is Kashgar."

"As you wish," Jiàn Zǒu said. "I do have contacts there who will help us move about. When you are ready, I will make the necessary arrangements."

Ehmet turned to peer out the grating again. "The guards are waving all the buses through, just as you told us they would."

"Money and blood grease the gears of this world," the snakehead said. "The drivers pay the guards well to let them pass unmolested."

Brakes and springs squawked as the jingle truck lurched forward, sending up a cloud of dust through the floorboards that threatened to choke the three men.

Above them, wealthy passengers from Islamabad and other affluent cities snapped photographs and gasped at the vistas of the Pamir Mountains. These men and a small number of women, each with a respectable male escort, sipped tea and chatted nervously about caravan thieves on the old Silk Road, ignorant of the fact that three fugitives hid in the hollow floor just inches beneath their feet.

From the time the first explosion had rocked the prison, Yaqub had felt caught up in a terrible, unstoppable wave. Stunned at the loss of their leader, Ali Kadir's men had ushered them quickly away from Dera Ismail Khan in an old Mercedes van, heading northeast along the Indus River. They had changed to a sedan in Rawalpindi, and then switched vehicles again in Abbottabad, this time to a large panel truck that carried a load of goats. Whatever the plan had been beyond that, it had died with Ali Kadir. In Abbottabad, the men seemed unsure of what to do next. Jiàn Zǒu had told them to go to Nagar where he said he had a contact. They reached the small village before daybreak.

Jiàn Zǒu had met with his contact, who'd shown them inside the jingle bus an hour before the first tourists arrived. It would be cramped to the point of crippling, he said, but under the present state of security in the country, drastic measures were a necessity. The bold and bloody escape had been a devastating blow to Pakistan in the court of public opinion—making the Feng brothers two of the most wanted men in the world.

Ehmet raised his head. "Do your contacts in Kashgar have food?" he said, loud enough to startle Yaqub, though there was no danger anyone above could hear him over the rattling jingle bus.

"Food?" Jiàn Zǒu stifled a cough amid the swirl of road dust.

"Yes, food." Ehmet nodded. "I have had nothing to eat since I snacked on Afaz the Biter."

Chapter 3

Pakistan, 6:35 AM

Forty minutes after they trotted out of K2 base camp, Quinn and Thibodaux had cut Abu Khalifa's lead to less than two hundred meters. Light from the rising sun crept down the mountains and across the valley floor, turning everything a brilliant gold.

"Chair Force," the big Marine said, never missing an opportunity to razz Quinn for being in what he considered the taxi-driving branch of the military. "You remember those pre-deployment training iterations they give you where every scenario devolves into a critically catastrophic shitstorm of death?"

Quinn shrugged as he moved. His friend's philosophical path was a wandering one. "I guess."

"Well, I'm here to tell you," Thibodaux said. "Every op I go on with you starts out that way."

"And?" Quinn said, waiting for the rest.

The Cajun grinned, batting his good eye. "I just wanted to say thanks." Chuckling despite the almost nonexistent air, he nodded down the trail toward their fleeing target. "I gotta tell you though, I am tired of this runnin' shit. What say we go ahead and give this guy a big hand hug around his neck?"

Quinn smiled. Jacques was good for keeping things light, even amid the chaos of battle. It helped him keep his mind off his daughter. "Not sure what he'll give us, but I hope we have a few minutes with him before we have to break off and go after the Feng brothers."

"Roger that," the big Cajun said, gulping for air, but powering through like a good Marine.

Snow-covered peaks tore at the belly of the sky like fangs. Many of the world's 8,000-meter giants surrounded the valley. The Gasherbrums, Broad Peak, and K2—the Mountain of Mountains—rose up around them, reminding the three tiny dots that were pursuers and pursued of how insignificant they truly were. It was no wonder this place was called the Throne Room of the Mountain Gods.

Quinn scanned the boulders ahead of the stumbling jihadist, searching for the hidden threats he knew were there. "See one, think two" was a philosophy that had kept him alive on countless occasions. There were few secrets in the tactical world anymore. The Internet was rife with training videos and war-fighting manuals that drew the veil of secrecy from even the most sacred of strategies. Posting a rear guard was far from a complicated procedure. Even a conscripted goatherd would remember to leave someone to watch his back trail. There was a high probability that the kill squad had left someone behind—and that someone was likely lurking in the shadows ahead, just waiting for Quinn and Thibodaux to enter his sight picture.

Hours of physical training left both Quinn and Thibodaux in excellent condition. They'd been living at the base camp long enough for their bodies to acclimatize, but prolonged jogging at 12,000 feet pushed them to their limits and slowed them to little more than a steady shuffle.

The valley narrowed ahead before spreading out along the river in a wide gravel bar, forming a little pass that made for a perfect choke point on their route. Going downhill, Quinn was able to keep the target in sight, but boulders the size of garage doors littered the riverbank, providing countless places for an ambush. Quinn took his eyes off the dangers ahead long enough to shoot a glance at Thibodaux. They were in the shadows, but the big man squinted his good eye as if he were staring into the sun. Like Quinn, he was watching Khalifa for some sort of reaction.

Quinn raised his fist the moment he saw the fleeing target's head snap to the right. Something—or someone—in the rocks had caught his attention.

Puffs of dirt and debris rose from the ground and surrounding rocks a half second later, sending Quinn and Thibodaux diving for the cover of a car-sized boulder. The staccato crack of gunfire echoed across valley walls.

His back against the rough stone, Jacques held the rifle flat to his chest. "Sound's bouncing all over these mountains," he said. "Hard to get a fix on 'em."

Quinn said nothing. He'd drawn his revolver the moment he'd seen the fleeing jihadi perk up. He wished for a rifle of his own, but posing as a cook made carrying a long gun impractical, so he made do with a rusty Colt revolver he'd traded for in Karachi. It came with half a box of relatively new .45 ACP ammo and two metal half-moon clips that held the rounds in the cylinder. Without his customary Kimber 10mm and a second Glock or Beretta, Quinn felt nearly naked with the six-shooter.

Thibodaux closed his good eye, listening intently as

he pinpointed a shooter's location, a hundred meters ahead in the boulders along the river. He swung the SCAR and pulled the trigger, silencing the would-be assassin with a well-placed shot. One down, a second shooter began to walk a series of bullets across the trail.

Thibodaux looked down at the Colt in Quinn's hand and grimaced. "Tell you what, Chair Force, how about you let me do the heavy lifting on this one. I'm not convinced that blunderbuss won't blow up in your hand and kill us both."

"How many rounds you have?" Quinn asked, nodding to the SCAR.

The Marine patted the magazine that jutted from the rifle's action. "Seven here," he said. "And another mag of twenty in my pocket. But, I don't reckon there are more than two or three bad guys up there."

The whap of rotors combined with the high metallic whine of aircraft engines drowned out the sound of gunfire. A hundred feet off the deck, two Alouette III helicopters, olive drab and bearing the green-and-white dot of the Pakistan Air Force, flared to slow and hover as they moved down the trail on the other side of the ambushers and directly in front of the fleeing jihadi. Designed for the rigors of operations at extremely high altitudes, the Aérospatiale Alouette IIIs were a favorite of both the Pakistan and Indian Air forces.

Quinn shielded his eyes with a forearm trying to block the swirling gray cloud of glacial dust. The lead chopper inched forward a few yards at a time, searching the rocks like a hunter kicking the grass to flush a bird. A moment later, a rocket hissed from the cylindrical pod on the Alouette's struts, slamming into the ambusher's nest. The blast was close enough that bits of stone and dead jihadist rained down on Quinn and Thibodaux where they knelt behind their boulder. The choppers loitered over the area for another full minute, no doubt using a FLIR or Forward Looking Infrared scope to search for remaining threats.

Quinn could see Khalifa through the dust, lying stunned on the gravel at the side of the trail, his uniform reduced to a pile of rags. The concussion had likely rendered him half deaf, but he was still alive.

Both Quinn and Thibodaux shielded their eyes as the Alouettes settled onto the gravel and the engine sounds whined down. A steady mountain wind pushed the dust away in a matter of moments, revealing a team of six extremely fit-looking men in maroon berets and camouflage battle dress. Each carried a Steyr AUG Bullpup rifle in his hands and a dour expression on his face.

"They don't look too awful happy," Jacques said, letting the butt of the rifle slide down to his boot toe, holding it by the barrel, but not giving it up completely. "Reckon they're here to help us or shoot us in the beak?"

"We're about to find out," Quinn said. "See the guy standing out front?"

"He's the one you told me went to the US Air Force Academy?" Thibodaux said. "The one with a mustache the size of a Kleenex box?"

"For a semester." Quinn nodded. "We were roommates."

"Friends then." Thibodaux nodded.

"There was one little thing." Quinn took a deep breath. "We had a little boxing match the last day of the semester."

"Great," Thibodaux groaned. "I guess I'll understand it if they shoot us then."

The apparent leader of the squad stood out front, arms folded across a narrow chest. A gleaming gold tooth

peeked from behind a bushy black mustache that looked
far too wide for his face. He'd always been thin, but the
years since the academy—and likely the weight of
command—had added depth to the hollows of his
cheeks. Two men slung their rifles and stepped forward
to grab the panting Abu Khalifa. One punched him in
the belly, doubling him over in pain before the other
cuffed his hands behind his back. The first soldier un-
slung his rifle and pointed it at Khalifa's head while the
other patted him down for weapons. When it was apparent that he didn't have any, they kicked his feet out
from under him to send him sprawling to the rocky
ground with no means to catch himself. He landed
with a thud and writhed on his side at the wing commander's feet. The commander studied the jihadist for
a moment from behind his big mustache, and then
turned to peer at Quinn. There was a glint of mischief
in his brown eyes. Hands clasped at the small of his
back, he breathed deeply from the mountain air as if he
owned the place.

And that was not far from wrong. A smile formed
on the man's face, just a hint at first, but by the time he
reached Quinn, it had turned into a full-blown grin.
The slender Pakistani embraced him in a full hug,
grabbing both shoulders and then stepping back to give
him a once-over.

"It has been too long," the man said.

"It has." Quinn smiled, glancing at Thibodaux.

"Jacques," he said. "I'd like you to meet Wing Commander Mandeep Gola of the Pakistan Air Force."

Thibodaux grinned, extending his hand. "I'll bet you
have some juicy stories to share."

"Apart from the one of him nearly killing me in
front of my parents?" Mandeep gave a deep belly laugh.
He steered Quinn and Thibodaux out of earshot of his

men. "As a matter of fact, I do know some interesting tales." His words clicked with heavily punctuated Pakistani English. "But I am afraid we must save the best ones for another time. My superiors report that the escaped brothers have killed a small contingent of military police on the road between Gilgit and Chitral."

Quinn nodded, picturing a map of Pakistan in his mind. "The Fengs were thought to have ties with al Qaeda cells operating out of some caves in Waziristan and even more across the border. You think they could be heading for Afghanistan?"

Mandeep smoothed his great mustache with a thumb and forefinger and sighed. "Many in my government believe just that. Or at least they say they believe so. But reports also say the security at Dera Ismail Khan prison was extremely tight. I have it on good authority that half the guard force had called in ill the night of the escape." He shrugged. "It took the help of someone with power and connections to ensure their escape in the first place. I see no reason those same powerful and connected entities would not work to deceive everyone regarding their direction of travel."

"Even killing their own guys," Thibodaux muttered, disgusted, but not really surprised. "That's messed up."

"Indeed," Gola said. "These killers have ties to Kashgar and my gut tells me that is the way they have gone." He smiled at Quinn. "Do you still trust in your gut, the way you did at the Academy?"

"I do," Quinn said. Even as a child growing up in Alaska, he'd learned that no matter what you called it, sixth sense, instinct, or a gut feeling—life offered subtle clues that only the subconscious could read. The Japanese called it *haragei*—art of the belly—and it was the foolish person that did not listen to it.

"There is a good chance that they have already crossed

the Khunjareb into China," Mandeep continued. "My government has set up a task force and the foreign ministry is working with Beijing for permission to send investigators into China."

"Politicians," Thibodaux scoffed. "How's that working out?"

"As one might expect, I am afraid." Mandeep smoothed his mustache in thought. "But at my lowly level, I maintain certain connections that help me circumvent such political entanglements. The Feng brothers' escape has made Pakistan a laughingstock. I wish to see these terrorists captured at once and I do not care who does it." He nodded toward his Alouette, brightening some. "My men will take custody of your prisoner. I've made arrangements to fly you across the border as far as Tashkurgen, where I meet with my counterpart in the PLA Air Force for a periodic lunch. I have taken the liberty of setting up ground transportation for you from there." Mandeep put a hand on Quinn's shoulder. "I know how much you like motorcycles, my friend, but was simply too rushed to find anything but a small van for you to use."

It made sense that the Fengs would go to a familiar area to roost. And getting as far as Tashkurgen by air would cut their time to Kashgar in half. He hated missing the opportunity to interrogate Khalifa. Quinn suspected Qasim Ranjhani—a terrorist with ties to President Hartman Drake—was behind the Concordia massacre and Khalifa was their first real lead to where he might be hiding.

The jihadist appeared to read Quinn's mind and looked up with a sneer from where he sat beside the Alouette's strut. "I am a man of no consequence," he mumbled in a voice much higher than Quinn had expected, as if reading from a prepared script. "You and

your kind are no more than dogs. Inshallah, we will
cleanse the earth of infid—"

Mandeep Gola's pistol seemed to leap into his hand.
He spun and put two rounds into the jihadist's face,
obliterating Quinn's chances of getting any information.

The wing commander holstered his pistol with an
exhausted groan. "We are already familiar with Abu
Khalifa's ties to the Taliban. He is one of fifteen men
responsible for the murder of the children of my friends.
Such a man's absence from the earth is far more bene-
ficial than any questionable intelligence he might have
provided."

Two of the soldiers picked up the mutilated body
and dragged it toward the other chopper. Mandeep shook
his head as if to clear it from the killing. The broad
smile crept back across his face as he looked at Quinn.

"Come," he said, disappearing around the left side
of the aircraft to give it a quick once-over before he
climbed in. "We should be on our way."

Ahead of Quinn on the Alouette's boarding ladder,
Thibodaux stopped to glance back at the second chopper where two of Mandeep Gola's men zipped the mess
that was Abu Khalifa into a body bag. A third Pakistani
stood by with his rifle across his chest, staring back
across the rocky terrain with a blank face.

The Cajun turned to Quinn.

"What do you think the odds are we find these
Uyghur bastards without getting ourselves cooked in a
Chinese pot?"

"Well," Quinn said as they climbed into the helicopter, "the Feng brothers blew up a train before they
were arrested, so everyone in the People's Liberation
Army who isn't aiming missiles at the US will focus
their resources on tracking them down. You're practi-

cally AWOL, and I'm being hunted by every police
organization known to mankind. Beyond that, we're
members of the United States military sneaking across
the border of a country with which we are on the brink
of war—out of uniform and with no official documents. That makes us spies in anybody's book."

"So . . ." Thibodaux winked his good eye. "You're
sayin' we have a chance."

"Yep." Quinn buckled his harness and was pressed
back in his seat as Mandeep added power to lift the
Alouette off the gravel. He watched the glaciers and
rock cliffs blur by the window of the chopper as they
headed toward Khunjareb Pass—and wondered if the
Chinese would bother to take him into custody, or put a
pistol to his head and shoot him on sight. "I'd say our
odds are outstanding."

Chapter 4

Vice President Lee McKeon shooed his secretary out of his small West Wing office so he could take the incoming call. Nearing sixty, Natalie Romano had been with him since his days as governor of Oregon. Though she knew nothing of his true background and plans, she was savvy enough not to snoop in affairs that didn't affect her directly. Had that not been the case, she would have been dead long before and that would have been a shame because good secretaries were difficult to find. She shut the door on her way out.

The cell in McKeon's pocket was not connected to the administration and, as such, was less of a problem should one of the many bothersome anti-administration groups that were springing up in Congress want to subpoena records. Even the President did not know about this phone.

A self-proclaimed Chindian, the former governor of Oregon was actually of Chinese and Pakistani descent, adopted and raised by a couple named McKeon. He was a tall and lanky man, and his resemblance to Abraham Lincoln was not lost on the American public. His political opponents often described him as cadaverous. He found it impossible to fold his long legs under the desk for any length of time and had to push the chair away so he could stretch out as he answered the call.

"Hello," he said, dispensing with his official title. Anyone who had this number knew who he really was.

"Peace be unto you," the caller said. It was Qasim Ranjhani, McKeon's distant cousin and right-hand man. Though both men used prepaid "burner" phones, they were careful to keep from using names in their conversations.

"And peace be unto to you," McKeon returned the traditional greeting.

"Our very good friend AK passed away during his recent struggle," Ranjhani said, a faint tightness in his voice conveying the emotion at the loss. McKeon knew AK was Ali Kadir and the "recent struggle" was the prison break at Dera Ismail Khan.

"That is unfortunate," the Vice President said, meaning it. Kadir was a trusted friend, dedicated to their cause—pious and unafraid.

"Indeed," Ranjhani said. "But that is not my reason for calling. I received a message from a friend in Pakistan only moments ago. He saw a man today who resembles the American fugitive you have been looking for."

"In Pakistan?" McKeon sat up straighter. The fugitive Ranjhani spoke of had to be Jericho Quinn.

"Yes, a short time ago in the mountains near Skardu," Ranjhani said. "Gaunt, athletic, with the eyes of a killer."

"That would be him," McKeon said. "And he is in custody then?"

"Unfortunately, no." Ranjhani drew a long, whistling breath through his nose, as he often did when he was about to divulge some new piece of great and important information. "He was last seen boarding a helicopter bound for China with my friend's America-loving wing commander."

"Does this friend of yours know where the fugitive was going in China?"

"Kashgar, he believes," Ranjhani said. "I have a contact there who can help us put an end to this problem."

"That would be welcome news." McKeon drummed long fingers on the desk, thinking. "Any word on our shipment from China?" Of all the things that occupied his mind as the Vice President, the shipment of the Black Dragon was at the very top. Apart from being the trigger in his overall plan, the weapon would also take care of an extremely bothersome nuisance once and for all.

"Indeed," Ranjhani said, the smile almost evident in his voice. "It is en route and on schedule. I do not anticipate any problems."

"Good to hear," McKeon said. His mind was already jumping back to the nagging problem of Jericho Quinn. "I have a thought. Your man in Kashgar should go forward, but we should not rely on him alone. This particular fugitive has proven too slippery for that. I'll get word to the Chinese that they have a dangerous killer hiding out in the Western provinces."

"The Chinese?" Ranjhani scoffed. "They do not trust anyone in your administration."

"Back channels, my friend," McKeon said. "Back channels. We'll nudge our friends in Pakistan to make the Chinese government aware of this trained assassin. Even now he's certainly plotting some evil terrorist act against their sovereignty and it's our duty to make them aware. The Chinese may believe him to be an agent of the American government, or they may think he's working in concert with the Fengs. I don't particularly care as long as they hunt him down and kill him."

Chapter 5

Pacific Ocean, 6:50 PM

Dickey Ng leaned on the painted steel railing alongside the raised house of the 900-foot mega ship, watching a wispy line of black smoke twist up from among the stacked containers on the deck below. Off the bow of the huge vessel, the surface of the indigo water jumped with small, confused waves, as if Neptune held his great cup of ocean with a shaky hand. Ng stood still for a long moment, pondering his four rules, the inviolable laws that had kept him alive and in business for the last eleven years.

Rule One: *Smuggle only one item at a time.*
Rule Two: *Never smuggle anything radioactive.*
Rule Three: *Never smuggle anything with a heartbeat.*
Rule Four: *Always accompany what he smuggled.*

Rule Four seemed all the more pertinent considering the development of this new plume of smoke. He made his way forward, padding down the metal stairs toward the rows and stacks of multicolored metal containers that took up the bulk of the ship. They were known as TEUs—or Twenty Foot Equivalent Units—and the CCC Loadstar carried over 13,000 of these ubiquitous metal shipping boxes.

Dickey Ng only cared about one of them. He'd followed PVMU 526604-1 from the time it had been loaded with palletized tractor parts in Guangzhou. A little money in the right hands made certain he was the one charged with "stuffing" the container, to ensure that the contents could not shift during the movement of the ship while in transit—and thus the last person to see it before it was sealed. He didn't know what was in the wooden crate marked with the red peony flower that he'd strapped to a wooden pallet of parts for small garden tractors, but he was fairly certain it was some sort of weapon. Weapons and art were his two most common assignments. There was no law against smugglers profiling their clients, and considering all the *inshallahs* and *alaikums* going on between the men who'd set up the transportation arrangements, he had a pretty good idea that he wasn't moving a piece of art. He was being paid two hundred and fifty thousand US dollars to see that the crate was delivered safely to the United States. His four rules made sure that would happen.

Making his way forward the length of two football fields without drawing the attention of the bridge watch took time. Ng moved slowly, staying low and out of sight in the narrow walkways between the towering stacks of metal boxes. He told himself the smoke was nothing. Perhaps it was only one of the sailors hiding out to smoke a cigar, or even some vent in one of the ship's systems that he was unaware of. He was, after all, a smuggler, not a sailor, and the only paying customer on the CCC Loadstar.

Flying the flag of the Marshall Islands, the mega ship operated with a crew of twenty-six but kept four cabins open for world travelers and adventure seekers. Ng had signed on in Guangzhou, staying out of the way during the frenetic first few days of the journey as the ship stopped to load more TEUs in several more Chinese ports, then Hong Kong, and finally Kogoshima in southern Japan before heading out to open sea. For the last ten days, life on the ship had settled into a comfortable routine of watches and chores for the crew—made up of primarily Malaysian sailors—and cigarettes and boredom for Ng.

Raised in the teeming streets of Singapore, Dickey Ng found it difficult to breathe with all the fresh air of the open sea. While it wasn't exactly quiet, the sounds were far too one-dimensional for him. He missed the frantic honk of traffic and the constant buzz of people milling in the back streets. Singapore was a nanny state, but it was his nanny state. Even in a place where nearly everything was against the law, there were so many people stacked on top of each other that a person could blend in, get lost in the crowd.

This was the same sentiment—and the reasoning—he used to complete every job he accepted.

There were plenty of people who could fill a shipping container with plastic dolls that were stuffed with Korean Ecstasy or teddy bears packed with Baggies of uncut heroin. Flat crates of Russian AK-47s fit perfectly in the hollow walls of refrigerated containers.

But customs officials knew all that as well as any smuggler. They tore apart a large cross section of Chinese-made dolls and ripped the stuffing out of the bears. The first place inspectors looked for hidden weapons were the hollow walls of reefer units. Every up-and-coming customs inspector he'd ever seen was looking, not so much for contraband, as to make a name for him or herself—to find that big haul of illicit goods that would garner them a fat promotion. If those goods had something to do with terrorism, their hero status would be set in stone. In the East, customs officials looked for bribes. In North America, they wanted to make the news.

So, Dickey Ng followed Rule One and got himself and whatever he happened to be moving lost amid the thirteen thousand twenty-foot-equivalent metal containers stacked on the CCC Loadstar—all part of the eight million moved from Asia to the United States every year.

Ng was around the corner, still fifty feet away from the origin of the smoke and unit PVMU 526604-1, when he smelled cooking fish. He smiled to himself. Azmin, the skinny deckhand, was well known for never getting enough to eat. Ng rounded the stacks to find the young Malay squatting on his haunches beside a can of burning Sterno, grilling a flying fish he must have found on the deck.

Ng began to relax, until Azmin looked up and met his eye.

"You are a watcher," the young man said, using the grease from his cooked fish to smooth his ridiculously sparse mustache. "I thought the smoke might bring you so we could have a talk. You don't remember me, do you?" He looked altogether too smug for Dickey Ng's taste. "But we met five years ago in Hong Kong. I was supposed to be on that ship but I got sick. You were a passenger then too, but you had a different name." Azmin shook his head and rose to his full height, doing his best to intimidate Ng. "I can't remember what your name was then, but it was different."

"What do you want, Azmin?" Ng said, pretending to be frightened.

The young sailor grinned, showing tobacco-stained teeth. "I want a piece of whatever you are getting for whatever it is you are doing. My family is poor. I only do this sailing shit to support my wife and kid, you know. I figure you must have something big going since you travel with a fake name and all. What is it? Gold? Precious stones? Cut me in and your secret's safe with me."

"How was the fish, Azmin?" Ng asked, cocking his head to one side.

Azmin just stared at him. "The fish?"

Ng struck fast, slamming the web of his hand into the young Malay's Adam's apple, stunning him and making him lift both hands defensively.

"Fish bones," Ng said. Shoving one shoulder at the same moment he pulled on the other, Ng spun the panicked sailor and snaked an arm around his neck, drawing him in like a constricting snake to squeeze the life out of him.

"I heard," Ng said, holding the young man firmly while he struggled, "that some people are so embarrassed when they begin to choke that they wander off and die alone. Such a pity . . ." Ng jerked his arm tighter across the faltering sailor's throat. "You were all the way out here in the stacks with no one to hear or see you or come help when you choked on a fish bone. It must have been awful to die . . . so alone." Feeling Azmin go limp in his arms, Ng held him for another full minute, and then slammed his head backwards against the edge of a container, just to be sure. "It's a violent thing," he muttered, "choking to death."

Ng stooped down beside the body and grabbed a

handful of cooked fish from the makeshift grill. Prying open Azmin's jaws, he shoved it in, using his finger to push it far back into the dead man's throat.

Finished, he wiped the grease from his hands on Azmin's filthy shirt and stood to make his way back to his cabin.

"Rule Five," he whispered to himself. "Never enter into a smuggling agreement with a fool."

Chapter 6

Zhongnanhai
Communist Party Headquarters, Beijing

Minister of State Security Wen Shou folded strong hands in the lap of his navy blue suit and listened to the leader of China vent about the impetuous actions of the United States. Wen rolled his lips slightly, keeping a passive face. A bitter word or even a frown at the wrong moment could very well become the match that lit the fuse of war. General Sun, the commander of the People's Liberation Army's Second Artillery Corps—and thus, China's ballistic nuclear missiles—and Admiral Jiang, commander of the PLA Navy Submarine Force, sat across the office from Wen, side by side in matching golden chairs to the right of the President's desk. The two military men were among the few leaders not presently under investigation for some sort of graft. It was not the lack of technology, weaponry, or troops that threatened his country's military. It was corruption.

The presidential office seemed meant to make visitors feel small. There was nothing to clutter the center of the spacious room—no busy coffee table or cozy

couches as in the American President's Oval Office—
just thirty feet of empty red carpet, plush and smooth
but for the faint outlines of footprints that had stood in
exactly the same spot in front of the President's antique
huanghuali wood desk. Wen found himself wondering
about the fate of the men who had worn those spots in the
carpet. To stand in front of the desk of a man as powerful
as the President—who simultaneously held the offices
of General Secretary of the Communist Party of China
and Chairman of the Central Military Committee—
seemed a perilous endeavor.

As the leader of the Ministry of State Security—pat-
terned after the former Soviet Union's KGB—Wen had
nearly unfettered power to jostle and manipulate the
lives of a billion citizens if he'd had the notion to do
such things—but President Chen Min could manipulate the lives of the manipulators themselves. And yet,
the man appeared to like him, telling Wen he valued his
"direct and unfiltered" counsel. Wen did not admit it,
but when a wise man spoke to the paramount leader of
The Peoples Republic of China, he always filtered his
counsel. A consummate diplomat and spy, Minister Wen
just did it better than the military men in the room.

Both General Sun and Admiral Jiang nodded thoughtfully at each word Chen spoke, as if they could not
have possibly said it better. The President paused for a
long moment, looking at his counselors over pursed lips,
as if he had a touch of indigestion.

Taking the silence as a cue to speak rather than pon-
der, General Sun leaned forward in his chair to drive
home his point. "My soldiers stand ready," he said. A
well-fed and jowly man, his thick fingers clutched a
large dress hat above his belly, next to the ribbons fes-
tooning his chest. "As a proud nation, we cannot be ex-

pected to suffer the indignities and bullying from the United States."

The minister kept a file on all of the most powerful military leaders. General Sun had not always been so fat. Before being promoted to the Second Artillery, he'd been fit enough to lead the Southern Broadswords, an elite group of special operations commandos based in Guangzhou. The pampered living of a general officer may have softened his body, but Wen had no doubt the man had retained his flint-hard resolve and tactical sensibilities.

"Perhaps," Wen interjected from his spot across the room, "they mean to goad us into firing the first shot— to make us the aggressors in a devastating war." He spoke to the President, unconcerned as to whether he convinced the general of anything or not. A sword, after all, was not meant to stay sheathed. Advice from the military would always contain a military option. It was the way of things.

"*Zhǔxí* Chen," General Sun continued, using the word that had meant *chairman* during Mao's day, but was now commonly translated as *president*. "The United States is well aware that it could not win a protracted war in our battle space. They are stretched thin with Korea and have neither the stomach nor means to occupy anything else east of Japan for any length of time, not with the world such as it is. They will try to utilize their carriers and submarine fleets to attack us from afar. So far, we have planned for little beyond denying them access to our waters. But Mr. President, national honor demands we take the fight—"

The President raised his hand, waving away the assault of words. General Sun fell silent immediately.

"I understand our national honor," Chen said, more

contemplative than angry. "And I am more than aware of the tactics the US will use in an air-sea battle. What I need are options—and a cogent plan of what to do in the face of this open hostility from the US. I cannot understand what is going on in the American President's head. It seems to me as though he is bent on war. The President is practically in bed with the Japanese. Two of the most notorious terrorists in our nation were handed over to the Pakistanis—who conveniently let them escape." He gazed out of the floor-to-ceiling windows to his left, breathing deeply, thinking on each word. "I wonder what the Americans would have done if we'd had bin Laden and handed him over to France. I have to tell you, gentlemen, even if I did not want a war, there are plenty in the Central Committee who think it is the wisest course of action—blood and treasure notwithstanding."

Wen had no love lost for the United States, but chose to look at things as they were, rather than as nationalist fervor wished them to be.

"Sir," he said, speaking evenly, mirroring the President's demeanor. "I agree with the general's point that after decades of fighting in the Middle East, Americans have no stomach for war—but I assure you, they have much less stomach for defeat. Even if our strikes disable US communications satellites and cripple their naval assets with the first salvo of nuclear missiles—a relatively blind and wounded United States would counterstrike with enough force from their surviving submarines and carriers that our losses would be in the millions."

"Perhaps it would be millions." General Sun sniffed dismissively. "But are those lives not a small price to pay to chase the US out of our waters for good?"

"Any victory would be a Pyrrhic one," Wen said, "At

the cost of so much blood and treasure that our economy would crumble—"

"Or perhaps the economy would grow." Admiral Jiang nodded thoughtfully. At sixty-six, he was the oldest man in the room by a decade. He was fit for his age, had a square jaw and military bearing—but he parted his jet-black hair in the middle, a habit that Wen found off-putting and distinctly un-Chinese. "The Americans flaunt their perceived power in our noses at every turn," the admiral said. "They appear to want a war. I do not need to remind you that though the side that shoots first, so to speak, may be judged the aggressor in the court of public opinion, that side will also have a considerable advantage in the fight."

General Sun leaned farther forward. "In an air-and-sea battle with the United States, first strike would be a necessity, sir. I believe, as do many of my colleagues, that we could endure the heavy losses sustained in such a conflict—even a nuclear war—as long as we make the primary move."

"Are these colleagues that agree with your assessment the same wise men who allowed a sensitive prototype weapon to be stolen from a poorly guarded warehouse in Penggu?" The President tipped his head slightly to one side, eyes locked on the general while he waited. This was not a rhetorical question.

Wen decided to step in, more to let the President know the status of the stolen weapon than to let the bloviating general off the hook. If Sun had his way, nuclear missiles would arc westward by nightfall.

"We have information that may lead us to the Black Dragon, sir," he said, careful not to give himself an impossible deadline to find something that was lost because of the military's inept security measures.

General Sun glared at the interruption and the news

that MSS possessed information that had not been shared with the army.

"This thing you've lost." The President leaned back in his chair addressing the question to anyone with an answer. "This Black Dragon. It's not nuclear, correct?"

"That is true," General Sun said. "But thermobaric weapons are sometimes called the 'poor man's nuclear device.' The effects are devastating."

Chen Min gave a thoughtful nod. "I understand the Americans do not have such a device."

"Not as such," Minister Wen said. "The US arsenal includes many thermobaric bombs. Their Javelin for instance is a shoulder-fired missile much like this one. But for its size, the Black Dragon is much more powerful. An ugly weapon."

"Ugly and useful," the general said.

"Ugly, useful, and small enough to make it difficult to locate, I'd imagine," the President said. "Please work in concert on this, gentlemen. I do not need to tell you what sort of problems it will cause if our own Black Dragon, say, made its way here to Beijing. There are those who would be happy to see such a thing deployed against this very office."

"Understood, sir," General Sun said. He took a deep breath, holding his hat in both hands. "Mr. President, I must speak frankly. I hold Minister Wen in the greatest of all possible esteem, but regarding our clear victory over the United States during a possible conflict, I have more faith in our country than he does. The minister's world is one of spies and deceit—which, I freely admit, is necessary for the security of our nation. The admiral and I operate in a world of honor and duty—a world of direct attack. We have a plan in place that will allow China more than any Pyrrhic victory." He looked at Jiang, who nodded in forceful agreement.

"Even as we speak, Mr. President," the admiral said, "if the Americans want war, we have assets in position to crush them."

"Very well," Chen Min said. He gave a flick of his hand as he stood, knocking a silver teapot off his desk in the process. All three men moved at once to pick up the pot, nearly knocking each other over in the process. The President stopped them with a look.

"Tea and blood are both impossible to retrieve once they have been spilled," he said. "Trust that I am not above spilling either if I see that it is the right move. In the meantime, someone find out what is going on in the mind of that fool America has for a President. And while you are at it, capture the Feng brothers and locate our missing weapon."

Wen did not say it in front of the others, but he had someone working on that very plan. He looked across the spacious office at the fallen teapot. The admiral caught his eye and gave him a pleasant nod. There was no doubt that he and the general had a plan of their own.

Chapter 7

Kashgar, China, 7:35 PM

Quinn swerved the stubby Wuling microvan to avoid a broken donkey cart and took the left lane to keep moving forward. Known as *mianbao che* or a breadbox car, the miniscule van was hardly larger than a compact car. Thibodaux had the passenger seat shoved back as far as he could and threatened to bust the thing off its rails to keep his knees from digging into the beige plastic dash.

They had come up from the isolated Chinese outpost of Tashkurgen on the Karakoram Highway from the southwest, leaving the drifting sands of the Taklaman Desert for the lush oasis-fed orchards of pistachios, walnuts, and almonds that began to spring up the closer they got to Kashgar. Great fields of millet and watermelon stretched on either side of the road in a patchwork of varying shades of verdant green as they drew nearer the city.

Jacques stared out the window, slouching with his knees canted sideways. He hadn't said a word in the last ten minutes—which, Quinn was certain, was some kind of record.

"Something on your mind?" Quinn asked.

"Did I tell you my cousin, Khaki, joined the FBI?"

Quinn shot him a surprised glance. "I thought she just got married to that Beaudine guy."

"She did," Thibodaux said. "They both got hired for the same academy. A buddy system or some such thing." He rolled his eyes. "Weird to think of it . . . Khaki Beaudine, FBI . . ."

Quinn shrugged. "The way things are going, it will be good to have someone you can trust on the inside."

"She's my cousin," Thibodaux said. "Who says I trust her?" His face darkened and he got to the meat of his worries. "You think Camille looks like Téa Leoni?"

"Same husky voice, maybe." Quinn couldn't help but chuckle at the random things that might be bouncing around in Jacques Thibodaux's brain at any given moment. "But the looks are 180 degrees off."

"Yeah." The big Cajun shrugged. "But I had a dream about Téa Leoni last night. Camille would shit a brimstone brick if she thought I had a thing for Téa Leoni."

Quinn rolled his eyes. "I think you've been away from home too long."

"I'm sorry, l'ami." Jacques gave a sheepish grin. For a guy who could bench 405, he had the embarrassed schoolboy thing down pretty good. "But this not being able to call her has me all screwed up. I don't mind tellin' you this dream scares my mule. Camille has a way of lookin' into my skull and finding out about shit like this."

Quinn shrugged, both hands on the steering wheel. "Good. Then maybe you can channel a little bit of your inner Camille the next time we need to get information out of somebody and pull something out of their skull."

"Whatever you say, Chair Force, but this is serious

business. I haven't had a dream about any woman besides Camille in years. Wooeeee!" He shook his head as if to purge any unclean thoughts about Téa Leoni. "Anyhow, don't you fret. I'll focus on not getting killed now that we're coming into civilization."

"Good idea," Quinn said, breathing a measured sigh of relief when he brought the van off the relatively light traffic of the Karakoram Highway and into the riot of evening commuters. The packed arterial road was a chorus of honks and shouts mingled with braying donkeys and no one took notice of Quinn's van, swerving or not.

"Funny," Thibodaux said, staring out the dusty window at the sprawling oasis of 350,000 people. "From the way you talked about it, I pictured this place as some Alibaba-ancient Silk Road caravan stop with magic carpets and shit."

"Yeah." Quinn nodded. "The Chinese government's knocking more and more old buildings down every day to make way for progress." Quinn sped up to get ahead of a motorized trike hauling a load of fat-bottomed sheep in the rusty bed. Once far enough ahead, he took another lane to turn on Renmin Road toward his old friend Dr. Gabrielle Deuben's neighborhood. "There won't be any of the old town left before too long." He took his eyes off the road long enough to shoot a glance at Thibodaux. "But believe me, there are still plenty of places for the Feng brothers to hide."

"We'll find 'em." Thibodaux grinned, tipping his head at the low sun that cast long shadows through the last pistachio grove before the land gave way completely to concrete and stone. "We got a while until dark."

Quinn smiled to himself, remembering the shadowed

mazes of alleys, dead-end roads, and walled courtyards that made up Kashgar's centuries-old neighborhoods.

"There are some places," he said, "where night falls well before dark."

Gabrielle Deuben's home was located in an apartment above her the clinic. Quinn parked the van a block down out of habit, backing in so he had plenty of room to drive away unimpeded if he had to leave in a hurry.

He'd not spoken to Deuben since she'd helped him and Garcia get across the Wakhan Corridor into Afghanistan nearly two years before. Any hotel would require a passport and he hoped the doctor would give them a place to rest their heads for a few minutes— along with any information she might have come across from the working girls she treated that would lead them to the Feng brothers. Quinn wasn't a hundred percent sure that she was even still in the same place, but her missionary zeal when it came to treating the ailments of the prostitutes and other poor in Central Asia made it a pretty sure bet. People like Deuben tended not to even go on vacation, afraid of what might happen to those in their charge if they went anywhere else. Tajik, Kyrgyz, Uyghur, and Chinese traveled for miles to have her treat their various ailments. Stern and to the point, she never held back on her pronouncements, but patients knew she cared about them. Why else would she stay and work with such a forsaken people? Quinn found himself asking himself the same question—and then he got out of the van.

A warm evening wind, heavy with the scent of cumin and roasting lamb, hit him in the face. Two-stroke engines vied for street positions with braying donkeys.

Birds chirped in the trees along the cobblestone street as if their volume knobs were turned up twice as loud as normal American or European birds. The smell of baking bread rolled out from under an awning just down from the van, making Thibodaux lick his lips.

"This place don't need no Aladdin's lamp to be magic," the Cajun said, casting a look up and down the bustling street. Women in colorful headscarves, some wearing Western dress, others in more traditional but equally colorful robes, towed kids dressed in T-shirts with American slogans. Fierce-looking men with sharp Turkic features and scraggly beards chatted under awnings along the side of the road. Some sharpened blades against spinning stones. Some sat for haircuts from other men. Others hacked at freshly killed carcasses of goat and mutton. Almost every adult male wore a four-cornered silk hat called a *doppa*.

The entrance to Gabrielle Deuben's clinic, a rough timber door, was located down a deserted side street behind a stall that sold hand-thrown pottery. A cardboard sign that said CLOSED in Uyghur and Chinese script hung behind a dusty window. It was dark inside. Quinn glanced at his Aquaracer. "It's just after eight o'clock Beijing time," he said. "Hopefully she's home and not off working in some Kyrgyz village."

Thibodaux doubled his fist. "Want me to huff and puff or just give it a knock?"

"Stand by a minute. She has another entrance around back, down the alley there." Quinn took a step back to look up at the second floor windows. He could see a light through the curtains and thought he saw movement, but couldn't be sure. He half expected to see Belvan Virk, Deuben's towering Sikh bodyguard, peek out. "Let's do our knocking around the corner, out of sight."

Leading the way, Thibodaux ran headlong into a waifish Chinese girl as she scuttled away from Deuben's back door. She kept her head down like a person who lived around things she really didn't want to witness. A handful of business cards fell from the pocket of her hand-knit wool vest, spilling across the dusty street.

Quinn stooped to pick them up and handed them back to her. A sinking pit pressed at his gut when he read one of the cards and realized she was a *dingdong xiaojie*, a "doorbell girl." At the low end of the hierarchy among prostitutes in China, a doorbell girl went room to room at hotels and apartments, ringing the bell or sliding her card under the door looking for work.

"Cindy Wei." Quinn read the name printed on the cards. "Are you okay?" He spoke in Mandarin, literally asking why her face color was not excited.

The pouting Cupid's bow of Cindy Wei's mouth was tinged with flecks of bright red lipstick and formed a smudged arrow that pointed upward to desperate eyes.

"Sorry," she said. "I am too sick to help you right now." She took the cards, mistaking Quinn's smile as a proposition for her services. She shot a quick look back down the alley to Deuben's door, then to the main street beyond Thibodaux as if looking for a way to escape. He completely dwarfed the tiny thing and she had to crane her body to see around him.

"You misunderstand me," Quinn said, trying to set the flighty girl's mind at ease. "The doctor is my friend. We're going to see her too."

Cindy Wei's eyes brightened, filling with tears. "Grigor!" She spat as if the name tasted bitter. "They call him The Mongol. He is up there with her now. He and his men . . ." She shook her head. "I must go. I have to find some medicine."

She tried to shuffle away, but Quinn grabbed her arm, a little rougher than he should have. He couldn't let her go without more information.

"The Mongol?" He gave a puzzled Thibodaux a quick thumbnail in English to bring him up to speed, then looked Cindy Wei in the eye. "Who is Grigor and what does he want with Dr. Deuben?"

"He is a cancer," Cindy Wei said, apparently accustomed to being grabbed by rough men. "A mixed-blood gangster. His father was Russian. He runs the Black Hotel racket from here to Urumqi." She used the euphemism "Black Hotel" to mean extortion or protection. "Everyone—the Chinese, the Uyghurs—they are all afraid of him. Even the army looks the other way. He is untouchable."

"And you saw Grigor with the doctor just now?" Quinn felt the white heat of anticipation rush to his core as his body prepared for a fight.

Cindy Wei shook her head, wincing at some memory. "One of the men that works for him. But Grigor was at the Chini Bagh Hotel last night. I accidentally knocked on his door. I never would have gone near the place if I had known The Mongol was in town. He's a filthy thing, worse than an animal." She pulled her collar away to show a necklace of purple bruises. "I hope he catches the drips from me!"

Quinn had known more than his fair share of prostitutes over the course of his career, but the way this sad young woman spoke so bluntly about the diseases of her trade sent a chill up his spine.

"So you didn't actually see him, but you think Grigor is here at the clinic now?" Quinn asked, trying to nudge Cindy Wei back on subject.

She nodded. "One of his men came to the door. I said I needed to see the doctor, but he didn't care. He told me she was busy and said to get lost. Grigor never goes anywhere without his men—and they never go anywhere without him. He is in there, probably making Doctor Deuben pay him money for his black hotel." Cindy Wei's face twisted into a squirming grimace. Quinn couldn't help but notice that she was just a few inches taller than his seven-year-old daughter and was maybe in her late teens.

"How many men did you see?" Quinn asked.

"I saw two," she said. "But he always travels with three." She held up her fingers, thumb folded in. She squirmed again. "I really have to pee."

"Go," Quinn said. "I'll tell Dr. Deuben to call you."

"Grigor will kill you," she said over her shoulder as she waddled away.

"We'll be fine," Quinn said.

"Four bad guys?" Thibodaux mused as Cindy Wei rounded the corner to the main street. "Against a United States Marine and one Air Force *pogue* . . . I reckon you're lucky to have me along, *l'ami*."

"According to Cindy Wei, this Grigor is supposed to be a stone-cold killer," Quinn said.

"I much prefer dealin' with killers," Thibodaux said as they trotted down the alley toward the clinic door. "It narrows down my strategy."

Chapter 8

CIA protective officer Adam Knight clung to the last two things that made any sense in his upside-down life—the Director's Detail identification pass that would get him onto the White House campus and a fervent desire to see the Vice President dead. He looked at his watch. Ten minutes and this would all be over. Best-case scenario, he'd spend the rest of his life in prison. Worst case, a bunch of his best friends would blow his head off.

In an agency that fed on secrets and innuendo like a mosquito sucked blood, it was a miracle that he'd been able to keep his downward spiral under wraps. Tall and fit, with the hint of a Boston accent, he'd risen through the ranks of the CIA's protective division to become the lead officer on the Fable detail, the code name given to Virginia Ross, the director of the Central Intelligence Agency. Some said he'd peaked early at only thirty-seven, but he'd been at the top of his game, doing what he loved for someone he genuinely admired. And then the director had been arrested on trumped-up charges by members of the Internal Defense Task Force—the administration's newly formed goon squad.

From the moment Knight had watched his boss—a woman he regarded as he would a favorite aunt—carted off like some sort of axe murderer, he'd heard nothing but rumors. She'd been taken to an undisclosed black site, he figured that, but he could find nothing concrete about what had happened to her. Some self-proclaimed "patriot" sites on the Internet said she'd been rescued after enduring terrible torture at the hands of the IDTF. According to them, she was now in hiding. If she was, she was doing it right, cutting off all contact with anyone in her former life. Knight hoped that was the case. Other sites reported that she was still locked away somewhere or even dead. He'd sworn to protect her with his life—and she had vanished under his watch. If half the stories floating around about the IDTF were true, she was as good as dead.

Every day another politician, reporter, or military officer who opposed the new administration in even the most trivial matters found themselves harassed or taken into custody by the Task Force. The assassinations of both the President and Vice President on the heels of so many recent terrorist attacks had many in the country swallowing whatever the government told them if they thought it might offer them a shred more safety.

Seething inside, Knight kept quiet and unnoticed in an agency that already prided itself on anonymity. He kept up the pretense of nose-to-the-grindstone devotion in his work and then assaulted his liver each night sharing drinks with acquaintances from every alphabet-soup agency he could think of. He kept the conversations light, noting every word but refusing to join in even

the most innocuous criticisms of the present administration. After each meeting, he'd return to his apartment and write a detailed description of any new
intelligence he'd gained. He spent hours on the Internet, browsing through a proxy server to find any trends
that might shed more light on what was going on in the
country. He was single, so no one was around to chide
him for living on seven Red Bulls and two hours of
sleep a day—or to witness his death spiral.

A law-and-order man to the core, it took Knight very
little time at all to realize Vice President McKeon was
the man behind the curtain—but two full weeks to get
his head wrapped around the fact that someone had to
kill him. It wasn't much of a leap for the protective
agent to realize that he was one of the handful of people who had the access, opportunity, and skill set to get
that job done. Once he'd made the decision to go ahead,
implementation was fairly straightforward.

Knight parked off G Street in a lot next to the World
Bank building, passing through security first at the
OEOB—the Old Executive Office Building—where
the Vice President had ceremonial offices and staff.
Knight knew McKeon would not be there. President
Drake was a buffoon who couldn't keep his pants zipped.
Someone had to run the country and it was common
knowledge that that someone was the crazy-eyed
Skeletor Vice President.

Knight put on a fake smile as he swiped his White
House Visitor ID badge. He said hello to the uniformed
Secret Service officer at the entry point, a young red-
head named Miller.

"You got a detail coming in?" the officer asked, re-
viewing his clipboard. The beautiful thing about being
with CIA protective division was that people rarely

questioned specifics, assuming most everything Knight did was above their clearance level.

"No," Knight said. "It's just me." He tapped the breast pocket of his suit jacket. "I'm trying to link up with Harper on Stovepipe's detail." He used the Secret Service code name for the VP—a nod to the fact that McKeon was tall and gaunt and often compared to Abraham Lincoln. "I lost a pair of Nationals tickets on a bet." He leaned in, confiding a secret. "Presidents Club seats."

"No shit? Behind home plate?" Miller's eyes lit up. He grinned and held out his hand, fingers fluttering. "I'm afraid you'll have to go ahead and leave those with me."

"Yeah, right," McKnight said. "I'd better give them to him myself so they don't . . . get lost."

A group of staffers came through the door in a herd behind him and Miller waved Knight through with a shake of his head. "Suit yourself. He's been over at Crown since 0700." The officer used the Secret Service code name for the executive offices in the White House.

Knight cut through the wide, polished halls of the OEOB, catching a muggy blast of morning air as he popped out on the other side. He stopped for a moment at the top of the broad steps leading down to the second set of security gates that would take him onto the White House campus. The thought occurred to him that once inside, he'd likely never see the sun again. Shoving such notions aside, he walked on. If he quit now, nothing would matter anymore. *He* wouldn't matter.

Knight kept up the smile, tapping his chest and repeating the story about the Nationals tickets at the outer gate and again at the West Wing entrance. He'd often accompanied Director Ross to meetings in the White House. He was on a first-name basis with most of the staff and they were accustomed to seeing him around.

He could hear Vice President McKeon's voice coming from around the corner, hypnotic and creepy even while he was yelling at someone. The uniformed Secret Service officer at the security screening station rolled his eyes and handed back Knight's credentials. "Welcome to my world," he said.

The National Security Advisor's office was to his immediate right—and the VP's office was just beyond it on the same side.

"Harper?" Knight asked, nodded to the doorway at his right.

"He was getting his ass chewed by the Chief of Staff the last time I saw him."

That made sense. In most administrations, the Chief of Staff was a powerful figure, running interference and dictating most of the President's schedule. But since Drake had assumed the presidency, McKeon had made certain he was the only one dictating anything to do with the President. The Chief of Staff, frustrated at being emasculated in his job, would strike out at anyone who couldn't do anything about it—like security.

Knight repeated the story about the tickets. "I just need to put these in his hand."

"Suit yourself," the officer said, and waved him through.

Visitors were required to be on a list, even with a pass, but security personnel were like postmen in their invisibility. It was accepted that they would lurk in halls and linger outside doors where important meetings took place. They were armed window dressing that was barely noticed and tolerated as a necessary evil until the shit hit the fan.

The best dignitary protection consisted of a series of concentric rings, like the layers of an onion—but there was little that could be done when the inside layer of the onion wanted to do the killing. Knight's plan was simple. He would walk straight up to the Vice President and empty his pistol into the man's chest.

Knight strode through the West Wing lobby with a purpose, locked on like a guided missile now that he was so close to his target. He followed McKeon's slightly nasal voice down the carpeted hall toward the Chief of Staff's office. Harper stepped out just as he passed the VP's secretary's office and nearly ran into him.

"Guys up front radioed to say you had some tickets for me?"

Knight put out his hand in what turned out to be an overly exuberant greeting, heart in his throat. He could plainly hear the Vice President talking just steps away around the corner in the Chief of Staff's office. He had to move now or risk losing the perfect moment—a moment that might never present itself again.

"Washington Nationals, buddy." He kept his voice at a whisper, the way protective agents become accustomed to speaking after years of working in the halls of government elite. "You won, I lost, so I'm here to pay up."

"What's this all about, Adam?" Harper gave him a quizzical look. "You could have just dropped them by my apartment."

Knight could feel the other agent's eyes boring into him, sizing him up as a possible threat. He had about half a second before he'd be asked to leave—politely at first, and then forcibly booted out the door. It was what he would have done had the roles been reversed.

"Well, I was in the area," Knight said, taking the tickets out of his jacket pocket and letting them fall to the ground.

All Harper had to do was look down. He did, watching the fluttering paper long enough to allow Knight to slip by him unimpeded.

Knight heard Harper's startled shout behind him as he shouldered his way past and rounded the corner through the door to the Chief of Staff's office, pistol already in his hand. Harper might shoot him in the back at any moment, but by then it would be too late.

Vice President Lee McKeon came into view an instant later, towering over the Chief of Staff's desk, pounding on a stack of files with the flat of his hand. He was less than fifteen feet away. It would be an easy shot.

Knight caught a flash of something out of place as he brought the gun to bear. It was dark and fast and moved obliquely along the inside wall—directly toward him. He stepped sideways to avoid this new threat, keeping his focus on McKeon. Before he could pull the trigger—or even take a breath—an Asian woman threw herself in front of him and loosed a chilling scream as if he'd already shot her.

Chapter 9

Kashgar

A dusty Land Rover sat parked in the shadows of the three-story brick wall outside the back entrance to Deuben's clinic. Thibodaux put a hand flat on the hood and raised the brow of his good eye. "Still warm," he whispered. "Your friend's got company all right."

A flurry of German curses, flung on the pointed voice of Gabrielle Deuben, poured through a crack in the second-story window above them.

"I don't know what she's saying," the big Cajun said, "but she don't sound like the happy sort of woman."

A muffled grunt followed, like someone being hit in the belly.

Quinn put a shoulder to the door. Locked. He stepped aside, making way for Thibodaux. Booting a door himself when the big Cajun was around was akin to using a teaspoon to dig a ditch. He could do it, but why?

"Now you can huff and puff," Quinn said.

It had been nearly two years, but Quinn still had a clear picture of the interior layout. Doors to the clinic and the small kitchen Deuben used as her personal office ran off the end of a short hallway. Just inside and to the right, blue cotton curtains covered the entrance to a set of timber stairs, roughhewn and nearly as steep as a ladder. They were ancient and creaky, a passive burglar alarm, but that mattered little since Thibodaux had put his boot to the back door with great effect, splintering the jamb with a loud crack in the process. Rather than creeping up, Quinn and Thibodaux bounded up the steps, hoping to reach the top before Grigor and his men had time to formulate a strategy.

Quinn heard a second gasp when he was mid stairway, followed by another torrent of German curses. He hit the top step at an all-out run.

The upstairs was comprised of a one large open room with what looked like a small bathroom off the far back corner. Two large timber support columns ran up to wooden ceiling beams in the middle of the twenty-by-twenty room. A bald Chinese man with his shirtsleeves rolled up over brawny forearms stood over Belvan Virk beside the column to Quinn's left. The muscular Sikh slumped in a chair, chin to chest, his bare feet and hands tied in place with thick cords. His face was a swollen mass of blood and bruises, but he managed a crooked smile when he looked up to see Quinn.

At the other end of the room, at the foot of a tidy double bed, Gabrielle Deuben was also tied to a chair. A tall man stood over her while two henchmen wearing jogging suits slouched on the foot of the bed, as if waiting for orders. Deuben wore only a thin cotton gown that had ripped in some earlier struggle and now hung well off a pale shoulder, exposing more than it covered. Deuben was far from being the sort to slump in defeat, but the tendons in her neck strained like knotted ropes as she arched her back and fought the ropes that held her in place. The Mongol's men had not been gentle when they'd tied her up and her hands and bare feet were purple from loss of circulation. Spittle dripped from her lips.

Deuben's face fell slack when she saw Virk's change in demeanor, but a smile of her own spread over her face when she followed the Sikh's gaze. Catching Quinn's eye, she shot a quick look at the tall man looming over her, as if to let him know this was the one behind her present troubles. This had to be Grigor The Mongol.

He was more thickly built than the others in his crew, and there was a natural curl to his head of shaggy black hair. His brows grew wild and bushy over deep-set eyes. An expensive leather vest covered a tailored white dress shirt, complete with gold cuff links. The shirt was unbuttoned halfway down the front, exposing a dozen gold chains draped across his hairless chest. He clutched a heavy riding crop of braided rawhide in a gloved hand. Far from a simple quirt or whip, the rough leather resembled a short version of a South African hippo or rhino skin *sjambok*, capable of flaying skin or worse.

It was easy to see how such a man might intimidate a more timid sort into doing business with his "black hotel." Full of his own perceived power, he misjudged the situation completely when he saw Quinn.

None of his men appeared to have a gun, but Quinn knew from hard experience how quickly a weapon could materialize.

Thibodaux had never really stopped moving when he reached the top of the stairs. He chose the man sweating over Virk as the object of his fury. A deep growl grew in the big Cajun as he plowed into the much smaller man. Lifting him high over his head by the belt and scruff of the neck he slammed the man into the floorboards like a bug against a windshield. A boot to the ear kept him there.

The two goons who had been sitting on the bed sprang to their feet and bore down on Quinn at a run. He side-stepped the leader like a matador, dropping to a crouch as the second man ran into him, intent on a tackle. The point of Quinn's shoulder caught the man low in the belly, driving the wind from his lungs. Quinn twisted slightly, matching the man's momentum while spring-ing upward at the same time, pushing with his legs. Upended, Quinn's would-be attacker flipped face-first into the wooden floor with a sickening thud. Quinn booted him hard in the ribs to keep him down.

The man who'd run past decided to keep going, yelling over his shoulder at his boss that he was going for help.

"Don't let him get away!" Quinn snapped, but Jacques was already sprinting toward the stairs.

Seeing one man abandon him and two more reduced to crumpled heaps on the floor, The Mongol turned to face Quinn. His mouth twisted into an unnatural twitchy half smile—he was a cruel man, now terrified for his own safety. He held the rawhide swagger stick like a sword above Deuben's head. "I will break her neck before you could reach me," he said.

"Shǎzi!" Quinn spoke in rapid-fire Chinese. "Idiot! Do you have any idea who this woman's friends are? You are fortunate that you have not truly harmed her. As circumstances stand now I will be able to take my boss one of your ears—to let him know you heard his message."

"My ear?" The twitch in Grigor's smirk boiled over into his right eye. "What are you talking about?"

Quinn stepped sideways toward the heavy timber support column nearest the bed. Grigor was forced to turn with him to keep him in sight.

Quinn yawned as if he was fatigued at the mundane

nature of the fight. "If you had hurt her," he said, "I would have been forced to return to my boss with your head. But taking heads is such an ugly business, best left to thuggish brutes."

"You are bluffing." The eye twitch grew into something that looked like full-blown apoplexy.

A muffled cry rose up from the stairwell when Jacques caught the fleeing member of The Mongol's crew. Quinn shrugged. "No help on the way, Grigor."

"You are dead," The Mongol whispered, his voice growling louder with every word. "Dead. Do you hear me? I will have you killed before you can flee the city."

Quinn looked at his fingernails, feigning boredom again. "I doubt your men will trust a leader with no ears."

Grigor's eyebrows shot upward. "You said one ear!"

"I did," Quinn goaded. "But you appear to be hard of hearing—"

Mentally undone, the gangster loosed a low growl. Rushing forward, he swung blindly with the leather crop.

His back to the column, Quinn had already decided to use the heavy timber as a weapon. With the end state of the fight already in his mind, it was a fairly simple matter to get from A to B with a man like Grigor who bullied his way through life on little more than bluster, bruised women, and brawn.

Quinn stepped inward, closing the distance to catch The Mongol's arm high at the shoulder, robbing his swing of power. At the same moment, Quinn pivoted, bringing the point of his elbow across the other man's jaw, cracking teeth and opening a two-inch gash in his cheek. Reversing directions, Quinn let his arm snake up and over the back of a staggered Grigor's neck, trapping the man under his armpit. Using his opponent's momentum against him, Quinn yanked backwards, slamming the top of Grigor's skull into the heavy column. There was a good chance such a blow would kill the man, but Quinn didn't have time to care. He felt Grigor go slack in his arm and let him fall.

Kicking the swagger stick out of reach, Quinn did a quick pat down to make certain there were no hidden pistols. Satisfied Grigor and the other two men posed no immediate threat, Quinn moved to check on Deuben.

She looked up at him with blinking wide gray eyes, her mouth agape. "Do you ever lose a fight?"

"Every time," Quinn said, rolling his shoulder and feeling the cartilage pop a little more than it had just a few moments before.

"See to Belvan first," Deuben said, her voice frayed from screaming threats at her tormentors.

Quinn drew a wicked, fat little blade called a Riot from his belt sheath and cut her loose first anyway. "He needs a doctor."

"I am fine, little brother," the big Sikh said, his words thick with Punjabi enunciation, despite his swollen face. He dabbed at a bloody lip once Quinn cut him loose as well. "Lucky for them you happened along when you did. I believe that one was about to injure his hand on the bones of my face."

Thibodaux lumbered in with the last member of Grigor's crew draped over his shoulder, out cold, arms trailing.

"This one decided he didn't want to leave so bad after all, *l'ami*," the Cajun grunted, tossing the limp body on the floor next to the others.

"Jacques Thibodaux," Quinn said, nodding toward Deuben, who now used her fingers to comb tenderly through the Sikh's long beard examining his wounds. "I'd like you to meet Dr. Gabrielle Deuben and her bodyguard, Belvan Virk."

Virk extended his hand. Deuben nodded, but continued to fuss over the Sikh, ignoring the fact that her thin cotton gown was torn from shoulder to hip. Soft tut-tuts and tender chidings said their relationship had moved well past the bodyguard and client relationship.

"It is a pleasure to meet the brother of a little brother," Virk said, eyes fluttering at the attention from the woman who was surely his lover.

Quinn gestured toward Grigor's body. Even unconscious, the man's mouth turned up in a crooked smirk. "Seems as though I've happened by again when you're in the middle of an adventure."

"This is Kashgar, Mr. Quinn," Deuben said. "The Wild West of China. Each and every day is fraught with this sort of adventure. You just happened by on a Tuesday." She let her hand linger on Virk's shoulder. "You're going to need stitches, *mein schatz.*"

Moving quickly as if she'd come to some decision, she strode across the room to the bed. Deuben possessed the sensibilities of a physician when it came to nudity—even her own. She peeled the gown over her head and tossed it in the corner garbage bin and stood naked while she searched through a basket of laundry for something else to wear.

"You have forgotten our company, my dear," Belvan said, who looked naked even in a pair of slacks without his customary turban and Sikh crest.

"Ha! I know how a man's brain works." She gave a dismissive laugh. "I was much less modest in that bit of torn gown than I am out of it completely."

"I do not blame her." Virk rolled his eyes at Quinn. "But with her experience, sometimes I wonder that she likes any men at all."

"I like the strong ones," Deuben said, glaring at the unconscious Grigor while she stepped into a pair of clean khaki pants. "It's the weak bastards who pretend to be strong at the expense of women who disgust me."

Across the room, Quinn saw Thibodaux shudder.

After pulling on a white T-shirt, Deuben grabbed a traveling medical kit out of the closet and opened it on the bed. She filled several small syringes from various ampules she got from the bag. Then, holding all but two of the syringes in her teeth, she squatted beside the still unconscious Russian. She used the first to inject something straight into his stomach and then gave him several small shots from the second on the side of his head and neck.

Moving from person to person, she gave each of the other three men a single injection in the hip, through their clothing.

"There," she said as she finished the last shot. "That should keep them all sedated, for the near term at least."

"You gave Grigor more shots," Thibodaux said, squinting as if he really didn't want to know the answer. "What was that all about?"

"'First, do no harm,'" Deuben said, groaning as she used the timber column to get to her feet. "I have taken an oath as a physician. The second syringe was a local anesthetic to make it less painful when you cut off his ear. If you wish to maintain the respect of a man like Grigor The Mongol, you must follow through on your word."

Chapter 10

Ran Kimura sensed the threat before she saw it, low, almost painful in her belly. Small in stature, she made up for her size with an uncanny skill from a lifetime of training. The edge of a dark tattoo showed above the low V at the open collar of her silk blouse. She'd been standing just inside the doorway to the Chief of Staff's office, waiting to follow McKeon toward the Oval. It was only by happenstance—and her abhorrence of being anywhere near the idiot President Drake for one second longer than she had to—that she'd waited instead of going on to meet him there.

She moved the instant the man entered the room—a place where he had no business being. She saw his hand sweep the tail of his suit jacket as he reached for his sidearm, already crouching slightly the way American law enforcement did when they prepared to shoot.

Going through a process sometimes called the OODA Loop—Observe, Orient, Decide, Act—it took the average police officer a little over two seconds to decide to draw and fire. Something out of the ordinary might disrupt this loop and make the actor have to start the process of orientation over, slowing the time toward action. Though the man, an agent from the way he moved, had already decided to kill McKeon, he was, in his heart, one of the good guys and wanted to do so without taking an innocent life.

Ran screamed as she moved, using the most fragile and terrified voice she could muster. Stunned by the cry, the agent paused for a split second, giving her time to spring forward, slamming the point of her shoulder into his floating ribs and driving him backwards. Her own hand shot to the collar of her light wool blazer during the rebound, snatching a razor-sharp thumb dagger from inside the reinforced lapel. A flick of her hand severed his carotid artery, spraying an immediate arc of blood across the room at the same moment his pistol cleared the holster. A consummate professional, Knight could have still shot and killed McKeon before he bled to death, but Ran was still moving. She ignored the swath of spraying blood and caught the hand that held his pistol as it rose toward the intended target. Letting the thumb dagger fall to the carpet, she trapped Knight's hand in hers, and stepped toward him, turned his wrist inward on itself in a tight circle. This *kote-gaeshi*, or wrist reversal, used Knight's own weight and momentum to snap the small bones in his wrist. His trigger finger convulsed when the weapon was turned, the round impacting him just below his diaphragm. Ran wrenched the gun away after the initial stunning round, putting three rapid shots into the man's neck to obliterate the work from her thumb dagger.

She pushed away, dropping the gun beside the dying man and falling to the floor in the process, soaking the seat of her slacks in his blood. She scooped up the thumb dagger and dropped it in the pocket of her blazer. She summoned a flood of tears— she used them just as effectively as she had the dagger and pistol.

The entire process, from Ran's scream to the attacker's head hitting the floor, took just under three seconds. A Secret Service agent named Harper burst into the room with pistol in hand. Legs splayed, tears streaming down a stricken face, Ran raised her open hands and turned her head away to keep from being shot.

Secret Service agents are trained to protect before they investigate. When he didn't find anyone to shoot, Harper grabbed the Vice President by the scruff of the neck and hustled him out the door away from the blood and into the arms of a cadre of arriving agents. Claxons sounded up and down the hall, calling for a general lockdown of the West Wing. Inside the Oval Office, the President's Secret Service detail would be surrounding him in a bristling phalanx of ballistic vests, pistols, and submachine guns and rushing him to the bunker.

Ran stopped crying immediately once she found herself alone in the room with the dead body and a pallid, trembling David Crosby. She stood to face the Chief of Staff, wiping her bloody hands on the thighs of her slacks, not because she was disgusted, but because blood was slick and she wanted to be ready if another threat presented itself.

"I want to know who this man was," she said, turning the dead man's ashen face toward her with the toe of her navy blue pump.

"Adam Knight," Crosby said, rolling his lips until they turned white. "He was the agent in charge of the CIA Director's detail. I should call the FBI."

"I'm sure the Secret Service is doing just that," the Japanese woman said.

Crosby's jaw hung slack. A wisp of thinning hair hung down across a pasty forehead. "That was amazing," he said. "That thing you did with his hand . . . you saved the Vice President's life."

"I panicked." Ran tried to downplay the speed with which she'd dispatched the shooter. It was much better if people thought her merely McKeon's sullen concubine rather than his protector. "And he was sloppy. Anyone could have done it."

It took the better part of an hour for Secret Service personnel from both POTUS and VPOTUS details to confer and decide to give the all clear for the White House campus. A team of agents from the Washington Field Office of the FBI—as well as Director Bodington himself—arrived twenty-one minutes after the shooting, but were forced to sit outside until the Secret Service decided to admit them. Once inside, they had complete control over everything but the President and Vice President's immediate security. Since the shooter was a government agent, albeit CIA and not their respective agencies, tensions regarding turf and jurisdiction ran into the stratosphere. Bureau agents milled about conducting interviews and casting looks of blame while the Secret Service personnel glared back at the interlopers who dared to invade their sacred ground.

After four hours and a heated Oval Office chat between Director Bodington and the President, all investigating agents decided they had all the evidence they needed.

President Drake demanded a meeting with McKeon and Ran in his personal study as he had the White House back to himself. The study was located off the Oval Office. It was more private, and absent the peephole in the door leading out to his personal secretary and body man's area.

Fuming at the dictatorial summons, McKeon found himself unsteady on his feet at having been so close to death. It wasn't so much that he was afraid of dying—he simply had too much left to do and did not want to see his father's legacy ruined because of some madman with a vendetta.

Hartman Drake fumed and paced in the tiny office like a caged cat wearing a bow tie. He'd tossed his suit jacket over the arm of a leather couch and worked to remove gold cuff links while he was on the move. He was not a tall man, but hours in the gym—hours when he should have been doing his job—had given him an incredible physique for a politician of any age. Veins bulged on the side of his bullish neck as if he'd pulled the bow tie too snug.

McKeon sat on the far end of the couch next to the window overlooking the Rose Garden, more exhausted than he'd been in a very long time. He'd already fielded a call from his wife, who'd heard about the shooting on the news. The call had set Ran even more on edge and she moved even closer to him, sitting all the way forward on the edge of the couch, her body taut as if she planned to spring up and fend off another attack at any moment.

She had changed out of her blood-soaked business suit and into a pair of jeans and a black cotton blouse with long sleeves. It looked hot for summer in DC but it hid the tattoos that covered her body from shoulder to just above the knee. In any case, McKeon was not at all sure that Ran felt normal sensations like hot and cold weather.

"What the hell happened?" Drake demanded, falling back in a thick leather chair and throwing his feet up on his desk. "I'm not about to set foot in Seattle if we can't even keep some crazy assassin from slipping into the White House. Best security in the world, my ass. Who was this guy?"

"The lead agent on Director Ross's protective detail," Ran offered, deadpan.

McKeon chose his words carefully. "We cannot cancel the trip to Seattle," he said. "The Japanese advance team has been here for a week. Plans have been set. I don't have to tell you how crucial this meeting is."

Drake waved away the words, ripping off his bow tie. "I am aware of how important it is." His eyes narrowed, glaring as if he was accusing McKeon of something.

"What is it?" McKeon asked, anger at the other man's impudence rising in his gut. "Say what's on your mind."

"This guy who got in," Drake said. "This assassin, he went after you?"

"A target of opportunity within the administration." McKeon rolled his eyes.

"No." Drake set his jaw like a bulldog, not buying any of it. "Everybody says this guy badged his way in here looking for an agent on your detail right from the beginning. That means you were the primary target."

McKeon shook his head in dismay. "Are you actually angry that the assassin didn't come to kill *you*?" He'd thought it impossible that Hartman Drake's self-absorbed delusions could ever surprise him.

"What I am angry about," Drake fumed, "is that the American people think you are the one running this show. I read the commentaries. Everyone's saying we're a co-presidency and calling me the Lieutenant Commander in Chief. It's bad enough that half the Congress insists on calling me 'Acting President.'"

McKeon shrugged. "Technically, you are the acting president. This is new ground constitutionally. But it

doesn't matter. You have the powers of the President
so—"

"Do I?" Drake spat. "Because I tried to call a cabinet meeting last week and David told me we couldn't
because you were not available! Do you hear what I'm
saying? I can't call a meeting to run the country because the VP isn't able to attend."

McKeon patted Ran softly on her knee, trying to
calm himself as much as her. Her entire body hummed
with pent up energy but Drake was too self-absorbed to
see it. Had he taken the time to really look at her, he
would have seen that the gleam in her eye and the particular crook of her lips meant she was on the verge of
punching him in the throat with her thumb dagger.

"What do you want me to say?" McKeon muttered.
"Shall I tell you that you are the wisest man I know and
say it was you who put together this entire plan to send
the United States spiraling into a terrible and final *Götterdämmerung*? Do you—?"

"You and your fifty-dollar words." Drake smirked,
shaking his head. "What the hell is a *Götterdämmerung*?"

McKeon stood to his full height and doubled his
fists. McKeon was normally composed to the point some
would consider bland, but Drake's idiocy caused his head
to shake. "You would have starved to death as a small
boy if my father had not taken you from your filthy
Tajik existence and placed you in a good home. . . ."
He clenched his teeth, breathing deeply to try and regain his composure. "What is it you want from me?"

"What I want," Drake said, lips quivering with a
mixture of fear and frustration, "is for you to treat me
with the respect I deserve. I am, after all, the most
powerful man on the planet—something it would do
you well to remember."

He reached behind the desk and picked up a gym bag. "I have to go to the gym and work off some steam," he said. "In the meantime, both of you get the hell out of my—"

A knock at the door cut him off.

"Mr. President." David Crosby's muffled voice came through the door. It was unlocked, but with Drake's tendency to bring pert female staffers back into his office, the Chief of Staff knew better than to open it uninvited. Drake invited him in.

"I'm sorry to bother you, Mr. President," Crosby said, looking relieved that he didn't have to sneak some girl out the back hallway. "You're needed in the Situation Room. Something to do with Chinese submarines."

"Dammit!" Drake dropped his gym bag in his desk chair.

"Do you want me in there?" McKeon smiled inside. "Or would you like me to let you handle this without me, Mr. President?" he said.

"Shut up," Drake said, grabbing his jacket but dispensing with the bow tie. "Of course, I want you in there."

Chapter 11

Kashgar, 8:40 PM

"I watch the news," Gabrielle said as her sure hands worked methodically to stitch the gash under Belvan Virk's left eye. She was noticeably more tender than she had been with the nubbin of skin left behind from Grigor's ear. "Ehmet Feng is a vile human being. I felt certain your government would dispatch someone like you to hunt down a man like him."

"Well, I am glad they sent you, little brother," Virk roared. He tried a smile but the swelling on his face was getting worse by the moment and he only managed a muffled wince through split lips.

"The Fengs have family in Kashgar," Quinn said, failing to mention that he was there without the backing of his government.

"Of course." Virk nodded, receiving a scolding cluck from Deuben as she pulled a suture tight. He closed his eyes and grimaced but kept going with his thought. "It stands to reason that they would come to roost among their Uyghur brethren."

"The Fengs are bad men," Deuben said, her voice humming with tension. "And your country had the little shits safely ensconced in an American prison. Who had the bright idea to hand them over to Pakistan?"

"Our very own President," Thibodaux said, teetering a little from watching the operation. He'd been fine smashing the faces that needed smashing during the fight, and hadn't flinched when Quinn had cut off Grigor's ear—but seeing anyone other than the enemy in pain had a tendency to give the big Cajun a serious case of the wobbles.

Quinn brought Virk and the doctor up to speed on the moles hiding within the highest levels of the US administration—including the President and VP. "It's all connected to that orphanage you told us about in the Wakhan Corridor when Ronnie Garcia and I were here," he said.

"Scheisse," Deuben cursed, as much about Virk's battered face as the situation. Starting on a second wound, she pressed the Sikh's beard to one side with her forearm as she closed a second gash, this one over the bridge of his nose. "Raising children up to hate America . . . That is actually pretty brilliant when you think of it. Though I suppose ISIS and others are doing the same thing now—just more overtly."

"You talk to a lot of working girls as part of your practice," Quinn said. "Can you think of any who might be connected to the Fengs—or anyone who might be a fugitive?"

"A fugitive around here?" Deuben chuckled. "We have no shortage of people wanted by the law in Western China. There have been killings in Kunming, bombings in Urumqi. . . . A local imam was recently hacked to death on the steps of Id Kah Mosque—for the offense of being too moderate. Things are worse than I've ever seen them—and that only gives the Chinese government all the more reason to march in lock-

step over the old city and crush what is left of the culture." She sighed. "It makes me . . . how do you say?
Lebensmüde . . . fatigued. Soon there will be no more
Western China—only China—one great block of concrete, each corner patrolled and kept in check by a
gang of uniformed soldiers."

Virk looked at Quinn and gave him a conspiratorial
wink.

" 'Four things greater than all things are,' " the Sikh
said, again using Kipling to make his point. " '. . .
Women and Horses and Power and War.' " He closed
his eye as Deuben pierced the apple of his cheek, just
above his beard, with her curved needle. "Our Gabrielle is no shrinking violet when it comes to espousing
her passions."

"Violets know nothing but the heels of wicked men,"
Deuben scoffed.

Quinn had seen firsthand on his last visit how deeply
entrenched the doctor was with the Uyghur cause. She
generally sided with them over the ethnic Han Chinese,
whom she saw as interlopers. She wanted no part in
any violent cause or revolution, but if Western China
had been a democracy, she'd surely have put out yard
signs touting the benefits of a free and separate Uyghur
state.

"If anyone knows the whereabouts of the Feng
brothers it would be Hajip," Virk said.

Thibodaux brightened at the sound of a name that
would move them forward. "You think this Hajip guy
will talk to us?"

"He'll try and kill you." Virk chuckled without moving his head while Deuben pulled the last of the sutures
tight. He waved his hand over the four unconscious
gangsters on the bedroom floor. "But I do not imagine
that will prove much of a deterrent for men like you."

"Hajip is active in the East Turkistan Islamic Movement," Deuben said. "To tell you truthfully, I am not certain why the Chinese have not already rounded him up."

"Sounds like a good place to start," Quinn said, shooting a glance at Thibodaux. "The Feng brothers are ETIM as well."

"Anyway," Deuben said. "Hajip will be easy to find. He takes the best spot for his *matang* cart across the street from the mosque."

It was not unheard of for *matang* dealers to use their large and intimidating knives to up the price of their fruit and nut confections after they'd hacked off a piece for a customer. It was delicious but sticky stuff, prone to pulling out fillings, even if the vendor wasn't the sort to rest a thumb on the balance scale and then haggle with his blade.

Virk groaned and let his head fall back in relief as Deuben finished with her needle. She stood and peeled off her blood-smeared latex gloves and tossed them in the garbage bin.

His full beard had cushioned many of the blows from his attacker, but precise sutures crossed much of the flesh of his cheeks like tiny sections of black train track.

"So you are finished torturing me then," the Sikh said.

"I am indeed." Deuben collapsed back on the bed, sitting with her hands in her lap. She looked up at Quinn. "Beijing has doubled our number of PLA soldiers, and that does not take into account the already huge presence of People's Armed Police and the roving packs of sanctioned thugs they use as leg breakers. Nationalist views are high on both sides all over China, but they burn especially bright here in the west. The average Han soldier will see you as Americans—the enemy. Most Uyghur people are hardworking folk who are happy to see a few tourist dollars—but separatists like Hajip are growing in number. To them, you are an infidel, less than human." She looked over the top of a prominent, though not unattractive nose. "Many of the people you meet tonight would be all too happy to see you dead."

"She is right, you know," Virk said, pulling aside his beard to study his wounded face in a hand mirror. He dabbed at the sutures with the tip of his finger, earning another scolding from Deuben.

"The Uyghurs are armed with religious zeal," he continued, "not to mention all manner of axes and knives. The Chinese soldiers have guns and the weight of law. Placing yourselves in between these two factions will be an extremely dangerous endeavor. It will require a . . . delicate touch."

Thibodaux winked his good eye. "That's us." He gave a sickly grin, nodding at the blood-soaked piece of gauze that held Grigor The Mongol's severed ear. "Delicate."

Chapter 12

The White House

Everyone stood when President Hartman Drake entered the situation room, but they kept their eyes glued to the door to make certain McKeon followed him in.

"What have we got?" Drake said, taking his seat at the head of the long table. McKeon sat to his immediate right, rolling his chair away slightly to give the President more space.

Admiral Ricks of the Joint Chiefs along with Secretary of Defense Andrew Filson sat across the table from McKeon. Forrest Beauchamp, the National Security Advisor, sat on the other side of McKeon from the President. The man spent most of his time writing vision statements and watching the television in his office—and that was just fine with the Vice President. When it came to national security, he didn't want anyone to have this idiot President's ear besides him.

Secretary Filson's face was flushed red and his tie was pulled to the side of his collar, as if he'd just been trying to hang himself before rushing to the meeting. McKeon never had been able to put a finger on the man. He seemed to have a difficult time sitting still and often rose from his chair when it was his turn to speak. The constant motion was off-putting, but McKeon made allowances because the man was a hawk when it came to military operations—and that is just what they needed under the present circumstances.

Filson put both hands flat on the leather desk blotter in front of him as if to steady himself, and nodded to the admiral.

"Mr. President, two of our Ocean Imaging satellites have picked up an inordinate amount of submarine traffic out of the Yulin Naval Base in China." He nodded toward a female Navy lieutenant named Robertson sitting at a laptop computer beside him. She had the short black hair and fine cheekbones Drake had a thing for and McKeon couldn't help but notice the President appeared to be more interested in her than he was in the briefing. A few keystrokes later, Robertson pulled up a map of southern China on the video monitor at the far end of the table.

"Mr. President," she said. "The PLA Navy keeps their submarines in caverns on the coast of Hainan Island off the southern coast of China. At present, we believe they have five working nuclear ballistic missile submarines, but those numbers could be low by as many as three. The water is fairly shallow there, maybe thirty to sixty fathoms so our OI birds have been able to—"

"Excuse me, OI?" Drake said, throwing her a flirtatious grin along with his question.

Robertson blushed. She'd obviously heard of the President's reputation. "Ocean Imaging," she said.

"Of course," Drake said. "Please go on, Lieutenant."

"Using lasers, synthetic aperture radar, and infrared, our birds are able to detect subs at that relatively shallow depth. Even when the sub itself is not visible, its wake stays viable for some time, allowing us to get a reading until the bottom drops away out in the South China Sea." She used the laptop to add a series of stars on the existing map, forming a rough triangle from the Philippines to the coast of Ecuador to just north of Hawaii. "We have picked up readings on remote buoys that are consistent with a great deal of submarine activity."

"Our assets?" McKeon asked, since Drake probably would not think of it in his lustful daze.

"We have Los Angeles Class Fast Attacks in the areas of concern," Admiral Ricks said, apparently happy someone was asking the right questions. He pointed toward the monitor with his fountain pen. "The *USS Boise*, the *Alexandria*, and the *Santa Fe* are all prowling, but so far, they have had no contact."

McKeon studied the chart, thinking over his strategy. This new intelligence was more perfect than he could have imagined.

"This much activity and only three submarines?"

"Three Fast Attacks checking out the areas from the buoy signals," the admiral said. "We have boats attached to carrier groups around the world, sir, as well as Ohio class ballistic missile submarines well within the range of China. At any given time, nearly a third of our boats are in for refit or servicing. Budget constraints of the last decade have seen orders for new submarines cancelled, leaving the fleet aging and diminished."

McKeon rubbed his chin as if he was musing over the possibilities. In truth, he'd been waiting for something like this. He turned to Drake and cleared his throat to draw the man's attention away from Lieutenant Robertson.

"Mr. President, considering the state of affairs with China, I think it's time to consider bringing the bulk of our naval forces to the Pacific."

"Mr. President," Secretary Filson said, giving an emphatic shake of his head. "China would see any such movement as a clear provocation."

"Because they'll see we know what they're up to," Drake said, shooting a glance at McKeon to show that, amazingly enough, he understood where he'd been going. "Who do we have in the Persian Gulf?"

"The Fifth Fleet," Admiral Ricks said, giving an almost imperceptible shake of his head. "But, sir, they're necessary to keep—"

"Put together a plan," Drake said. "I want a full briefing on contingencies for moving them into the Pacific by close of business today." He smiled at the admiral's aide. "Now, Lieutenant . . . Robertson," he said, looking at the pretty young officer's name tag. "I'd like to be a little more up to speed on this Ocean Imaging technology. Do you think you could bring your computer to the Oval and enlighten me?"

"I . . . uh . . . suppose," the young woman stammered. She turned to her immediate boss. "With your permission, Admiral Ricks."

"He outranks me," Ricks said, grimacing at the thought.

"Mr. President," Secretary Filson said, bouncing his fist on the table. "I must advise against positioning too many of our forces in one area. The United States faces threats from all over the world. Some are perhaps even deadlier than China."

McKeon gave Filson a serene nod. It was the smartest thing he'd ever heard the warmongering fool say.

Chapter 13

Ehmet Feng tied the father of the family to a chair and killed him last—slowly, after he'd been made to watch his wife and children beg and scream for their lives. Feng's clothing was covered in blood, but he was the same size as his victim. The man's wife had been a fine housekeeper before Ehmet had killed her, so it would not be a problem to find something freshly laundered that he could wear.

Yaqub had grown used to the cruelty of his brother over the years. Ehmet had a strict code of eye-for-an-eye justice. Even as a child, the slightest breach of trust brought more suffering and pain than Yaqub had thought possible—but something had happened to Ehmet in prison, as if some terrible demon had been released.

This man was an informant, the man responsible for telling Chinese authorities their identities after the train bombing in Urumqi—and, because of that, for their eventual capture by the Americans in Afghanistan. Death, even a slow death, had come as a mercy to the traitor. Ehmet had forced him to watch the killing of his wife and two small children. Yaqub could understand the reasoning behind it, but there was something broken inside his brother, something that looked for reasons to punish—and then relished the opportunity like others relished a delicious dessert. It made Yaqub want to sleep behind a locked door at night, for fear of what his brother might do.

Finished with the gruesome butchery, Ehmet dropped the knife in the bound man's lap and looked up at a silent Jiàn Zǒu, who sat at a small kitchen table with a pile of papers and passports. The woman of the house had been preparing a late evening meal when they'd arrived and the snakehead had pushed all the food to the side to give himself room to work. As far as Yaqub could tell, Jiàn Zǒu wasn't so much surprised by his brother's violent activity as he was put out by the time it took when he felt they should be on the move. Head bent over a passport now, pen in hand, he seemed to have blocked out the wailing and death that had just taken place a few feet away from where he sat.

Ehmet waved a hand in front of his face to shoo away a fly that had already followed the scent of blood through the open balcony window of the traitor's apartment. "I am ready to go now if you have the arrangements made."

Jiàn Zǒu shook his head without looking up.

"What were you doing while I was busy here?" Ehmet's face darkened. "You have not made arrangements?"

The Chinese man suddenly pushed back from the table. "If you are done with this business," he said. "A Tajik friend of mine has arranged passage on a cargo flight in a few hours."

Ehmet leaned against a wall and wiped the blood from his hands on rag he'd gotten from the kitchen. He glared at Jiàn Zǒu through narrow eyes. Yaqub knew from growing up with Ehmet that with him it was not so much what you said, as how you said it. "You don't approve of my actions?" he said, giving Jiàn Zŏu a confrontational shrug.

"I personally do not care who you butcher along our route," Jiàn Zŏu said. "Your actions are your business. Getting us out of China is mine."

"Well said, Mr. Zŏu," Ehmet said, rifling through the dead man's closet for a clean shirt. "As long as you remember your business, we may all live through the week."

Yaqub considered the job that lay ahead and decided the odds of any of them living more than a few days were extremely slim, no matter what Jiàn Zŏu did or did not remember.

Chapter 14

"You know," Thibodaux said as they watched Hajip from a safe spot in the crowded twilight, fifty meters from where he ran his *matang* cart. "Just once, I wouldn't mind comin' to an interesting place like this and having a little time to mosey along and enjoy the atmosphere. Camille could do a mean belly dance in one or two of these silk scarves."

Since all of China operated on Beijing time, it was late in the west by the time the sun actually set. Uyghur people operated on their own unofficial time, two hours earlier than Beijing, making it just after nine. While people in the capital might be retiring for the night, the Kashgar night market still hummed with activity.

"Buy her a scarf," Quinn said, breathing in the scent of barbecued lamb. Beside him, a man used a blackened piece of a cardboard box to fan a grill covered with sputtering kabobs. "It'll fit in your pocket. It's getting late, even on Uyghur time, but I'm sure we still have a few minutes before our guy closes up his cart." Quinn nodded toward the adjacent stall where a sharp-eyed woman stood surrounded by wooden rods that held dozens of colorful Uzbek scarves. The apples of her round cheeks were red as if she'd just run a foot-race and her blue eyes gleamed under the string of electric lights as if she'd won the race. A stray lock of auburn hair peeked from her head scarf. Her lips turned up in the tiniest of grins as she surely identified Jacques as a man to whom she could sell an entire sack-ful of scarves. "I'd offer her about half of her asking price," Quinn said, knowing a pushover like Jacques would likely pay double. "You go on. I'll keep an eye on our guy."

Quinn bought himself a small cup of *durap*—a mix-ture of shaved ice, yogurt, and lemon juice. His mouth watered for some of the grilled meat and naan bread, but the likelihood of impending violence made him stick with something on the lighter side.

He paid two yuan to the smiling Uyghur—who looked a lot like his uncle—and walked with his paper cup of *durap* to stand under a mulberry tree and watch. Hajip was tall and he moved through the crowd hawk-ing his nougatlike *matang* with the purposeful air of a man accustomed to getting his way. Gabrielle had been right. Hajip did take the best spot for his cart—but there were really no bad spots among the sounds and sights and smells that made up Kashgar's night market.

Strings of electric lights and open flames from bar-becue grills illuminated the night. A vast sea of stalls selling everything from goat testicles to pirated DVDs of Hollywood movies lined the road under the shadow of the yellow towers of Id Kah—the oldest and largest mosque in China. A few feet from Quinn, an ancient man in a ratty suit jacket and a white silk *doppa* sat cross-legged under a gas lantern selling refurbished leather shoes from a pile spread out before him. Not five yards away, another man, similarly dressed, knelt on the sidewalk over a hogtied ram, directing blood from the gurgling animal's freshly slit throat into a plastic bucket. Beyond this gruesome scene, a Uyghur girl of seven or eight helped her father sell scoops from a pristine white mountain of ice cream.

The smell of fried, grilled, and boiled meat permeated the air, mulling with saffron and garlic and a thousand other spices that flooded Quinn with memories of bazaar and bizarre.

"Mighty short trip from the sidewalk to the stove," Jacques muttered, tossing his head toward where the bleeding ram gave its last dying gurgles. "Pretty damn fresh."

"How much did you pay?" Quinn asked, raising an eye at the two red silk Uzbek scarves Jacques held wadded in his fist.

"I don't want to talk about it," the big Cajun grumbled.

Quinn was about to rib his friend more—but down the block, Hajip answered a call on his mobile phone. He talked for a short time, and then appeared to hang up and make another call that lasted only a few seconds. A moment later, he lifted the handles of his cart and shoved his way through the crowd.

Quinn took the last drink of his melted yogurt and set the wadded paper cup on top of a barrel that overflowed with similar trash. Thibodaux stuffed the scarves in his back pocket. Without a word between them, the two men began to follow, moving slowly as if to look at merchandise, but always keeping an eye on Hajip.

Quinn's hope was to keep the Uyghur in sight, but half a block past the last stalls of the night market the *matang* vendor took a quick right down a side alley. By the time they reached the corner, he had vanished. Quinn thought he heard voices in the darkness and held up his fist, motioning for Thibodaux to stop. Somewhere ahead, the wheels of not one, but two *matang* carts squeaked down the quiet street.

"He's joined up with a friend," Thibodaux whispered. "Maybe that's who he called."

Three blocks later the alley broadened and split into three different directions disappearing down pitch-black pathways between ancient buildings of leaning brick and slumping stone that had surely been here when Kashgar was still a thriving oasis for camel caravans. The voices fell silent, but the squeaking of the cartwheels continued. If Hajip had been better at maintenance they would have lost him.

Feeble pools of yellow lamplight spilled out here and there from windows at various heights in the ancient brick walls. Family sounds filtered down to street level with the reserved quiet of a people used to living in such close proximity and pretending not to know each other's business. Padding slowly and knowing that the big Cajun had his back, Quinn rounded the corner of a crumbling three-story building in time to watch Hajip open the twin wooden doors of what looked like some kind of warehouse or a barn. Another *matang* vendor followed behind him, pushing an identical cart. The building was dark until Hajip entered and switched on a light.

"Looks like there's just the two of them," Thibodaux whispered from where they crouched at the corner.

A dog barked in the distance. The sizzle of frying meat popped through the window above, close enough for them to feel the splatter of grease through open shutters and taste the spiced mutton on the warm evening air.

"You see what you can find out from the other guy while I talk to Hajip," Quinn said, moving toward the warehouse in a shuffling crouch. He knew Thibodaux well enough to be certain the big Marine would prefer head-on action to all this sneaking around.

"I know you got rid of that exploding blunderbuss," Thibodaux said as they moved toward the door. "But these guys are famous for their big-ass knives. I don't guess you've got another pistol up your sleeve."

"This is Kashgar." Quinn grabbed the door handle, ready to go. "There'll be plenty of knives for us."

Hajip had locked the main doors behind him and Jericho had to use the chisel point of his Riot to jimmy the flimsy lock. From the outside the place looked to be as big as a deep three-car garage. Easing from the darkness into the lighted warehouse allowed Quinn to make it fifteen feet from Hajip before he even looked up from his cart. Quinn was surprised to see that the man's eyes and nose were red from crying.

Thibodaux faded to the right as soon as they came in, cutting off the second Uyghur, a burly young man who was built like a farmhand. Both Thibodaux and Quinn moved quickly, closing the distance while their surprised targets were still busy trying to figure out what was going on. Quinn's heavy black beard and olive complexion gave him the ambiguous ethnicity that might make him a Central Asian, but the sight of the giant Cajun momentarily stunned the two Uyghur men.

Quinn was nearly on top of Hajip when the Uyghur snatched up the heavy cleaver he used to hack off pieces of *matang*. Dozens of blades of various shapes and sizes were strewn over several other carts parked alongside Hajip's. Quinn snatched up a long, but relatively thin blade compared to the cleaver. He didn't plan on a fencing match. There was too much danger of an errant slash from Hajip connecting with something vital.

Quinn knew from harsh experience that human bodies were little more than flimsy, blood-filled balloons. Movie knife fights featured a lot of clanging metal, thrusts and parries, and sparks for show. Showing a knife as a defensive threat—as Hajip was doing now—was all well and good, but a real-world knife attack was more like an assault with a club—a sharp and pointed club, but still a club. An attack was usually over in a matter of seconds with one party completely overwhelmed.

Mean and intimidating as it was, the cleaver was heavy and its weight and momentum made Hajip's movements clumsy. Whatever had caused him to cry likely weighed on his mind and slowed him down even more. Quinn feinted left. Hajip took the bait, slashing wildly with the unwieldy *matang* blade. Quinn stepped offline, parrying the attacking arm out of the way with his right, and then clobbered Hajip in the neck with a quick left hook. Stunned, the Uyghur fell sideways, slamming against the edge of his metal cart on the way to the ground, his right arm snapping with a sickening pop.

"That didn't take long," Thibodaux observed, standing over his unconscious opponent. "I guess waving at customers with a big honking knife don't provide for much combat experience."

Quinn kicked the blade out of the way and grabbed a roll of plastic wrap from Hajip's *matang* cart. Two minutes later both Uyghurs looked like angry cocoons leaning against the back wall. Their arms were secured to their sides, and they were wrapped from chest to ankle in most of the industrial-size roll of plastic.

Awake now, Hajip fired off a furious string in Uyghur. Bloodshot eyes locked on his unconscious friend. Quinn hopped up to sit on the edge of the cart. He didn't understand the words, but got the gist of them.

"His shoulder is torn up," Quinn said in Mandarin. "But he's still alive."

Hajip glared with the white-hot hatred of a powerless man. A thin trickle of blood ran from his nose. His right eye was a little off-kilter—evidence of the power of Quinn's left hook. His face was pale, likely from the pain of the broken arm he received during the fall.

"So," Quinn said, speaking in Mandarin. "Do you know why I'm here?"

The Uyghur stared back but said nothing.

"What's bothering you, Hajip?" Quinn said, hands resting beside his thighs as his legs dangled off the cart.

"I am tied like a goose," the Uyghur spat. "That is what's bothering me." His Mandarin was fluent, but spoken in short, choppy sentences, as if distasteful to speak.

Quinn gave a slow nod, pondering which way to go with the questioning.

Snot flowed down the Uyghur's nose. He was unable to rub his eyes, which brimmed with more tears. As interrogations went, someone or something had done half of Quinn's job for him. Hajip was distraught, too distracted to keep up much of a lie.

"Let me get straight to the yolk of the egg, as they say," Quinn said.

"That is a good idea," Hajip said. "If you mean to take my head, so be it. I am prepared to die."

Quinn shook his head. "I'm not interested in killing you." he said, "As a matter of fact, I understand you are the man who can help me find the Feng brothers."

The Uyghur began to thrash at the mention of the

name, straining against the plastic wrap and beating
the back of his head against the wall. Tendons strained
at his neck. His face flushed red behind his wispy
beard. Unable to free himself, he finally stopped long
enough to glare at Quinn, panting. Spittle hung from
his lips. His eyes burned with the rage of a tortured
man.

"Ehmet Feng will burn in Hell!" he spat.

This was not the reaction Quinn had expected. He
scooted forward to the edge of the cart. "You have seen
Feng tonight?"

"Haaaa!" The Uyghur let loose a pitiful, heart-
broken cry. "He would be dead if I had." Hajip threw
back his head again, screaming towards the rafters
through clenched teeth. "I swear I will put a blade through
Ehmet Feng's black heart."

"Hey!" Quinn patted the man on his cheek to keep
his attention. "Listen to me. You want to get Ehmet
Feng, then tell me where I can find him."

"You must believe me when I tell you," Hajip said
through clenched teeth. "If I knew where that dog was,
I would not be here. I would cut his throat, just as he
did my brother."

Quinn slid off the cart. "Why would Feng kill your
brother?"

Hajip looked up through grief-stricken eyes. "Ehmet
believed my brother betrayed him to the authorities,
that he is the reason they were arrested." Hajip shook
his head, tears welling again. "The last scene to reach
my brother's eyes was that of Ehmet Feng murdering
his children. . . ."

"When did this happen?" Quinn moved in so he was
just inches from the other man's face. "Who gave you
this information?" he whispered.

"Ehmet called my mobile to gloat." The Uyghur's

head fell to his chest—he was crying in earnest now. "He murdered my brother while I stood on the street, selling confections like an old fool."

"That was the call you received out on the street a few moments ago?"

Hajip nodded toward the unconscious man beside him. "My cousin and I had a plan to find the dog and avenge my brother, until you showed up."

Quinn took a deep breath and considered his options. He felt for the poor man. The loss of a brother would be devastating, but a pat on the shoulder was all the solace he could afford. If the Fengs had committed bloody murders in the last hour, they were still in the area.

"Where would you look first?" Quinn said.

"I do not know." Hajip choked back his sobs. "I was insane with grief when I received the call. I am not sure it's even possible to find him. He has cousins in Kashgar, but the police will be watching them. He is much too smart to turn to any of them."

"Where then?" Quinn said. "What did you plan to do before my friend and I entered the picture?"

"Habibullah," the Uyghur said.

Thibodaux mouthed the word several times, getting it in his head.

"A Tajik," Hajip went on. "Habibullah is powerful, a man with many connections. If you want a new identity, Habibullah is the man to see. He would know if someone assisted Ehmet Feng."

"That's a start," Quinn said, feeling the familiar flutter of an impending hunt. "Let's go and talk to him."

"Oh," Hajip said, giving an emphatic shake of his head as he spoke in a distraught and rapid-fire pace. "It is too late to speak with Habibullah tonight. He will be sleeping by now. His men would slaughter us if we woke him. The only way to get near Habibullah is to have business with Habibullah. Even then you must go through his men. I could have spoken with him early tomorrow. . . ." Hajip's gaze shifted to his right side and lingered at his injured arm as if all was lost. "But your interference has ruined my chance to speak with Habibullah!"

"Damn," Thibodaux whistled under his breath. "I can't understand a word, but this guy sure likes to say 'Habibullah.'"

The unconscious man began to stir.

"Ayeee!" Hajip threw his head back and cried. "You have broken my arm! I will never be able to get near Habibullah!"

Thibodaux stepped up, taking Hajip's sudden rise in tone for a threat. "Blah, blah, blah, Habib-blah-blah-bulla! You best calm your ass down, down fast, fast."

"It's okay, Jacques," Quinn said, and translated the last to bring the Cajun up to speed before turning to face the Uyghur. "Why does your broken arm keep you from talking with Habibullah?"

Hajip rattled off his plan in Mandarin, sobbing as much as he spoke. Quinn thought for a moment, then came back with a plan of his own. The Uyghur stopped crying and fired back with a string of curses. When he was finished, Quinn spoke again, and then stepped back, rubbing his chin in thought.

"Dammit, *l'ami,* but you make my head ache." Thibodaux rubbed his temples. "I know a scoff when I hear it in any language. It sounded to me like you're trying to convince this guy of something and he ain't buying any."

"You picked up on that, did you?" Quinn grinned.

"*Arrete toi,*" Thibodaux said, shaking his head. *Stop, you.* "Every time you get that look in your eye—"

"What look?" Quinn's mind was already racing, making plans.

"Don't make me pass you a slap, Chair Force. You know what I'm talking about." Thibodaux peered at him with his good eye. "That look that says you think you have superpowers. It's a bad, bad look, I'm telling you straight. What are you plannin'? Pistols at dawn with Habibullah because you broke this dipshit's arm?"

"A duel . . ." Quinn looked up and gave his friend a sly smile. "I wish it were something that easy."

Chapter 15

Former CIA Clandestine Services Officer Joey Benavides hoisted a doughy leg out of the passenger side of his partner's government-issued Jeep Patriot and unfolded himself onto the quiet residential sidewalk. The little car seemed to squeak with relief as the pressure was taken off the suspension.

Joey B's partner, former IRS agent Roy Gant, wore a gray blazer that was at least one size too small and caused his fleshy arms to ride up a little farther away from his body than they should have. Agents of the Internal Defense Task Force weren't known for strict adherence to dress codes, but Gant was one of the few who were slovenly enough to make even Benavides look acceptable. He didn't even bother to tuck in his shirttail.

A girl on a bicycle, one of the legions of snot-nose kids Benavides saw terrorizing the neighborhoods this time of year, cruised by on the sidewalk.

"I hate summer," Gant grumbled, glaring at the little girl as she sped down the street.

"Okay, we're looking for the Thib-o-day-ox residence," Benavides said, spitting into the gutter as he hitched his slacks over a sagging belly.

"Rhymes with dough," his partner corrected. "Thib-o-daux."

"Whatever."

Joey B stuffed the errant tail of his white shirt back where it was supposed to be. Task Force agents weren't required to wear ties—which was a good thing, because Benavides hadn't been able to button the top button on any of his dress shirts in six months. Leaning back into the Jeep, he shrugged on a wrinkled sport coat to cover his sidearm and nodded his jowly head toward the house halfway down the block so his equally corpulent partner would know where they were going.

Younger than Gant by at least fifteen years, Benavides took the lead as they walked to the house. Gant, who didn't appear to care, plodded along behind with his head down, a hand in one pocket.

"The boss is gonna have my ass if we don't find something on Garcia," Gant muttered as they cut across a freshly mowed yard.

The grass was littered with mutilated pieces of green toy soldiers and Hot Wheels cars as if the toys had been mowed over. Plastic guns and wooden swords hung from the handlebars of two bicycles parked in a barren flower bed beside the front porch. "I'm seriously thinking he might take me out back and shoot me."

"Mr. Walter is a son of a bitch," Benavides said. "But I doubt he'd shoot you, even if you did let a traitor slip away on your watch."

Gant stopped in the middle of the sidewalk. He did that sometimes, just stopped moving in the middle of a sentence for no apparent reason. Benavides hated working with him. "Have you heard from Craig Thorson lately?"

"No. Why?"

"Exactly." Gant nodded as if it should all be so clear. "Thorson let some numbers slip to a Senate staffer about the IDTF budget. Nothing big, but Walter didn't approve it beforehand so he got pissed—and Thorson hasn't been answering calls or e-mails for two weeks."

In reality, Benavides had no doubt the top supervisory agent within the Vice President's newly formed Task Force would have no problem shooting a colleague in the back of the head. Hell, the sadistic whack job probably had a couple of people chained up in his basement. It was just not something Benavides wanted to talk about. If he agreed with Gant, the other agent might twist his words around and call him a traitor— earning him a bullet in the brain from Walter.

Benavides thought about it a second too long and gave a shivering shrug. "Come on. Let's go see what this bitch knows." He read the name he'd written in pen on the palm of his hand, pronouncing it correctly this time. "Camille Thibodaux. The boss says her husband did some work with Garcia. He's supposed to be a gunny in the Marine Corps, but he happens to be deployed so we can take our time if his wife decides to get pissy with us. If she knows something about Veronica Garcia, we'll get it out of her."

Benavides was grinning at the prospect by the time he stepped up on the porch and rang the bell.

A curvaceous woman with dark hair and brooding brown eyes flung open the door—as if she'd been lurking there, waiting. Barefoot, she wore a pair of loose basketball shorts and a red USMC T-shirt. He let his eyes play up and down over the swells of the shirt, then back to the fresh red polish on the woman's toenails. A snotty toddler clung to the leg of her shorts, pushing them up and giving the agents a tantalizing peek at his mama's muscular thigh. In between ogling her legs and her toes, Benavides had the fleeting thought that this woman kept her right hand out of sight. She might actually have a weapon hidden back there. Marine wives were a tricky bunch.

Both agents held up their credential cases. It could be pretty gratifying to see people wilt with fear at the IDTF badge.

"You're not in any trouble," Gant said, raising his hand as if it was even possible to calm the fury in this woman's eyes.

"I know I'm not," Camille Thibodaux said. "Because I haven't done anything wrong."

"Be that as it may." Gant shrugged. "We need to talk to you about a person of interest named Veronica Garcia. Sometimes goes by Ronnie. She a friend of yours?"

"Never heard of her," Camille Thibodaux said.

"I see," Benavides sighed. "You know, people like Ronnie Garcia tend to have a short shelf life. And you know what they say about one bad apple. I think it'd be a shame if her problems spilled over into your problems. . . ."

"I don't really give a damn about what you think." Her baby began to squall and she took a moment to reach down and pat him on the head. "It's okay, sugar. These men just made Mama use a Bible word." The door swung open a hair farther, allowing Benavides to get his foot inside.

"Here's how this is going to—" He stopped in midsentence, staring at a large family photo that hung on the wall beside a framed black-and-white photo of some Marines from another war. Along with an ungodly number of kids, the studio portrait showed Camille holding the arm of a mountainous USMC gunnery sergeant. The crew cut and black eye patch filled Benavides with immediate dread. This was one of two men who'd bashed out his teeth and blackmailed him into cooperating to help with the escape of the traitor and former director of the CIA, Virginia Ross. He'd never given Benavides his name.

"Thibodaux . . ." Joey B mused under his breath. So that was his name. It made sense. He fought the growing urge to crow. This Marine Corps shithead had spoken his bullying threats with a Cajun accent. And now he'd gone and gotten himself deployed with no one to look after his sexy little wifey.

"So," Benavides said, smiling sweetly. He removed his foot from the doorway. "You've never heard of Ms. Garcia?"

"I have not," Camille Thibodaux said, her lips clenched in an obvious lie.

"Okay then." Benavides shrugged, looking at a baffled Gant. "Someone must have gotten their wires crossed back at HQ. We'll just be on our way."

Mrs. Thibodaux slammed the door, leaving the two men standing on her porch.

"What the hell was that all about?" Gant asked.

"This bitch knows something," Benavides said as they walked back to the Jeep. "But she isn't going to crack with the direct approach. Trust me on this one, bud. I want to try something with more of a personal touch."

Chapter 16

Veronica "Ronnie" Garcia sat with six others around a long plastic table, all watching a small flat-screen monitor mounted on the wall at the far end of the bunker. She felt herself tense as the image of two state police helicopters passed across the screen, picked up by the skyward cameras over the wooded compound. The group was deep underground and the earth outside the thick concrete cooled the piped air, forcing each of those in attendance to wear a Windbreaker or light jacket. Ronnie, without thinking, had slipped into a tight, long-sleeved cardigan. It was one of Jericho's favorites, but the reasons he liked it were the same reasons that would bring her so much grief from their host, the owner of the bunker.

"These overflights are becoming more frequent," Winfield Palmer said to Garcia from across the table. Garcia and Jericho's former boss, he'd served as the National Security Advisor before the President and Vice President had been assassinated. Even now, as a fugitive with a terrible head cold, he still carried himself like a man who was completely in charge of the room. It was troubling to Garcia that something like a common cold could find its way past Win Palmer's concrete persona. He'd been the President's confidant and advisor, the power behind the power for as long as she'd known him—ever robust and full of confidence-inspiring vigor. He was still strong, despite his illness, but the stress of this life was chipping away at his base. When the coughing subsided, he turned to the elderly man in faded Carhartts who stood slightly behind him against the back wall of the cellar. "Have you heard any chatter around town?"

"Everybody round here knows I hate the G," the man against the wall said, abbreviating "government" as if he couldn't bear for the word to cross his lips. His name was Sam Hawthorne and he owned nearly three square miles of the Pennsylvania woodland where Garcia and the others had holed up. At seventy-one, he still stood ramrod straight with big, farmer's hands that matched a husky, six-foot build. "No one in their right mind would think I'd hide the likes of you. Hell, if you'd told me a year ago that Sam Hawthorne would be aiding and abetting a bunch of DC spies turned Sons of Liberty, I'd said you were full of shit."

"Sam!" Wilma Hawthorne chided, looking up from where she sat in the corner working over a hooped cross-stitch project. "Watch your mouth. We have guests." She was an apple-shaped woman with silver hair and a quiet smile.

"Spies from the G," Sam said under his breath. "Guests my ass."

A self-proclaimed doomsday prepper, Hawthorne had been suspicious of the federal government during every one of the eleven presidential administrations since he was old enough to make it to a ballot box. The current occupant of the White House validated all his years of ranting, curtailing freedom of the press and tightening the grip on personal freedoms in the name of greater security. When President Drake had issued the executive order creating the Internal Defense Task Force, even the normally pensive and peace-loving Wilma Hawthorne had seen the new secret police force for what it was—an American Gestapo. She had stood up from the television and found her way to the gun safe to strap on her favorite Makarov pistol and was rarely seen without it.

The Hawthornes had spent the last forty-six years building up the rural property Wilma had inherited from her mother. Years spent raising three sons and living a life that was what Sam called "on/off" the grid—having just enough connectivity to keep from raising suspicion with authorities, but with plenty of safe rooms, underground bunkers, and escape tunnels to keep an intrusive G guessing if they did ever decided to raid the place and take away all his guns. Palmer's consistent comparison of their movement to the Revolutionary War's Sons of Liberty seemed to appeal to Hawthorne's notion of a patriotic fight against the G.

"Likely just a routine flight," Melissa Ryan, the former Secretary of State, said from the chair on the other side of Garcia. "But I'd suggest a couple of us stay in the rooms below at any given time so we're all not captured should we get raided." In her early fifties, Ryan still looked like a cover girl in her formfitting jeans and signature silk blouse under her red Mountain Hardwear Windbreaker. It was no secret that she and Palmer had been an item for several years. It had broken the hearts of many an eligible bachelor when *DC Magazine* had named them one of the top most influential couples in the country. In addition to being beautiful, Melissa Ryan was also one of the brightest minds on the planet. If they were going to do anything to bring down the present administration they needed all the brainpower they could cobble together. It was Ryan's connections that had made the introductions to the Hawthornes, and her particular diplomatic skills that made Hawthorne, if only grudgingly, agree to aid and abet former bureaucrats from the G.

"I agree," the former Director of the Central Intelligence Agency said. Virginia Ross stood against the concrete wall near the Hawthornes, hands behind her back, listening. "These people are evil, but they are not stupid." Ross said little but when she did, it carried a lot of weight. A fugitive now, she'd been arrested on trumped-up charges by an IDTF agent named Walter, stripped of her clothing and tortured in an attempt to find Palmer and the others deemed to be a threat to the administration. Garcia and Thibodaux had masterminded her escape. She was now not only on the run, but a celebrity in the underground movement to topple President Hartman Drake and his regime. Ronnie had been part of her rescue, had seen firsthand the effects of the inhuman treatment the poor woman had received at the hands of Agent Walter. The cruelty had only managed to bolster Ross's resolve to fight.

Garcia caught the eye of Emiko Miyagi, the strange little Japanese woman who was Jericho's martial arts trainer and confidant. Miyagi was attractive in the way a handsome blade was attractive—dangerous, and quite useful in the right hands. Garcia had known her for over a year now, received defensive tactics instruction from her at Camp Peary during CIA basic, and worked alongside her on several bloody missions. She still couldn't quite put her finger on this woman. If she hadn't known better, Garcia might have been jealous of the time Miyagi spent with Jericho. She wasn't worried that they'd ever been romantic—but, Ronnie knew, there were things far more intimate than romance. She couldn't help but think that this Japanese warrior woman was able to see far more deeply into Jericho Quinn's soul than she would ever find possible.

"Evil," Miyagi said, wasting no further words since everyone was in agreement.

Palmer unwrapped a menthol cough drop and popped it in his mouth, narrowing his eyes the way he did when Garcia knew he wanted to get back to business. He was a normally vibrant man, but the illness, along with months of playing cat and mouse with the administration's goons had caused him to lose most of what was left of his close-cropped gray hair. His once ruddy complexion bordered on ashen and his posture had stooped noticeably from the time when Garcia had first met him. Wearing a shawl collar cardigan against the chill of the underground, he looked more like an exhausted college professor than the West Point graduate and close confidant of the man who'd been the most powerful man on earth.

Since they'd come to the farm, Palmer had decided to hold all their important meetings in the bunker rather than the more comfortable farmhouse. Hawthorne had built the thing like a SCIF or Sensitive Compartmented Information Facility. No two-way communication took place from the facility. Cells and radios were left topside and radio frequency detectors at the door made sure everyone stayed honest. Twelve feet beneath the surface under two feet of concrete, fresh air was drawn in and stale air was piped out through a series of vents that came up through the floor of an empty barn over a hundred meters away. The bunker could be accessed through a false floor in an equally well-hidden panic room entered by sliding back a portion of the kitchen counter. Even Garcia, who'd been through training in all manner of unbelievable things at Camp Peary, had found the designs amazing. Paranoia caused people to take drastic measures—but it was hard to say Sam Hawthorne's paranoia was unwarranted, considering their present situation.

"I got in touch with Jennifer on the Hill this morning," Palmer said, bringing the meeting back on topic once the cough drop began to do its job. He looked at Garcia. "Senator Gorski and Congressman Dillman have agreed to meet you this evening."

"Why don't you just send one of these girls in to shoot the son of a bitch President in the eye?" Hawthorne groused, giving a sidelong look toward Garcia. "The busty one looks like she's shot people before." His wife raised a chastising eyebrow at his cursing, but adjusted the Makarov on her hip and resumed her cross-stitch without saying anything.

Garcia smiled at the old man. Miyagi had much more experience in the shooting department, and the intensity in her eyes bore it out, but Hawthorne made no secret that he had a little crush on Ronnie. At least twice a day he'd lament that none of his sons had married a healthy girl with "breeder's hips" like hers. Ronnie just shrugged it off. Her deadbeat ex-husband had described her as having a "ghetto booty." "Breeder's hips" seemed more pleasant than that—and anyway, Jericho didn't seem to mind them. In any case, Hawthorne was committing all sorts of crimes by just letting fugitives from the G stay at his place, so she put up with a little leering and a comment or two. He was harmless enough at seventy, but she was sure he'd been a handful for Miss Wilma back in his prime.

Palmer swallowed to stifle a cough. "Garcia is plenty capable of shooting a man in the eye," he said quietly, "or killing him in a variety of ways if he were to give her any trouble. There are many who would be willing to take on that job, but it's not that simple. Both the President and Vice President are guarded by arguably the most highly trained protective agency in the world." Palmer paused for effect. "And I should know. They protected me for a time while I was National Security Advisor. They're good men and women and too many would get hurt if we made an attempt now."

"Fox News said there was a gunman in the White House today," Hawthorne said. "They're saying the target was the VP. Sure the shooter wasn't yours?"

Virginia Ross shook her head, her chin quivered like she might break into tears. "No," she said, "that was a good friend of mine acting on his own volition. His loss is a blow to the country. I can tell you that much."

"At any rate," Palmer said, "the G, as you call it, has enough checks and balances that even moles like Drake and McKeon can't bring it down easily. They have to chip away, nudging us toward a war that will inflate the economy, devalue the dollar, and ultimately cost millions of American lives. Slowly and methodically, they have raised the stakes on the evil of the masked terrorist who shoots dozens or bombs hundreds. It takes both houses of Congress to bring up impeachment charges. I think the senator and congressman can swing enough of their people our way—as long as we give them something they can sink their teeth into—something more than the mere suggestion the POTUS and VPOTUS are warmongering moles. Miss Garcia can lay out the evidence we have, including Drake's connection to a Pakistani terrorist." Palmer shrugged and crunched through the last of his cough drop. "It's thin, but I'm hopeful that impeachment will send a signal to China that the entire country isn't in lockstep."

"You think the meeting could be a trap?" Garcia asked, focusing on her immediate mission. She wasn't afraid, but alliances in Washington were historically fluid. Lately, they blew like dandelion fuzz in an ever-changing political wind.

"These two were handpicked to keep that from happening." Palmer shook his head. "Deborah Gorski went to college in Fairbanks with Quinn's mother. Her father was a senator before her and gave Quinn his nomination to the Air Force Academy. Personal ties beat credentials at this point. Mike Dillman was a plebe my senior year at West Point. We worked on a number of missions well before the good citizens of Indiana decided to elect him to Congress. I trust him the way Quinn trusts Jacques."

"Roger that," Garcia said, knowing no better analogy for trust. She glanced at the Tag Heuer Aquaracer Quinn had given her for her last birthday. "What time are they meeting me?"

"They know to walk down York Street in Gettysburg at six. They'll look for your mark, and then wait at the area you designate. You contact them after you're sure they don't have a tail. Miyagi will pull countersurveillance." Palmer stood, ready for everyone to get to work. "To tell you the truth, I'm surprised this administration hasn't imploded already. The problem with conspiracies is that they rot from within."

"I don't know." Sam Hawthorne shrugged. "This Sons of Liberty shit you're doing ain't nothing if it's not a conspiracy—and, apart from your croup, it looks pretty damn healthy to me."

Ronnie reached back out of habit, touching the small 9mm Kahr pistol tucked over her right kidney, inside the waistband of her jeans. Even under the thin cashmere sweater, it was all but invisible. Breeder's hips or ghetto booty, being built on the athletic side of zaftig made it easier to hide a pistol—or at the very least more unlikely that anyone would notice that particular little bulge when there were so many other bulges to ogle.

Melissa Ryan must have seen her index the pistol and came up to put a hand on her shoulder. Garcia had liked her from the moment they'd met—nearly everyone did. She had a tantalizing smile that drew people to her and seemed to say to men and women alike, "Oh, my darling, if only I was yours and you were mine. . . ."

"Not to worry, dear," Ryan said, flashing the smile. Garcia caught the jasmine hint of Chanel as she drew alongside. Ryan exuded elegance even in a bunker. "Gettysburg streets are crowded with tourists from all over the world this time of year," she said. "You should be fine. Just try not to draw any attention to yourself."

"You women talk like such a thing is even possible," Hawthorne scoffed, taking advantage of the setup from Ryan. "This sweet little Lipstick and Lead gonna draw attention like a—"

"That is enough, Sam!" Wilma stomped her little foot without looking up from her cross-stitch. "Leave the poor girl alone or you won't be seeing much of anything, let alone a female hip."

Hawthorne hung his head. "I'm just saying, let me come with if you want so I can look out for them. Folks are gonna look at her. It's the damn truth and she knows it."

"I'll be fine, Sam," Ronnie said, driving him to his wife with a lingering kiss on the cheek. "Thanks for your concern."

Garcia waited for the others to leave the bunker so she could talk to Palmer alone for a second. "Heard anything from Jericho?" she asked.

Palmer popped another cough drop, which he immediately chewed to pieces. "Not since yesterday." He didn't go so far as to tell her not to worry. That would have been pointless. He did give her an uncharacteristic smile. "This will all be over soon, Veronica. You're doing great. I always knew you would."

"Cut the sentiment, boss." She grinned. "It scares the shit out of me."

"Yeah." Palmer stifled a cough. "You're right. Get to work."

Chapter 17

The day was still pink and new when Quinn and Thibodaux arrived at the open field adjacent to the livestock market. The sun wouldn't clear the eastern horizon for another half hour but the area around the outer edges of the field was already filled with intently focused men and excited horses.

Gabriella Deuben had invited them to spend what was left of the night in the bottom floor of her clinic, but Quinn had been unable to purge his mind of the whirlwind of thoughts. Images of his seven-year-old daughter, Mattie, tormented his mind, chasing away any semblance of sleep. She was stashed away with friends in Russia to keep her safe, and operational security meant that he rarely even got to speak with her. In the end, he lay on the makeshift pallet and tried to rest his body if not his mind, finally drifting off a scant hour before he had to get up. He could get by for weeks on three hours a night, but one left him groggy and slow and wishing he'd just stayed awake. His father, a commercial fisherman in Alaska, was fond of saying that the older he got, the more mortal he felt. The older Quinn got, the more he understood his old man.

Quinn shut the driver's door to the little micro van and rubbed his hands together against the chill. A rusted set of five-tier bleachers like Quinn remembered from his Little League days listed heavily, looking like it might collapse at any moment under the weight of dozens of spectators who'd crammed themselves on the ancient metal benches. Frenetic *dutar* music twanged over a crackling loudspeaker. Men who seemed to have no regard for personal space shouted exuberantly whether they were half a field apart or standing nose to nose. Volkswagens, Citreons, and rusted Toyota trucks ringed the expansive dirt field. Many of the vehicles had livestock trailers in tow.

A constant line of traffic flowed in from the city, sending a curtain of dust drifting sideways against the sunrise. More and more cars arrived, each spilling out more spectators. When the rickety bleachers were full, spectators began to line up ten and twelve deep around the field. Grown men and boys stood packed together munching on snacks and chatting with each other. The smell of hot bread and sweet chai worked to chase away the chill in the morning air. A squad of uniformed Chinese soldiers had even come to watch the action from folding chairs set up in an open-backed six-by-six troop truck similar to a US deuce and a half.

Horses groaned and stomped as fierce-looking riders tugged their rigging tight before climbing into their saddles. Some of these men wore padded Soviet-era tanker helmets; most wore hats fashioned from leather and ringed in fur or wool. Thick, quilted clothing was the uniform of the day. All but the youngest few had wild beards. A ragtag bunch, they possessed the intense focus of professional athletes.

"There's Hajip," Quinn said, nodding toward the Uyghur, who stood beside a tall dapple-gray horse. His arm hung in a homemade sling of colorful cloth.

"Chair Force," Thibodaux said, shaking his head, lips turned down in a disgusted frown. "I seem to remember you saying this would be like a rodeo."

"It is," Quinn said, nodding to a line of nickering horses.

The big Cajun pointed a flat hand toward a group of men standing over a shaggy black goat. One held the bleating animal's head by the horns while another man ran a long blade across its throat, slaughtering in the traditional Islamic fashion without stunning it before the cut. The animal struggled as it bled to death, and then the man with the knife hacked off the head. A long-haired child of five or six swooped in and grabbed the head the moment it was free of the animal, carrying it away as if he'd won a prize. A third man squatting at the rear end of the goat slit the animal's belly and removed the paunch. He took a heavy needle and thread from the lapel of his jacket and began to sew up the carcass before the child with the head had even made it back to his family.

"Warning," Thibodaux said in a mock announcer's voice. "Animals will be mutilated during the filming of this movie. . . ." He breathed a heavy sigh. "There's a hell of a lot of goat killin' going on in this damn country, I'll tell you that. I ain't never been to a rodeo where full-growed men chop off a goat's head, then fight over the body."

"Well," Quinn said as they came up beside Hajip. "Now you can say you have. I told you *buzkashi* means 'goat bashing.' What did you think it would be like?"

"I don't know," Thibodaux said. "Maybe a pointy

oval ball made of goatskin that you kick, throw, or carry down the field."

"It's a rough game," Quinn said. "But this is a rough country. The big games are played in the winter, so it's easier on the horses. But according to Hajip, they hold a competition once a month early in the morning like this while it's still cool enough."

"Ain't that just the luck," Thibodaux muttered.

"As-salamu alaykum," Hajip said through clenched teeth as the men approached. Eyes still red and brimming with vengeance for the murder of his brother, the Uyghur glared at Quinn as a necessary evil. He pointed to a burly man riding an equally burly bay among the other riders. "That one," he said. "That is Habibullah."

Quinn took a moment to think, patting the tall gray's flank while he sized up the Tajik. Habibullah was built like a tank, with broad shoulders and a bull neck that rivaled Thibodaux's. High cheekbones and a wispy beard over a strong jaw worked with the peaked fur hat and padded clothing to make him look like one of Genghis Khan's soldiers. Massive hands clutched the reins, wheeling the horse back and forth to show the animal and everyone watching who was in charge. Quinn's gray appeared to notice whom Quinn was looking at, and stared intently in the same direction as if studying Habibullah's much larger mount.

Thibodaux stepped up and took the gray by the bridle. "Now let's all just hang on a second," he said. "You fall off your horse out there and you'll be stomped to puddin'. Tell me again why you don't just go up and ask this Habibullah guy which way the Feng brothers went and we can be done with it. He's a big dude, but if he decides he don't want to talk to you, I'll ask him."

Quinn translated this into Mandarin for Hajip. It was

a valid question, and one that bore repeating, though Quinn already knew the answer.

"Our ways are not your ways," the Uyghur said in Chinese. "All is honor with Habibullah." Quinn translated for Jacques as he spoke. "His word—even with men like the Fengs—is a matter of honor. But, to him, the game of *buzkashi* is also a matter of honor. If we work with him, he is more likely to help us. You see how his horse has a bit of red cloth tied to the bridle?"

Quinn nodded. "As does mine."

"That mean you're on the same team?" Thibodaux was keeping up well for all the back-and-forth translation.

"Yes and no," Hajip said. "All the riders with red bits of cloth may indeed work together, helping one get the *buz* back to the goal. On the other hand, they may just as easily decide to work independently, fighting with any and everyone else on the field for their own chance at glory. The object of the game is to carry the *buz* down the field around the flag and then bring it back to deposit it in the circle. Only the rider who scores with the *buz* is paid a prize. It is his responsibility to pay the rest of his team—or not. Any rider may lean down and pick up the carcass so long as he remains in the saddle, or he may wait until someone else retrieves the animal and then steal it from him." He shot Quinn a challenging look as if all of this might be too much for him. "You said you ride. Did you not?"

"I've been riding since I was four," Quinn said truthfully, though the bulk of his riding experience had been in high school. His mother had taken up riding and it had been something they could do together when she hadn't been out on the fishing boat with his dad. Quinn found that he loved horses nearly as much as he loved motorcycles and, as a natural athlete, found sitting one fairly intuitive. "Don't worry about me."

Thibodaux scoffed and shook his head, watching a procession of men on foot make their way through the crowd and fling the goat carcass among the waiting horses. The animals stomped and kicked at the thing, obviously trained to treat it with a sort of contempt.

"Very well," Hajip said, looking only half convinced. "Do you see how the riders carry small leather whips and riding crops between their teeth?"

"I do," Quinn said, already thinking on what kind of platform the back of a horse would make in a fight.

"In the strictest rules of *buzkashi*," the Uyghur continued, "it is forbidden for one rider to strike another with a whip or any part of the body. But, I must confess that these men do not often choose to conform to the strictest sense of the rules, especially at these summer contests. I count twenty riders this morning. Most of them know each other, if not by name, then at least by reputation. None of them know you. Some of the spectators are prone to the forbidden vice of gambling. A popular wager is on how many will leave the field because of broken bones. If I were a gambler, I would bet on at least one third.

"The Afghans say the *buz* belongs to the horse." The Uyghur looked Quinn in the eye. "And these horses are bred to believe that as well. They develop rivalries with each other and are prone to bite and kick. Aggressive does not come close to describing them." He patted the gray on its rump. "This horse is worth at least twenty thousand American dollars and will likely make my family many times that over its lifespan. It belonged to my brother."

"I still say we wait until the game is over and have a sit-down with this guy." Thibodaux set his jaw, looking

at Quinn. He shook his head in disgust. "You're looking forward to this. . . ."

"You are strong men," Hajip said, "cunning and handy
with your fists. But there are only two of you. When
the game is over, Habibullah and his men will leave.
There is no way short of killing him that you could
stop him if he does not wish to be stopped."

The Uyghur handed Quinn a leather tanker helmet.
It smelled like someone had tried to cover the scent of
blood and sweat with a bottle of condensed Aqua Velva
cologne. Quinn strapped it on anyway, not knowing
how many more bashed noggins he could afford at his
age.

"Now go," the Hajip said. "Help Habibullah get the
buz to the circle. Allah willing, he will see you are riding
my brother's horse and point us toward Ehmet Feng."

Thibodaux patted Quinn on the knee. "All right, my
goat-bashing buddy. You watch yourself out there."

"Don't get all emotional on me." Quinn winked.

"It ain't emotion," Jacques said. "I'm too big to fit
behind the wheel of that midget clown van. There won't
be anybody to drive me around if you get turned into
hoof jelly."

"I'll be fine." Quinn scanned the field of shouting
riders and nickering horses, already forming the basics
of a plan. Wheeling the gray on its haunches, he shot a
glance down at Thibodaux, then back at a broad rider
with a sun-burnished face beside Habibullah. "See that
guy on the black horse?"

The Cajun nodded.

"His name is Muzra," Hajip said. "A competent
horseman and Habibullah's most trusted lieutenant."

"Keep an eye on him," Quinn said to Thibodaux. "In
about two minutes he's not going to like me very much."

Chapter 18

Ronnie Garcia pretended to window-shop, strolling from store to store with the pockets of tourists who were in town after a long day at the battlefield looking for something to eat. She watched a young college-age woman leading a group of three or four families on a walking tour of downtown. Ronnie was sure the tour had all kinds of interesting history behind it, but ambling through a bunch of pastel brick buildings had to pale next to a day at the hallowed grounds like Cemetery Ridge, the Round Tops, and the Copse of Trees from where General Pickett led his ill-fated charge.

The point of choosing Gettysburg for the meeting was that anyone suspicious would be more likely to stand out. But Ronnie hadn't considered the fact that she, herself, could look quite suspicious loitering around alone in the quiet little town. She did her best to blend in as much as possible while scanning passersby for weapons and intent to do her harm. Her instructors had taught her during CIA countersurveillance training that everyone had quirks. Trying to be too average only made one draw more attention. A female instructor had gone so far as to point out that while Ronnie's biggest problem was her figure, it was also her greatest asset. This instructor, a longtime operative herself, observed that if Ronnie were to rob a bank, some witnesses might not remember her deeply tanned complexion. Others would fail to note the thick, ebony hair that she'd inherited from her Cuban mother or the broad shoulders and high cheekbones of her Russian father. But any adult that saw her would recall her figure. "T and A," the instructor had noted, running a manicured hand over her own shapely rear end. "Hard to put these particular Talents and Assets in a lineup, kiddo. Remember to use them responsibly."

Ronnie had learned early as a young woman that few people she met, particularly the men, would spend much time looking at her face.

The comforting whine of Miyagi's Ducati revved behind her, toward the traffic circle and Lincoln Square. Garcia found it comforting to know she was there—a mother hen on a motorcycle . . . with a sword.

The weather was hot and extremely muggy compared to the canned air of the bunker. Garcia had exchanged the cashmere for a light blue button-down oxford and the loosest pair of jeans she owned. Her ex called them her "mom jeans." Half expecting her meeting to turn into a run for her life, she opted for a light pair of Nike sneakers instead of more fashionable shoes. Far from formfitting, the outfit still drew plenty of nods from passersby, both male and female.

She was fairly certain she hadn't been followed but used a half dozen countersurveillance measures in any case, doubling back on herself and stopping at intersections through two complete light cycles as if her car had stalled. If anyone had known where she was, Palmer and everyone else would have all been dead in a ditch somewhere. Her concern was that someone would follow the delegation. Palmer had briefed his friend, Congressman Dillman, on how to watch for surveillance. Dillman supposedly had considerable experience in combat, but like Thibodaux had pointed out that from his experiences in both, combat and tradecraft were about as far apart as a tickle and a slap. Their lack of covert experience notwithstanding, both Gorski and Dillman appeared to be extremely intelligent people. Ronnie was depending on that to keep them all alive.

All associated with the effort to bring down the administration were careful not to carry anything that would incriminate them or tie them to any organized effort. They committed information to memory, sent notes in encrypted e-mails, and used old-fashioned dead drops, but recruiting powerful politicians to the cause—convincing them to move forward and actually put themselves at risk—meant certain lines needed to be crossed.

Garcia had to take risks to show the others that certain risks were worth taking. The encrypted IronKey flash drive in her pocket contained photos and detailed charts that tied the Vice President to the Pakistani Qasim Ranjhani, and medical records connecting President Drake to known terrorist plotter Dr. Nazeer Badeeb. Any one piece of it would no doubt get her shot if found in her possession, but the fact that she was willing to hand carry the thumb drive to the meeting and look the congressional delegation in the eye when she handed it over should carry some weight. She would explain the contents during their meeting, and then provide the delegation with a password after they parted company.

Garcia stopped to look in the window of a shop selling Civil War chess sets, thinking idly of her parents.

Revolution and civil war had been constant topics in her home. Her father, a rule-keeping Russian who taught math and science under the Soviet-backed education system in Havana, saw no room for anything but unwavering loyalty to the party. A devoted Cuban wife, her mother was the daughter of a man who had been a successful grapefruit plantation owner before Castro. Ronnie never acted on it, but the blood of a revolutionary ran deep within her veins. She missed them both to the point of tears.

Mind snapping back to the moment, Garcia reversed direction, wanting to make one more pass down the street. Miyagi kept coming, off her bike now and looking like a tourist in crisp white slacks and a navy T-shirt. She wore a white ball cap to match her slacks and dark shades that mercifully shielded others from the intensity of her eyes. The two women passed, acknowledging each other with the polite nod of two strangers and nothing more. No one else on the sidewalk knew that inside Miyagi's oblong messenger case was a Japanese short sword that had tasted more than its share of blood. Garcia smiled to herself, thinking how odd it was that she found such a thing comforting.

Halfway down the block, she paused in front of a small café that sold Dutch apple pie and scrapple. Lifting her hand from the pocket of her jeans, she let a red crayon fall to the ground. Without looking down, she used the heel of her Nike to grind the wax into a small circle on the sidewalk. Satisfied she'd left a mark small enough to go unnoticed by most, but large enough to get the attention of anyone who was looking for it, she made her way across the street to another espresso shop. Ordering her third cup of coffee for the evening, she took a seat by the window to wait.

Chapter 19

Kashgar

Settling deeply into the high-back saddle, Quinn gave the big gray its head and "smooched," the universal human-to-horse signal that it was time to move out. The animal lurched forward, breaking easily into a fast lope toward the dust-choked scrum of other horses. Cheers erupted from the sidelines. He was a stranger, but he was also a *buzkashi* rider, and that was enough—for now.

Quinn vaguely remembered that there was a Japanese martial art called *bajutsu*—fighting while on horseback. Other than seeing the word in a book about medieval samurai, he'd never taken the time to delve any deeper into the subject. He could, however sit a horse very well—and he knew how to fight even better.

His mother had taught him years before that a quick "preflight" of an unfamiliar horse could save a lot of heartache and what she called an "involuntary-rapid-aerial-dismount" down the road. Quinn leaned back in the saddle as soon as the gelding was well into its stride, lifting the reins and applying just enough pressure forward of the girth with his legs to bring the big

animal to a sliding stop. The horse reared, pawing the
air with its forefeet as if on command. Quinn leaned
forward immediately, throwing his weight over the horse's
bowed neck, patting the snorting animal and urging it
back into a canter, this time gaining speed until they
reached the mob of other animals that stomped and
screamed around the carcass of the dead goat. Not
nearly as smooth as a motorcycle, the horse was never-
theless nearly as push-button in the way it responded to
Quinn's movements. His mother had always stressed
for him to be as light as possible with any command.
Thankfully, Hajip's brother must have had the same
sentiment when it came to horsemanship. It took little
more than a change in leg pressure for the gray to
"bend" around Quinn's thigh, collect its haunches, and
launch in the direction Quinn wanted to go as surely as
a guided missile.

The game had already begun and at least twenty
other horses and riders pushed and shoved at each other
in a bloody melee of hooves and knees and whistling
leather quirts. Habibullah and his two men sat on the
outer edges of the scrum, watching and waiting patiently for someone else to do the initial work and pick
up the carcass. Quinn rode as if he intended to drive
straight into the center mass, shifting the weight at the
last minute to turn the horse straight for Habibullah's
man on the black horse. Muzra was the larger of the
two sidekicks, so Quinn had decided to get him out of
the way first and take his spot on the team.

A shout rose up from the mob as a rider finally
scooped up the carcass. Fending off the sudden rain of
quirts and whips, the hapless man began to shove and
whip his way through the packed scrum. He leaned
back as he rode, using a leg to help prop up the flopping body of the headless goat as he tried to put dis-

tance between himself and the crowd. With all eyes on the carcass, Quinn focused on Muzra, bringing the gray just off the big black's nose. Muzra was unconcerned with the oncoming rider since he wasn't in possession of the goat. Quinn found it fairly easy to scrape in close, using his knee to shove the other man's leg back and out of his stirrup, upending him and tossing him out of the saddle. The gray got in on the action, biting at the big black's flank as he went by. Quinn gave the other horse a swat on the rump with his quirt, sending it trotting off the field and leaving Muzra lying on his back in the dirt. The action moved down the field at breakneck pace and though Muzra must have a pretty good idea that it had been Quinn who unseated him, there was nothing he could do about it, even if he'd been sure.

Habibullah made his move as the other riders strung out toward the pivot flag, each either running interference for the man who held the carcass or trying to get into a position to steal it. Obviously knowing that rider would have to come back toward the circle after he rounded the flag, the Tajik slowed, lurking on the near side, aiming to intercept. Habibullah's remaining helper, an agile man who seemed to have been born on the back of a horse, drifted easily to his right while Quinn galloped the gray up alongside on his left. Habibullah turned in the saddle, giving him a wary look.

Holding the leather quirt in his teeth and leaning forward over the gray's head to give it plenty of speed, Quinn smiled and gestured at the oncoming rider with his right hand as if to say "all yours."

A *buzkashi* rider cannot be a timid man, but looking up and seeing the hulking Habibullah and two sidekicks bearing down on him made the rider who held the carcass flinch and cut right in an attempt to dart around.

This put him broadside to the oncoming horses and allowed Habibullah to crash in, driving his larger bay into other animal. Horses squealed and collided as dozens of hooves pounded the earth. Centrifugal force threw dirt and dung and the tail end of the carcass into the air as the horses spun from the momentum. Quinn was able to squirt by on his gray, hazing three opposing riders out of the way so Habibullah could snatch the flopping *buz* as he plowed by. The startled rider had to use both hands to stay in the saddle and surrendered the goat without a fight.

Now, with the goat in his possession, Habibullah tucked the quirt between his teeth and spurred the bay back toward the flag at the far end of the field.

The next round had a similar outcome with Quinn using the gray to haze away other riders so the big Tajik could gain the point. Muzra was able to rejoin the contest, but Quinn had proven himself Habibullah's ally by then, so it didn't matter.

The sun was well up by the time the third round commenced. Mirages of morning heat began to drift up from the hard-packed dirt. Bits jangled and leather groaned as riders wheeled their horses, all bathed in sweat, waiting. A portable speaker on the sidelines crackled and a static-filled voice made an announcement in Uyghur. Quinn couldn't understand the words but knew this was the last round. The horses were too valuable to risk in the heat.

A horn blew and the riders, Habibullah included, flung themselves at the battered goat carcass intent on finishing the game with honor. Caught up in the fierce competition, Quinn did not see the newcomers until they were almost on top of him. There were two of them, throwing up trails of yellow dust as they brought their horses in at a gallop from a row of trucks to the south.

Quinn spun his horse, getting a quick 360 look, and saw a third horse, nostrils flaring on its huge black head, bearing directly at him from the sidelines. Something in the rider's hands caught a glint of the morning sun. At fifty feet Quinn could see it wasn't a riding crop but a two-foot length of metal rod.

Caught between the scrum behind him and the newcomers, Quinn spurred the gray forward, urging the big animal directly at the two men galloping toward him, and creating some distance between himself and the man on the black horse. The oncoming riders slowed, circling Quinn like wolves, pestering the gray with their quirts and pushing him toward the man with the spear. Quinn swung with his quirt, hearing it whistle past the intended target. The gray gave an energetic hop and cow-kicked at the nearest rider, missing but keeping him at bay.

To an onlooker, the three horses circling around Quinn against the backdrop of other horses vying for the carcass looked to be an extension of the game. But Quinn saw it for what it was, a direct attack.

Quinn lifted the reins, using his heel to urge another kick from the big gray. Snorting and trailing a line of slobber, the horse gave little hop, and then lashed out, hooves connecting with the thigh of the nearest rider with a crack like a gunshot.

Relaxing the reins, Quinn turned the gray to face the man on the black, shouldering past and narrowly missing a stab in the thigh. Two more new riders tore out from the sidelines, each carrying their own short spear. Both smiled crooked smiles, the way a lion surely looks at an impala before bringing it down. He gave a fleeting thought to making a break for it, but the black horse was fresh and showing his back would only turn Quinn into an easier target.

Spinning again, Quinn realized his only option was to use the other *buzkashi* players as a shield and look for a chance to put some distance between himself and the armed riders.

He might have made it had Habibullah not retrieved the carcass and run directly at him. The entire scrum of twenty horses followed, coming at Quinn from behind, carrying him like a wave toward the man on the black. Quinn twisted in the saddle as they washed together, but there was nowhere for him to go.

He felt a dull thud as the point of the metal rod impacted his shoulder, shoving him backwards but not quite unseating him. Quinn felt no pain, but the familiar rush of adrenaline said he'd been hit. He rolled his shoulder and flexed his hand to make sure there'd been no serious damage to the tendons or ligaments, turning the gray at the same time to put its rump toward the assailant. Gathering the reins, he collected the horse, urging it to bring its hindquarters up without moving forward. Snorting like a warhorse, the big gray arched its powerful neck and gave a hop before letting fly a backward kick with both hooves. Metal shoes snapped against the black horse's ribs, cracking like a gunshot and catching the hapless rider's knee. He yowled in pain, slumping forward in the saddle in an effort to keep his seat and maneuver out of the way in the swirling mass of screaming horses and shouting riders.

Quinn began to feel light-headed as he spurred the gray through the oncoming riders past Habibullah and his men. He reached to touch his shoulder and his fingers came back wet with blood. Some sort of claxon began to sound, hollow as if set deep inside his head. His vision began to narrow. Swaying in the saddle, he heard angry voices shouting something in Chinese. There was a gunshot and Quinn in his daze wondered if he'd been hit. His shoulder was on fire. He could hear engines, see the blurred image of the big six-by-six truck full of PLA soldiers rolling onto the field. Horses stomped and nickered, not understanding why the game had stopped as uniformed officials poured onto the grounds. Rough hands clamored for Quinn, dragging him from the saddle as he blinked stupidly, using all his energy in an effort just to remain conscious. Shoved flat on his back, he could see nothing but a small circle of sky above the angry faces of soldiers who held him down.

A Chinese woman in dark glasses hovered over him and ripped away his padded shirt, slapping away his hand as it lifted it in a feeble attempt to defend himself.

"Get away from me!" he tried to yell but managed little more than a whisper. Too weak to resist, he could no longer even raise his head.

"Hold him!" The woman in glasses hissed, drawing a blade from her belt.

Quinn felt the world close in around him as she plunged the knife into his chest.

Chapter 20

Vice President Lee McKeon stared across the white linen tablecloth at the Japanese woman and picked at his pheasant and pasta without looking down. Still brooding over Drake's recent growth of a spine, McKeon had skimmed over the portion of the menu that said the dish was seasoned with fennel. The chef in the Navy Mess must have bought it by the bushel—and then used half of his purchase in this serving alone.

The mess, located within a stone's toss from the Situation Room, was actually only open for seating during breakfast and lunch—making takeout orders for dinner—but none of the staff had argued when the Vice President sat down with his companion.

"I wish you'd let me sort out your wife," Ran said, chewing a bite of bourbon-glazed salmon as her eyes flicked around the empty dining room. McKeon was certain that the assassination attempt had put her on edge, but there was little that could put her off a meal. Ran Kimura ate little, but she ate often, a function of all her physical activity, he supposed. Had it not been for McKeon's own case of nerves the thought would have made him smile.

"The situation with my wife will work itself out in time," he said, pushing away the plate. "Right now I'm more concerned with getting word from China."

"About our friend Jericho Quinn?" Ran scoffed, chasing a bite of salmon around the plate with her fork, catlike. "You should have let me handle him personally from the beginning."

"It should be a fairly easy endeavor at this point," McKeon said, resolving to swear off fennel for the foreseeable future. "My sources say they have him located, and, for all practical purposes, cornered."

"As they have in times past." Ran's lips turned up in a sarcastic smirk. "I prefer to do things myself. All this talking to others gives me a headache."

McKeon cocked his head to one side. "But if you left, then who would look after me?"

"I suppose that if I had been gone this morning, Agent Knight would have been successful." Ran shrugged, nodding in thought. "That would have been unfortunate."

"Unfortunate, indeed." Looking into her dark eyes, McKeon was taken back to that night years before, when Ran had come within a hair of taking his head. Her father's organization had been hired by a rival to kill Qasim Ranjhani, a Pakistani fixer who was actually McKeon's distant cousin. McKeon had been the governor of Oregon at the time. His father's plan was still in its infancy and McKeon had been visiting with Ranjhani when Ran had slipped into the room, sword in hand, completely naked so as not to stain her clothing with blood from the planned slaughter. Certain he was about to be killed, McKeon had found himself transfixed by the incredibly intricate black and green ink of the tattoo that covered this beautiful woman from shoulder to mid thigh like a bodysuit. Coincidentally, Ranjhani had been in the toilet so McKeon faced her alone. Instead of striking him dead at once, she had paused, studying his face as her sword moved slowly, back and forth like the tip of a hunting cat's tail, bleeding off coiled energy.

The look in her eyes at that moment was one he often recalled and one that he would never forget.

"Why did you not kill me?" he said, blurting the words much louder than he'd intended. A nearby Navy steward looked at him, then turned away so as not to be rude. "I only know that you stopped," McKeon continued, quieter now. "What I do not know is why."

"Because you frightened me." Ran blotted at her lips with a linen napkin, leaving a telltale pink stain of lipstick. "And I am not an easy person to frighten."

"Me, frighten you?" he said. "That's laughable. I know I'm tall, but in a physical confrontation I would be worse than useless. That night . . . I was unarmed and you held a sword that you have proven you know how to use all too well. What was it about me that could have possibly frightened you?"

Ran stared at him, her oval face serene. She wore very little makeup, the natural flush of her cheeks providing plenty of contrast. "My father was a strong man," she said, hands placed flat on either side of her plate as if she were meditating. "There was a time when I was younger that I thought he might be invincible. Over the years I learned that his heart was like iron and there was truly no room in it for me. I was led to believe that my target, Qasim Ranjhani, worked for a man who was as violent as my father was strong, a man who had some grand notion of global jihad—a new world for which he was willing to fight and die. I found the idea of a person with such lofty, impossible goals to be intriguing. When I came into the room that evening, I realized you were that man. I saw in you a similar strength that I'd seen in my father." She leaned forward, almost imperceptibly, just enough that he caught a sultry glimpse of tattoo at the edge of her collar. "But I saw in you one fatal flaw."

"And what was that?" he asked.

Ran leaned back and dabbed at her lips with the napkin again. "Even with all your grand plans of death and war," she said, "your heart had room for someone else. I never saw that in my father."

"So that is what kept me alive?" He forced a smile.

"So far." She shrugged. "Time will tell."

He wanted to ask her what she supposed she was going to get from following a man like him. He could understand it if she was after a man with power, but his mission was to bring down the very government that he now led. He was Muslim and she was *kafir*, an infidel from a nation of idol worshipers. His actions might be permissible under the principle of *Muruna*, a doctrine that allowed believers to suspend Sharia law in order to further Islam. But a woman like Ran who had covered herself in tattoos and held her head up like a man during conversations would be stoned or hanged once the law was reestablished.

In the end, he supposed that they both realized the likelihood either of them would live that long was very slim. The cell phone in his shirt pocket began to buzz, momentarily saving him from his philosophic self-flagellation.

"Yes," he said, expecting it would be his secretary or the Chief of Staff. He felt a surge of anticipation when he heard Glen Walter's voice. The IDTF agent was too intelligent to call unless there was something interesting going on.

"Mr. Vice President," Walter said. "I'd like to brief you on a matter if you have a moment." There was an urgency in his voice that made McKeon sit up straighter in his chair.

"By all means, Glen," he said. "Brief away." He flipped his slender fingers at Ran to bring her in closer so she could hear both sides of the conversation.

"I've taken the liberty of assigning agents to keep tabs on various members of Congress who have voiced vocal opposition to the administration—"

"Wise," McKeon said, genuinely impressed.

"Thank you, Mr. Vice President," Walter said. If he was happy with the praise he didn't gush over it. "But that's not the end of it. The two agents I have on Senator Gorski from Alaska just called in. Seems she's driven up to Gettysburg this evening with Congressman Dillman."

"An affair?" McKeon asked, raising an eyebrow at Ran.

"That could be it, sir," Agent Walter said. "But it doesn't really jibe with their personalities or backgrounds. Gorski is driving and my agents say she's executing various countersurveillance maneuvers— doubling back, slowing down and speeding up, taking exits and then getting right back on the freeway. It's as though they are trying to shake a tail."

"So," McKeon said, "you believe they are meeting someone."

"I do, sir," Walter said. "There's always the possibility that it's some sort of decoy or ruse, but I think they're going to meet someone from the conspiracy."

When Walter spoke of "the conspiracy," he was referring to Winfield Palmer and his little group of patriots. Of course, Walter had no idea of anything really. He was only loyal because he enjoyed being nasty to people. Working for McKeon and the administration gave him the opportunity to do things that would have otherwise seen him strapped to an execution table with a needle in his vein.

McKeon took a deep breath and pressed his forehead against Ran's. "This is good news," he said. "Are you there in Gettysburg?"

Walter cleared his throat. "Unfortunately no, sir. I'm in San Diego on another matter."

"Very well," McKeon sighed, looking at Ran. "I'm going to send someone to meet the agents you have on scene. I trust you to have them handle this swiftly and surely. They should use whatever force they deem necessary."

"Of course, sir," Walter said. "They'll scoop up whoever they find. I'll book the next flight back."

McKeon ended the call and smiled. He would have kissed Ran on the forehead had it not been for the Navy steward. "Take Marine One and get to Gettysburg as quickly as possible. I don't want our IDTF idiots to squander this opportunity."

Ran leaned closer. "Your pet President is in a pissy mood," she said. "What if he does not want me to borrow his private helicopter?"

"Then kill him," McKeon whispered, only half joking. "But get out there now. I want Winfield Palmer in a prison cell or in the ground."

Chapter 21

A stark white light bored into Quinn's subconscious, needling him awake from an uneasy dream. Every muscle in his body ached as if he had the flu. At least he knew he wasn't dead. His eyes felt as if they'd been rubbed with sand. Blurry images of Chinese soldiers in green Army uniforms spun in his head, bringing waves of nausea. He blinked, letting his eyes grow accustomed to the light, and found that a tube ran from a catheter in the back of his left wrist to an IV rack at the head of a metal hospital bed. The clang of a chain leg restraint told him he was secured in place by more than a flimsy IV line.

A Chinese woman peered at Quinn over the top of an English copy of *The Economist*. She looked to be in her late twenties and was pretty, as guards went, with thick black hair piled into a loose bun over an oval face. Black-framed glasses—the kind of glasses that looked like they belonged to a person who might read *The Economist* in someone else's hospital room—clung to a smallish nose.

Quinn recognized her immediately as the woman who'd stabbed him just before he passed out.

Her eyes flicked up at the rattle of the leg irons. An audible gasp escaped her lips when she saw Quinn—as if she was surprised that he woke up. She glanced at her watch, then tossed the magazine on the side table and scooted her chair closer.

"How are you feeling, Mr. Quinn?" She spoke in English.

Quinn licked his lips, taking the time to steady his racing mind before he spoke. She knew his name. That was something, since the only identification he carried was a Moroccan passport. He wondered how much he'd babbled while he'd been unconscious.

"I guess I'm okay," he said, "considering the fact that you stabbed me." His throat was on fire. He'd been through enough surgeries in his life to recognize the residual pain a breathing tube left in his throat. The bandages on his chest and shoulder confirmed his suspicions. "What happened?"

She gave a little sigh, like she was about to explain something to a child. "Do you know how every story involving politics begins in China?"

"How?" Quinn raised an eyebrow, playing along.

The woman shot a worried gaze over one shoulder, and then the other, before turning back to Quinn. "Just like that."

"Hmmm," Quinn grunted. "That might be funny if I wasn't chained to a hospital bed."

"You were poisoned, Mr. Quinn," the woman said.

Quinn ran his fingers along the bandage on his chest. That explained the nausea and the fact that he'd blacked out from such a superficial wound. "The man with the spear. Who is he?"

"A Pakistani," the woman said. "Unfortunately he did not survive his arrest."

"That figures," Quinn said, letting his head fall back against the stiff hospital pillow, eyes closed as another wave of nausea passed. "There were at least four more," he said. "Did you get them?"

"Perhaps," the woman said. "We made a large number of arrests, seventeen in all. Three fought back and were killed by authorities. Identifications are still ongoing."

"What kind of poison?"

"Bì má dú sù," she said in Mandarin. "Ricin." She leaned over the edge of the bed, as if she wanted to keep their conversation between them alone. Strands of black hair escaped the utilitarian bun and fell across her forehead. Flushed cheekbones were set high, over a strong jawline. She shot a glance at the door over her shoulder every few seconds, as if still trying to illustrate her earlier joke. "It is a fairly easy substance to procure from the common castor bean. The Pakistani rider was able to inject you with a small pellet from a specially designed metal rod. Crude in its operation, but it would have been effective enough had we not been watching you."

Quinn put his hand flat on his chest, feeling the surgical wound. He was fortunate this woman had known to look for a ricin pellet. A fleck the size of a pinhead could kill a man. Vomiting, bloody diarrhea, seizures, kidney failure—there was nothing noble about death caused by ricin. The KGB had used it to assassinate a Bulgarian dissident by stabbing him in the thigh with a pellet-shooting umbrella.

"Are you sure you got it all?" he said.

"I removed one pellet while you were still on the

buzkashi field," the woman said. "The doctors here could not locate any more with their scanners. They did some exploratory digging, which I am certain you will feel when the anesthetic wears off, but they did not find anything else. They believe there was only one. The spear was painted with some sort of sedative or I fear you would have fought until you were dead."

Quinn reached for a cup of water on the side table. It was room temperature but brought some relief to his sore throat. "This Pakistani," Quinn said. "Might he have been one of Habibullah's men?"

The Chinese woman shook her head. "I do not believe so," she said. "We have Habibullah in custody. We will certainly ask him."

Quinn took another sip of water. A Pakistani. It made sense. One of Mandeep Gola's men must have recognized him and been working for the other side. "How long have I been out?"

"A few hours." The woman glanced down at her lap. "You spoke of someone named Veronica while you were still under sedation . . . in terms that were quite tender."

Quinn took a deep breath, steadying himself by assessing his surroundings, careful not to say anything that would confirm any of his unconscious babbling.

The door leading out of the room was shut and had no window, but it was safe to assume there was at least one more guard posted outside. The furniture and bed linens were worn and shabby and though the room looked clean, it didn't have the sterile smell common to hospitals in the United States.

Dressed in nothing but a flimsy cotton hospital gown, Quinn was in a private room in a culture where multi-patient wards were the norm. His only contact was this woman who, though she seemed willing to answer his questions, was surely a government agent. She was tall and trimly built, but well-muscled like she'd just finished boot camp. She wore fashionable jeans and a tight black T-shirt. The imprint of a pistol was clearly visible at the waist of her khaki journalist vest. Quinn couldn't see her shoes from his vantage point on the bed, but was sure they were at once stylish and utilitarian. There was a sort of awkwardness about the woman, as if she was working from a script, and didn't quite have all the lines memorized.

He took another sip of the water.

"You seemed to worry a great deal about your friends while you were out," the woman said. "Quite noble."

"My friends . . ." Quinn wondered if Jacques had been able to make it back to Deuben's clinic.

"You are thinking of Gunnery Sergeant Thibodaux," the woman said. "He is fine."

Quinn moved his leg under the sheet, rattling the chains that secured him to the bed. "Is he also a prisoner?"

The woman glanced at her watch. "He departed on a flight to Urumqi while you were still in surgery. He will be on his way to New York within the hour."

Quinn thought about that for a moment. "Was he under guard when you left him?"

"What difference does that make?" she asked. "He is safe, I assure you."

Quinn leaned back against the pillow, eyes closed. Thibodaux would never get on a plane and leave the country if he knew Quinn was still alive and being held against his will.

"Your friend will not come to set you free. He will return to the United States as instructed. I told him my plans concerning you. He did not like them, but he appeared to understand that there were no other options."

The woman's mobile phone gave a quiet chime. She

smiled softly when she looked at it, like she'd seen a photo of a small child or a puppy.

"My name is Song," she said, almost as an afterthought.

"Well, Song," Quinn said. "As much as I appreciate you digging the poison pellet out of my chest, I wouldn't mind it if you took these leg irons off."

She nodded as if this was an understandable request, but just stood there beside the bed, making no move to release him.

"Are you in pain?" she asked, touching his bandages like a concerned relative.

"I feel fine," Quinn said, following Song's gaze to the side of his face. He reached up to find a series of tiny needles had been inserted in various points of his ear.

"I believe your Air Force calls this Battlefield Acupuncture," Song said. "I instructed the surgeon to keep you as free from pain medication as possible. We need to move soon, so I thought this treatment more prudent."

Some called it a godsend, others deemed it quackery, but apart from his sore throat he was relatively pain free for coming out of surgery where a doctor had just spent a considerable amount of time digging around in his chest. He studied Song's face, noticing the tiny, tension lines at the corners of a smallish mouth, the fleeting twitch in her golden brown eyes. Though in her twenties, she reminded Quinn of his seven-year-old daughter, Mattie, when she was hiding something that might embarrass her.

Quinn swallowed, grimacing a little but feeling better by the moment. "You said we need to move quickly?"

Song gave a solemn nod. "You are an impressive tactician, Mr. Jericho Quinn." She held up her phone to show a photo of the Interpol Red Notice seeking his immediate arrest. The US Marshals, who'd placed him on their Fifteen Most Wanted List, had used his OSI credential photo for the wanted poster. "It says here that you are a dangerous fugitive, but I believe you and I are after the same thing."

"So you're looking for a handcuff key as well?" Quinn said.

She rolled her lips, as if holding in the words she wanted to speak. At length, she removed the black glasses and stuffed them in the pocket of her vest, sitting back down to slump in her chair with a resigned sigh. "The man you followed to the warehouse—Hajip Mohommed—has been the subject of my investigation for the past month. We had cameras and listening devices installed inside his warehouse three weeks ago, so I was able to see and hear much of your conversation last night"

"And what is it you think I'm—?"

The hi-lo tone of approaching police cars wailed in the distance. Song frowned, cocking her head toward the window.

"We should work together," she said.

"I'd be interested to hear what you have in mind," Quinn said. "But I'm chained to the bed."

"The fact is," Song said, "just like your friend Thibodaux, you really have no choice."

"There's always a choice."

"Quite so." Song shrugged. "But not always a good one."

She turned in her seat, shouting a curt order for the agent she had posted outside. A middle-aged man wearing the same style of khaki vest poked his head in the room, hand on the door.

"Go down and meet Colonel Wu when he arrives," she snapped. "I am fine here."

The other agent paused for a moment, studying Quinn. "Yes, of course . . . right away," he said, with a subordinate bob of his head and shoulders before ducking back out the door.

Song stood as the sirens drew closer. "As I said, I believe you and I are after the same thing." She took a handcuff key from her vest pocket and unlocked the leg irons and nodded toward a metal cabinet. "You will find fresh clothing in there."

Quinn pulled the IV from the back of his hand and replaced the bandage over the weeping needle puncture. He swung his legs off the bed and took a moment to let the room stop spinning before standing to check inside the cabinet. The woman was telling the truth. She did not turn around and eyed him without embarrassment as he stepped out of the hospital gown and into a new pair of khaki slacks. There were two shirts, a navy three-button polo and a red-and-white striped rugby shirt. She'd done a good job on the slacks, but the shirts were a couple of sizes too large.

"The blue one first," Song said, nodding to the polo as she took out her phone. "But hurry."

Quinn pulled the shirt over his head, stifling a groan as he lifted his arms. The stabbing, the surgery, and the fall from the galloping horse had taken a toll on his body that the acupuncture only dimmed.

She put on her glasses again. Reaching into the pocket of her vest, she took out a moistened towelette and raised it toward his face. "May I?"

Quinn gave her a puzzled look. "May you what?"

"You seem the sort of man who would break my hand if I touch your face without permission. This picture is for your new passport. Consider me your . . . what is the word . . . your stylist."

Quinn turned to the side, giving her a wary eye, but

he let her rub the towelette across the bridge of his nose and up between his eyebrows. He grimaced as she made a single swipe across the apple of his left cheek.

"I feel like my mother's giving me a spit bath before church," he said.

"'Spit bath,'" Song mused, stepping back to check her work. "I've never heard that before." Returning the towelette to her vest pocket, she reached up to fluff out Quinn's hair so it covered the acupuncture needles in his left ear. "That should do it," she said.

She used her phone to snap several photographs. Deeming them passport worthy, she nodded at the rugby shirt on the bed. "Now change quickly. It would raise suspicions if you are dressed in the same shirt you are wearing in your passport photograph."

Even this small bit of repetition brought welcome relief to his muscles. He hunched his shoulders back and forth, stretching. "Where am I going with this new passport?"

"Maybe nowhere," she said, staring at the scars that mapped his upper body. "I am not certain." She saw him catch her eye and looked away toward the window. "You must hurry," she said. "Not everyone in my government thinks as I do. Colonel Wu is the regional commander of the People's Armed Police. Once he arrives, things will be much more difficult. I will tell him you escaped your restraints while I was in the restroom." She waved a slender hand toward the door. Quinn noticed for the first time that she had pink polish on her nails. "Turn left as you exit, then take the service elevator at the end of the hallway to the basement. When you leave the elevator, go straight until you reach the double doors that will take you to outside. The People's Park is one block to the north." She looked at him, waiting for him to confirm that he understood her instructions, as if she was accustomed to repeating directions for people who didn't listen. "Colonel Wu believes females are worthless as field agents so he will quite happily believe the story of your escape. I'll tell him I watched out the window as you got in a car heading east, toward the expressway."

Quinn entertained the fleeting thought that she might be setting him up to be shot during an attempted escape.

"You must trust me." She looked at her watch. "I will meet you in one hour in front of the Blue Sky Hotel. It's on Jiefang Road alongside the park."

"You said we are after the same thing." He slipped on a new pair of Nike running shoes as he spoke, keeping an eye on the woman.

"When you questioned Hajip, you asked him about the Feng brothers," Song said. "Like you, I am trying to forestall a war between our two countries."

"So, you're Army?" Quinn asked.

"MSS," she said. Both an intelligence and enforcement organization, the Ministry of State Security was China's version of the KGB—with the same reputation for being heavy-handed toward their own citizens. Her lips set in a tight line. "Now hurry. But make no mistake, if my assessment of you is wrong—and you try to run, the combined forces of the police and the People's Liberation Army will hunt you down and kill you."

"And what if you're right?" Quinn asked, looking over his shoulder after a quick peek into the empty hall. "What if we are after the same thing?"

"Then many of those same people will be hunting us both."

Chapter 22

Gettysburg, 7:55 PM

Ronnie Garcia set her espresso on the table beside a folded copy of the *Gettysburg Times* crossword and watched Congressman Mike Dillman pause outside the shop across the street. He wore a baseball hat pulled low over sandy gray hair. Even from her vantage point a hundred feet away, his large handlebar mustache made it easy to identify him. He studied the crayon mark on the sidewalk just long enough to make Ronnie uncomfortable before ducking into the coffee shop.

Sue Gorski walked close behind him. A slender woman with the short, well-styled hair of someone used to the public eye, the senator from Alaska was dressed much like Ronnie in a crisp button-down oxford blouse and light slacks. She wore dark glasses, likely for the same reason Dillman wore the cap, though they looked less like a disguise and more like a fashionable piece of her normal wardrobe. Looking up and down the street, she ducked into the shop behind the congressman.

Garcia waited ten more minutes as tourists flowed back and forth in front of the espresso shop. Six patrons came and went, each carrying a cup of something they'd purchased inside. Garcia hit the tiny Bluetooth bud in her left ear and called Miyagi.

"How does it look out there?"

"Clear as of yet," the Japanese woman said. "But any followers could merely be waiting."

"I'll give it five more minutes," Garcia said, noting the time on her Aquaracer. "Let me know if you see anything odd."

"Of course," Miyagi said, ending the call.

Ronnie felt stupid even as she said the words. Emiko Miyagi had been her teacher at The Farm. There was no doubt she would let Garcia know if she saw something out of place.

Five minutes clicked by with no screech of tires or scream of IDTF sirens. Ronnie took the time to take what Thibodaux called a combat pee and get rid of all the coffee she'd been downing during her wait. Finished, she grabbed the newspaper from her table and stepped back out into the summer heat and flow of pedestrian traffic. The smell of someone grilling hot dogs made her stomach growl and she realized she hadn't eaten in hours. Instead of heading directly over to the waiting delegation, she walked down the street, crossing at the corner and window-shopping her way back to the espresso shop, keeping a weather eye open for surveillance.

Knowing she was at the point where she'd have to commit or walk on by, Garcia took a deep breath and walked inside. The harsh clang of a cowbell gave her a start as she stepped through the door into the air-conditioned shop. She half expected to be surrounded the moment she walked in but was greeted by a pert little barista with fuchsia hair and a nose ring.

Full to the gills with coffee and feeling more than a

little jittery, Garcia ordered a peach Italian soda and approached the waiting congressional delegation. She'd never met either of them, but was happy they'd chosen a table in the back corner near the door to a small kitchen, under the dusty mount of a deer head.

Cool drink in hand, she put on a broad smile and walked up to the table.

"Mind if I sit down?" she said, sipping on the soda through a straw daubed with her wine-colored lipstick.

Congressman Dillman, ever the gentleman, stood and pointed an open hand to the empty chair with its back to the wall. "I thought we'd save you the gunfighter seat," he said.

Senator Gorski smiled. She had a kind face but Garcia could see the tension around her normally laughing eyes and mouth. She was not cut out for this sort of meeting.

"Thank you for meeting me," Garcia said, keeping her tone and actions light, even as the topic of her conversation turned to treason.

Ten minutes later Senator Gorski looked up from the diagram of terrorist connections Ronnie had sketched on her napkin.

"Well then," she said, demonstrating the poise under pressure that had earned her three terms in the senate. "Everything you say sounds plausible. The President's support is waning, but even those who would believe the charges would need hard proof to convict. A photo with a known terrorist is damaging, but I'm not sure it constitutes a high crime or misdemeanor. Too easy to explain away. I think we might get more mileage with charges of warmongering."

"I understand," Garcia said, turning to Dillman. "Congressman, do you think you have a majority?"

He smoothed his mustache and nodded. "Enough for an impeachment? Yes, I'm sure we do."

"The people I work with believe that will be the shot across the bow we'd need," Ronnie said. "It will let the Chinese know that not everyone in this country is quite so eager for war."

"Not to mention putting the administration on the defensive," Gorski mused. "Even if they aren't convicted."

"Not that it makes a difference," Dillman said, "but having these particular men on the defensive is bound to be extremely dangerous for the people that put them there."

"No doubt," Garcia said. "This is dangerous for all of us, but the alternative is unthinkable."

Gorski stood, pushing the napkin back across the table at Garcia, smart enough not to carry something so damning on her person. "Please tell Mr. Palmer that he has our support."

Mike Dillman stood as well. "And tell the old warhorse when this is over he owes me a beer."

"When this is over—" Ronnie said, as Miyagi's voice crackled over her earbud.

"You have visitors," she said through the electronic crackle. "Two SUVs rolling up in front—"

"Roger that." Garcia pointed her open hand toward the kitchen entrance. Jaw set and scanning for options, she repeated Miyagi's warning to Dillman and Gorski. "You understand I cannot let them arrest me," she said.

"We do," Dillman said as a pudgy man with greasy black curls walked in from the back to block her way. Another agent, this one older, but in no better physical shape, brought up the rear. Since neither looked like much of a runner, they'd probably resort to guns right off the bat.

"Benavides!" Garcia whispered, recognizing the lead IDTF agent. Jacques had forced the witless idiot to help rescue the Director of the CIA from a secret prison.

"Well, well, well," Joey B said, his words dripping with condescension. "Sweet Meat. You're looking kind of pale without your big Cajun friend."

Garcia choked back a gasp. It killed her that this pompous bastard was able to get such an emotional response. He was a weak man. She knew that, but weaklings were especially dangerous when they got the upper hand. Virginia Ross had recounted his cruel treatment while she was in custody. Ronnie knew what he was actually capable of—and what was in store for her if they got her alone.

"Turn your ass around so I can pat you down for weapons." Benavides gave her a lecherous wink. "With all you got going on, this might take a while."

"Here now!" Congressman Dillman stepped in between Agent Benavides and Garcia. "There's no call for that sort of talk."

"Step aside, Granddad." Benavides flicked a fat hand like he was shooing away a fly. "This is a federal investigation."

Garcia glanced behind her, seeing two more agents come through the front door. Both were on the heavy side, but not as soft as Joey B and his partner. One had the flat nose of a street fighter and there was likely a good deal of muscle hiding under his bulk. Benavides and his partner were definitely the weak link in the arrest team. Frozen like a deer in the path of an oncoming car, she thought of drawing her pistol and shooting her way out. Action was always faster than reaction so her odds were actually pretty good. At the very least, she'd have the satisfaction of shooting Benavides in the eye before falling in a hail of bullets. But that would leave Gorski and Dillman at the mercy of the IDTF.

Joey B gave her another leering stare. "It would be a surprise if you could hide a weapon in those jeans," he said.

"Son," Dillman said, blocking the agent's way with his hip. "Do you have any idea who I am?"

Not quite as soft as he looked, Benavides planted the flat of his hand against Dillman's chest and shoved him back into his chair. "I believe I do," he said. "You're the dumb bastard from Indiana about to be arrested for treason."

Older than Benavides by at least two decades, Mike Dillman was still a military man. Garcia saw the flash of indignation in his eyes and moved to protect Senator Gorski from what was about to happen.

Dillman rebounded the moment he hit the chair, springing back to his feet to clobber a startled Joey Benavides with a wicked right hook. Dillman pressed his advantage, driving the agent backwards and giving Garcia time to draw her gun and drag Senator Gorski toward the rear door. With any luck the bulk of the IDTF backup team would be out front.

"Stop her!" Benavides screamed, even as Mike Dillman backed him against the wall and pummeled him with blows. A new agent, this one younger and in much better shape than the others, bounded in through the kitchen, colliding with Garcia and sending her sprawling onto the floor with the senator. Scrambling to her feet, she caught a fleeting glimpse of something dark that seemed to fly toward the congressman. The young agent hit her hard in the neck with an expandable baton, missing her head, but staggering her. She pushed off a table, catching him on the chin with the point of her elbow and buying some time. A pitiful cry came from her right. She looked up in time to see a fierce Asian woman standing over Dillman. Her heart rose, thinking it was Miyagi, but something wasn't right. This woman looked like Emiko but was much younger, with a darkness that was palpable, even from across the room.

A blade glinted in the muted light as the woman used her dagger to great effect, gutting the congressman where he stood.

Dillman staggered backwards, blood-drenched fingers clutching his abdomen. Benavides climbed to his feet and spat on the floor. He dabbed at his bloody lip before drawing his pistol and shooting the congressman three times in the head. The bullets tore away much of the poor man's skull but he was a tough bird and even with the gruesome damage, it took a moment for him to stop moving. The barista screamed, clutching her fuchsia hair as she dropped behind the counter.

"Come on!" Ronnie prodded Senator Gorski, who stood transfixed by the awful sight of her friend. An instant later, Ronnie heard the familiar crackle of a Taser. A searing pain arced from her buttocks to her shoulder as the twin barbs sent fifty thousand volts through her muscles. Toppling like a downed tree, she fell headlong on the floor, her body, from forehead to toes, arched stiff as a plank, as it tensed from the electricity. After five agonizing seconds, the shock abated and she collapsed, panting for air.

"Hit her again," Benavides spat, his voice slurred from the beating. "I want this bitch tenderized."

She flailed her hands behind her back, hoping to sweep the thin electrical wires away, but it was too late. Her body arched again and she was clenching her jaw so hard she thought it might pop out of place. A grunting scream felt forced from her throat. The shock abated and she collapsed drooling, her cheek pressed against the carpet. A shadow crossed her face and she expected to feel handcuffs at any moment. Instead, she felt a stab of pain as someone jabbed a needle into her neck. Gorski's terrified scream faded into nothingness.

Chapter 23

Three minutes earlier

Emiko Miyagi stood from her sidewalk table halfway down the block and across the street the moment she saw the maroon SUV. It had normal license plates, but the small black puck antenna on top identified it as being wired for a two-way radio, equipment civilian cars were unlikely to have. A balding man wearing a fishing vest stepped out of the passenger side, hitching up his slacks and exposing a dangling pair of handcuffs that were stuffed in his waistband. Miyagi shot a glance over her shoulder to see another SUV arrive, this one white and bulging with more men in tactical gear and ill-fitting suits.

She warned Garcia on the radio, simultaneously drawing the short sword from behind her back. Holding it with the point down, parallel to her thigh, she padded up quickly behind the white SUV. She'd counted six men, two in the lead and four in the white follow car. Formidable, but their superior numbers made them complacent. She was able to kill the first three before the fourth realized she was even there. She drew the blade across the fourth man's throat as she ran to help Garcia.

In front of her, a younger agent pushed open the door of the espresso shop, exiting to the street. He waved the maroon SUV forward with a flick of the pistol in his hand. Miyagi, still fifty feet away, picked up the pace as two more agents followed him out. One carried an unconscious Garcia over his shoulders like a sack of potatoes. Another dragged a handcuffed Senator Sue Gorski toward the second SUV. A young Japanese woman followed them out.

Emiko slowed, struggling to keep a grip on the short sword as she looked at the face she'd not seen for two decades—the face of her own daughter. The bearing, the walk—the resemblance was unmistakable.

"Ran!" Miyagi gasped, head spinning. Like herself, the young woman's clothing was swathed in blood.

The younger woman's head shot up when she heard her name, glaring. She too stumbled, shaking her head as if to clear her vision. Shoving the agent with Garcia into the waiting SUV, she froze, dagger in hand. She cocked her head to one side, entranced.

"Ran?" Miyagi said again.

The younger woman shook it off, and jumped in the front passenger seat. Benavides dragged Senator Gorski into the back, sending the remaining two agents to take care of Miyagi as the SUV sped away.

Both agents began to shoot immediately, oblivious of the crowd of pedestrians that had gathered to watch the spectacle. Miyagi sprang sideways, letting her blade clatter to the sidewalk. She drew her own sidearm, desperate not to lose sight of the departing SUV. Her Ducati was parked around the corner. If she could see to these two remaining agents, she'd be plenty fast enough to follow and see where they took Garcia.

Two more IDTF agents rolled up in a black Crown Victoria sedan, bailing out behind the cover of their car and sending Miyagi diving into a nearby shoe store. Rather than trying to capture her, the agents simply kept her pinned for two minutes before speeding away in the opposite direction of the maroon SUV.

Sirens began to wail as onlookers figured out this wasn't some reenactment or street performance and called 911. Miyagi pushed her way through the gathering crowd, down the street to her Ducati. The SUV, Ronnie Garcia, and Senator Gorski were long gone. Miyagi had seen Dillman's body as she'd run past the espresso shop and known from the blood on Ran's clothing that she'd been the one to murder him.

Straddling the bike, Miyagi caught her breath as she punched a number into her cell. The shock of finally seeing her daughter after so many years combined with the frustration at having lost Garcia. Her shoulders shook uncontrollably, and for the first time in many years she felt as if she might break down.

Winfield Palmer picked up on the first ring. "Yes."

"All is lost," Miyagi said, clearing the catch in her throat. "I repeat. All is lost."

Chapter 24

Quinn sat on a concrete bench under the mottled shade of a mulberry tree along Jiefieng Road. He'd chosen to wait in the shadows so he could see the portico to the Blue Sky Hotel and still remain out of sight of any curious People's Armed Police cruisers. His head throbbed like he'd gone three rounds with Mike Tyson and his stomach still threatened to rebel at any moment from the recent anesthesia. The spinning uncertainty was even worse. It made him crazy to think of the block of time that was simply missing from his memory. Even as a youth, he'd possessed a severe aversion to being out of control, preferring a local anesthetic even to fix a compound fracture of his lower leg from a motorcycle wreck.

He leaned back against the cool concrete of the bench and worked on his breathing to calm his nerves—in for five, holding for five, then out for five. There'd been three hundred RMB in the pocket of the slacks Song had given him. It wasn't enough to escape the country—about fifty US dollars—but he'd been able to buy some lychee-flavored bubble tea. Even that hurt his throat, but he didn't know when he'd have the opportunity to eat again and hoped the sweet tapioca and milk would provide some energy and soothe his stomach.

A horn honked on the road and he looked up to see Song pull alongside the curb in a dusty tan VW Santana. She reached across the seat and flung open the passenger door as if she'd always expected him to be waiting in the trees.

Quinn climbed in and shut the door, trying not to look as sick as he felt. Midday traffic poured back and forth in a mad rush as if half the residents of Kashgar were streaming into the city while the other half fled. Song made liberal use of her horn and nosed her way into the melee in the particular way of someone unafraid of authority—or getting run down by a bus—before heading north.

"You told me to meet you at the Blue Sky Hotel," Quinn said. "How did you know to pick me up here?"

Song tipped her head to look at him over the top of her black sunglasses. "This is where I would have waited. Anyway, I brought you a steamed bun." She pushed a grease-stained sack across the seat. She wore the same jeans, T-shirt, and loose vest as before, but had let her hair down so it hung past her shoulders. Quinn thought it looked much better down, but he kept it to himself. Style tips weren't something you shared with communist spies—even ones who seemed a little muddled as to their own identity.

"I'm assuming you have a lead on the Fengs' whereabouts," he said. He considered the steamed bun, but his gurgling stomach made him stick with his bubble tea.

"Habibullah seems to know more than he was telling us at first," she said. "My assistant is talking to him now."

"Are we going there?" Quinn asked, wondering what sort of conversation her assistant was having with the big Tajik. They crossed the muddy waters of the Tuman River. Ugly concrete buildings rose up like gray cancers among the pink-brown bastions of old Kashgar. It was easy to see why Gabrielle Deuben got so worked up about the city's takeover.

"No," Song said, watching a group of Uyghur youth eye her as she took a corner into one of the few remaining stone and brick neighborhoods down near the river. "We are going to Hajip's brother's house."

"The one the Fengs murdered?"

"The same," Song said.

Quinn gazed out the window, saying nothing. It made sense to go to the last place the Fengs had been seen. An experienced tracker and hunter, it ate at him that he hadn't thought of it.

"What do you know of the Fengs, Mr. Quinn?" Song made a tight turn and they rumbled slowly down the narrow ally, tires popping against the cobblestones. Women in colorful scarves stopped sweeping and stood in their doorways. Children leaned out of second-story windows as they passed, boring holes in them with their eyes.

"There were three of them—" Quinn grimaced as Song hit one of the ancient city's numerous potholes, deep enough that the battlefield acupuncture didn't stop the pain in his shoulder. He continued once he'd caught his breath. "One apparently died in prison shortly after the US turned them over to Pakistan. Their father was Hui Chinese, mother was Uyghur, both deceased. US intelligence says they were trained at an al Qaeda camp in Yemen."

Song nodded. "Our intelligence confirms only Ehmet attended the terrorist camp. Yaqub is the eldest, but he is more of a follower. Ehmet ran away when he was not yet thirteen to seek glory in Yemen. Yaqub would have been recruited as a suicide bomber had he attended such training. It is not uncommon to use more slow-witted youth in such a way. Ehmet's complete disregard for human life apparently demonstrated great promise to his teachers. He began sawing the heads off people he considers infidels while the ISIS darlings we are watching on the news these days were still attending European boarding schools.

"The odd thing," Song continued, "is that there does not seem to be any pivotal event that turned Ehmet into a killer. His parents died while he was in Guantanamo Bay, but he was already responsible for hundreds of deaths long before he was arrested by your military. Though he may be a believer, it is my belief that his jihad provides him a convenient vehicle to further his lust for blood and death."

"Maybe," Quinn said, thinking that he'd met a great many evil men and he'd given up trying to figure out what tragic event had made them that way. Some people were simply born broken.

"In any case," Song said. "Ehmet Feng is a fighting machine. Our sources say he absorbed the weapon practice and hand-to-hand training in Yemen as a natural. I am a hundred seventy-two centimeters—you would say five eight. I believe Ehmet to be significantly shorter than I am. But many soldiers and police officers have paid a heavy price for underestimating him because of his size."

"I try not to underestimate anyone," Quinn said.

Song turned, deadpan. "Except men on horseback carrying spears." Quinn thought it might be her attempt at humor, but couldn't be sure.

Song brought the Volkswagen to a stop in front of a

slumping brick building that looked like all the other brick buildings in old Kashgar. Quinn had expected to see a Chinese soldier or two standing guard, but the narrow street was eerily empty.

"I am at a loss," he said, taking advantage of the moment. "You appear to know a great deal about me while I know nothing about you but your name and employer."

Song kept both hands on the wheel and stared straight ahead. "It is enough to know that I am a very good at what I do—and I will do whatever it takes to stop Ehmet Feng."

"As will I," Quinn said.

"I am counting on that." She glanced down at the sack containing the steamed bun. "You should eat. I don't know how you are around blood, but there is a lot of it in there. It may ruin your appetite."

Quinn felt his stomach groan again. "I'll be fine," he said, and left the steamed bun on the seat.

Light streamed in through several open windows, throwing spotlights on great pools of drying blood on the tile floor of the main room. The bodies of the victims were gone, but the authorities hadn't done anything about the blood and other gore, leaving that for the family to take care of. Uyghur on Uyghur crime, hardly worth a lengthy investigation. Hajip was tied to a terrorist group, and his brother, thought by many to be an informant, was associated closely enough with terrorists that he could inform on them. It was a win in the eyes of the local police.

"Hajip's brother had two children, eleven and seven years of age," Song said, shaking her head at the individual pools of blood on the floor. "It looks as though Ehmet killed them first and made the father observe their deaths."

"Ehmet Feng is a bad man." Quinn held up his hand, stopping her from giving him any more description that might make him think more of his own daughter. "I don't need to be convinced of that."

"I have seen some horrible things," Song whispered, "But the people who would do something like this . . ." Her eyes scanned the room, looking for answers to questions Quinn knew were unanswerable.

He stepped over a black pool of blood, drying in a shaft of light from window, to reach a small wooden desk at the corner of the area that served as a kitchen and dining room. A pile of sliced carrots, a diced onion, some raisins sat on a cutting board beside a wooden bowl of chopped and shriveled lamb. Hajip's sister-in-law had been surprised in the middle of preparing *polo*—the Uyghur word for pilaf. Everything had been shoved to one side, spilling a clay bowl of uncooked rice. Someone had sat there during the murders. A potato, cut in half but still unpeeled, lay on the table beside the bowl of lamb.

"Odd," Quinn said.

Song looked up. "What?"

"Probably nothing." Quinn shook his head. "Do you like Uyghur food?"

"I do," she said.

"Ever had polo made with potatoes?"

"Not often." She turned up her nose. "Potatoes and rice. Too much starch."

"I think so too," Quinn said, picking up the potato half and looking at the sliced end. The other half had turned black and shriveled like a prune, but the cut end of this one had been facedown on the table and remained moist, if a little discolored. He held it up to Song. "Got a piece of paper?"

She took a notebook from her vest pocket and stepped gingerly over the blood, looking a little unsteady.

"A potato stamp." She nodded, squinting as if she was only now able to see what he was holding and understood what he was talking about. Quinn wondered just how necessary the glasses were for her to see anything. She passed him the notebook.

"Exactly." Quinn breathed softly against the cut portion of the potato to give it a little more moisture, before pressing it firmly against a blank page of Song's notebook.

"What is the American slang?" she mused, watching him work before she answered her own question. "*Old school.*"

Quinn left the potato pressed in place a few seconds. "Old school, indeed."

A potato stamp was a well-known trick used by professional forgers before the advent of inkjet printers. The cut end of a potato could be used to lift the ink of a stamp from a genuine passport or other document and transfer it to a phony one.

Quinn lifted the potato off the page to find the vague outline of a Chinese immigration exit stamp. It told them the Fengs were leaving China. But it didn't give them any clue as to where they were going.

Song made a quick call on her mobile phone, relaying the new information in rapid-fire snippets. She looked at Quinn as she spoke, knowing he understood Mandarin, and apparently not caring.

"Yes," she said, "Tell the stupid Habibullah that we know they are leaving the country—" Her face dark-

ened and she spun, facing away from Quinn, speaking
through clenched teeth. "He said what?"

She rocked forward on her toes, almost imperceptibly as she listened to the call. Her voice suddenly dropped
and Quinn could only make out a few of her words.
"You're sure that's what he said?" She turned back toward Quinn, still talking on the phone "Very well,
then do what you must," she said. "Tell him you will
cut off his balls if he does not help us." The interroga-
tor was evidently in the room with Habibullah so Song
stayed on the line to get her answer. A moment later,
she rolled her eyes in disbelief. "Is that so? He will
not?" She brightened, suddenly struck with an idea.
"Inform Mr. Habibullah that I will be generous and
give him fifteen seconds to tell me what I want to
know or I will personally drive out and shoot his *buzkashi* horse. . . . Yes, tell him now. I will hold."

Quinn whistled under his breath. "I wish you could
have gotten to know Jacques. You would have scared
him to death."

"I once had the adventure of purchasing a new car in
America," Song said, holding the phone away from her
face. "The finance manager was a very stern woman,
frightening really. When I need to be so, I merely imagine her."

Quinn raised an eyebrow. "So it's an act?"

"Yes and no." Song shrugged. "The mystery of where
the charade ends and the action begins . . . That is what
makes women frightening. Don't you think?"

Song put the mobile phone back to her ear, rescuing
Quinn from a philosophy talk worthy of Thibodaux.

"Very good," Song said, thanking the caller for the
information before she ended the call. "Apparently,"
she said, giving Quinn a sly shrug, "Habibullah values

his *buzkashi* horse over his balls. According to him, the Fengs are en route to Dubrovnik."

"Croatia." Quinn tapped the cut potato against the table, considering the options before them. "Do you plan to notify the local officials?"

Song was already weaving her way through blood puddles on her way to the car. She turned to glance back over her shoulder. "I don't even plan to notify my own officials."

"Smart."

The breakup of Yugoslavia and the Balkan wars had been devastating to the population, but organized crime and the smuggling of everything from heroin to humans had flourished in the vacuum left in the rule of law. Generational gangs of criminals had developed such deep and pervasive roots that even the relatively stable new government found it easier to live with them in a sort of uneasy truce. It was not the sort of place where you wanted to tip your hand.

"My kid brother has a friend who married a Croatian girl," Quinn said. "They've been living over there for a couple years. He can help us out with transportation if you can get us the travel documents and a way there."

"I will arrange private transport. With any luck, that will keep us out of the official databases," Song said. "Fortunately, I have a few trusted resources within the party. Our passports will not exactly be genuine, but we won't need to utilize a potato."

Chapter 25

Ronnie Garcia awoke certain she was being suffo-cated. Struggling to maintain her composure in the darkness of the cloth hood, she battled the urge to scream, lying still and willing herself to relax. Listening and feeling the situation, she strained to bring her cloudy brain into focus and to remember what had happened to get her here with a bag over her head. She moved her jaw slightly against the coarse material and pressed back the panic of the unknown. Muffled voices spoke now and again, but in her drug- and shock-induced haze, she couldn't make out the words.

Her hands were cuffed behind her back and she lay on her side. The top of her head rubbed against what felt like the handle of a car door. A gentle swaying sensation told her she was in a moving vehicle. It was impossible to tell where they were since she had no reference to how much time had passed since leaving Gettysburg. Her mouth felt stuffed with dry cotton and her body ached deeply into the bone.

A hand ran slowly along her hip, lingering at the small of her back where her shirt had come up. Whoever sat beside her had decided to have a good feel while he thought she was unconscious.

"Knock it off," an unfamiliar voice said.

The hand moved away and Joey Benavides spoke. "Mr. Walter wouldn't care. He'll do more than touch her ass and you know it."

Ronnie fought the urge to recoil, knowing it was better that these men thought her still unconscious.

"Whatever," the other voice said. "But that's for him to decide."

Clenching her eyes shut against the darkness of the hood, Ronnie slowed her breathing and listened. She remembered Miyagi's training—"*Do not wait for someone to swoop in and save you. Such thoughts are nonsense, the stuff of fairy tales. Be your own rescue. . . .*"

Ronnie ignored her throbbing hands and shoulders to focus on what she could hear.

The sound of other vehicles whirring past came from her left so they appeared to be traveling on an undivided road. She held her breath, straining to pick up something else, the sound of a church bell or a train—anything that might help provide her with a fix on her location. All she got was more traffic noise and the sickening odor of Joey Benavides's hair gel.

The swaying car was hypnotic. She was about to give in to a dazed sleep when she felt the SUV begin to climb. It didn't mean anything at first, but then they slowed, as if caught in a traffic jam. Ronnie could hear other cars nearby, each slowing in turn. Her body rocked in the seat as they SUV came to a rolling stop before accelerating again.

Ronnie waited for the sound she felt sure would come next. She smiled inside the bag when, seconds later, she heard the rhythmic thump of a pavement joint,

formed where the sections of a bridge or overpass came
together. They had slowed for a tollbooth. Even in the
darkness of her hood, she could picture it. The problem
was there were countless bridges and tollbooths in the
DC area. The rhythmic thump of tires passing over the
joints was still going strong two minutes later, allowing
Garcia to rule out all but the widest rivers. *So*, she
thought, *We're going east over oceans and bays*. She
began to run through all the bridges she could think of
near DC, still counting the seconds as she listened to
the thumps. Roughly four minutes after the noise
began, the road smoothed.

A four-mile-long bridge. They had to be crossing
the Chesapeake. Garcia pictured the terrifyingly long
two-lane Bay Bridge. She'd crossed it with Jericho on a
trip to Ocean City—which he'd found too crowded,
promising to someday take her to a chillier but much
less populated beach in Alaska.

She felt the car rumble again as they crossed a second, shorter bridge. She pictured Kent Island and the
Narrows that separated the Bay Bridge from the Delmarva Peninsula—the dangling bulb of land consisting
of pieces of Delaware, Maryland, and Virginia. The almost imperceptible smell of sweet corn, maturing, but
still in the field, confirmed her guess. She felt the SUV
turn to the right, taking them farther south. The pit in
her stomach grew as she realized there was little down
there but fields, forest, and backwater—with plenty of
remote acreage to keep someone stashed away for a
very long time.

An hour later, the SUV began to sway and bump as
they turned down some uneven road. Branches scraped
the doors as they drove down an even narrower lane,
before finally coming to a stop.

"Shake your moneymaker, little dove," Benavides said, giving Garcia a hard slap on the rump before dragging her from the car. "Time to rise and shine."

Unable to adjust to moving her stiff muscles, she collapsed in a heap. Still bagged, she sprawled into the cool mud, clambering blindly to regain her footing. Benavides took her actions as an attempt to escape and slapped her on the back of the head, sending her face-first into the mud. The wet muck against her face had the effect of a water board and she rolled on her side, wheezing in an attempt to draw enough air through the plastered cloth. The men chuckled while they let her suffer for what seemed like forever. Instead of removing the hood, rough hands simply spun it, giving her neck a rug burn, but putting a relatively clean portion of cloth over her mouth and nose.

Someone grabbed her by either arm and began drag her forward. The sudden shock of cool around her ankles terrified her as every horrible scenario flooded her brain: Alone, handcuffed and hooded with brutal men in the middle of nowhere—and now being led into the water. The thick odor of decaying vegetation seeped through the hood. Cicadas buzzed in the trees. Her Cuban mother would have called the little bugs *chicharra.* . . . Ronnie choked back a sob. Of course, she would think of her mother at a time like this. People always thought of their mothers when they were about to die.

She screamed, planting her feet in the mud and refusing to take another step.

"Shut her up," Benavides said, sloshing up from somewhere behind her. "Bitch," he spat just inches from her ear. "Get in the skiff before I change my mind and start your R2I before Mr. Walter gets here."

R2I was short for Resistance to Interrogation—but implied the measures used to see that such resistance did not occur. Her legs began to wobble at the thought. Sleep deprivation, withholding food, constant light and noise, forced nudity, and all manner of debasing treatment—the list of what one human being could do to another was limited only by the imagination—and she was certain Agent Walter had a vivid one when it came to making people suffer.

Ronnie half stepped, half fell over the side of a metal skiff that crunched against the gravel a few feet off the bank. Once over the side, someone, likely Joey Benavides, kicked her hard in the tailbone, sending her crashing into the floor of the skiff.

"Take her out to the boat and put her in the cage until he gets here," Benavides said.

"You're not coming?" another man asked, sounding surprised but not upset. Ronnie could imagine that there were few people in the world who really wanted a creep like Joey B hanging around.

"Don't worry," Benavides said. "I'll be back before the boss gets here. I don't want to miss any of the fun, but I got a date with a little Italian dish."

"A date?" the other man scoffed.

"Yeah," Benavides's syrupy voice made Ronnie cringe. "Her husband's out of town. We got us a short window of opportunity to really get to, you know, spend some quality time together."

Chapter 26

Yaqub Feng sat in the rearmost seat of the window-less Chevrolet van at once terrified and thrilled by the proximity of the young woman crammed in beside him. Surely still in her teens, she wore a great deal of green eye makeup. She sucked on a mint that did little to hide the horrible breath that came with being dragged from her bed and put to work in the van. Forcing a pained smile, she shifted back and forth as if she had a stomachache.

A commercial flight from Kashgar to Dubrovnik took nearly twenty-four hours, but Jiàn Zǒu had used his connections to get them aboard a direct cargo flight taking just over seven hours. They'd arrived in the wee hours of the morning, likely about the time the girls had fallen asleep from their duties the night before.

Ehmet sat at the far end of the seat, talking on a mo-bile phone while he terrorized the girl who was crammed between him and Yaqub's redhead. He wore a hooked, claw-like blade fitted to a leather cuff that laced around his palm. Ehmet had a sense for all things deadly, and noticed it in the center console when they'd been picked up at the airport. He began to toy with it immediately, dropping veiled hints until Scuric, the Croatian driver, had gifted it to him. Called a *Srbosjek* or "Serb cutter," the hooked blade was designed to harvest wheat, but during World War II it had earned a reputation as a weapon for cutting thousands of Serbian throats.

The bony child next to Ehmet knew exactly what it was and shrank from the evil blade as if it was on fire. Ehmet moved his eyebrows up and down, mocking her fear as he drew the dull backside of the tip across the pale flesh of her trembling shoulder. The pitiful redhead next to Yaqub watched in a sort of blank stupor, as if she could not comprehend where exactly she was or why she was there. Jiàn Zǒu sat in the next seat forward, eyes watching the road. He'd declined the offer of a woman, earning him a string of derisive curses from Ehmet. Yaqub watched the sick thing rocking in pain beside him and wished he would have declined as well.

Anton Scuric, the Croat behind the wheel, glanced in the rearview mirror as he turned the van up a winding single-track into the scrubby limestone hills an hour northwest of Dubrovnik. A bald man with a crooked smile, he had a long and oddly misshapen skull—as if his head had been run sideways through the wringer on an old-time washing machine. A red-and-white checkerboard tattoo of the Croat flag covered the side of his neck, but he seemed far more gangster businessman than ardent nationalist. Scuric had made a small fortune during the Homeland War, smuggling the guns and drugs that were so plentiful when staples like food and heating fuel were in such short supply. He traded with fellow Croats, Serbians, and even Bosniak Muslims, but drew the line at working with Gypsies. Still, Jiàn Zǒu had thought it best to keep secret the fact that the Fengs were Muslim, just to be on the safe side.

According to the snakehead, Scuric was the best in the business when it came to fraudulent passports— equal parts scientist and artist. Apparently, the two men had a long history and Scuric was more than happy to work on credit providing them with passports made from stolen Hong Kong SAR blank documents—for double his usual fee. Apparently, the Croat had found it lucrative to use his established smuggling routes to traffic in humans as well as drugs. The Serbian girls he'd thrown in out of the goodness of his heart. Yaqub did not see much added value.

It had been over a year since Yaqub had been so near a woman. It was hot outside the swaying van and though the air-conditioning was blowing at full force, the young Uyghur felt himself sweating through his shirt. He wasn't sure if it was the cloud of dust that sifted up through the floor or the smell of cheap alcohol and per-fume drifting up from the child beside him, but if they had to travel much longer, he knew he would be sick.

He patted the trembling young woman on the thigh, below the hem of her tight shorts where it dug into her pale skin. He'd hoped that the touch might convey some sort of understanding between them, perhaps let her know that he was not an animal, that he did not intend to hurt her. Maybe she might even enjoy her time with him. She winced at his touch, but turned her head to look at him, as if she'd been warned to be cooperative. Her green eyes were wide, overflowing with tears and terror. Saliva dried at the pinched corners of her heav-ily rouged lips.

"Where are you from?" Yaqub asked in halting Eng-lish.

"Bosnia," she whispered. "I find work . . . Italia."

"Shut up, Amna," Scuric barked from the behind the wheel. "You have found work here." He launched into a stream of invective Yaqub did not understand. It did not matter. Her name alone put a pit in his stomach. Amna meant "safety" in Arabic. From Bosnia with an Arabic name, she was not Serbian after all but a Bosniak Muslim. Still, Yaqub thought, struggling for a way to console his nagging conscience, she must have done something very sinful to end up working as a prostitute in another country.

He closed his eyes so he didn't have to look at her, and focused on his brother's conversation.

". . . Is that so? . . . Well, someone will have to kill them then." Ehmet laughed maniacally as if he'd just made the world's funniest joke. "It may as well be us. I am telling you it would be good practice. . . . Of course, I understand." He handed the phone up to Jiàn Zǒu. "Here," Ehmet said. "He wants to discuss the details."

Ehmet pulled the girl closer and nibbled on her cheek, biting hard enough to make her yelp. He shoved her away, brandishing the Serb cutter before leaning over the seat to look out the windshield for a moment and then falling back into the seat. He let his head fall sideways to peer at Yaqub. It was Ehmet's way, always moving, unable to sit still for very long.

"Why so glum, my brother?" he said in English so the girls would be able to understand him. "We have our mission before us and a night with these acceptable if not overly beautiful whores." He elbowed his girl in the ribs. "You are much too skinny, but at least you have good teeth. Smile a little more and maybe I can forget the rest of you." He looked up at Yaqub. "Ranjhani tells me that a private aircraft filed a flight plan to

Dubrovnik a few hours after we left Kashgar. It seems that the people following us are a determined lot."

"Do we know who they are?" Yaqub said, wondering who could be after them so fast—surely not the Pakistanis.

"He gave me some name," Ehmet said, "but it meant nothing to me. I told him to let us kill them but he assured me that he will take care of it. Evidently, he has some Albanians who owe him a favor."

Ehmet turned to look directly at Yaqub, suddenly very serious. He switched to Chinese. "Why is your countenance so dark, my brother?"

Yaqub shot a glance at the quivering girl beside him. "You know that I am fully committed to our jihad. Our cause is just . . . but this . . . We are good Muslims. To lay with a woman when we would die as martyrs seems to me a grave sin."

Ehmet leaned forward, nodding toward Scuric, the Croatian driver. "Many here hate Islam," he said, still in Chinese. "Mohammed himself, peace be unto him, has said that it is better to play the sinner than to be discovered."

Yaqub nodded. *Taqiyya,* or lying to deceive a nonbeliever like Scuric, was not only acceptable but just and honorable as well.

"Besides," Ehmet said, as he pushed up his girl's short skirt and gave her thigh a pinch. "As far as lies go, this is most pleasant."

Jiàn Zǒu ended the call and turned to pass the phone back to Ehmet. He opened his mouth to speak, but turned back around without a word.

"Go ahead and act like our eunuch friend if you want, brother." Ehmet laughed, smiling at both girls. "But these whores have chosen their sinful lives. Allah will certainly punish them, so why not be the instrument of that punishment?"

Amna, surely feeling the intent if not the actual meaning of Ehmet's words, scooted closer to Yaqub so her red hair trailed along his shoulder. She looked up at him and batted gaudy lashes. "You seem kind," she whispered in halting English.

I am kind, Yaqub thought, but that did not matter The girls had already heard too much—and even if they hadn't, he'd known the girls were as good as dead the moment his brother had first picked up the Serb cutter.

Chapter 27

Croatia, 10:05 AM

Quinn shifted in the deep leather seat and opened his eyes. He'd learned from commercial fishing with his father in Alaska, and then later at the United States Air Force Academy, that sleep was a fleeting commodity. It was imperative to grab whatever snippets came his way, even if it meant closing his eyes around a Chinese spy. He still did not trust Song, if that was even her real name, but if she wanted him dead, she'd already had ample opportunity to make that happen.

She'd made a point to remind him that much of the People's Liberation Army would be hot on their trail now that they were working together, but she apparently still had enough connections to score them a ride to Dubrovnik on a Citation X. The smell of rich leather and new carpet made Quinn think the sleek business jet had just rolled off the assembly line. Song assured him it was privately owned, but the airplane smelled too much like government. It would be a rare private citizen who would loan their twenty-million-dollar aircraft to fugitive spies. More likely the Citation X was an MSS plane, registered to some dummy corporation or innocuous agency, like Winfield Palmer flagged the Challenger he used as an OGA for his OGAs—Other Governmental Aircraft for Other Governmental Agents. The Bombardier Challenger was a fine aircraft, but Quinn was certain Palmer would bristle when he found out the Chinese were jetting around near Mach speeds in the comfort of the world's fastest business jet.

"You are awake," Song said, looking over a folded map of the Balkans. "Good. We are almost there." She wore the thick black glasses again and a pair of white earbuds that led to her phone.

Quinn stretched, arms above his head, feeling the familiar tightness in the scars across his ribs, and the nagging pain from the recent injury to his shoulder. He wondered, as he often did lately when he moved, how long it would be before the broken parts just stayed broken. He'd already noticed a certain lag in healing that hadn't been there when he was younger and racing motorcycles with his brother.

He covered a yawn, rubbing his eyes at the blinding light that streamed into the cabin. "That was quick," he said, glancing out the Citation's round window at the blue-green waters of the Adriatic below.

"The Citation X is fast," she said, glancing down at her map again. "But I told the pilot to put the spurs to her."

Quinn stifled a chuckle at the idiom.

"What is it?" Song said, cocking her head. "Did I say something wrong?" She pulled one of the buds from her ear and something that sounded suspiciously like the Zac Brown Band spilled out. A Chinese spy who listened to country music—that explained a lot and raised an entirely new set of questions.

"Not at all," he said. "Not at all."

She tapped the phone to pause her song and removed

the other earbud, wrapping up the cord and shoving phone and all in the pocket of her vest. "Your friend will pick us up at the airport?"

"That's the plan," Quinn said.

"You trust this man?"

"My brother does."

She took a deep breath, peering over her glasses. Quinn could imagine her scolding a small child about homework.

"And you trust your brother's taste in friends?" she said.

"I do." Quinn thought of the Denizens, Bo Quinn's motorcycle club that operated on the rough edges of legality. "Most of them anyway."

He'd met Mike "Buzz Saw" Bursaw many times, and though he knew little about the man's background, Quinn was certain he was completely devoted to Bo— and he could fight, which might come in handy on this go-around. Quinn's brother had actually introduced Bursaw to the Croatian woman who would later become his wife, when he'd hired her to waitress at the club's bar outside Dallas. Buzz Saw had traveled home with his new bride and ingratiated himself with his father-in-law enough that the old man had offered to set him up in business in order to keep his daughter and any grandchildren that might come along nearby. Bursaw knew Quinn was a government agent and that he frequently worked outside the lines. None of that seemed to bother him.

Quinn hadn't told him everything when he'd called that morning, just enough to let him know they were looking for a set of Chinese brothers who would arrive sometime before they did.

Song gazed out the window, obviously mulling this

all over. "I hope he is as trustworthy as you believe him to be."

"I trust him more than I trust the locals," Quinn said.

"You know what they say," Song said. "That where Italy is a state with a mafia, Croatia is a mafia with a state."

What do you expect from a country that invented the necktie? Quinn thought, though he kept it to himself.

Song stuffed the map in a small nylon messenger bag, rummaging around for a few seconds before pulling out Quinn's Riot, still in its Kydex sheath.

"Here," she said, sliding it across the oval teak table between them. "You seem to be more comfortable when you have a knife."

Quinn took the blocky little knife and clipped it to his belt on the left side between three and four o'clock, pulling the tail of the rugby shirt over the green G10 handle. He was pretty sure she gave it to him so it wouldn't be in her bag when they passed through customs and immigration. Quinn didn't really care as long as he had his knife back. A body pat down was less likely than a bag search, and if it came to that, a knife on his belt would be the least of his worries.

"I don't suppose you have an extra pistol in there, do you?" he asked, nodding at her open purse.

"I don't even have one for myself," Song said. "But, we are in the black market arms capital of Eastern Europe. I feel certain something will turn up."

The Citation X banked west on final approach to Čilipi Airport. Dubrovnik's dazzling umber rooftops came into view—the clay tiles new and bright since the Yugoslav bombardment of the recent war. Quinn looked out the window at the mazes and warrens of the old walled city and took a deep breath. Croatia was thriving, Dubrovnik was beautiful, the food was excellent, and the people were friendly. But Quinn had been to Croatia twice before—both times looking for war criminals, evil men, the thought of whom brought the same flood of adrenaline he felt prior to a fight. Song was right. Some kind of gun would turn up. He just hoped he was at the right end of it when it did.

Chapter 28

Quinn flashed a benign smile at the harried female officer behind the Croatian immigration desk. Thankfully, their arrival coincided with that of a packed Alitalia Airbus and United flight carrying a large television production crew, so he and Song were able to blend in with the crowd. Quinn had trimmed his dark beard back to stubble so he looked slightly different than the photo Song had taken of him in the hospital—not a bad deviation. Things that were too perfect and stories that were too pat were all the more likely to raise suspicion. The immigration officer glanced up at him, incredibly stone-faced for such a young woman who could not yet have been thirty. She perused him a moment, then studied the Australian passport that Song had provided.

"Business or pleasure, Mr. Martin?" she asked in accented English, raising the passport to compare the photograph with Quinn's face.

"Here on holiday," Quinn said, turning up the volume on the smile. Whether it was based on fact or not, the world expected Australians to be a hard-drinking and good-hearted lot. For whatever reason, people trusted someone with an accent from down under. Song had chosen Australian passports for two simple reasons— Australian citizens did not require entry visas in most countries around the world, and more important, they did not plan to visit Australia. A paramount rule— tradecraft 101 when traveling on fraudulent documents—was never to enter a country using that same country's papers. The look, feel, and security features were too well-known—and it was far more likely the home country would have a list of stolen passports in their database.

"Welcome to Croatia," the young woman said, sliding back his passport, then flipping her fingers toward the long queue. "Next!"

Quinn took a moment to worry about how effective the Chinese government was at manufacturing false passports—and wondered how many "Australians" were in the United States, preparing for coming war. He saw Kevin Bursaw standing outside customs and filed the problem away as something to mention to Palmer later— if he lived through the next few days.

"That's him," Quinn said as Song pulled her suitcase up to walk beside him and they approached a smiling man. "I told him you were my girlfriend, but he has an inkling of what I do, so expect a little bit of eyebrow raising."

"Of course," Song said. She looped her arm through Quinn's, naturally, as if she belonged there.

"Hey, buddy," Bursaw said, careful not to call Quinn by any name. He was a broad-shouldered man, well over six and half feet tall, with a brooding black goatee and a polished bald head. He smiled and enveloped Quinn in a back-slapping brotherhood handshake common to men who'd fought side by side. "Let me help you with your bags."

"I got mine." Quinn nodded at Song's roller bag. "And she's pretty particular about hers." In truth, Quinn's bag was stuffed with clothing Song had cobbled together at the last minute to alleviate suspicion at Croatian customs if they were searched. Normal people traveled with more than a knife.

"We're parked outside." Bursaw pointed with an open hand toward the far lot, out front and across from the taxi stands. He lumbered along, looking a little thicker around the middle than he'd been as an outlaw biker.

"Married life's been good to you," Quinn said, waiting until they reached the car to discuss anything important.

"It has indeed," Bursaw said, rubbing the belly beneath his T-shirt. "A beautiful wife who knows her way around the kitchen, two great kids, and a father-in-law who hasn't beaten me to death yet." He pressed a button on his key fob and the lights flashed on a dark blue Mercedes minivan. He lifted the rear hatch and tossed the suitcases in back. "Business is booming too. We got a big tour group staying with us right now so you're lucky we have a room for you. It's crowded but that's also a good thing because Petra always cooks up her famous *janjetina s ražnja* on the last night of any tour—which happens to be tonight." He kissed the tips of his fingers. "Petra makes the best lamb on a spit this side of . . . well, anyplace. You're welcome to join us. Couple of oddballs in the group, but by and large, just a bunch of folks who like to ride."

"That would be nice." Quinn opened the back door for Song, then took the front seat. "It all depends on how the day turns out. Did you happen to see the guys I talked to you about on the phone?"

"I did." Bursaw left airport parking to pull out onto

the narrow two-lane and head northwest toward Dubrovnik. Scrubby limestone hills rolled up above them
to their right. The Adriatic stretched out in a deep blue
blanket to the left. "They got here about two hours
ago."

Quinn felt the surge of adrenaline at being so close.
He shot a glance at Song. Her mouth was set in a flat
line.

"There was something though," Bursaw said. "Those
two Chinese guys you wanted me to watch turned out
to be three Chinese guys."

"Three?" Song said.

"Yep." Bursaw glanced over his left shoulder before
passing a Russian Lada that belched an endless cloud
of gray smoke. "A local guy named Anton Scuric picked
all three of them up and headed north. Scuric's bad
news. His grandfather was Ustashi during World War
II. He somehow escaped being hanged for war crimes
and was able to teach young Anton everything he
knew." He shot a glance at Quinn. "You know about the
Ustashi?"

Quinn nodded. "They out-Nazied a lot of Nazis
when it came to cruelty in the name of nationalism."

"The ISIS of their day," Bursaw said. "Killing people with hammers, sawing off heads—they were really
big on the whole beheading thing. The stories my
father-in-law tells me . . ." He gave a little shudder. "It
would curl my hair if I had any."

"So," Song said from the backseat, gazing out the
window in thought. "This man, Anton Scuric, he is
very much like his grandfather, the Ustashi?"

"In a lot of ways," Brusaw said. "I'm sure he's handy
with a hammer, but it's the smell of money that moves
him, not nationalism. The collapse of the Soviet Union
and the breakup of Yugoslavia opened up a lot of op-

portunity for people who had the right mix of savvy and meanness. I gotta tell you, there are people here in Eastern Europe who have elevated smuggling to a fine art—guns, drugs, girls, kids, cigarettes. . . . You name it and shitheads like Scuric can figure out a way to get it where it needs to go. And, they're not afraid to stomp anyone who gets in their way."

Song leaned forward now, over the seat between the two men. "Where does this man Scuric hang his hat?"

"That's the problem," Bursaw said. "He's a smuggler, so he's a slippery one. He's got safe houses and holding spots in the mountains from here all the way up the coast to Pula. He's successful enough so I'm sure he's got stash sites in Italy as well. Cops know all about him. You can check with them."

"We'd better handle this off the books," Quinn said. "Let's say this guy Scuric took someone you cared about. Where would you look for him first?"

Bursaw thought for a minute. "He's got a big boat he calls the *Perunika*. Keeps her anchored about twenty kilometers outside the city. I've seen him taking party girls back and forth in his little raft when I was going by on the bike. I'll draw you a map."

"How will I recognize him when I see him?" Quinn asked.

Bursaw laughed. "You couldn't miss him if you tried. Just find the ugliest dude in the room and that'll be him. Got a haircut like mine but his face is . . . I don't know, all crooked and shit, like somebody stomped on him as a kid."

The Bursaws' three-story inn of whitewashed stone sat in the lap of a small valley. Scrubby oaks dotted the limestone hills. Twin girls—four years old if Quinn did his math correctly—played in a tire swing under the canopy of a huge beech tree to the right of the inn. Beyond the tree, an older man with a snap-brim driving cap carried a set of tires over his shoulder into an open shed that served as a stable for several motorcycles. The entire scene was awash in dazzling sunlight. People, buildings, and hills glowed with the hazy aura of a colorized photograph.

The little girls' mother stepped out of the inn through an open side door the moment the van rumbled up on the cobblestone driveway. Flashing a toothy grin at Quinn, Petra Bursaw walked toward him shaking her head and drying her hands on an apron. She was tall, almost six feet, with auburn hair and eyes blue-green as if they'd been dipped straight from the Adriatic. As talented with a wrench as she was in the kitchen, she wore a loose mechanic's shirt and a pair of well-worn jeans under the apron.

Petra induced a flurry of giggles from the twins when she reached Quinn and crushed him in an all-enveloping hug. Grabbing him by both shoulders, she held him back at arm's length.

"Just making sure you are intact," she said, giving him a motherly once-over. A Baltic accent—that sounded somewhere between Italian and Russian—added spice to her flawless English. "The life you lead has a way of stealing bits and pieces."

"Of your soul," Kevin Bursaw said, like he knew more than he admitted.

Quinn chuckled but let the comments slide. There was no way to argue with them anyway. Instead, he introduced Song to Petra.

"She's pretty," Petra said, winking. "I like her."

Quinn looked at Song, who merely smiled and left any explanations to him.

It didn't matter. There was no time for lengthy explanations anyway. "Bo says you have the BMW rental concession here," he said to Bursaw. "You have an extra GS laying around?"

"Afraid not," Bursaw said. "They're all out with the paying customers at the moment." He flicked his hand toward the shed. "Follow me. I figured you'd want something comfortable anyway since you're riding two up. I took the liberty of having my father-in-law get the GTL ready for you."

Quinn looked at the monstrous ivory BMW touring bike parked on a center stand under the edge of the shed—all 800 pounds and 1600 ccs of her.

"That's not a motorcycle," Quinn said under his breath. "That's a space station." The bike was big, but it was flashy, liable to stand out more than Quinn wanted. Behind the monster was another, smaller bike covered with a soft cotton sheet. He could just make out the shining black front fender and the outline of a fat round headlight. "Is that what I think it is?"

Bursaw grinned like a proud father and gave Quinn a smiling nod as he pulled back the cotton cover. "A 1972 Toaster Tank."

Quinn ventured farther into the shed to get a better look at the shiny little bike. A BMW 75/5 sported a 750 cc engine and carried nearly five gallons of fuel in a tank that gave the bike its nickname because of a resemblance to the kitchen appliance. His voice grew quiet, almost reverent. "This one would fit the bill."

"No way." Bursaw shook his head. "Not the Slash-5. I just got her rebuilt."

"Kevin," Petra chided. "How often does Jericho come to visit? Let him take your precious bike. What's the worst that could happen?"

"Oh," Bursaw said, "that just shows how little you

know. He'll probably be trying to do a Steve McQueen over some barbed-wire fence by sundown."

Petra waved her husband away. She clucked at him in Croatian with the universal tone understood by husbands the world over. "My father will get you the key," she said to Quinn, before turning to Song. "I have helmet and a jacket that should fit you, my dear."

Chapter 29

The White House, 6:30 AM

Ran Kimura normally found herself calmed, emotionally blank after a bloody conflict. Before or after, she was not the type to wander without purpose. She either stood and waited patiently, or moved directly to her intended objective. That was before she had come face-to-face with her mother. Now she paced the length of the Oval Office, moving like the works of a precise clock in front of the fireplace, looking up only to stare holes in Drake and decide if whether or not she should cut his throat.

Of course, she'd known of Emiko Miyagi's existence. She had seen more than one photograph, but pictures were nothing like a face-to-face encounter.

Ran had almost dropped her dagger when she'd come out of the coffee shop in Gettysburg. The look in her mother's eyes hit her like a cold slap. Frozen and defenseless for far too long in her line of work, Ran realized the woman could have killed her had she been so inclined. She wondered though if her mother even realized it. It was terrifying, demoralizing—and Ran hated the woman for it.

Drake leaned back in the chair with his feet up on the Resolute Desk. He droned on and on about something but Ran chose to ignore him, knowing that if she focused on even a word he said, it would send her into a rage. McKeon must have sensed this and glanced up from the couch to put a hand over his phone to shush the President. He gave Ran a look as well, but she waved him off and kept walking. He might as well waste his attention on training an angry cobra. When she decided she'd had enough, Drake would be dead before anyone else in the room could blink. There was something about him, a palpable smell that made Ran's blood boil with rage. She hated the way he used his position to prey on young women, she loathed him for his ignorance . . . and she absolutely despised his stupid bow tie. It was early, so Drake was still in his gym clothes. Had he been wearing one of his signature ties, she might not have been able to stop herself. McKeon needed the idiot in place at least for another day—and that was the only reason Ran left him alive.

McKeon turned back to the phone conversation, springing up from the sofa as he spoke to pace on the opposite side of the room from Ran. He'd barely been able to contain his giddiness since the arrest. It had imbued him with an energy that made the muscles in his angular face appear to twitch with anticipation, his words breathless and rushed. Veronica Garcia was in custody. It was only a matter of time before Palmer, Virginia Ross, and all the other conspirators were brought in as well. The death of Mike Dillman would serve notice to others in Congress about the danger of crossing the administration. The IDTF would sweat Senator Gorski to see what she knew before making her disappear on a more permanent basis. He hadn't said as much, but Ran knew the way he worked.

"Whatever you have to do," McKeon said. "I don't have to remind you how important this is." He'd already given Glen Walter carte blanche in his treatment of the prisoners but wanted to make it perfectly clear. As long as one arrest kept leading to another, all the gloves should come off during interrogations. The arrests not only yielded valuable intelligence, but had the added effect of destabilizing alliances and derailing any attempted putsch.

"Call me when she gives you something," McKeon said, nodding his head like a child about to open a present. "No, I don't care about the hour." He ended the call. "This is outstanding. Walter will be there this evening."

"Holy hell, Lee," Drake scoffed. "Do you realize you are actually rubbing your hands together like some kind of fiendish villain? You might give some thought to the whole vice-presidential bearing thing."

Ran spun in her tracks, her chest heaving.

McKeon stepped in between her and the President's desk, resting a hand on her shoulder. "I know," he whispered. "Forget about—"

She cut him off with a voice as sharp as her dagger. "I must do something to settle my mind, something productive."

Drake chuckled. "I could probably find you a sack of kittens to kill. Shit like that seems to calm you down."

McKeon's hand tightened on her shoulder. She let him keep it there and shut her eyes, working to control her breathing. She was a professional, dispassionate, and would not let her anger at this fool prove otherwise.

"I think I will go to Oregon," she said, opening her eyes to gauge McKeon's reaction. "Everything is happening quickly. It's time for me to sort out your wife."

McKeon let his hand fall away. "I need you with me," he said, a little too quickly. A flash of something

Ran hadn't noticed before crossed his face. The familiar beguiling look returned to his eyes. He spoke so both she and Drake could hear. "Things *are* happening fast, but they are happening just as we have hoped they would. In two days' time, the President of the United States will stand with the newly elected Prime Minister of Japan and reassert our support for Japan's claim to the Senkaku Islands—and publicly condemn China's blatant aggression towards her weaker neighbors, who happen to be our allies. China will see it for what it is—a declaration of war without the actual words. The Fifth Fleet will be out of the Arabian Sea by that time, on its way to the Pacific. I do not know if the United States is strong enough to win a war against China, but I am certain she cannot do it while leaving assets in the Middle East."

"The venue is a concern," Drake said, suddenly serious. "That Kobe bell is too out in the open. I'd prefer we moved it to a more secure location like the Japan Cultural Center. At least it's got walls. In case you haven't noticed, our actions have garnered me an enemy or two."

And I should be at the top of that list, Ran thought but kept it to herself.

"That is fine," McKeon said. "The location is of no consequence. The message is the important thing. I'll have David inform the Secret Service."

"After the speech then," Ran said, still watching McKeon's eyes.

"What?

Ran glared at him. "After the speech, I will sort out your wife. Having her in the picture exhausts me."

McKeon pulled away, laughing, avoiding her eyes. He did many things, but he never avoided her eyes. "Oh, dear Ran," he said. "I have the situation with my wife under control. Trust me. Everything will work out as it must."

Chapter 30

Croatia

A half hour after they'd arrived at the Bursaws' inn, Quinn straddled the little BMW 75/5 under the shade of the beech tree and planted his feet for Song to climb on behind him. She assured him she'd ridden before, but the tentative look in her eye said her experience had likely been on little more than a scooter. Kevin and Petra Bursaw had outfitted them with riding jackets, helmets, and leather gloves from the extras they had accumulated over the years of running a motorcycle touring company.

Quinn, who had crashed more bikes than many people have ridden, opted for a black full-face helmet and an armored mesh jacket—following his father's advice to plan for the wreck instead of the ride. The jacket had started life as khaki in color but hours under the sun had combined with road grime and bug guts to give the material a natural camouflage that blended with the scrub and limestone of the surrounding hills. Song wore a more stylish half helmet, yellow to match the bike's bumblebee paint job. Petra loaned her a pair of goggles since the shorty helmet didn't have a face shield. The breezes rolling in off the sea would be just cool enough to make her kidskin jacket comfortable once they were riding. The lightweight leather was stylish, but was also discreetly armored at the elbows and spine, giving her some protection in the event they suffered an involuntary get-off.

Quinn thought about asking Kevin Bursaw if he had a pistol but decided against it since he was already apparently taking the man's favorite bike. Petra stuffed a couple of sandwiches and a pair of binoculars in a small knapsack and gave it to Song.

"I am not sure what you're doing," Petra said. "And to be completely honest, it is probably better that way. But the sandwiches will help you blend in while you are doing it."

Quinn put a hand to his helmet in a sloppy salute and then eased out on the clutch, rattling down the cobblestone toward the *Državna Cesta* D8, a narrow ribbon of highway that ran along the coast of Adriatic Sea. Song scooted up close, squeezing with her long thighs and clenching her fists around his gut as if she was trying to save him from choking. She proved to be a quick learner and relaxed by degrees with each passing mile once they hit the highway.

Traffic was light and other motorcycles made up a good deal of what little there was.

It had been so long since Quinn had been on the back of a bike that he was almost sorry when he came out of a lean on a sweeping corner and saw Anton Scuric's boat come into view. Song tensed behind him, seeing the boat as well, at anchor a quarter mile out in the aquamarine water, right where Kevin Bursaw said it would be.

Quinn downshifted and turned the bike onto a small

gravel turnout on a wooded hill that overlooked the
ocean some hundred meters below. They'd passed a
small dirt lane not quite a mile back and Quinn assumed
it was the service road for anyone going to or from the
vessel.

Song slid off the bike immediately, using the binoculars to scan the ocean like a tourist, but not paying an
inordinate amount of attention to the boat. Three other
bikes—big American Harleys that stood out from the
quieter European stuff—chuffed past on the highway behind them. Quinn straddled the bike, happy the Harleys
moved on down the road. He slouched on the handlebars
with the side stand down, waiting for his turn with the
binoculars.

"I see no one onboard," Song said before handing
them to Quinn.

Quinn used the binoculars with one hand, shielding
them against a low western sun with the other. Song
was right. There might be people on the boat, but there
was no one on deck.

The *Perunika* was a "gullet." Originally Turkish
trading vessels, the sleek wooden schooners were often
used on the Adriatic as charter operations—or for
smuggling. This one was on the large end of the scale.
Judging from the size of the wheelhouse, Quinn estimated it at around ninety feet in length. *Perunika* had
started life as a sailing vessel but the masts and all the
associated lines and stays had been removed to make
for a cleaner deck. The oak planks were varnished and
she looked to be in decent shape with accents and trim
painted bright white and deep blue.

"Some kind of pier down along the rocks," Quinn
said, scanning. "Looks like he's got a small inflatable
tied up there. Nice engine . . . looks fairly new." He

lowered the binoculars and passed back them to Song.
"Awfully tempting for a thief. Odd that Scuric would
leave it tied up and unattended for very long."

"Unless everyone is so frightened they leave his
things alone." Song took a look through the glasses as
she spoke. "You think the Fengs are on this boat?"

"I don't know," Quinn said. "But I'm betting whoever
left that dinghy there won't be gone long. Let's stash the
bike and go down for a closer look."

Quinn pushed the Beemer over the gravel lip, using
the brake and clutch to move downhill in a controlled
roll toward a stand of fragrant cedars. He skirted large
stones and piles of toilet paper that lay like landmines
in the tufted grass, left over from roadside toilet
emergencies. Song followed along behind him with
the pack.

Braking when he reached the trees, Quinn eased the
bike through the dense underbrush and leaned it against a
gnarled cedar trunk, making certain the front tire was
pointing uphill so he wouldn't have to do a lot of jockey-
ing if he had to climb up and get back onto the road in
a hurry. It was not difficult work, but Quinn found he
was sweating by the time he was finished and chalked
it up to the aftereffects of the surgery in China. Song
noticed and looped the binoculars around her neck,
helping him pile brush over the bike.

The cedar grove covered most of the hillside, giving
them adequate concealment as they made their way to
the shoreline. There was no trail, but the brush and rocks
gave them passable footing even as it grew steeper
above the beach. Quinn slid to a stop just inside the tree
line. Crouching in the mottled shadows beside Song, he
studied the *Perunika* where she bobbed at anchor. He
thought he caught the sight of movement through the

curtains in the raised salon, but the deck remained empty and quiet.

Song sat beside him, making a note in a small notebook. He couldn't help but wonder if it was some observation about him she planned to send back to her bosses. He certainly had some observations of his own.

"I'm guessing most of my background is attached to the Interpol Red Notice," he said, his words buzzing against his hands as they held the binoculars.

"Quite a lot of it." Song put the notebook in her lap and toyed at the peeling bark of a nearby cedar tree. "Air Force Combat Rescue Officer, OSI agent, multilingual, accomplished in hand-to-hand fighting, that sort of thing. But the report does tend to highlight the fact that you are a rogue killer."

"I'd argue the rogue part," Quinn said. He played the binoculars back down to the inflatable as he formulated a plan. Song was hard to get a handle on, but she seemed smart enough to judge him on his actions, not something she read in some intelligence file.

The gray dinghy bobbed in the blue-green water alongside a weathered wooden plank. This Spartan boarding ramp was affixed to a rusted set of metal arms that had been driven into a concrete jetty ages before. A riprap breakwater ran from the shoreline in a stunted J, wrapping around the dinghy and decaying concrete dock to form a protective nest from direct waves. The dinghy itself looked to be around twelve feet, made of tough Hypalon with a single board seat fixed amidships across the pontoons. What looked like an ice chest was just forward of a small outboard motor where the driver would sit while steering with the tiller. A red plastic fuel tank, faded and much older than the boat, sat beside the ice chest on an inflatable rubber floor. Quinn had ridden in identical little boats hundreds of times in Alaska.

"So, you know about me." He lowered the binoculars and turned to face Song. "Tell me a little about yourself."

Song peeled away more bark from the cedar tree. "There is no need—"

"Not so," Quinn interrupted her. "You're an operative from a country that has significant issues with US policy—I get that. But at this very moment, politics are a long way down my list of things to worry over. What I need to know is if I can depend on you in a fight. Tell me about your training, where you came from."

Song studied him, breathing deeply, but saying nothing. She had the amazing ability to look him in the eye as if she were listening and then go on like she'd not heard a single word.

"We should take turns keeping watch," she said at length. "It may be some time before this Scuric shows up."

As a rule, Quinn found silence profoundly more enjoyable than chatter, but six hours of sweating shoulder to shoulder in the rocks and trees with a silent woman he did not know began to wear on him. Several times, she began to hum some song he didn't recognize, but always caught herself, clenching her teeth as if she had almost given up a state secret. When she did speak, it was only to tell him she was going deeper into the trees for a bathroom break.

He breathed a sigh of relief when the welcome sound of a vehicle filtered through the trees. Action trumped silence every time. Tires crunched on the gravel as the vehicle turned off the D8 Highway above and began to wind its way down the service road toward the dinghy.

Quinn folded the motorcycle jacket he'd been using to pad the rocky ground and stuffed it behind a tree. Crouching so he would remain hidden but able to move quickly, he decided to give it one more try with Song as Scuric drew closer. "Seriously," he said. "They give MSS agents some tactical training, right? Just make something up. It'll make me feel better."

"Of course, we are trained," Song said. "But mostly in computers and the writing of reports."

Quinn's mouth fell open.

"I joke," Song said. "Don't worry so much."

Suspension springs squeaked and groaned as the vehicle drew closer. A large panel van creaked to a stop along the edge of the gravel single track twenty meters above the dinghy. The driver stayed behind the wheel while the passenger in the front seat got out and came around to slide open the side door, revealing two red-headed women, both bound with duct tape at the wrists and ankles. Gaunt and cowering, neither looked to be even twenty years old. The man, obviously Scuric from Bursaw's description of his misshapen head, leaned in and cut the two women free with some kind of hook attached to his hand. Scuric motioned them out and pointed toward the dinghy. One of the women tried to run as soon as her feet hit the ground. The driver, a younger man wearing a backward cap and a cigarette hanging out of a pouty mouth, stayed slumped behind the wheel and shook his head in disgust. Scuric caught the fleeing prisoner easily and cuffed her in the back of the head, sending her flying face-first into the gravel.

Quinn felt a pang of pity for the girl, but her actions gave him just the break he needed to move.

"Okay," he said, peeling the rugby shirt over his head. "Scuric's taking them out to the boat. The dinghy motor is going to die shortly after he gets it going. When it does, I need you to be ready to take care of the driver. Make some noise and get Scuric's attention focused on you."

Song stared through the trees at the van, frozen in thought.

"Got it?" Quinn asked.

"Yes. Got it." Song blinked, and then turned suddenly toward him. "What are you going to do?"

"What somebody should have done to this guy a long time ago."

Staying low as he moved through the trees toward the far side of the jetty, away from the dinghy, Quinn hit the beach at a run. He pushed away any thought of Song's capability. If she couldn't do her job, it was only a matter of time before they were both dead anyway.

He dove noiselessly into the water, sliding through the blue-green sea with hardly even a splash. It was cool compared to the evening air and gave his body the shock he needed to cover the thirty feet to the end of the rocks in a matter of seconds.

Thankfully, the two women were not the kind to go peacefully and Scuric had to pester and prod them along the road, cursing to keep them in line at the same time Quinn swam around the end of the jetty and kicked his way to the stern of the inflatable. Even from nearly fifty meters away, Quinn could see the print of a pistol under the Croatian's shirt.

A stiff ocean breeze added a light chop to the surface of the water and with the sun to the west, Quinn felt certain Scuric wouldn't be able to see him. The bottom dropped away fast off, which made it easier to get around than floundering in shallow water. Using the skeg of the outboard motor as a step, Quinn waited with his nose just above the surface at the pointed back corner of the pontoon until Scuric turned his head to chide one of the balking girls. While the Croatian was looking back, Quinn reached over and popped loose the rubber line between the motor and the plastic fuel tank. He left it slightly attached.

Quinn considered just reaching across the pontoon and dragging Scuric overboard when he arrived, but the water was deep, giving him no leverage but for the weight of his body. His hands would be wet, so there was too big a chance that the Croatian would just shrug him off. The sidearm combined with the crystal-clear water made things too iffy for a direct assault.

Quinn drew the Riot from the scabbard on his belt and let himself sink back to nose-level in the cool water, bobbing out of sight at the rear of the inflatable. Anton Scuric cursed and shoved, threatening the two young women as he forced them toward the little boat. When they made it to the concrete jetty, Quinn ducked silently beneath the surface and slipped under the pontoon.

The plan was simple—but he had only one chance to make it work.

Chapter 31

The chain-link cage made it impossible for Ronnie Garcia to straighten her legs. Thin orange scrubs did nothing to protect her from the rough galvanized wire.

Her captors had taken her clothing as soon as she'd gotten on the boat, before they'd even taken off the hood. At once dazed and terrified, she'd balked at the instructions to disrobe. She'd always planned to fight under such circumstances—she was full of all sorts of worthless plans. In reality, there were just too many hands, pushing and shoving and ripping away her clothing to get it around the handcuffs. Naked with knees drawn up to her chest and her hands behind her back on the cold metal plate of the floor, Garcia had screamed threats and Cuban curses until her throat was raw. She braced herself for the worst, but they'd just stopped, snickering like cruel schoolboys at her predicament. Someone punched her hard in the kidney before removing the handcuffs.

"Get dressed," a bored voice said.

She'd ripped away the hood to find herself alone in the room with a pudgy middle-aged man. He had a bulbous red nose and sagging eyelids as if he'd been up on an all-night bender. Blinded by the glaring artificial light of a bare bulb, she couldn't tell if the man was scared she might try something or if he just wanted to take the opportunity to punch a girl. When he'd given her a stiff kick in the hip as he shoved her into the metal dog crate, she decided it was a little bit of both. He'd tossed the orange scrubs in before locking the gate and then disappeared through an oval metal hatch without another word. The door gave an eerie squeak as he dogged it shut from the outside.

That had been hours ago.

Ronnie arched her back, first tensing and then relaxing each muscle group in turn, starting with her feet and working upward until she reached her shoulders—a sort of static yoga that kept her from losing her mind— for the moment at least. The prison crate would have been fine for a large dog, but was intended to make human confinement as uncomfortable as possible without causing immediate physical injury. They called it "stress positioning"—and it was aptly named. Ronnie knew there would come a time when she'd welcome a beating if it meant she got to stretch her legs.

She estimated her cage to be no more than three and a half feet across, which made it little more than five feet from corner to corner, forcing Ronnie to keep her knees bent when on her back or on her side. She could sit up so long as she hunched her shoulders and dipped her head like a pouting child, but the rough link floor dug into her buttocks, bringing tears to her eyes in a matter of minutes. She found that lying on her back and planting her knees and shoulders against the floor helped spread out the pressure points and alleviate the pain for a time, but it wouldn't be long before her muscles fell victim to the confinement, cramping into painful spasms.

The fact that they'd given her something to wear was a relief. It gave her captors something to take away—but she shoved that thought from her mind. There were too many things they could, and likely would, do for her to dwell on it in too much detail. Instead, she'd occupied her mind by planning her escape—no matter how remote the possibility.

Jericho had been a stickler for EDC or "everyday carry" from the moment she'd met him—so much so that he'd remind her that if she caught him without a firearm, a knife, a light source, and something to make fire, he would owe her a steak dinner. In addition to his EDC, he customarily had a second blade and a variety of shims, picks, and keys secreted away in his clothing. Garcia had been following his example when she'd been taken, carrying her customary Kahr PM9 pistol inside the waistband of her jeans and a Bond Arms derringer called a Snake Slayer in a Flashbang holster suspended beneath her bra. Though it offered her only two extra shots, she'd fitted the little Snake Slayer with three-inch barrels chambered for .410 shotgun shells. Loaded with buckshot, it made for a perfect get-off-me gun. In addition to the pistols, Ronnie carried a wicked little curved blade Quinn's knife-maker friends in Alaska called The Scorn, a metal handcuff shim, and a plastic cuff key laced into her shoes.

Now, she was left with nothing but her wits and a set of orange hospital scrubs that made her feel like the victim in an ISIS beheading video.

She knew she was on some kind of boat, a big one judging from the number of stairs she'd been forced to climb when they shoved her out of the skiff. Still hooded, she'd been led along some kind of deck, through a hatch with a lip tall enough to trip over, then down another set of clanging metal stairs to the bowels of the boat. She could feel the periodic swaying and hear the clanking chain of a vessel at anchor.

The walls of the brightly lit room, maybe twenty feet across at their widest point, sloped rapidly inward, leading Ronnie to believe her dog crate prison was located near the bow. The steady knock of an auxiliary engine thrummed behind the bulkhead nearest the same hatch where the fat bully had disappeared. Tall shelves stacked with engine parts, oil, and hydraulic fluid ran along both of the sloping exterior walls. A metal ventilation grate on the bulkhead above her had been sealed over with canned foam, leaving the air dank and cloyingly still. The overpowering smells of diesel fuel and the dirty bilge coming up through the floor grate filled the humid enclosure and made Ronnie feel as if she was being poached.

Lost in thought, she nearly jumped out of her skin when she heard the hatch squeak open. Two men stooped to enter one at a time. First in was the same doughy bully who'd punched her in the back. Next came a younger man she'd not seen before. He had bright red hair and a disarming smile that reminded Ronnie of a *GQ* model. She might have said he looked kind had he not been a willing party to keeping her in a cage. The redheaded pretty boy carried a bottle of water and an energy bar. He squatted down next to the crate and waved the water back and forth, taunting her.

"So this is the sweet thing they're all talking about," he said. This one must have held some sway in terms of leadership on the boat because he carried her Scorn on his belt. He took the Snake Slayer out of his front pocket and twirled it around his finger by the trigger guard like a kid pretending to be an Old West gunfighter. "A girl could hide a little pistol like this in all sorts of places," he said, leering through the chain link.

"Maybe I should give you a little more thorough search. . . ."

Garcia let her eyes play up and down the young man, imagining the joy she'd feel when she planted her fist in his throat. She said nothing. It would do no good to antagonize her captors, but she didn't intend to cooperate with them either. She knew the drill. He wasn't likely to give her the food or water, no matter what she did.

GQ stared at her for a long moment, his leering grin growing more sickening the longer she looked at it. Ronnie fought the urge to cower when he stuffed away the derringer and took a key from his pocket. He unlocked the two padlocks that secured the front of the cage that acted as a door and threw the water bottle and protein bar inside. Once he'd locked it again, he pulled out the Scorn and began to run the curved blade along the outside of the cage, clicking against the wire while he hovered over her.

"Evidently, you're some kind of badass high-value target who should scare the shit out of me," *GQ* said, reaching in to tickle her shoulder through the chain link with his left hand. She flinched and he jerked away, grinning at the game. "If it was up to me you'd be wearing nothing but French maid panties and chained to the galley makin' us sammiches."

"You're a sick little man, *postalita*," Ronnie blurted out, resolving to bite his fingers off if he was ever stupid enough to stick them through the wire again.

"Whatever." *GQ* looked over his shoulder at his partner. He stuck the Scorn back in its sheath and rubbed his hands together as if he was eager to start some new game. "You bring 'em?"

For the first time since they'd come through the hatch,

Ronnie realized the fat one had kept his hands behind his back, out of her sight.

"You mean these?" The other man grinned. He was fat enough that he couldn't manage a smile without squinting his eyes. He produced two cattle prods, each comprised of a battery box and a set of metal forks at the end of a two-foot fiberglass rod. He held up both devices and nodded at GQ. "Choose your weapon."

Ronnie felt as if she might vomit. Months of training, hours of lectures, nothing prepared a person for this. She pressed herself against the cage, drawing her arms and legs inward, as far away from the two men as she could get.

"We have a job to do," GQ said, taking one of the cattle prods and whooshing it back and forth through the air like a sword. He looked at Garcia and shrugged. "Just following orders."

"Orders?" Ronnie heard herself whispering.

"Yep," GQ said. He moved to the other side of the cage, opposite the end where the pudgy agent had taken up a position with his prod. "Our orders are to . . . soften you up before Mr. Walter gets here. So, we're gonna play us a little game of bitch hockey, and you get to be the puck."

Garcia wanted to scream, to cry out for her father, for Jericho. She'd read the manuals. She'd watched the videos. There would be a time when her mind would come unwound, when she'd be able to do little but whimper, but that time was not yet. So, she clenched her teeth and waited for them to begin.

Chapter 32

Croatia

Anton Scuric gave the shorter of the two Bosnian har-lots a healthy smack to the back of her skinny neck to keep her in line. He never should have cut the stupid women loose, but he couldn't afford for merchandise to drown if they fell out of the boat. And his reward for being nice was that one of the bitches kept trying to run away—that after he'd bought their passage from their pitiful peasant lives in Bosnia and Herzegovina. On top of that, he'd spent the money to feed and house them while they were on their way to new jobs with nice men in Rome. *No good deed goes unpunished*, he thought to himself as he shoved the boohooing girls down the wooden planking and into the bobbing inflatable. They cursed and cried as if he'd thrown them off a cliff—which is what he felt like doing. Neither could likely swim, so they cowered in the bow of the dinghy instead of trying to escape. It would be easy from here.

Still standing on the weathered dock, Scuric lit a cigarette with shaking fingers. He was used to the thrill of a good operation—smuggling was his life and the excitement of it was a draw equal to the money. But his recent business with the Chinese had set him on edge. Watching them go, he couldn't help but feel as if he'd been exposed to some deadly plague. He didn't mind that they'd killed their girls. He'd been well paid, more than he'd have gotten for the little whores anyway—but the smaller man, the one called Ehmet, had looked at Scuric as if he would have been happy to kill him as well, just for the fun of it.

Shuddering, the Croatian stepped into the boat and cursed at the girls, ordering them to cast off the bow line. The tall one just glared at him. He threatened to cut their heads off and the little one yanked the rope free, nearly falling out of the boat in the process. Both women began to sob, clutching each other and glancing up at Scuric as if he might actually follow through on his threat. He was beginning to wish he'd let the Chinese monsters have these girls as well. It would have been a monetary loss, but at least he could be home having a beer and watching soccer instead of taking another trip up the coast to Sibenik to drop off the goods.

Scuric did his best to ignore the wailing women, turning on his seat to give the motor a yank. It roared to life on the second pull. He settled back on the ice chest and gave the throttle a little twist to nose the boat out toward his gullet. Maybe he'd even treat himself to a round or two with the merchandise to calm his nerves. The tall one had a face like a squirrel, but the little one had potential.

A moment later, the motor coughed, then went silent, leaving the dinghy bobbing in the water just feet from the dock.

Cursing to himself, Scuric turned to give the motor another pull. Nothing. He checked the choke lever, then glanced at the fuel line. It looked okay, but he tugged anyway and was relieved to see the connector had slipped loose. An easy fix—

A frantic yell from the shore jerked his attention back toward the van. A woman with dark hair stood beside the driver's door, waving her arms. Pavol was nowhere to be seen. A chill ran up his spine when he saw that she looked Asian, bringing back the horrible recollection of the Chinese monsters.

A burble in the water, like a fish feeding off the surface, drew his attention back to the boat. The inflatable gave a little rock, as if it had been hit by the wake of a passing ship. Scuric grabbed the running line along the pontoon to steady himself. A fleeting notion that something wasn't right hit him at the same moment something pierced the rubber floor at his feet. There was a loud zipping sound as the floor yawned open like a gaping black mouth. He saw only a shadow in the water, then a hand shot up from the depths followed by the cruelest face Scuric had ever seen.

Screaming in abject terror, the Croatian pedaled backwards, hands flung forward to fend off this smiling demon from the deep. The wet hand snatched him by the ankle and yanked him downward, pulling him beneath the surface in mid scream.

Above, two terrified women huddled at the bow of the boat, staring into the black water where the floor used to be. Absent Scuric's cursing, there was no sound but the wind and lapping waves.

Quinn had come up for air alongside the dinghy as soon as he felt Scuric take his seat on the ice chest. When the Croatian put the boat in gear and headed away from the dock, Quinn had simply let his body trail, hanging on for the short ride with little more than his nose above water. Turning away from the dock, the extra drag was hardly noticeable in a small inflatable loaded down with three people. Quinn had ducked under the surface the moment the engine died and hovered under the rear of the little boat, just forward of the transom, giving Song time to do her job.

There was plenty of light in the clear water and Quinn could easily make out the indentations of Scuric's feet on the inflatable floor when he braced himself to give the motor another pull. Quinn counted to five before driving the Riot's thick tonto blade up through the rubber floor and drawing it around in a quick, sweeping arc just forward of where Scuric sat. The Croatian's weight did most of the work opening up the hole as Quinn swam up and grabbed him around both ankles. Filling his lungs with air while Scuric shrieked out his last bit of oxygen, Quinn dragged the surprised smuggler beneath the surface, trapping the man's arms against his sides as he swam toward the sandy ocean floor, ten feet below.

Scuric's scream trailed upward in a silver cloud of bubbles with the last of his breath. Quinn couldn't help but smile to himself. The idiot probably still hadn't realized that it was a human being that had him and not some mermaid seeking revenge for all the women he'd sold into slavery.

Driving downward with slow, steady kicks, Quinn held Scuric's face against the rocky bottom until he ceased to struggle, then another half minute for good measure. When he felt sure the Croatian was still revivable but beyond fighting, Quinn swam behind him and grabbed him around the neck in a less friendly version of a rescue tow. Snatching the pistol from Scuric's belt, he kicked his way upward.

He could hear the girls screaming before he even reached the surface. Still cowering in the front of the gutted dinghy, they calmed immediately when they saw their tormentor in a headlock. Any enemy of Scuric's was likely an ally. Quinn dragged the sputtering Croatian onto the rocks and turned him on his side so he could vomit out the seawater he'd gulped in his panic. Quinn wiped the water off his face and motioned the girls to come out of the boat with a nod of his head.

"You speak English?" he asked.

The shorter of the two gave him a hesitating nod. "Some little." She looked at the pistol but her eyes played along the myriad of bullet and blade scars that covered his torso, sizing him up.

"What's your name?" Quinn said, stuffing the gun in his waistband to get it out of sight and free up his hands to deal with Scuric. Water streamed from his jeans, making a pool on the white rocks at his feet.

"Belma," the girl said.

"Okay, Belma," Quinn said, stooping to take a look at Scuric's wallet. A quick count showed it fat with a few waterlogged Croatian kuna and nearly 5,000 euros in large bills. "Can you find your way back home?"

She nodded at Scuric. "He take . . . passport."

Of course, Quinn thought. It was a common practice for human traffickers and pimps to hold a woman's passport to keep her in check. A quick search of Scuric's front pocket found the documents safe in a plastic bag. As Quinn suspected, the girls were from Bosnia, caught up in a prostitution scheme when they'd been promised jobs as nannies or housekeepers.

Song jogged down the concrete dock as Quinn handed the passports back to the girls, along with the wad of wet money from Scuric's wallet.

"Don't trust men like this anymore," he said. "Now take this and go."

Belma's deep green eyes flew wide when she saw the bills. "Home?" she stammered, unsure of what he meant. "Yes? I go home?"

"Yes, you can go home," Quinn said. He looked up at Song. "The driver?"

She nodded, leaving the man's fate to Quinn's imagination. "They may take the van. The keys are in the ignition."

Quinn instructed the girls to drive only to the nearest bus station where they should ditch the van and take a bus back into Bosnia. Still stunned from their brush with the cruelest of futures, they shuffled away quickly, jumping into the van and spraying gravel as they sought to put the whole episode behind them.

Quinn dragged Scuric into the thick foliage just up from the jetty and out of sight from anyone on the anchored *Perunika*. He press-checked the chamber of the pistol and released the magazine to make certain that it was full. The Hrvatski Samorkres HS2000 handgun was sold under license to Springfield Armory in the United States as an XD or X-treme Duty Pistol. Scuric's gun was an XDS, meant for concealment rather than as a primary battle weapon. The subcompact single-stack carried only six rounds of .45 ACP ammunition, including the one in the chamber. Quinn found a second magazine in the same pocket where Scuric had kept the girls' passports. Song had taken an identical pistol from the van driver and now pointed it at Scuric as she squatted beside his shoulder opposite Quinn.

"The Fengs," Song hissed. "Where are they?"

"Why?" Scuric wagged his head, gaining some of his swagger back after the underwater ordeal. "Did one of them run off and leave you at the altar?"

Quinn planted his palm straight down against the man's nose, bringing a sputtering string of curses. Quinn snapped his fingers above the man's face. "Listen up," he said. "Are the Fengs on the boat?"

Scuric blinked, his eyes watering from the blow. "You are both dead."

Quinn gave a chuckling shrug. "You aren't doing much to convince me to keep you alive."

"Quickly," Song snapped, sending a hammer fist into the man's unprotected groin. "Are the Fengs on the boat?"

Scuric drew himself into a ball and moaned. He shook his head. "Gone . . ."

Quinn cuffed him in the face to keep his attention. "Listen to me," he said. "Where did they go?"

"I tell you the truth," Scuric groaned. "All of it. I just help with passport sometimes. New names—I'll give them to you—all Hong Kong SAR blanks. Good shit. Really, I have no idea where they go."

It never failed to amaze Quinn that tough guys who bullied women caved so quickly during a comparatively mild interrogation. "The one with the weasel nose," he said. "Who is he?"

"A snakehead," Scuric said. "I only ever call him Jiàn." The Croatian brightened as if he had news that might save him. "I do some business with Jiàn, moving people sometimes. He don't know I learned some Chinese when I move Afghan heroin sometimes. Him and Fengs, they talked freely on the mobile. . . ." His voice trailed off.

"And," Quinn prompted, "what did they say?"

"I tell you, you let me go?"

"I only want to find the Fengs," Quinn lied. "I have no problem with you."

"They are going to meet someone named 'Big Business.'"

"That makes no sense," Quinn said, looking up at Song.

She shook her head. "Tell me what you heard in Chinese."

"He said '*Da Ye.*'" Scuric nodded his misshapen head. "That means 'big business,' right?"

"Da Ye." Song looked at Quinn, shaking her head as if she didn't want to believe it. "Big Uncle."

"Who's Big Uncle?" Quinn asked.

"A triad boss your FBI has been hunting for more than a decade. They know he exists, but have no idea what he looks like. Very notorious."

Quinn smiled, trying to imagine someone being a little bit notorious. "And how about the Ministry of State Security?" he asked.

"Oh, we know exactly who he is," Song said. "But he causes problems for your FBI. That's no problem for us. When last I heard, he was in Madrid." She took the cell phone from her vest pocket and moved a half step away to make a call.

"Those Fengs," Scuric said quietly to Quinn as if they were partners now that Song was otherwise engaged. "They are, how you say it? Bad news. I fed them and, you know, showed them hospitality since I worked with Jiàn sometimes. They used two of my girls before they left. That little Ehmet Feng, he's . . . wrong in the head. He carved up both girls with Serb cutter once they finish with . . . you know, hospitality. Sick bastard killed them all like it was nothing."

"I wonder where he got a Serb cutter?" Quinn felt the urge to kick the Croatian in his crooked head. Song turned and stared down at him in disgust, the phone still to her ear. Scuric noticed her darkening mood and changed tack.

"I heard the little shit, Ehmet, say something else on the phone," he said. "Wherever they are going, they have some big plan." He nodded for effect. "They talked about something called the Black Dragon. Some kind of Chinese weapon—"

Song's pistol barked twice as she put two quick rounds in the man's heart. Stunned, Scuric's mouth opened and closed like a dying fish with a stomped head.

Quinn, who was surprised by little in the world, jumped at the sudden gunfire. He leveled his pistol at Song and glared. "What was that?"

Song put her gun slowly on the ground and raised both hands. "A man who would stand by and do nothing while another murdered two young girls is a murderer himself."

"No argument there," Quinn said, glancing through the foliage at the beach. He wondered who else had heard the shots. "Still—"

"He had knowledge of sensitive Chinese technology." She cut him off with a dismissive shrug, as if she shot people every day, but Quinn could see the worry lines at the corners of her mouth had deepened. She wasn't used to this. "My government cannot allow that information to leak."

Quinn took a deep breath. "Well, it sounds like the entire weapon has leaked and is in the wind. I doubt Scuric's rudimentary knowledge posed much of a threat."

"Not any longer," she said, her lip giving the slightest of quivers.

"We could easily find ourselves up against this weapon of yours," Quinn said. "I would have liked to hear a little more about it."

"I can tell you what you need to know," she said. "An overabundance of knowledge could get you killed."

"I can see that," Quinn said. "But what about the Fengs? Hard to question a man with two .45 slugs in his chest."

"It does not matter." Song stooped to pick up her pistol, apparently satisfied Quinn wasn't going to shoot her—though he hadn't quite made up his mind. She waved a hand toward the trees where the motorcycle was hidden. "If they are going to see Big Uncle, I know where to find them."

Chapter 33

Spotsylvania, 2:30 PM

Camille Thibodaux was in the kitchen, surrounded by two bushels of green beans, when the doorbell rang. She ignored it, focusing instead on the sound of the pressure cooker with her first canning batch, hissing and rattling on the stove. Glass quart jars packed with fresh beans lined the counter space on both sides of the stainless-steel sink. A cloud of steam rolled out of the dishwasher when she opened the door to take out a load of newly washed jars. She pushed a lock of dark hair out of her eyes with her arm, and removed the rack of jars, flipping the dishwasher door shut with her foot.

She didn't wear a watch, so she glanced at her cell phone that lay on the counter beside a thick wooden cutting board to check the time when the bell rang again, wondering who could be dropping by at this time of day. Government agents and the homeowners' association Nazis tended to knock, apparently feeling the sound of their fists on the door was more intimidating than a wimpy chime. Church folk or salesmen rang the doorbell. It was that time of year again when the bug boys and security system installers descended on the DC area like locusts. They were mostly harmless, clean-cut young men from the Rocky Mountains, but it wouldn't hurt them to wait a little minute.

The bell rang a third time, bringing shouts of "Door, Mama!" from the younger boys, who knew not to open it themselves under penalty of a swat on the butt with a Hot Wheels track.

Beads of sweat trickled down Camille's back as she hoisted the jars onto the counter, wetting her green Marine Corps T-shirt. She'd still not lost all her weight from the last baby so T-shirts and loose sweats made up most of her wardrobe. Canning pole beans was far too hot an undertaking for sweats, so she'd slipped into a pair of basketball shorts and some well-worn Saucony runners. The older boys were out playing and the younger three were watching cartoons in the basement—giving Camille some much needed time to work.

With the special pay addendum gone that Jacques had been getting before the administration change, she had to pull out all the stops to feed seven hungry boys on a Corps salary. One of the guys at the Spotsylvania Farmers' Market was a former Marine and knew the drill of making ends meet. He'd given her a killer deal on pole beans. Camille spent a good deal of each summer canning produce to feed her boys—and Jacques whenever he decided to come home. Always a worker, she enjoyed the industry of home production. It gave her something to take her mind off the worry over her husband, who was, it seemed, always trying to find the most dangerous people in the most awful places on earth to spend his time with.

The doorbell rang again, followed by a soft, civilized knock. She felt a pang of guilt for not answering sooner. Looking at the buckets and jars of beans, she did some math in her head as she dried her hands on a dishtowel and made her way down the hall toward the door. According to Jacques's grandmother's canning recipe book, she had enough beans to make twenty-eight quarts—four canner batches—with maybe a few left over to make a couple of jars of her pickled beans. Jacques loved pickled green beans.

She was thinking of how much Jacques loved pickled beans when she opened the door.

Camille tensed when she recognized the IDTF agent with greasy black curls from the day before. She slammed the door in his face, half expecting that he'd kick it in. Instead, he gave another soft knock.

"Mrs. Thibodaux," he said. "Please listen to me. I'm a friend of your husband."

She stood behind the closed door, considering making a run for the pistol. "I'm listening," she said.

"I've come alone," the man said, "without my partner. I'm here unofficially, as a friend."

She looked through the peephole. "What about my husband, Mr . . . ?"

"Benavides," the man said, smiling. "Joey Benavides. I did some work with the Gunny."

Jacques had never mentioned a Joey Benavides, but that was not unusual. He'd worked with Jericho Quinn for several months before she'd even heard him say the man's name out loud. Now you'd think the two had grown up together.

Sighing, she pulled open the door. If he was not what he said he was, he'd just kick it in anyway.

"What is it you want, Mr. Benavides?"

"I need to get word to your husband," the tubby agent said, glancing over his shoulder, up and down the street. "Look, I'm taking a big risk. If my boss finds out I came here like this, it could cost me my job . . . or worse. Could I please come inside for a couple of minutes?"

Something about this guy still raised her hackles, but he had asked permission. Even when he'd come the day before with his partner, he seemed more bark than bite. Against her better judgment she stepped back. "Come in then," she said.

The timer on the stove began to beep as soon as she'd shut the door. "I need to get the pressure cooker," she said, nodding up the hallway. "We can talk in the kitchen."

"Sure," Benavides said, smiling. He seemed extremely interested in their family photos, pausing here and there, as an old friend might to catch up after a long absence.

Camille turned down the heat under the pressure cooker and picked up the stubby paring knife to cut the ends off the green beans before stuffing them in the hot jars from the dishwasher. Doing something with her hands helped her focus. "I'm all ears."

"I don't know how much your husband has told you about our present situation," Benavides said, sidling up next to her at the counter.

Camille noticed right off that Joey Benavides was what Jacques called a "close talker." The man's idea of personal space was measured in single digits.

"You want some water or sweet tea?" Camille asked, taking a half step away.

"Sure," he said, stammering as he tried to get back on his train of thought. "Tea . . . that would be great. Anyway, I'm not sure who to trust anymore. That's why—"

Camille held up her paring knife, using her elbow to gain back a little more of her space as she pointed toward the fridge. "The pitcher's in there. Help yourself."

"Okay," he said. "Thanks . . . I mean, sure, that'd be good. You want some?"

"Sweet tea," she said, "In the blue pitcher." She told him where the glasses were and continued to cut beans from a seemingly endless pile.

"Your husband and I thought we could get things back on track." Benavides filled two glasses with tea as he spoke, then returned the pitcher to the fridge. "With Ronnie Garcia in custody, I need to get word to him ASAP."

Camille nearly dropped the knife at the mention of Ronnie's name, but kept cutting beans as if it meant nothing to her. She glanced up in time to see Benavides reach into the pocket of his slacks and bring out a small pill, which he dropped into one of the tea glasses.

"You need sugar or anything?" he asked, swirling the doped glass in his hand, presumably giving whatever he'd slipped her time to dissolve.

"You're sure enough not from the South," she said forcing a smile. "It's *sweet* tea. The sugar's already in it."

"Oh, yeah." Benavides winced. "Of course."

Camille continued to play naïve while her mind raced for the next move. She was stupid, stupid, stupid to let this guy in her house. Whatever she did, she had to do it in a hurry, before he realized she knew anything. Jacques always said most people lost a fight while they're standing around deciding what to do. Maybe the pill was a vitamin or something, and he meant it for himself. Maybe . . .

She made up her mind when he held the doped tea glass out for her to take.

Her paring knife caught him where his thumb met his forefinger, just behind the glass. Bringing her left arm across, Camille used both hands to drive the blade downward, screaming at the top of her lungs.

"*Porca Vacca!*" The Italian curse was one hundred percent fear, but it had the startling effect of a war cry.

The glass of sweet tea crashed from Joey B's hand as her knife pegged him to the wooden cutting board. His own gurgling screech rose above hers when he looked down and saw blood pouring from the wound.

"You biiiittchh!" he shrieked. "I'm—"

She cut him off with a quart jar full of green beans to the side of his head. Sinking like a sack of sand, he fell to the kitchen floor in a pile of blood, beans, and broken glass. The heavy cutting board, still attached to his hand with the knife, followed him down and bashed him in the head.

Her mind racing to figure out what Jacques would do, Camille bent quickly to snatch the pistol from a holster on the man's belt. She took a step back with trembling knees. She'd just stabbed a federal officer— maybe even killed him with the jar. Then she thought, maybe she *should* kill him. He had tried to drug her, but there was no going back from what she'd done.

"Mama?"

Her oldest son's voice nearly sent her out of her skin. He was twelve, and already sounded a lot like his father. She spun, biting her lip to keep from breaking down right then and there.

"Mama," the boy repeated. All three of her older sons had come in from the yard and stood wide-eyed in the doorway to the kitchen.

Denny, the third in line at eight years old, had gone pale. "You're bleeding. . . ."

She glanced down to see blood running out of her hand and dripping off the point of her elbow. The jar must have cut her when she hit Benavides in the head. She grabbed a paper towel and pressed it to the wound. It was not as bad as it looked, but it might take a while to stanch the blood.

"Help me, boys," she said, as if she'd just asked them to bring up some laundry. "We need to get this bad man into the bedroom and tie him up."

Dan, the second oldest nodded. "Want me to call 911?"

She shook her head. "This man is a policeman," she said, wrapping her hand with a towel as she spoke. "But trust me, he's a bad one. He was trying to hurt your mama."

All three boys bristled at that and looked ready to stomp Joey B where he lay.

"Come on," she said, "he's a big guy. It's going to take all four of us to move him."

Ten minutes later, Camille Thibodaux and her sons of twelve, ten, and eight had dragged, rolled, and lifted Joey Benavides onto her bed. She'd considered using the guest bed, but her four-poster had strong oak rails at the head and foot, giving her something to chain his arms and legs to. Jacques's grandfather had been the sheriff of Terrebonne Parish, and Camille had been able to find two pairs of his old handcuffs in the drawer where Jacques kept what he called his "important tactical shit."

She used ropes and duct tape to secure Joey's ankles, sure it cut off his circulation, but she didn't really care.

Satisfied Benavides wouldn't be able to escape when he woke up, Camille stepped back to try to work out what to do next. If he'd told anyone he was here, she was screwed. Help would be along anytime. But considering the fact that he'd tried to drug her instead of arrest her, she hoped his visit was unofficial and off the books.

The three boys stood behind her, flushed and glowing that they'd be able to tell their dad about being men of the house while he was gone. Jacques had instilled in them from birth that "protector of the mama" was the highest of callings.

Camille handed Dan the keys to Joey B's sedan, holding up the ignition key so he'd know which one it was, and told him to drive the car around back so it was off the street and out of sight. At ten, he was the best driver of all the boys and often took the wheel when they went to their grandpa's farm in Louisiana. Besides that, she wasn't about to leave them alone in the house with this creep, even if he was tied up.

She sent the other two boys to clean up the glass in the kitchen and picked up her cell phone with trembling hands to make another futile attempt at calling Jacques. He rarely spoke of it, but she knew his life was full of stabbing and head bashing. He would surely know what to do. Benavides had said that Ronnie Garcia was in custody. Though Camille didn't know everything, she was smart enough to read between the lines and see that if IDTF agents had found Ronnie, everyone she was associated with was in mortal danger.

She got Jacques's voice mail, listened to all of it just to hear his voice, then tried again, holding on to hope while it rang. Still nothing. Cursing under her breath in staccato Italian, she paced back and forth, her eyes locked on the unconscious man tied to her bed.

"Come on, Jacques," she said, barely holding her sobs at bay. It was all over the Internet what these IDTF guys did to their prisoners. The thought of it made her sick to her stomach. Jacques and Jericho were both AWOL so they would be no help. It was up to her to figure out what to do to help Ronnie. She was smart and relatively fit, but she knew she couldn't do this by herself—whatever it was she was doing.

With no one else to call, she scrolled through her list of contacts and took a deep breath before punching in the number to the last person on earth who should want to help Veronica Garcia.

Chapter 34

Croatia, 9:50 PM

It was dark by the time Quinn rode the Toaster Tank Beemer up the cobblestone road in front of the Bursaws' inn. From the looks of things, the party had been going on for some time.

Petra's father played raucous folk music on his accordion beside two men about his age on a wooden stage they'd dragged up under the canopy of the beech tree. One man played the violin, another a long-necked stringed instrument called a *tamburica* that sounded to Quinn much like a mandolin.

Song sat on the back of the bike for a long moment after Quinn rolled to a stop and lowered the side stand. Arms locked around his waist, she seemed frozen in place, her eyes glued to the musicians. The end of a number broke the spell and Quinn felt her shake herself as if shooing away a stray thought. He steadied the bike while he waited for her to swing a leg off and step back.

"I need to make arrangements," she said, removing her helmet and running a hand through her hair as she started for the door. "I'll be down in a moment."

She bounded through the milling crowd as if she couldn't wait to get away from Quinn now that she was out of her stupor.

Kevin Bursaw stood chatting with a small crowd of men under a string of white and red lights, the colors of the Croatian flag. Nibbling from a paper plate piled high with food, he looked up and waved at Quinn, motioning him over.

The lights draped from the high eaves of the three-story inn to the beech tree, across to the motorcycle shed, then back to the inn, forming a lighted stable for two dozen adventure motorcycles and half again as many people. Beaked GSs and larger GS Adventures made up the bulk of the bikes since Bursaw had the BMW concession, but the herd was dotted with a handful of KTMs, Yamahas, and Triumphs. They all looked aggressive and predatory. Two black Corvettes and a gleaming lime-green Dodge Challenger Hellcat sat parked along the edge of the road facing the lighted stable as if they were looking over the bikes.

Quinn peeled off his helmet and hung it on the Toaster's handlebars. The incredibly thick and herby odor of spit-roasted lamb hit him full in the face and caused his mouth to water. He knew he'd have to make excuses and get going, but he also had to eat. The heady smells of fresh bread and cooking meat made him realize his body was running on reserve. Off the bike, he arched his back, popping his neck from side to side. The wind on the ride back had almost dried his wet jeans but left him chilled and exhausted down to his bones. Some sort of nourishment was fast becoming an imperative.

Petra had outdone herself with two long tables of assorted Croatian dishes. There was a long line crowded around the lamb so Quinn grabbed a piece of crusty bread and a small fish grilled simply in olive oil and herbs. He ate it in two bites while he walked over to let Kevin know his prized Toaster Tank Beemer was, amazingly enough, still intact.

"Hey, man," Bursaw said, shaking Quinn's hand when he walked up, still careful to let him pick the name he wanted to use to be introduced. Bursaw gestured to a rangy-looking man with a blond goatee to his left. "You'll have to forgive my nephew, Craig," he said. "He won't shut up about his new muscle car."

"John Martin," Quinn said, using the name on his Australian passport. "Pleasure to meet you."

"American muscle, Uncle Kevin," Craig said. A lit cigarette drooped from the corners of his grinning lips. Though he spoke excellent English, his Balkan accent gave him away as being from Petra's side of the family. He didn't look much younger than Kevin. He nodded proudly and gestured toward the shiny green Dodge with the glowing cigarette. "Just picked her up from the customs lot three days ago. She is a 2015 SRT Hellcat. She has a 707 horsepower Hemi engine, capable of zero to sixty miles per hour in three seconds—"

"Yeah." Kevin laughed, "And it cost you more than my house." He stuffed a bite of cheese and *pršut*, the prosciutto-like cured meat of Croatia, into his mouth.

Bursaw's nephew, whose real name was Crepko, but who had changed his name to Craig because he loved American things, swung the red and black key fobs in his hand and gave a resigned shrug. "Maybe my car is expensive, but I had the money." He wagged his head and jabbed at him with the cigarette to make his point. "And don't tell me you don't want to take her out on the road and let her speak to you, Uncle. Perhaps Aunt Petra would not allow you because the women would flock like birds to such a sexy machine. . . ."

Song walked up and touched Quinn's arm. He didn't mind small talk if it was about motors and speed.

"I need to talk to you, dear," she said. Her voice was tense, pointed.

The other men raised their eyebrows and gave Quinn a knowing nod. They stepped away to give the couple space.

"I am informed that Big Uncle is no longer in Madrid," she whispered. Her eyes darted from guest to guest as she spoke. "He has set up shop in the United States."

"Okay." Quinn nodded thoughtfully. "So the Fengs *are* going to the US. Do you know where?"

"Washington," she said.

"The capital," Quinn mused.

Song shook her head. "The state. Big Uncle now runs his triad from Seattle."

"Interesting," Quinn said, his brain going into overdrive. He went over the long list of possible targets in the Northwest—military bases, nuclear facilities, the major cities themselves.

"We need to get to Seattle then," he said. "And in the meantime, you need to tell me more about this Black Dragon so we can consider where they might hit."

Song folded her arms tightly across her chest and stood silently in front of him. To others in the group it probably looked like they were having a fight instead of discussing how to avert a war between their two countries. Quinn couldn't help but notice that even in their present situation Song's shoulders bounced and bobbed to the lilt of the music, as if she might break out dancing at any moment. Her foot tapped along with the beat.

"Come on," he said. "I'll get Kevin to take us to the airport."

Song shook her head, rolling her lips as if she wanted

to make sure she didn't let the wrong words slip out. "There are no flights for another seven hours."

"The Citation?" Quinn said.

"Already tasked with another mission," she said.

"A mission more important than this?"

"I warned you," she said. "There are those within my government who believe war with the United States would work to the eventual benefit of China. My allies grow fewer in number with each passing hour. Very soon it may just be me and you."

"I'm still an undecided in that regard," Quinn said.

"In any case," she said, still watching the band. "We are booked on a British Airways flight to Seattle in the morning."

"Nothing to do but wait then," Quinn said. He paused, looking directly at Song. "Do you play?"

Her head snapped around. "What?"

"We're talking about World War Done and you haven't taken your eyes off those musicians."

She bowed her head and gave him a sheepish nod. "The violin," she said. "Back at the university. I was quite good at it. I studied fiddle music in the United States my second year, intending to make it my profession before my present job . . . occurred."

"The fiddle," Quinn mused. "That explains the country music."

Kevin Bursaw walked back up in the middle of the conversation. He looked at Quinn. "Bo never told me you play the fiddle."

Quinn laughed. "I couldn't even play the triangle." He nodded at Song. "She's the fiddle player."

Bursaw held his paper plate with one hand and put two fingers to his mouth in a piercing whistle, bringing the band to a stop. "Papa," he yelled across the crowd. "We have a beautiful young lady here who plays the

fiddle. Do you think Silvano would mind if she had a
try?"

All eyes turned in their direction, giving Song no
way out. She flashed Quinn a pinched look that said
she might shoot him.

Bursaw noticed the look as well and picked up a ball
of fried dough crusted in sugar as they watched Song
step up on the portable stage. "Make sure and try Petra's
fritule before your girlfriend cuts your guts out."

The three musicians gave Song the stage, happy for
a short break to partake of the feast. Quinn watched in
rapt attention as she raised Silvano's violin to her shoulder, and, after a few plucks of tuning, launched into a
frantic buzz of "Flight of the Bumblebee." Everyone at
the party stopped what they were doing as the notes
swarmed from the strings. Then, as if the bees had
turned back on themselves, the violin transformed into
fiddle. A few notes later and the eerie screams and
groans of "The Devil Went Down to Georgia" began to
spill from her bow. The crowd of riders erupted in
whistles and applause when she finished. Song bowed,
then moved to climb down off the stage, but a chant
rose up, begging her to continue. Quinn found himself
shouting along with the crowd, hoping to convince her
to play another, if only for her own sake.

Song smiled shyly. It was a look that Quinn hadn't
seen on her before, but it suited her well, making her
appear more like an actual human being.

"One more," she shouted back over the crowd.

"Two more!" the people pled.

She actually blushed. "One more."

Quinn found himself grinning. He looked at Bursaw
and said, "She's with me."

The crowd fell silent, watching, leaning in toward
the music as Song's bow coaxed out a haunting tune

that Quinn didn't recognize. It sounded like a cross between Mannheim Steamroller techno and Old World
folk. The locals in the crowd launched into a frenzy of
cheers. When she finished, Bursaw's father-in-law tried
to convince her to join the band.

It took Song almost two minutes to wade through
her new admirers and work her way back to Quinn. She
gave him a good-natured jab in the ribs with her elbow,
in a much better mood than when she had left.

Bursaw looked at her with a gaping mouth. "How
did you know how to play 'Croatian Rhapsody'?"

"Is that what it's called?" Song shrugged. "I heard it
at the airport when we arrived." She looked at Quinn as
if she wasn't some kind of musical genius. "We have
an early day. I think I'll go to bed."

"I'll be up in a minute," he said. "Don't lock me
out."

"Why, because you made me play in front of everyone?" She smiled.

He watched her walk away, still trying to get a handle on what made her tick. As soon as she made it inside, he turned to Bursaw. "Do you have a phone I can
borrow for a couple of international calls? I'll pay to
cover the cost."

Bursaw reached in his pocket and handed over his
smartphone. "Knock yourself out," he said. "I have to
call my parents every other day or they flip out. I got an
international plan."

Quinn took the mobile and walked beyond the beech
tree, away from the noise of the crowd. The moon was
nearly full and each stone and shrub cast long shadows
on the silver limestone of the hillside. Far enough away
that he felt he could speak freely, he punched in the pre-
arranged emergency number for Palmer. If the Fengs
had something planned for Seattle, he had to tell some-

one. It would take him nearly twenty-four hours just to get there, and though the Fengs were apparently traveling commercially as well, they had a good ten-hour head start—and a lot could happen in ten hours.

There was no answer, so Quinn ended the call and tried again, mentally willing his old boss to pick up. He gave up after ten rings, immediately punching in the last number he had for Garcia. They hadn't spoken in almost a month, and though Quinn told himself he needed to get in touch with Palmer through whatever means possible, he had to admit that he was glad to have an excuse to check in with her. She was the most low-maintenance girl he'd ever even heard of, but he'd learned from the wisdom of Jacques Thibodaux that low maintenance didn't mean no maintenance.

He tried her twice as well, getting nothing but empty rings both times. He tried both Miyagi and then Jacques next with the same result. Everyone had gone dark. He needed to get word to someone on the West Coast and thought of calling Bo, but decided to wait on that. Great to have around as backup, Bo and his club were just as likely to start World War III as prevent it if sent in unsupervised.

A sickening realization that something was very wrong began to creep over Quinn. He'd found himself in some very lonely spots over the course of his life— remote hunts on the barren Alaska tundra, outside the wire at forward operating bases in the Middle East— but here, standing on this moonlit hillside in Eastern Europe, the aloneness was oppressive. He worked for the most powerful nation on earth—or at least he had— a nation with the fastest aircraft, the most advanced satellites, and the most sophisticated war-fighting apparatus on the planet, and still, he found himself waiting for a seat on a commercial airline and dependent on a mercurial enemy agent to complete his mission.

A sudden commotion at the party drew his attention back toward the lights. The sound of a revving engine grew louder. Gravel crunched in the darkness as a vehicle ground to a quick stop. At first he thought it might be Bursaw's nephew showing off the muscle car, but the engine sound was more mowl than roar. The unmistakable sound of a scream rose above the noise of music and dancing.

Out of habit, Jericho stuffed the phone in his back pocket to free up both hands and began to trot back toward the party—toward the sound of danger. The band's Croatian folk song came to an abrupt stop. As he reached the beech tree, he realized everyone had turned to look toward the back of the inn where the browlike taillights of an Alpha Romeo Giulietta sedan flashed in the darkness. Quinn saw Stilvano, the violinist, run toward the sedan, and then crumple under the pop of gunfire. Kevin Bursaw, who had already drawn a pistol, ran toward the house where his twin daughters were sleeping. The Giulietta's tires squealed as it sped away in a rooster tail of spraying gravel.

Quinn, who'd come in diagonally from the tree, intercepted Bursaw and they reached the back driveway at the same moment. Bursaw stopped in his tracks, pistol in hand watching the taillights flash between the trees down the road to the highway and Dubrovnik.

"They took her," he said, panting.

"Took who?"

"Song," Bursaw said, nodding toward a lifeless body that sprawled along the gravel drive. "Looks like she killed one of them, but I saw her face in the back window of the car as they pulled away. They got her."

The fleeing car was too far away to chase on foot, so Quinn spun on his heels immediately, running for the stable of motorcycles out front.

"It's probably a trap," Bursaw panted, struggling to keep up.

"Of course, it's a trap," Quinn said.

Bursaw dug in his pocket as they broke through the crowd and nodded toward a blue GS, gleaming under the red and white lights. "That one is mine. It's plenty fast."

"Fast isn't enough." Quinn shook his head, going straight for Bursaw's nephew. "Sorry, Craig," he said, snatching the astonished man's car keys from his hand and sprinting for the Hellcat. "I need fast and brutal."

Chapter 35

Camille Thibodaux nearly jumped out of her skin at the sound of the doorbell. The boys were down in the basement watching cartoons with strict instructions to stay there. She snatched a five-shot Ruger .357 revolver Jacques had given her from the gun safe above the medicine cabinet in her master bathroom and held it behind her right thigh while she went to answer the door. She was fairly certain she knew who it was, but considering the fact that she had a government agent tied to her bed, the gun seemed a prudent measure. Hand on the knob, she rehearsed the lines she'd played over and over in her head since making the call, then took a deep breath and opened the door.

"Hi," Kimberly Quinn said, her voice perkier than her face said it should be. "Sorry it took me a minute to get here. My physical therapist was busy torturing me."

It was easy to see what had attracted Jericho to his ex-wife. She was petite and pretty—Jacques called her "pretite"—with flaxen hair and blue eyes that were large and round, if a little on the accusatory side. She wore a loose black T-shirt that said: I FIGHT LIKE A GIRL!

in bold pink letters. Her khaki capris said she didn't care about hiding the above-the-knee metal prosthetic that had replaced the leg she'd lost to a sniper months before. She carried a large purse slung over one shoulder and a metal cane in the opposite hand. Camille knew she'd been able to walk without a cane until a kidnapping attempt on her daughter in Crystal City had reinjured her leg and sent her back to physical therapy. The same incident had also made it impossible for her to travel with her daughter, who was now stashed with friends in Russia to protect her from the present administration. The fact that she was separated from her child pressed Kim Quinn down more than even the loss of her leg. Camille could not imagine how she'd react if she had to give up her kids, even for a week. Mattie Quinn had been gone over a month.

Kim smiled, but it was forced, following the civilized norms of talking to the wife of your ex-husband's best friend. "You said this was something important?"

Camille pushed the door open wider, looking up and down the residential street in front of her house before stepping back inside. "Come on in," she said. "Were you followed?"

"No," Kim said, grimacing a little at the question. "I don't think so."

Camille couldn't really blame her. Jacques worked with Jericho on a daily basis, and as such they'd become entwined in his new life. His friends were their friends—and that included his girlfriend, Veronica Garcia. Camille had met Kim Quinn several times, and even liked her, but she didn't know her well, and certainly not well enough to ask her to do what she was about to.

"I'll cut right to it," Camille said as soon as she'd shut the door. "How much do you know about what Jericho and Jacques do for a living?"

Kim's blue eyes flew wide at the sight of the re-volver. "Sorry," Camille said, "this'll make a little more sense in a minute."

Kim appeared to relax a notch. "I know some, of course," she said. "How could I not? I mean he's taken our daughter halfway around the world. Are they all right?"

Camille nodded quickly. "They're fine," she said, the rest gushing out like a waterfall. "At least I think so. To tell you the truth I don't know. I don't know anything really. I haven't heard from Jacques in over two weeks, but the last time we spoke, they were both doing okay. He told me he had to go dark for a while. I understand, but you never get used to something like that."

Kim nodded. "I hear that."

"I'm sorry I had to drag you into this," Camille said, getting control of her emotions. "But I literally don't know who else to call."

"How much do *you* know about what they do?" Kim asked.

"Jacques is a talker," she said, "but he knows how to keep a secret too. I know they're into things that aren't exactly in the published job description for the Marine Corps or OSI."

"No kidding," Kim said, shivering a little.

"Again . . ." Camille said, the rehearsed words sounding stupid in her head now, "I'm sorry to get you involved, but—"

"Involved in what?"

A muffled cry, followed by a series of hollow thumps came from down the hall.

"Come with me," Camille said, nodding toward the sound. "It's easier if I just show you."

* * *

All the blood drained from Kimberly Quinn's face when she saw the man tied spread-eagled to Camille's bed. She spun as quickly as she could on the prosthetic leg to leave the bedroom and walked back toward the front door. Even after Camille explained what had happened, she insisted that they call the police. It took five agonizing minutes to convince her that the agent tied to the bed had something to do with the work Jacques and Jericho did—something in which they were both already deeply embroiled. He was IDTF, Camille had reasoned. The police would believe his story over hers, no matter the circumstances.

Ten minutes after she'd arrived, Kim Quinn gave her tentative agreement to help. After spending two minutes in the room with Joey Benavides, any reservations flew out the window.

"Do you bitches have any idea who you're dealing with?" Benavides said, finally working himself free of the gag Camille had stuffed in his mouth. He arched his back in time with his words, like a flopping fish trying to make a point. "Let! Me! Go!"

His wrists were red and swollen from his thrashing to get free of the cuffs. The sheets were sodden with blood that wept from the stab wound in his right hand. Even as his face was stricken with terror, he resorted to threats and hollow bravado to try to get his way. He leered at Kim, eyeing her prosthetic leg with a vaporous smirk. "Can you hear what I'm telling you? Gimp your ass over here and turn me loose."

Kim ignored him, her arms folded across her chest, thinking. She looked up suddenly, startling Camille. "Jericho hides little lock pick thingies and blades in the seams of his clothes," she said, nodding at Benavides.

"You're right," Camille said. "I hadn't thought of

that." She went to Jacques's drawer of "Important Tactical Shit" in his bureau. Among the dozens of assorted knives, she found one with a small and very sharp curved blade.

Benavides resisted when she'd first started, but the sight of Kim standing back with the revolver aimed at his head, and Camille with the razor-sharp blade a whisper away from his soapy flesh left him a silent, trembling blob. Camille was horrified to find a small pistol in a holster on the man's ankle as she cut away his slacks. Thankfully, she'd not given him a chance to get to it. Not wanting to chance missing another weapon, she even took his socks.

"And that," Kim nodded to the heavy gold necklace around Joey's thick neck. Camille grimaced as she reached to pick it up from the matted thatch of curly black hair on his flabby chest. Jacques had plenty of chest hair, but he also had lots of muscle. Joey looked more like a fuzzy, half-deflated beach ball. She yanked the necklace away, snapping the clasp so she wouldn't have to get too close.

Shuddering, she threw the necklace and shredded clothes in the corner of the bedroom and then locked the pistol in the closet safe. Her boys were smart and knew about gun safety, but they were still boys. Even with a man tied to her bed, she didn't want more than one gun out at a time.

Now wearing only a dingy pair of briefs, Joey B transitioned from threats to tears. A ponderous belly rippled in time with his pleading sobs.

"Pleeeeeease," he whimpered. "You have to let me go."

Camille whispered something in Kim's ear. She nodded slowly, thinking things through, and then stepped out of the room. Camille leaned toward the door. "Ask Dan!" she shouted. "He'll know where Jacques keeps it." She turned back to a quiet Joey B. "You mentioned that Ronnie Garcia has been arrested."

He looked up at her, rolling carpy lips until they turned white.

Camille bumped the bed with her hip. "Where is she?"

Benavides clenched his eyes shut. "I can't tell you that."

"Sure you can," she said. "I'm just a weak little housewife. What harm could it do?"

Benavides turned his face away. "That would get us all killed."

"You let me worry about that," Camille said, trying to mimic Jacques's tone. "Where is Ronnie Garcia?"

"I'm telling you I don't know!" he wailed.

"No," Camille said. "You told me you couldn't tell me. That's different. I'm thinking you're the sort of creep who would make it his business to know where they put the pretty women."

Kim walked in, lugging a red metal toolbox with both hands. She looked at Camille and gave it a rattle to get Joey's attention.

His head snapped around. His lips quivered. "What's that for?"

Kim shrugged. "You know," she said. "A little of this, a little of that." Camille was surprised at this new steely calm in her voice.

"It's not too late to turn back." Joey began to hyperventilate, eyes pleading to Kim. "You didn't stab me. You're not the one who tied me to the bed. You don't have to be a part of this."

Kim took a deep breath. "Jericho always says I should trust my gut instinct," she said. "And my gut tells me you are somehow connected with the people who shot me."

Joey began to writhe wildly, popping loose the fitted

sheet from the mattress. "No," he said. "I'm not. I got no idea what happened to you. I don't even know you. I am IDTF. You have to let me go!"

Camille took the toolbox from Kim and set it on the ground at their feet without a word.

Joey Benavides watched in abject horror as the two women ducked down beside the bed, and out of his sight. The stab wound made his hand feel like it was being eaten by ants and throbbed enough to make him lose his mind. His wrists were about to snap into pieces and he was pretty sure he'd sprained both his ankles fighting against the ropes. Unable to see over the edge of the bed, he raised his head and strained to hear what these crazy women were saying over the rapid thudding of his heartbeat in his ears. They whispered so he caught only snippets of muffled conversation.

". . . No, no, not that one," the blond one said.

A series of clanks and bangs followed before Camille Thibodaux stood, holding a ballpeen hammer. The blonde used a chair to pull herself up. Her eyes were cruel and devoid of forgiveness. She grasped a large pair of channel-lock pliers like a club.

"Now, wait, wait, wait," Joey stammered, feeling as if he was coming unhinged. "I . . . you . . . I mean I didn't mean any harm. . . ."

"*Beh*," Camille said, in the Italian equivalent of a verbal shrug. "I'm sure you didn't expect it to come to this," she said. "I would have been so docile and compliant if only you'd been able to get that roofie into my sweet tea without me catching you."

"Wait, wait, wait," he pleaded, "what about your kids?" He licked his lips. "You can't do this with little kids in the house."

Camille gave him a pitiless smile. "My husband and I make a lot of noise in this room. That's why we have so many kids. He made sure the door was heavy enough to deaden any sound." Her laugh was cold and heartless. "Besides, they're boys. They wouldn't notice a stick of dynamite if it went off in the middle of their cartoons."

The room began to close in around Benavides. He'd been in his share of bad fights. He'd thought his boss might shoot him. Hell, he'd even been afraid Jacques Thibodaux was going to kill him, but he'd never in his life been as terrified of anything as he was of these two insane women. The blond one didn't say much, just held the heavy pliers like she intended to start yanking off important parts. He began to jerk against his restraints in earnest, past the point of feeling any pain.

Camille stepped to the edge of the bed, studying his knees with her cruel black eyes. Nearly out of his mind, he locked on the ballpeen hammer. "Wh . . . what are you going to do with that?"

"To tell you the truth," she whispered. "I don't really know. Guess we'll just keep trying stuff 'til we hit on something that does the trick."

Chapter 36

Croatia

Quinn moved on autopilot, carried forward by instinct more than any actual plan. He slid behind the wheel and hit the Hellcat's ignition, bringing the beast to life with a burbling roar. Bursaw's nephew had both the red and black fobs on his keychain. When both proximity chips were in the vehicle, the more aggressive red key always won, all but screaming orders at the onboard computer, and awakening all 707 horses under the hood. The predatory *blat* of the supercharged 6.2 Hemi engine alone was enough to send the crowd stepping back as if they were afraid of being eaten.

Quinn whipped the wheel hard over, giving the muscle car enough gas to drift the rear tires to the right and point the nose in the direction of the fleeing Alfa Romeo Giulietta. It didn't take much and he lifted his foot just enough to stop the drift, straightened the wheels, and then poured on the throttle.

The blower kicked in with a rising whine and the car sprang to life around him, as if it had caught the scent of new prey. Throwing him back against the bolstered

leather seat, the Hellcat tore across the cobblestone
drive in a shrieking squall of smoke and gravel. Less than
a minute from the time the door shut on the Giulietta to
speed away with Song, Quinn fishtailed the screaming
Hellcat off the gravel and onto the paved highway toward Dubrovnik. It was late and thankfully there was
no oncoming traffic, so he was able to use the entire
road, drifting through the first long, arcing curve to the
south, just in time to see the lights of the Giulietta wink
out as they crested a hill, a quarter mile ahead.

Quinn used the paddle shifters to take the car down
a gear, applying steady throttle to get maximum speed
but without the smoking burnout that the powerful Hellcat was famous for. The effect was like being strapped to
the back of a bullet with the Challenger eating up the
distance to the fleeing sedan in a matter of seconds.
Quinn let off the gas as the easily recognizable rear
lights of the Giulietta loomed ahead in the darkness
like two long number sixes tipped on their faces.

Song was nowhere in sight and Quinn assumed the
two men visible through the rear hatch had pushed her
down in the backseat. An arm appeared out the rear
passenger window, buffeted heavily by the wind, and
began to shoot at him. Quinn gave a tight chuckle despite the situation. Shooting backwards, in the dark,
and from a moving car was useless.

Tracking in close like a guided missile on the Giulietta's tail, Quinn took a quick moment to tap check
Anton Scuric's pistol he'd stuffed in his waistband,
making certain it was still in place. In the middle of a
long, slow curve, the little Giulietta used up the entire
road. The little family car swayed and rocked back and
forth to keep the heavier Dodge from passing. It
seemed obvious that the driver wanted to be followed
so he could lead Quinn into a trap, but he could not

have expected to be overtaken so quickly, likely miles from any reinforcements.

Coming out of the turn and into the straightaway, Quinn took the Hellcat down a gear and feinted as if to pass on the right. The moment the Giulietta's driver moved to cut him off, Quinn rolled quickly to the left, shooting the Hellcat forward between the fleeing sedan and the mountainside.

Nosing in along the Giulietta's left flank, front fender to rear quarter panel, Quinn yanked the heavy Dodge to the right, aggressively nudging the lighter sedan just behind the back wheel and causing it to come untracked. He mouthed the words he'd used when first learning the PIT or "Precision Immobilization Technique," toning down his aggressive driving as soon as the Alfa Romeo began to spin out and wrap around the hood of the Dodge to slam into the rocks to the left, facing in the other direction.

"GET!" Quinn barked when the cars made initial contact. And then, more softly, he said, "Out . . . of . . . my . . . way," as he steered through the collision to make certain he didn't end up spinning out of control himself.

With the Alfa Romeo behind him, Quinn took his foot completely off the gas, tapping the brake to bleed off speed. When the speedometer needle dropped below forty, he gave the wheel a slight flick to the right, shifting the weight off the inside wheels, then cranked it ninety degrees to the left and stomped the emergency brake. The back wheels broke loose, coming around in a semi-controlled "bootlegger's" turn. Machinelike, he released the emergency brake and rolled on the gas, closing the distance back to the smoking Giulietta in a quick breath.

The little sedan had rolled up on its side, snapping

an axle before colliding with a boulder and falling back to rest on all four tires. The driver, a tall and bony man wearing dark clothing, had just flung open his door and was climbing out with a pistol in hand when Quinn bailed out of the Hellcat, shooting him twice, center mass. He dropped to his knees and the gun slid away into the darkness. Quinn spent the third and fourth of the XDs' six rounds on the backseat passenger who'd been shooting at him during the chase. He came out of the Giulietta on the far side, taking potshots and moving at a crouch—but not quite low enough. Quinn's first round missed, but the second struck him in the back of his head.

Two rounds left. He had the extra magazine, but that would take time—something that was always in short supply during a gunfight.

The remaining kidnapper dragged Song out of the car, a pistol shoved under the base of her chin with such force that it caused her to gag. Blood ran from her nose in the glare of the Hellcat's headlights. Her eyes hung half open and she slumped as if she could barely keep her feet.

"We have stalemate," the man behind her said in heavily accented English. Albanian, Quinn guessed from his accent. A hired gun. He was sweating from fear and the effort of holding Song upright. "What now?"

Fifteen feet away, Quinn answered by shooting him in the exposed knee, relying on the gunfighter's mantra to shoot the target that was available until a better one presented itself—and one did. The man's shattered leg buckled at once, causing him to list sideways, reflexively throwing out his hands, including the one with the pistol, to catch himself. The sixth and final round from Quinn's XDs caught the man above his eye as his head tilted out from behind Song. He toppled into the

ditch and Song collapsed to the ground. She raised a
hand to shield her eyes from the headlights. Quinn dug
into his pocket for the extra magazine and reloaded as
he knelt down beside her, checking for wounds.

"I am fine," she said, attempting to shrug him off,
but grimacing at the pain. "My head was so full of that
stupid music, they were able to catch me by surprise."

Quinn looked up and down the highway, pulling Song
to her feet. "Let's get out of here before someone comes
along and we have to explain all these dead kidnappers.
I'm not sure my Australian passport will hold up under
that kind of scrutiny."

Kevin Bursaw's mouth hung open when the Challenger growled back up the cobblestone drive in front
of the inn with Song inside. His nephew, Craig, ran out
to open the door, grinning from ear to ear.

"Thanks," Quinn said, handing him the key fobs.
"There'll be a little damage to the front fender. I won't
blame you if you're angry—"

"Do you joke?" Craig said. "They will write songs
about my Hellcat. No way you could save the girl in
lesser vehicle. My muscle car, she is now famous."

Quinn moved to open the passenger door for Song.
"I'd really appreciate it if you didn't, you know, spread
that around."

Craig waved off the comment. "All the people here
know. That is enough for me."

Kevin Bursaw stepped up and put a hand on Quinn's
shoulder while Petra helped Song inside.

"Stilvano?" Quinn asked, wondering about the fate
of the fiddle player who'd fallen to the kidnapper's
gunfire when he ran to rescue Song.

"Right through the love handle," Bursaw said. "It'll

hurt like hell for a while, but he'll have a nice scar to show the grannies he likes to flirt with." Bursaw looked past Quinn, mulling over some kind of plan. "We need to get you both out of here. Just in case those guys send back some of their friends. I'll move my wife and kids for a few days until this blows over. The cops will have the road back to the airport blocked any time now. My father-in-law keeps a small cabin cruiser moored down in the bay below us. We'll take you around to the city in that. It'll be a safe place to wait until your flight leaves."

"I'm really sorry about all this," Quinn said. "I'm kind of a magnet for bloody murder."

"Your brother always told me you had superpowers." Bursaw chuckled. "Boy, was he right. We should call you Action Man. I never saw anyone react that fast— and I spent the better part of my life around bikers and other Type A personalities."

Quinn shrugged. Sometimes, there was just nothing to say.

"I happened to look at my watch when you ripped away in Craig's Challenger," Bursaw said. "You know you had the car and the girl back in under six minutes? Hell, Jericho, there are people at this party still chewing the same bite of food."

Chapter 37

Camille Thibodaux thought she would feel some kind of elation at holding the power to hurt this evil man in her hands. He'd tried to drug her—and she shuddered to think what else he had in mind. Instead, she felt sick to her stomach. It was in her nature to yell at Jacques with fiery Italian curses, and even threaten the boys with all sorts of mayhem if they didn't do their chores, but actual violence, that was her husband's department. She did not know for sure what he and Jericho Quinn did on their little secret missions, but looking down at the quivering lump of hairy lard who wore nothing but a sagging pair of briefs, she assumed it had something to do with people like this.

There would be no bluffing with this man. If she said she was going to hit him with the hammer, she would have to hit him with the hammer. The trick was neither she nor Kim knew where to begin. In the end, Camille supposed it was the clinical once-over she gave Benavides while deciding on an appropriate target that made the man spill the beans.

"Wait, wait, wait," he sobbed, flopping and arching

so much he nearly wriggled out of his underwear. "I'll tell you . . . I'll tell you what I know." His eyes rolled back in his head, unable to even look at the hammer anymore. "Just . . . please, put the tools away."

"That's all we ask," Camille said, shooting a look at Kim, who narrowed her eyes and gave a slow nod.

"Where is she then?" Kim said, seeming a little disappointed that she wouldn't get to pinch him somewhere painful with the pliers.

"She's being held at a black site," Joey groaned. "It's a boat really. Mr. Walter has us put certain high-value prisoners there. The ones he wants to keep out of sight." He craned his neck to watch her put the hammer back in the toolbox. "There are a shitload of guards. It's impossible for you to get her out."

Camille had heard Jacques talk about black sites and prison boats, but she'd assumed such awful places were overseas, a long way from American soil.

"Impossible?" Kim fumed, still holding the channel locks. "As impossible as knocking out an IDTF agent and tying him to a bed?"

"You let us worry about what we can and can't do," Camille said, grateful for Kim's bravado. "You just answer our questions."

Joey swallowed hard, sniffing back his tears. "Yes," he sobbed. "Sure. Absolutely."

Camille leaned in close enough she could smell the sickening odor of sweat that beaded beneath the mat of hair on his quivering body.

"Now, where is this boat?"

"Southwest of Salisbury . . . In Maryland, out on the Delmarva." His words were now spewing like a geyser. "I mean, we get to it from the Delmarva side of the Chesapeake, but the boat's actually anchored off Bloodsworth Island. The Navy used to do artillery practice there so it's off limits to civilians."

"I'm going to ask you this one time," Camille said, stooping to pick up the hammer again so Benavides would know she was serious. "There are Internet stories of the horrible things IDTF agents did to the Director of the CIA. Are those reports true? Did your people really strip and torture a fifty-year-old woman?"

Joey's head fell to the side, nodding as he looked away. "It was always on Mr. Walter's orders. All any of us ever do is follow his orders."

Camille let the hammer fall back into the metal toolbox with a loud crash. The sudden noise brought a squeaky fart from the terrified Benavides. His head fell back on the mattress when he realized she wasn't going to hit him for his confession.

Camille shook her head in disgust and motioned for Kim to follow her to the walk-in closet at the far end of the bedroom. "What do you think?" she whispered. "These are the same guys that took Virginia Ross. That means Ronnie Garcia is in real trouble."

"Isn't there anyone you can trust to call?" Kim said.

"Jacques keeps work stuff separate from our family as much as he can. I don't even know how many other guys in the Corps know what he's up to most of the time."

"I was just thinking about something Jericho always says." Kim gave a heavy sigh, as if she'd finally come to understand some mystery that had been eluding her. "He says if you're going to make a mistake, you should err on the side of action."

Camille threw her head back and laughed out loud. She looked up at the ceiling and shook her head.

"What?" Kim asked. "What's so funny?"

"I'm probably the first woman in my family to ever contemplate hiring a babysitter so she can go break a friend out of a secret boat-prison. I guess that counts as erring on the side of action all right." Camille stretched up on her tiptoes and began to search through the shoe-boxes on the closet shelf above the rack of dresses that she never wore anymore. "Got it," she said at length, finding the holster Jacques had given her, along with the little stainless-steel .357 he'd wanted much worse than she had. She remembered it was called a "Small of the Back" holster, or SOB, because those were the exact words that came to her mind when she saw Jacques had given her a gun for a present.

Peeking around the corner to make sure Benavides was still on the mattress where she'd left him, Camille stepped out of the loose basketball shorts and into a pair of heavy-duty Carhartt pants she wore to work in the yard. She rarely wore a belt and had to rummage around on the floor behind piles of clothing and boxed knickknacks, before she found a wide leather one that still fit her.

"Sorry you had to see in my closet," Camille said as she fed the belt through the loops and then the holster so it wouldn't slide around, just like Jacques had shown her. "I just throw junk in here to get it out of the way. . . ."

"Have you got another gun?" Kim said, mesmerized by the little revolver. "I only have one leg, but you have to let me do something to help. These guys are the reason my little girl is hiding out halfway around the world."

Camille gave her a leather belt from the pile on the floor. It was smaller but looked like it would probably fit Kim. "There's a gun and holster in the bathroom gun safe." Camille rolled her eyes. "I know. Right? Don't even ask."

"Remember who I used to be married to." Kim took the belt and gave a nervous laugh. "A toilet gun safe doesn't seem odd at—"

The sudden chime of the doorbell nearly sent Camille falling into the rack of dresses. The color bled from Kim's face. Out in the bedroom, Joey Benavides began to scream for help at the top of his shattered voice.

Camille ran to the bedside and grabbed the hammer from the toolbox. "You better hush, mister," she hissed.

The door was solid core but anyone standing near the window would be able to hear his yelling outside. If it was another IDTF agent, they were finished.

Benavides was obviously smart enough to know that this might be his only chance for escape. Leaning over the bed, Camille struggled to stuff the gag back in his mouth. He arched his body and jerked his head back and forth like a baby not wanting to eat his peas, all the while shrieking for help as if he was being burned alive. In a near meltdown panic, Kim began to whip him with the belt across the pale flesh of his thighs, which only added to his terror and made him scream even louder.

Realizing the situation called for desperate measures, Camille sprang onto the bed and threw herself astride Joey B so she knelt on his chest, trapping his head between her knees. He bucked and bounced beneath her, but she was finally able to stuff the gag between his teeth without getting bitten. She'd just pulled back her hand when she heard the bedroom doorknob rattle behind her. Terrified, and still straddling Joey B's naked chest, she turned to find all six feet, four inches of her husband filling the doorway.

"Jacques!" Camille said, frozen in place. "Sweetie, I can explain."

Thibodaux leaned a massive arm against the door-frame and cocked his head to one side, taking in the scene.

"Oh, Boo, you're wearin' the gun I bought you." He grinned, nodding to the revolver on her hip. "I don't believe I ever wanted you more."

Chapter 38

"What do you think Petra's father did to afford such a yacht?" Song said, sitting beside Quinn on the plush leather settee. It was U-shaped and took up much of the spacious salon. She'd taken a shower as soon as they'd boarded the boat and her hair was still wet and shone like obsidian under the wall sconce above her head. Bursaw was up with his father-in-law, just visible through a narrow hatchway, eerie silhouettes in the muted red light of the wheelhouse as they steered the forty-seven-foot cruiser through the black waters of the Adriatic.

"He seems comfortable enough running at night with no lights," Quinn said. "So I have a guess." He sat on the long side of the settee, at a right angle to Song, knee to knee.

Quinn's father had owned several fishing boats over the years. They were beamy things, working vessels, and they weren't cheap, but compared to this one they looked like a wall tent next to a five-star hotel. Quinn guessed it was at least a million-dollar boat. Pricy for a man who helped his son-in-law tend to motorcycle tires. Quinn didn't care.

Petra was in the forward cabin, down a short flight of stairs beneath the wheelhouse, trying to get her daughters to sleep after all the commotion. Quinn and Song had the salon to themselves.

Quinn rubbed his eyes, willing himself to stay awake. He'd always been fine when he was moving forward, running or riding toward a goal, but waiting sapped his strength more quickly than a fight. He looked at his watch. It was well after midnight. That put it after seven a.m. in China. It was no wonder he was exhausted. Including his time under anesthesia in the Kashgar hospital and the catnap he'd taken on the flight into Croatia, he'd gone over forty-eight hours on less than six hours of fitful or drug-induced sleep.

Song stared blankly across the interior of the boat, miles away and locked in thought.

"We have to check in at the airport in just over three hours," he said. "Bursaw says we've still got a good two hours on the boat. You should catch some sleep."

Locks of damp hair mopped the shoulders of the clean white T-shirt.

"Why do you do this?" she asked, still staring off into space.

Quinn raised a brow. "What do you mean?"

"You know . . . *this*." Song waved both hands around in a flourish. "This thing we are doing."

"I—"

"I do it because my government says I must," she said. "I think you do it because you can."

"Maybe," Quinn said.

"Please forgive me," she said, letting her head fall sideways so she was leaning back against the cushion but looking at him. "We Chinese can be very direct. What I mean to say is that you do this because you are capable." A single tear had formed and then dried on her cheek, as if it had given up.

She stretched her legs, staring at her feet, still bare from the shower. They were small for her height and Quinn was surprised to see her toenails were painted a girlish pink. "I do not think I was cut out for this type of work."

"You seem exceptionally good at it," Quinn said.

Song took a deep breath and opened her mouth to speak before looking away as if she'd changed her mind.

"You played the violin in high school?" Quinn offered, hoping to get her to talk some more about her past, to learn more about this woman in whose hands he was placing his safety.

"I did," she said, turning back to him and shaking off whatever funk had been about to overwhelm her. "And now I do not."

Quinn started to mention her incredible performance at the Bursaws' party, but decided it might open up old wounds. Instead, he changed his tack. "You promised to tell me more about the Black Dragon."

"Indeed." Song slumped in her seat, seemingly relieved to discuss anything but her past. "It's a shoulder-fired weapon resembling one of your American Javelin or Predator antitank missiles. I cannot divulge the specifics of the design, but it delivers a warhead capable of fifteen times the destructive power of an equivalent weight of a conventional high-explosive charge."

"Thermobaric?" Quinn asked, committing every word to memory so he could make a record later.

"I am afraid so."

Having any sort of explosive shot at you was bad enough, but thermobaric devices were particularly unpleasant. An explosive charge dispersed a cloud of fuel—like fluoridated aluminum or ethylene oxide. Anyone near the ignition point would be obliterated as the vaporized fuel used existing oxygen in the air to explode. Thermobaric devices tended to burn a fraction of a second slower than conventional weapons. The pressure wave in any enclosed space, along with the vacuum that followed, took care of anyone else, rupturing lungs, crushing internal organs, and destroying the inner ear. Blindness was not uncommon, but as devastating as the small devices were, the shock and pressure caused little damage to the brain so the victims were left blinded and conscious for seconds or even minutes while they suffocated to death.

"What's the size of the missile?" Quinn said.

She chewed on her lip, eyes twinkling in the diffused light of the boat. "Classified."

"We're past that," Quinn said. "I need to know so I can figure out possible targets."

"Approximately twenty kilos," she sighed.

Quinn did the math. If the entire device weighed just shy of forty-five pounds, the warhead itself was likely to be well over twenty. The Marines had taken out entire mansions in Iraq with a single eighteen-pounder from a Javelin—and Song said this one was even stronger.

"What's the fuel?"

"Really," she said. "That is secret informa—"

"If we plan to stop this, I need to know what you know."

"Beryllium," she said at length. "This device is a prototype, but believe me, it functions even better than the designers had hoped."

"I have to make a phone call," Quinn said, checking the time on his Aquaracer. "It will take us almost a full day to reach Seattle. I have friends who can work on this from that end."

Song sat up, hands folded at her knees. "If your government finds out that such a weapon will be used on US soil, I am afraid war is a forgone conclusion."

"There's a fine line between war and peace," Quinn said, almost to himself. "We are bound to cross it many times before we're done."

Chapter 39

Spotsylvania

Thibodaux braced himself in the doorway as Camille snapped out of her stupor and scrambled off the bed to launch herself into his arms.

"You're home!" She burst into tears, burying her head against his neck. "I can explain all this, you know."

Thibodaux patted her on the back and winked across her shoulder at an embarrassed Kim, who still stood at the foot of the bed with the leather belt hanging limply in her hand.

"Don't you worry about it, *ma chère*," he said. "I'd like to think we have the sort of relationship that if you came home and found me straddlin' a hairy, fat man, you'd trust I had my reasons." His grin turned sour when he focused on the man in his bed. "I'd say Joey B's the one who has some 'splainin' to do."

Camille pulled away. "So you do know him?"

"Joey, Joey, Joey . . . *Zeerahb saleau!*" Jacques nodded, giving Benavides a long, burning glare: "Disgusting, sloppy thing. What have you gone and let these gals do to you? I mean this is some kinky shit."

Joey's face twisted as if in agony and he began to bawl like a baby.

Camille put a hand on Thibodaux's chest. "Don't you want to know what happened?"

"I do," Jacques said. "But not in front of the sob-slobberer. Hang on a sec." He towered over the bed and yanked the gag out of Joey B's mouth. "Okay, shitbird, you have bled all over my sheets. You know what that means?"

Benavides shook his head, tears pressing between his lashes as a pitiful squeak escaped his lips.

Thibodaux leaned in close so he was only inches from the man's face. "It means I gotta buy me a new mattress—and this mattress means a lot to me. There ain't much to keep me from shooting you in the eye if you make another peep without permission. Understand?"

Joey nodded emphatically but kept his mouth shut.

"*Boop!* Right there," Thibodaux said, putting the tip of his index finger to Joey's clenched eye. "Keep that in mind."

Camille all but collapsed into her husband's arms as they left the bedroom with Kim leading the way.

Jacques chuckled softly. "What are you ladies planning, armed up like that with gun belts and such?"

"Hon," Camille said, taking her husband's hand. "They have Ronnie Garcia."

Jacques stood while both women collapsed back on the couch. Camille explained everything with a gush of emotion.

"*Oo ye yi*," Jacques said under his breath when she was finished. "You girls did good." He shook his head and shot a glance toward the TV room. "The little boogs are gonna need some therapy, but I'm so proud of you." He looked at his watch. "Y'all can go ahead and stand down."

"What are you going to do about Ronnie?" Kim asked.

"Well," he said, "I'm working on a plan and it involves our little cupcake in there."

"I'm not going to like it, am I?" Camille said.

"Probably not, Boo," Thibodaux said, tipping his head toward Benavides, "but he's not gonna think too much of it either."

Fifteen minutes later, Thibodaux stood in the living room holding the handle to a large black rolling duffel that contained all his scuba gear. He kept everything in the bedroom except for the tank, to keep his boys from boogering up the sensitive gauges and regulators.

Joey B slouched beside him, head down, dressed in a pair of sweats and a T-shirt. The women had cut away his clothing looking for weapons, and they were the only things Jacques had that would fit him.

Camille looked up with terrified eyes when she saw that Benavides was no longer restrained.

Jacques held up his big hand to calm her. "Don't worry, Cornmeal. He knows I'm lookin' for a reason to put a boot in his ass." He smacked Joey on the back of the head. "Go ahead," he said. "Say what we talked about."

"I'm sorry," Benavides whispered. "I apologize for making you stab me in the hand."

Thibodaux raised the brow over his good eye. "And?"

"And for making you knock me out with a jar of pole beans."

Jacques kissed his wife good-bye and gave Kim a hug because that's the way he did business. He told her Jericho was fine the last he saw him—though that wasn't really true since he'd just been stabbed with a poison pellet and was being held prisoner in a Chinese hospital. He figured Kim was too fragile to hear the piddly details.

"That feels better," Benavides sniffed as he walked through the garage and opened the passenger door to get into his Audi sedan. "Apologizing—making amends—that's the first step, right?"

Jacques froze in his tracks, a half step behind the greasy IDTF agent. "I wanna ask you something," the big Cajun said. "What was it you intended to do to my bride after you drugged her?"

Benavides hung his head. "Look," he said. "I'm really, really sorry. I swear. I'll resign from the Task Force."

Thibodaux shook his head. "Not 'til you help me get my friend back."

"I just can't." Benavides began to blubber again. "I can't go out to the boat. Mr. Walter gets back tonight."

"Look at me, cupcake." Thibodaux snapped his fingers. "You come to my house thinking to drug and do Lord knows what to my wife. Helping me get Garcia back is your only chance to save your worthless ass—and it's a slim one even then."

Thibodaux's cell phone buzzed in his vest pocket. He held up his hand to silence the blubbering IDTF agent. He spoke for a moment before hanging up and returning the phone to his pocket.

"That was my badass Japanese friend." He smiled. "She's meeting us in Salisbury. I think you're gonna really like her. She's a buck-twenty soaking wet but seventy-five pounds of that is balls. . . ."

The phone rang again almost as soon as he put it away. A wave of relief flooded over Thibodaux as he heard Quinn's voice on the other end of the line. Quinn

filled him in quickly on the trip out of China, a weapon
called the Black Dragon, and the need to get to Seattle.

"We won't be able to get there for another nineteen-
plus hours," Quinn said on the other end of the line. "I
could use some eyes and ears ahead of us—and I need
the blue go-bag I keep stashed in the hotel."

"I hear you, *l'ami*," Jacques said, "but we've kinda
got us a little situation here." He motioned for Joey B
to start the car and begin driving. The "I'll-shoot-you-
in-the-ass-if-you-try-anything," was implied with the
glare from his good eye.

"Your signal's cutting in and out," Quinn said, his
voice crackling with static. "I can barely hear you. Can
you get someone to ship me the duffel by Gold Streak
if you're not able to bring it out? I've tried to call the
others, but I'm not getting through to anyone."

"I said we've got a situation," Thibodaux said again,
louder this time. He filled Quinn in, doing his best to assure him they'd get Ronnie back—though both of them
had seen enough friends die to know some rescues went
well and others devolved into catastrophic shitstorms
of death. He smacked Joey B on the back of the head
when he hung up, for no reason but to keep him on his
toes.

Chapter 40

Near Bloodsworth Island

Ronnie felt like she'd been in the cage for days. Fear, pain, the glaring white light, and the constant thrum of the boat's auxiliary engine kept her from getting anything but fragments of nightmare-filled sleep. She busied her mind working through every method of escape she could think of. "Look broken but stay strong," became her mantra—to make her captors think they had beaten her.

"You can do this, *chica*," she sniffed, dragging herself out of the pity party she'd been having and working to channel a healthy dose of inner fury. She lay on her back, studying a tubular steel bar that was suspended from a pulley on the ceiling. Handcuffs were affixed to either end of the bar with strong U bolts. She followed a heavy cable from the center of the bar, over the pulley, then back down to an electric winch on the far bulkhead. A dozen different scenarios and possible uses for the awful thing ran through her mind, but she shoved them away, trying to focus on the immediate situation.

She'd been over every inch of her cage, noting the wire ties and brackets that held the six panels together. When she was a little girl, her father had a small hunting dog he kept in a kennel much like the one where Ronnie found herself now. The dog hated the kennel and eventually, when left to its own devices for long enough, figured out the weak spots in the chain link and gnawed and pulled and tugged until it escaped.

The cameras located at each corner of the room made it difficult to work overtly on any portion of the cage, but Ronnie found that by rocking back and forth and periodically twisting her hair like she'd lost her mind, she could cover her movements and work one of the metal wire door ties back and forth without any of her guards rushing in to check on her escape attempt. She imagined them slouching in front of a bunch of fuzzy monitors while they whiled away the hours surfing porn. The fact that they were working for the IDTF identified them as less than the cream of the crop from any of their respective heritage agencies.

The squeak of the metal hatch sent Ronnie cringing to the back corner of her cage, as far away from the door as she could get. The redheaded *GQ* and the older one, whom she'd learned was named Gant, stooped to come in and swung the hatch shut behind them. Each carried the cattle prod they used to "soften her up" prior to letting her out to go to the bathroom—which was nothing but a filthy five-gallon bucket next to the V formed by the bow of the boat.

Both men attacked their duties with gusto, laughing and cursing as they applied the metal probes through the wire mesh of her cage. Once she'd writhed and screamed for what seemed like hours, beaten down to their satisfaction, Gant unlocked one side of the gate and dropped in a set of handcuffs.

"Mr. Walter is on his way," *GQ* said, giving Ronnie a crackling jolt to the rump as she hustled by on her way to the bucket. "These little shock sticks will be a pleasant memory compared to the shit he does."

The men leered and giggled like idiots while Ronnie did her business in the bucket. She walked back with her head higher when she was finished, holding the cuffs up for one of them to remove.

"Nope," Gant said. "Not until you're back inside."

Ronnie groaned but complied, bending to climb back in the cage and bracing herself for the swift kick that Gant always gave her. For some reason, he seemed to have it in for her worse than *GQ*. The younger agent held the cattle prod under his arm and squatted to take off her handcuffs as she held her wrists out through the half open door. Ronnie gave him a sidelong glare and silently whispered, "Watermelon," once she caught his eye.

It meant nothing. Ronnie's father had taught her to mouth "watermelon" over and over when she didn't know the words to a song. Several boys in college had thought she was flirting with them. There was something, they said, about the way her tongue flicked across her teeth when she said it. It worked on *GQ* as well, because he did a double take and looked like he was having a hard time swallowing when he locked the cage. She guessed he would come back as soon as he got rid of Gant.

Twisting her hair with one hand as soon as the hatch squeaked shut, she used it to form a curtain to block her work on the metal hinge tie from the view of the cameras. She bent it back and forth until her fingers bled.

* * *

Thankfully, it took nearly two hours for *GQ* to re-turn, and by that time, Ronnie had worked the metal enough that she felt sure it would snap if given the right amount of pressure.

He wasted no time, getting straight to the point. "What was it you said to me before?"

"I have to go to the bathroom again," Ronnie said, tongue to her top teeth as if she was saying "water-melon" again.

"Nice try." He sneered. "You had your chance. If you need to go, do it in there."

Ronnie bowed her head, avoiding eye contact for fear her true emotions would bubble over and she'd scare him off. She'd purposely ripped the top of her scrubs a good foot down the center during her last bout against the cattle prods and she breathed deeply for ef-fect. The sight of her heaving chest should cloud the kid's mind. "Mr. Walter isn't going to want me all filthy," she said. "Come on. Please?"

"You know this is going to cost you?" *GQ* fished in his pocket for the key.

"Maybe you should go get that other guy," she said, retreating a little from his hungry gaze.

"We'll be fine," he said, his voice thick and gravelly. "Just you and me."

"What about the cameras?"

"Forget the cameras," he said. "I'm the one watching them. There's nobody there to bug us. Now put these on." Like he'd done each time before, *GQ* unlocked one side of the door and opened it just wide enough to drop in the handcuffs.

Garcia planted both feet against the other end of the door and kicked as hard as she could the moment the cuffs hit her hands. It took her two tries but the entire door fell away, slamming into *GQ*'s legs at mid-shin.

She scrambled out of the cage, using the handcuffs like a pair of brass knuckles and swinging with deadly accuracy at the kid's jawbone. Stunned, he pedaled backwards, blinking in dismay. Ronnie followed up with a low tackle, driving him backwards and taking him to the floor. His head slammed against a vent pipe with a satisfying thud, but he was still moving and far from finished.

A cold rush of adrenaline—and the sure knowledge that she was fighting for her life—kept Garcia moving with a burst of renewed energy. But adrenaline could only do so much, and she realized as soon as *GQ* began to fight back that she had very little in the way of reserves. She had to finish this quickly.

Falling face-first into *GQ*'s chest, Ronnie made a grab for the Scorn tucked into his belt. Her hand brushed the grip as he bucked his hips, rolling her onto her back and reversing their positions before she even knew what was happening. Her hands were trapped between them, low but unable to get to the Scorn and too far from his face to claw his eyes out. She tried to post a foot and throw him, tried to use the momentum of his movements against him, taking advantage of the power in her legs, but nothing worked.

"Just relax, babe," he said, chest pressed to hers, panting in her ear. She could smell the cheese crackers on his breath. "It might even be fun if you'd quit jumping around."

Garcia turned her head so she didn't have to look at him. She's been too slow to keep him from getting his hooks in—latching his feet around her lower legs and allowing him to rest the weight of his entire body low on her belly while still keeping his hands free. He planted a palm on the metal floor, slamming his right fist into her jaw. A shower of sparks exploded inside her head, but to her surprise she didn't pass out. *GQ* was mean, but he wasn't particularly good at hitting.

Momentarily rejuvenated by the realization that she was still alive, Ronnie put all her energy into bucking her hips, throwing *GQ* just high enough so she could work her hand down to his crotch. Miyagi called it "squeezing the kiwis." Ronnie decided it would be more productive to twist and pull. *GQ*'s eyes flew wide. A curdled growl spilled from his lips as he hit her again, pressing down to stop the squeezing.

"You fight like a girl," he groaned, laughing through a twisted grimace as the pain of her attack began to ebb. "Girls always go for the nuts. . . ."

Garcia smiled. She'd given his kiwis a good enough squeeze he hadn't felt it when her other hand moved to the Snake Slayer. She'd already pulled it from his waistband and cocked it before *GQ* realized she wasn't still trying to tear off his balls.

"I guess you're right," she whispered as she pulled the trigger, sending four rounds of .36 caliber buckshot ripping through his belly, destroying his diaphragm and turning his right lung into Swiss cheese. "I do fight like a girl."

She'd shoved the little derringer directly into *GQ*'s flesh under the point of his breastbone when she pulled the trigger. His organs absorbed the lion's share of the report, expanding gas and burning gunpowder doing nearly as much damage as the buckshot.

GQ gurgled, pushing himself away as if Garcia was on fire, backpedaling to get distance from whatever had bitten him. His mouth hung open and he looked down at the blossom of blood forming on his shirt. Ronnie pressed her advantage as he gathered himself up to scream for help, driving him backwards with a hard smack to the temple with the heavy barrel of the

Snake Slayer. She could have shot him again, but wanted to save the second round for whoever was on the other side of the door.

Fearful he had the cattle prod or some other weapon in a back pocket, Ronnie slapped away his pitiful attempts to fend her off. She fell against him and grabbed the Scorn with her left hand. The hawklike blade cleared the Kydex sheath with a welcome *snick*. In the same fluid movement, she drew the knife across the inside of *GQ*'s thighs, slashing viciously with all the speed and violence she could muster. Clothing, flesh, and arteries zipped and tore before the razor-sharp blade. With both femoral arteries cut and half a lung gone, *GQ* struggled for only a moment in a rapidly growing pool of his own blood before blinking his vaporous eyes for the last time.

Ronnie rolled gasping onto her side, Scorn in one hand, Snake Slayer in the other, blinking up at the bright light above her. Even the suspended metal bar was not quite as terrifying now that she was free of her cage.

Taking a brief moment to catch her breath, she moved to the hatch, bouncing up and down on her feet to regain movement and circulation after the endless hours of confinement. She had no idea what or who was on the other side, or if they'd heard the gunshot or *GQ*'s dying cries. What she did know was that she was going to get off this boat, even if she only had a little hawkbill blade and single shot in her pistol.

Chapter 41

Joey B let loose a flurry of curses, jumping sideways in the darkness as some kind of snake slithered out from under the beached skiff and disappeared into the heavy undergrowth along the muddy bank. Thibodaux took the opportunity to smack him on the back of the head on general principles.

"Couyon!" the big Cajun hissed. "Calm your ass down!" He zipped up the diagonal closure of his black dry suit and shrugged on a "wing" type buoyancy compensator and small tank.

Emiko Miyagi moved fluidly around the skiff, stowing her short sword along the gunnel within easy reach of where she would be sitting. Joey swallowed hard as he eyed the glinting two-foot blade.

"Scary shit, huh, Cupcake," Thibodaux said. "A gun don't necessarily do it for some people." He tipped his head toward Miyagi and her sword. "She likes to be more hands on when she works."

Thibodaux adjusted the straps of his harness over a separate gun belt and thigh holster so he could dump the dive gear when the time came without interfering with the rig. He carried a Glock 19 with a Gemtech suppressor in the holster. With subsonic 9mm ammo, the weapon would make little more noise than a good handclap. A short-barreled H&K MP10 was on a breakaway harness across his chest. Also suppressed, the rifle would be sure to announce his position if he had to use the weapon.

Miyagi was also armed with a Glock 19, as well as the short sword that she preferred to any firearm. She also carried a small dagger in her sleeve that he'd seen her use with amazing effectiveness.

Chest still heaving like he was about to burst out in tears, Joey B spun the combinations on two heavy-duty padlocks, and reached under the lip of the gunnel back near the transom and flipped a kill switch in the fuel line, meant to discourage theft of the boats since they were left along the shore. The bow scraped against gravel as Jacques helped him shove the aluminum skiff out into the water.

"Um . . . ma'am." Joey cleared his throat, holding a piece of black cloth out toward Miyagi as if she might bite him. "You'll have to wear the bag over your head for this to work. There's a gap in it so you can see."

Miyagi grabbed the bag from his hand and tossed it in the boat next to her seat without a word.

Thibodaux peered into the darkness through a set of IR binoculars, watching another skiff come up alongside the prison boat. "Your boss just got there," he said, his voice buzzing into his hands as they held the binoculars. "He's getting onboard now."

"Look," Joey B said, wobbling on his legs, clutching the side of the boat to keep from keeling over in the mud. "I . . . I really can't go out there."

"You ever seen a man gutted, Cupcake?" Thibodaux asked, moving in close so there would be no misunderstanding.

Benavides gulped loudly enough that Thibodaux was sure they heard it clear out on the boat.

"Well, let me tell you," the Marine continued. "I have and it ain't pretty. Depending on how the belly is cut, the guts, they just come poppin' on out. No way to hold 'em in really . . . try as you may."

"Why are you telling me this?" Benavides began to hyperventilate.

"Think about it," Thibodaux hissed, slinging spit in the other man's face as he talked. "I come within an inch of shooting you in the eye every time I think about what you were going to do to my wife. There is literally one thing keeping me from opening you up right damn now, and that is you getting us out to that boat. So you want to see your own entrails today?" He paused for effect. "No? Then get your ass in the boat. But I gotta warn you, Ms. Miyagi ain't as nice as I am."

Joey climbed into the skiff. "My life is shit," he sobbed.

"Yes, it is," Thibodaux said, sloshing in beside the boat and pushing it out into deeper water. "And it ain't likely to get better if you don't quit with the boohoos."

Once Joey was settled in next to the tiller with Miyagi, Thibodaux slipped on a pair of black jet fins to help steer his body as the boat towed him along low in the water and out of sight. The spring-steel heels on the fins fit easily over the rock boots he wore with his dry suit and would be easy to ditch along with the tank and harness once they got to the prison boat.

The water pressure increased against the thin laminated suit as they moved out over his head, pinching him in several unmentionable places. He touched the valve on his chest to jet a layer of air from his tank into the suit, relieving the pressure. It had been so long, he had forgotten that diving could be a cup sport.

"*Baka yaro!*" Miyagi said in sharp, dismissive Japanese, speaking to Benavides for the first time since they'd linked up in Salisbury: Fool! "You drive this boat slow and steady. If you lose my friend, your intestines will be the least of your worries."

Thibodaux couldn't help but shudder—but he was sure happy to have this little woman along. Wrapping a short piece of webbing around his wrist, he looked up at Miyagi.

"*Laissez les bon temps roulet!*" he said, before slipping the regulator in his mouth and giving her a thumbs-up.

Let the good times roll.

Chapter 42

The heavy steel hatch flew open the moment Ronnie turned the handle, knocking her backwards and sending her sliding across the metal floor on her butt. She tried to bring the Snake Slayer to bear on the dark form of a man, but the hard leads of a cattle prod impacted squarely in the center of her throat. The Snake Slayer skittered across the grating, useless and out of reach. She looked up to see Glen Walter's smirking face as he loomed over her.

Boots stomped and clanged, sounding hollow in the small metal room. Focused intently on Walter and the blue arcs of electricity coming from the end of the cattle prod, Garcia was vaguely aware of other men climbing through the hatch.

Walter said something in an odd, disembodied voice. It sounded as if he was speaking in slow motion as he pressed the prod to her neck, driving her head backwards so it slammed against the floor. Someone kicked her hard in the ribs, stunning her heart and saving her from the pain of the crackling voltage as darkness closed in around her.

* * *

The effect of the heart shot was only momentary and
Garcia came to with a gasp in a jerky panic. Another bag
had been placed over her head. Cold metal cut into her
wrists. The electric winch whined in the corner. The
cable clicked and twanged as it drew the restraint bar
up toward the ceiling, stretching her arms high over her
head until only the balls of her bare feet touched the
floor. Another shock came out of nowhere. She writhed
sideways, nearly wrenching her shoulders from their
sockets.

Screaming inside the hood until she could no longer
breathe, she let her head loll forward, panting. The
weight of her spent body hung against her wrists.

"Do you ever hunt, Ms. Garcia?" Walter's syrupy
voice buzzed next to her ear through the heavy hood.

"I . . . wh . . . I . . ." she gasped. "What?"

"Do you hunt?" Agent Walter said again.

"Hunt?" she said, trying to catch her breath.

"It doesn't matter," Walter said. "But if you had ever
field dressed an animal, you would know that the
shoulder is a unique joint."

Blind inside the hood, Garcia recoiled as he ran his
fingers along the shoulder of her scrubs.

"A little change in angle," he continued. "A half an
inch more lift—and you'll never be able to lift your
arms again. Do you understand?"

"Understand?" Garcia spat, her voice muffled inside
the hood. "I understand that you are beating the shit
out of me for no reason."

"I only point it out about your shoulder," Agent Walter said, "so you remember not to jerk too much during
the procedure—"

"What procedure?" Ronnie could hear her heart in her ears. "What are you talking about?"

"No one told you?" Walter chuckled.

Garcia heard the scrape of boots against the floor and braced herself for another round of shocks from the cattle prod. The next sound nearly caused her to pass out—the slosh of water in a bucket.

Without warning someone grabbed the back of the cloth hood, catching her hair and yanking her head back and downward so she faced the ceiling. Suspended from the metal crossbar by both hands and standing on tiptoe there was nothing she could do to fight it.

She heard Walter say, "Go," an instant before water began to splash against the cloth stretched over her face. She tried to draw in air, but the large weave of the bag made her get nothing but water. She'd seen this done before. All they needed was a thin stream. A trained professional could make a bucket last far longer than a person's lungs could hold out. Ronnie coughed and spit and croaked for air, forgetting the pain in her shoulders or even where she was.

And then it was over. The water stopped and the unseen hand released her head, letting her fall forward to gain enough of a gap in the hood so she could suck in great, wheezing gasps. She gagged as much as she breathed, heaving, fighting the urge to vomit inside the bag—but at least she had air.

An instant later the bag was snatched away, causing her to recoil at the sudden brightness. She squinted at Agent Walter, who stood in front of her with a smug grin.

He touched her with the cattle prod, caressing her chest, but did not shock her this time.

Ronnie let her head roll back and forth, a line of

bloody drool trailing from her chin. "What do you want from me?"

"The administration wants Winfield Palmer," he said. "And the traitor Virginia Ross."

"I can't figure it out," Ronnie said, her words slurred as if she'd been on a three-day drunk. "Do you even know who Drake and McKeon are?" She watched his face for any sort of reaction.

"Please," Walter chuckled. "You'll have to do better than some Internet conspiracy theory."

"I got proof, *mijo*." Ronnie sighed, tired of ducking questions, exhausted from the games. "These guys want us in a shooting war."

Agent Walter brushed a flap of hair out of his eyes and patted the cattle prod against his open hand, smiling.

"You don't give a shit, do you?" Ronnie said, genuinely surprised. She'd thought Agent Walter to be a more integral part of the plan, but something was off about the look in his eyes—a telltale glint as if he was processing some new information. "You're not a mole, you're just a pathetic thug, a sadist with a government sponsor."

"I guess none of that really matters right now, sweetheart." He waved the prod in front of her face, brushing her lips with the metal probes. "Tell me where Palmer is and maybe we can be more . . . civilized—"

"Glen Walters"—Ronnie gave a derisive laugh, spitting a clot of blood on the floor—"civilized!"

"The name is *Walter*!" the man snapped, leaning in to make his point. "No 's.'"

Ronnie lunged forward as far as the cable would let her, head butting him in the nose. Blood gushed from his nose as he reacted by grabbing her by both shoulders and kneeing her savagely in the groin. Screaming in pain, she slumped against the chains, putting all her weight on her shoulders, nearly passing out from the sickening shock of the blow.

Walter ripped a handkerchief from his pocket and dabbed at his nose. His chest heaved in anger. "I'm going to break you in two, sweetheart," he said.

Ronnie raised her head, blood and spittle drooling from cracked lips. The intense pain welling up in her groin brought on a new clarity, an odd peace of mind at what she knew she had to do. Her words sputtered out in a mix of sobs and maniacal giggles. "Why . . . why . . . you mad at me? 'Cause I hurt your nose or 'cause I forgot the 's'?" She let her head loll again, mimicking his Southern accent with a hint of Forrest Gump. "The name is Walter!" Her laugh turned to scorn. "No shit . . ."

"Ronnie, Ronnie, Ronnie," Walter said, obviously working to stay calm as he dabbed at his bloody nose. "Everyone who could help you is either on a different continent or hiding to save their own skin. You have no idea of the things I'm capable—"

"*Maldita sea!*" Ronnie's head jerked up so quickly that it caused Walter to take a half step back. "You gonna talk me to death? Go ahead and do what you gotta do."

Chapter 43

Thibodaux let his body glide in the wake of the skiff as Benavides turned wide to come up alongside the prison boat, a looming shadow in the black water.

A halogen light turned on at their approach, illuminating Joey Benavides and a slouching Emiko Miyagi, who wore the cutout hood and held her hands together behind her back as if she was restrained. In truth, she held the short sword vertically under a light jacket to keep it out of sight. With the scuba regulator in his mouth, Thibodaux was able to stay low on the shadowed side of the skiff, with just his mask and the top of his head above the surface.

Two men, each wearing uniform navy blue polos and khaki slacks, waved up the new arrival, their grins visible in the light as they saw it was a female prisoner. Both had short weapons Jacques thought were H&K UMPs, but he couldn't be sure from his vantage point.

"Who's this?" One of the men said, throwing Joey a line.

"Miyagi," Joey said. "She's wanted as part of all that shit with Winfield Palmer."

"Good catch." The other man whistled under his breath. "Maybe this will calm down the boss. He was in a pissy mood when he got here and then that Cuban bitch killed Stig." He snapped his fingers at Miyagi, ordering her to stand up.

"I . . . I am afraid I'll fall," she said, shuffling her feet. Jacques swam under the skiff, waiting just beneath the boarding steps.

"Clumsy bitch," the man nearest the skiff mumbled, reaching to grab a handful of Miyagi's shirt. Lurking in the shadows at the rear of the skiff, Thibodaux watched as the man dragged her aboard, assisted by the second guard. Neither of them checked her handcuffs, but Thibodaux knew that only postponed their deaths until they were past the cameras that covered the boarding ladder. Joey Benavides was all knees and elbows as he followed Miyagi up on deck—his face stricken with fear. He looked like he might topple overboard at any moment.

Once he knew Miyagi had everything well in hand, Thibodaux ducked beneath the surface and swam through the dark water to the aft swim-step where he would have a clear line of fire to the agent standing night guard up on the top deck. Bracing his elbows on the edge of the step, he tilted the barrel to let any water drain, then aimed at the orange glow of the cigarette where it illuminated the guard's sweating face. He fired once, watching the man sway for a moment before slumping forward to disappear behind the metal railing. Far from Hollywood-quiet, subsonic ammo and a heavier recoil spring would render the suppressed Glock's single report little more than a question mark to anyone who happened to be listening out on deck. The thud of the guard falling above was likely to raise more suspicion.

Less than half a minute from the time Miyagi stepped

aboard, Thibodaux returned the Glock to the holster. Still in water, he shrugged off the dive gear and clipped it to a cleat on the rear corner of the step, leaving it accessible in the event he and Miyagi needed to make a wet exit in a hurry.

The dry suit didn't absorb water like neoprene so he was able to move quickly once he'd pressed himself up on the fantail. He left the Glock holstered, relying on the MP 10 now that he was aboard. The suppressor on the H&K was really more to protect his hearing than silence the weapon. Harsh experience had taught him that the adrenaline-pumping environment of close-quarters battle made it all too easy for someone to assume they hadn't been shot if they didn't hear a loud bang—even with three or four slugs in the belly. Oh, they would go down eventually, but a man could stir up a lot of mayhem before he realized he was actually dead.

Miyagi met Thibodaux as he rounded the corner of the main house, padding up the narrow companionway past the boarding gate to the main entrance to the vessel. He had to step over the body of a very dead Joey Benavides.

He looked up at Miyagi.

"He lost his nerve the moment the door opened," she whispered. "As I knew he would."

Thibodaux wasted no more thoughts on the sleazy turd, following the little Japanese woman in through the open door.

Boats, even relatively small vessels in the seventy-foot range like this one, made acceptable black site prisons because they could be moved. They were basically surrounded by their own moat, making them difficult to approach. The disadvantage was lack of space, with no room for the two-door mantrap-style entries of a conventional prison facility. On a prison boat, there might be a camera on the main door and a guard behind it, but once inside, you were right on top of him. Miyagi had taken care of the inside man, the guards who had greeted her, and Benavides the moment the door had opened.

According to Benavides, they were holding Garcia belowdecks, forward, where Agent Walter liked to do his work. There were supposed to be other prisoners as well, behind the engine room in tiny cells that ran on either side of the boat all the way aft. Senator Gorski would be there if she was still alive.

Miyagi led with her blade, moving silently. Thibodaux brought up the rear, ready to employ the H&K when it became necessary. A circular staircase ran downward to their right, disappearing into darkness. It would lead to the cells Benavides told them about. A wooden bulkhead obscured the view to their left, toward the bow of the boat. Thibodaux could hear voices, laughing about something. It soon became evident they were playing some kind of card game.

Miyagi inched sideways, cutting the pie until she could get a visual on what was around the corner. She ducked back and held up three fingers—letting Jacques know there were three guards. The knocking thrum of the auxiliary engine, along with their own conversation, left the guards unable to hear their compatriots fall less than twenty feet away.

Miyagi let the blade of her short sword trail behind her, as if she was dragging it along. Thibodaux had watched her do such a thing many times, just before she attacked.

Chapter 44

Garcia's head felt like it was filled with burning coals. Every joint in her body was stretched, ready to snap. She was certain something in her wrist had already broken. Walter grabbed the back of her hair, yanking her head to keep her from head-butting him again. His arm pressed against her shoulder, driving downward and putting unbearable pressure on it.

"Virginia Ross," he whispered into her ear, his face close enough she could smell the onions from his dinner. "Point me to her."

The pain in her shoulder was so great Garcia could barely comprehend the question. Any words she could have mustered were covered in panting sobs.

Walter eased up a hair, bringing a measure of relief.

"You know," he said, "I took it easy on her because of her office. You don't have that luxury." He reached into his pocket with his free hand and drew out a small insulin syringe. "So I guess we find ourselves at a crossroads. Will you be the traitor who gives up her fellow conspirators and spends the rest of her days in prison, or will the authorities find the shell of your once beautiful body, scarred and abused by the men who supplied you with drugs?"

"You sadistic bastard!" Ronnie spat. She screamed when Walter bore down again with his arm, grinding her teeth until she thought they might shatter.

He thumbed the flesh of her neck with the hand that held the syringe. "Have you ever heard of Krokodil?"

Ronnie felt her knees give out at the word. Named for the scaly skin of its users, Krokodil was nasty stuff. It had been developed as a cheap heroin substitute in Russia, where codeine was available over the counter. It might contain hydrochloric acid, red phosphorous, lighter fluid, and even gasoline. As addictive as meth, depending on the batch, it had a tendency to eat away flesh at the injection site, exposing bone.

Walter laughed in her ear. "You'll still be sexy for a day or two," he said. "Long enough for my purposes. But I have quite a supply of this stuff. It won't be long before I'm tired of you. You'll be so nasty by then even Joey B won't want you—and that's saying something."

Ronnie rolled her eyes sideways to stare at the needle. Palmer and the others would already be moving, but she knew too much that could hurt them. She had to do something to make Walter angry enough to kill her before she talked.

Chapter 45

Counting Joey Benavides, there were nine bodies on the boat by the time Thibodaux and Miyagi made it to the hatch outside where Ronnie was being held. But for the guard on the top deck, Miyagi had taken care of all of them with her sword. Thibodaux, a man who had taken many lives himself since joining the Marine Corps was still amazed by the deadly, machinelike grace this woman displayed in battle.

They'd seen Garcia on the monitor and knew she was alone behind the hatch with Agent Walter. The image was fuzzy and they couldn't be sure what he had in his hand, but it looked like a knife. Whatever he held, Walter was still oblivious to the fact that he had no more friends on his boat.

Miyagi shoved open the hatch, allowing Thibodaux in first with his weapon since silence was no longer an issue. Walter stood with his back to the hatch. Garcia was directly behind him, arms above her head, attached to a four-foot metal bar. There was too big a chance that the 10mm bullets would rip through Walter's body and hit her for Thibodaux to shoot. Stepping forward enough to let Miyagi in behind him, he dropped to one knee and raised the muzzle of the H&K upward, releasing a burst of a half-dozen rounds at the pulley that held the handcuff bar suspended.

Ronnie rolled her eyes upward at the creak of the opening hatch, vaguely wondering which of the guards had come to watch the show. Through the mental haze of her torture, she saw a familiar eye patch—but out of context, she couldn't place it. When Emiko Miyagi flowed in next like the unstoppable force that she was, Ronnie felt her heart begin to race. Adrenaline flooded her limbs. Reanimated, her head snapped up and she spat a mixture of blood and bile into Agent Walter's eyes. She didn't care if he hit her again, as long as his attention was toward her and not the hatch.

She could see Thibodaux over Walter's shoulder and watched him take a knee as he aimed the H&K. Gunfire rattled the room. Brass clattered against the metal deck. The cable above her head gave a loud twang as it parted under the barrage of lead.

Ronnie collapsed on top of Walter as he fell backwards, bashing him in the face again and again with the bar. The first blow separated his nose at the bridge, peeling it downward so hung more off than on. Subsequent blows broke several teeth. Screaming in a voice an octave higher than before, he tried to throw her off, but Miyagi pinned him to the deck with an extremely painful but non-life-threatening sword through his shoulder above the collarbone. Jacques stood on the opposite hand while he bent to release Ronnie from the cuffs.

Ronnie screamed through the pain in her shoulders as she snatched up the fallen syringe and held it above

Walter's eye. Her hand shook. Her chest heaved. Every fiber of her body wanted to kill him and be done with it.

"Tell us what you know about Drake and McKeon," she said, a line of spittle dangling from her lips as she looked down at this man who'd been about to rape and murder her. Fury alone helped her keep a grip on the syringe.

Walter shook his head. He opened his mouth to speak, but no words came out.

"Who's running them?" She pressed the tip of the needle against his eyelid with a trembling hand, bringing a flood of tears. "What's their endgame?"

"McKeon hates the President," Walter all but shrieked. He panted, regaining a measure of his composure. "They're not working on anything together. I can swear to that."

Thibodaux stomped on the man's wrist. "*Cochons!*" he spat. "Quit tellin' us what they ain't doing."

"Okay, Okay . . ." Walter nodded quickly, catching his breath. "I know McKeon and his wife are running the show."

"You mean the Japanese girl?" Miyagi ground her blade back and forth in the wound to get his attention.

Walter clenched his eyes at the new wave of pain. "The scary tatted one?" He shook her head. "No. You'd think he was with her as much as she's with him, but he and his wife . . . they have some seriously long talks."

"And you know this how?" Thibodaux asked, raising the brow on his good eye.

"He thinks his burner phone is secret." Walter took a deep breath. "Knowing things, keeping tabs . . . it's what I do. Life insurance. You know?"

"So what's their plan?" Ronnie said. She was fading fast and was afraid she might pass out at any moment.

"I'm not up on the phone all the time," he said, blowing blood-bubbles out the wound in the bridge of his nose. "I just listen in . . . now and again. He talks to someone in Pakistan, I can tell you that much."

"You're going to have to tell us a lot more than that," Ronnie said.

"I will," Walter said. "I swear it. I'll tell us everything I know."

"Oh," Ronnie said, injecting the contents of the syringe into the man's neck. "I know you will."

She fell into Thibodaux's arms while Miyagi rolled the drug-addled Walter onto his belly and handcuffed him behind his back.

Ronnie felt her eyes sag. "Senator Gorski," she said, looking up at Jacques and forcing herself to stay focused. "Did you find her?"

Thibodaux nodded. "Monitors up top show several prisoners in cells on the lower deck. I'm pretty sure one of them is her." He looked hard at Ronnie. "What's that stuff you just gave him?"

"Krokodil," she said, regretting the hasty action. "I know I shouldn't have taken the risk."

"Hell, one dose won't kill him." Thibodaux helped her to her feet, nodding to the dead *GQ* in the corner. "That your doing?"

Garcia tried to stand, nearly passing out from the searing pain in her shoulders. The episode with *GQ* seemed ages ago. Out of habit, ingrained from months of training, she took a deep breath and stooped to find the Snake Slayer where it lay just inside the hatch.

"Looks to me like you went easy on Walter," Thibodaux said. He put a big hand on her shoulder. "You good to go, kiddo?"

Garcia flipped up the derringer's twin barrels, checking to see that it was still loaded with one shell before aiming it at Walter's belly for a moment of fantasy. "I'm walking off the boat with this piece of shit in chains." She prodded Walter with her bare foot to make sure he saw her with the pistol. "I am outstanding."

Chapter 46

The Feng brothers stood with Jiàn Zǒu under the eave of a small wooden shelter at the edge of the floating docks, waiting. Torn boat advertisements and commercial fishing notices were tacked to the plywood walls. Something that was not quite rain but a little more than mist drifted by on gray curtains under the feeble light. The smells of engine oil and low tide hung in cool air of the parking lot. The damp, combined with the darkness and an unknown future, sent a chill through Yaqub's spine that shook his entire body. He could make out the dark shapes of a dozen boats floating on an even blacker ocean fifty meters down a grated incline in the small harbor.

"Where is he?" Ehmet said, looking toward the water. He'd pulled the collar of a wool sweater up around his neck against the cool air.

Jiàn Zǒu nodded down the ramp. "There," he said.

A stocky man with long blond hair that stuck out like sheaves of wheat straw from a wool watch cap sauntered toward them. The coal of a stubby cigar illuminated a wide face and thick orange beard. High rubber boots squeaked and chattered on the metal grating. A pistol hung on a loose belt from baggy pants, as if he'd strapped it on as an afterthought.

The newcomer eyed the three men through the blossom of cigar smoke that surrounded his face, mixing with the mist. "I'm Gruber," he grunted, clenching the cigar in teeth that were as yellow as his hair. "I understand you need a ride under the radar."

"We do," Jiàn Zǒu said, extending his hand. "Half the money is in your account. I'll release the other half before we leave your vessel."

"Wait," Ehmet Feng said. "You do not know this man?"

Gruber raised a bushy eyebrow.

Jiàn Zǒu sighed. "Movement like this requires that we adapt." He nodded to the skipper. "My friend vouches for him."

"You are not even Chinese," Ehmet said.

"I'm a businessman," Gruber said. "And I got no love lost for the States. My great grandfather was moving cargo between Canada and the US over a century ago. If you wanna sneak a puny load of BC bud past the authorities, I'm not your guy. Something bigger . . . important enough to pay for . . . well, that's a different kettle of fish altogether. My family knows the location of inlets, caves, and hidey-holes that Canadian and US Customs have never even heard of—and that stuff don't come cheap." He puffed the cigar to life, then spoke without taking it out of his mouth. "But if you got other transportation, I got plenty to do. . . ."

Jiàn Zǒu cleared his throat. "No," he said. "We do need your services, and are more than happy to pay for them."

"That's nice." Gruber smiled. "I got three girlfriends scattered up and down the coast and they all seem to like the most expensive shit." He nodded down the ramp. "I'm ready when you are."

Ehmet raised his hand. "And how do you get past the authorities? I have studied the maps and charts. Even with your caves and secret routes, we must still eventually come into areas where US Customs boats do routine and random patrol."

"Studied the charts, have you?" Gruber gave Jiàn Zǒu a knowing smile.

"I have," Ehmet said, glaring.

"I hate it when customers study the charts. . . ." Gruber muttered before leaning back his head to blow a plume of smoke into the air. "You are right though," he said. "There's a hell of a lot of water out there, but the feds are getting smarter. Sometimes I swear it's like their patrol boats are running a blockade between the San Juan Islands and Anacortes. Some nights, the odds of getting through are less than fifty-fifty. They're all looking to stop the next vessel full of weed coming across the border or hoping to save the lives of a bunch of poor illegals crammed into a shipping container like cordwood. Every one of them is on the hunt for that big arrest that will make their career."

Yaqub's mouth hung open. He took a half step closer to his brother. "If the authorities are so numerous, then what do you plan to do?"

Gruber winked. The coal of his cigar brought an otherworldly glow to his face.

"Simple," he said. "We give them exactly what they want."

Chapter 47

Paris

Quinn turned on the phone Kevin Bursaw had given him the moment the plane touched down at de Gaulle. As rushed as he felt to reach Seattle, Quinn was grateful for the chance to finally get a sit-rep about Ronnie. He glanced at Song while he waited to get a signal. She'd passed out the moment they'd reached altitude leaving Zagreb, telling him flying on commercial aircraft were one of the few times she could relax. Quinn had scratched flying off his list of relaxing endeavors just a few months before. Still, he was exhausted as well, and fell into a semi-conscious doze for much of the three-hour flight, letting his subconscious work through his long list of unanswered questions.

He got the signal as the Croatia Air pilot turned the little turboprop down the taxiway and headed toward the gate where they would transfer to a British Airways flight direct to Seattle. They wouldn't leave the airport so they didn't have to clear French Immigration.

Jacques picked up on the second ring.

"L'ami," the big Cajun sighed, as if relieved to finally get the call. "We got her," he said. "She's whole."

Jericho let his head fall against the seatback. He closed his eyes, feeling his throat tighten at the news. He took a deep breath, working to regain his composure. "Thank you," he said, the catch noticeable in his throat. "Is she there?"

"She is," Thibodaux said. "But first things first . . . and this is where things get tricky. Your number-two buddy inside the Beltway . . ."

Quinn knew he meant Vice President McKeon. "Okay," he said.

"Looks like his wife is part of it too, and Number One ain't really in the loop, so to speak."

"Understood," Quinn said, running through the possible scenarios. "Can you get in touch with the boss?"

"He's gone dark," Thibodaux said. "But I've got Butterfly with me. She's taking us to his location as we speak. I'll get our girl all settled, then come runnin' your way."

Quinn ran down a thumbnail sketch of what he knew about the weapon, highlighting its size and destructive capabilities.

"Got it," Jacques said when he was finished. "I'll pass it up the food chain so they can get the big giant brains working on possible targets. Anything else?"

"Not that I can think of," Quinn said. "I'm sure we'll have more after we get there."

"That bein' the case," Thibodaux said. "I got somebody here who wants to talk to you."

Ronnie came on the phone a moment later, her voice breathless and frail, like she was sedated.

"Hey, Mango," she said. "You doin' okay?"

Quinn let his head fall backwards again. "I'm fine," he said. No words seemed adequate, no question quite right. "Are you okay?" he whispered.

There was a long pause, as if she needed to figure out how to answer. "I been better," she finally said. "But I'll mend. Sorry I got myself caught."

Quinn felt some of the tension in his neck begin to ease at the sound of her voice. There was so much more he wanted to say, but the phone didn't seem like the venue.

"I'll see you soon," he said at length, closing his eyes again and hoping it wasn't a lie.

Chapter 48

Ran Kimura squared her shoulders and cleared her mind, gently placing the black lacquered sheath on the carpet to her left, parallel to her body. Every movement with the katana, whether in practice or during the shedding of blood, she executed with reverence and perfection. She knelt in a position known as *kiza*, ignoring the Vice President, who was still in bed at the other end of the room. With the balls of her feet touching the floor and her toes flexed forward, Ran found *kiza* a much more active stance than formal *seiza* kneeling that put the tops of the feet down toward the floor and, to Ran's way of thinking, the kneeler in a much more subservient position. Subservient she was not. Meditation in *kiza* allowed her to focus while still maintaining the ability to rise and move quickly.

Both she and McKeon were early risers, often stirring by four a.m. But where she preferred to get out of bed quickly, falling into an established regimen of exercise and battle drill, he liked to linger in his pillows, checking e-mails and watching her. With his wife still attending to her social obligations in Oregon, they spent every night together. Once his wife returned, Ran intended to make certain the troublesome woman wasn't in the way for long.

Awake for over an hour now, McKeon had grown bored with the news on his phone and propped his pillow against the cherrywood headboard to get a better view. His tan arm trailed across her side of the bed. Long legs bent slightly, lifting the end of the tangled sheets to expose his feet. Though he was a heartbeat away from the Presidency—and arguably the most powerful man on earth—he knew enough to keep quiet while he watched.

Pink capris and a black sleeveless T-shirt accentuated powerful thighs and strong shoulders. She'd pinned up her hair, allowing a peek at the snarling *komainu* or "foo dog" that covered her back. The scoop neckline revealed the ropelike blacks and greens that that formed the borders of her tattoo. Known as a *munewari*, the ink had been applied traditionally, by hand with a repetitive stabbing from a bundle of ink-dipped needles tied to a bamboo stick with silk thread. Scenes of feudal Japan covered her chest and torso but left a five-inch gap of untouched skin down the centerline of her body, allowing her to wear clothing that blended in more easily with the rest of polite society.

She had wanted a full-body tattoo like her father—to prove that she too was capable of enduring the repetitive pain that often took over a decade to complete. Her father had suggested the gapped *munewari* and instructed the tattoo artist to stop the design at mid-thigh and shoulders, like shorts and capped sleeves. Of course, she had yielded to such a powerful being, but had still been able to prove her stoicism and endurance by undergoing *taubushi*—complete tattooing of the tender flesh of her underarms. The weekly process of an excruciatingly painful assault with a bundle of needles took two months to complete. Even during the long days in between visits, when her skin was so sore it would have left the toughest of men whimpering—she had not uttered a sound. Each time she raised her arms in battle, any opponent would know they were dealing with a woman who could endure unfathomable pain.

She'd been fourteen years old—and her father had commissioned a new sword because of her bravery.

Leaning forward with her hands flat on the carpet in front of her, she thought of her father. Her feelings were impossible to put into words. Reverence, veneration, fear, hate—any one of them would do, depending on the moment.

But whatever her feelings for the man, there were few wiser in the ways of battle. He had taught her that a gymnasium was unnecessary in her practice. Like him, she preferred movements that utilized her own body weight, building strength while retaining her ability to move quickly—for power in battle came when strength was combined with speed.

She was practical enough to remain proficient with a firearm, but preferred the sword for its fluid movement and the concentration required for its use. Each morning, before she picked up the blade, she spent five minutes dry-firing the small Smith and Wesson revolver that was rarely out of her reach. Push-ups, handstands, sit-ups, yoga poses all had merit and kept her sharp—and she did them all first, saving the blade work, her favorite, for last.

She picked up the katana by the lacquered scabbard in her left hand, then placed it flat on the carpet in front of her, handle facing to her right. Both hands on the carpet behind the blade, she bowed deeply, then picked up the sword and placed the scabbard along her hip, as if she meant to slide it in a belt.

Most practitioners of any art involving a Japanese sword dressed the part, wearing a robe-like judo *gi* and *hakama*, the flowing pantaloons of a medieval samurai. Her father had stressed the old way, requiring his disciples to dress in traditional clothing when on the grounds of his estate—in order to "keep their minds right." Ran found such a notion preposterous. She fought and killed in the real world—not some fantastical notion of the past. Her work was often presented to her when she was wearing a dress. Sometimes, when she had the opportunity to prepare, she wore nothing at all to keep from soiling her clothing in blood. A martial system that offered a convenient heavy-duty collar to grab or a long hem that hid the movement of the feet was more akin to a dance than a true martial way.

Ran's father had taught her many things, but she'd learned on her own that the art of killing required no costume, no tradition, merely a will to follow through.

Drawing energy from her center, Ran used the sword and scabbard as one, first pushing straight backwards, imagining an opponent behind her. She left the scabbard to the rear, drawing the blade in a fluid motion, listening for and feeling the familiar hiss as it leapt into the air. Slashing sideways with one hand, she let the scabbard fall to the floor as she stepped forward on her right foot, bringing the blade straight down the centerline with both hands. Rising, she spun to finish the imagined opponent behind her, then dropped in an instant back to one knee, letting the sword trail behind her and slightly to one side. It was a taunting technique and one of the few things she remembered about her mother's fighting style.

Death in a black T-shirt and pink capris.

McKeon's cell phone began to ring.

Ran considered cutting the thing in half. Distractions occurred during battle, so she followed through with her movements until she'd returned the katana to its sheath.

She resumed the *kiza* position, holding the katana at her side, breathing deeply to center her spirit as she listened to McKeon's side of the conversation.

From the corner of her eye she watched McKeon brighten at the call, as if it was good news. He returned a traditional Muslim greeting in English—". . . and peace be unto you . . ."—as he customarily did when the other party had given him an *"As-Salaamu."* He swung his long legs off the bed so he was facing away from Ran and kept his voice low. The call was over quickly and he shoved the sheets aside to walk naked to the bathroom. The smile on his face was visible in the mirror through the open door. It was the soft sort of smile he wore when he spoke to her in the shadows.

"Was it Ranjhani?" she asked.

McKeon half turned, dragged from some deep thought. The smile vanished from his lips. He nodded, the phone still in his hand as he walked. "Ranjhani," he repeated when a simple yes would have sufficed. "I wish I had time to watch the rest of your workout, my dear," he said, settling into his old self. "But there is a lot to finish before the trip this afternoon."

"Certainly," she said, her hand convulsing on the hilt of the sword, feeling the linen wraps, the roughness of the ray skin.

She knelt again, struggling to clear her mind. She listened for the hiss of the shower, the telltale metal scrape as McKeon slid the curtain open, then shut again after he'd stepped inside.

Peeling the T-shirt up over her head, Ran stepped out of the capris, one leg at a time so she wasn't hobbled—as her father had taught her—the samurai way so she minimized the time she was vulnerable to attack. She was not actually afraid that someone might jump her while she was changing clothes, but a state of awareness, she had been taught, must be practiced at all times and in all things.

She folded her clothes in a neat pile and set them on the foot of the bed. She placed her sword beside them, covered by the sheets, but where she could reach it quickly if the need arose. Naked and bathed in sweat from her workout, she stepped quietly into the bathroom as if to join McKeon in the shower. Steam rolled over the top of the curtain, fogging the mirror even with the door open, and muting the dark images of her tattoos.

McKeon's cell phone was beside the sink where he'd left it. Ran was stealthy if she was anything, accustomed to padding up behind her victims and slitting their throats before they even knew she was there. Gliding across the cool tile to grab the phone was child's play and she was back in the bedroom in a flash.

Ran had watched McKeon enter the code enough that it took her only two tries to unlock the phone. She checked the list of recent calls and didn't recognize the last number. The fact that there was a record at all was curious. She'd assumed Ranjhani was savvy enough to use a phone with no caller ID.

She closed her eyes, running through the possibilities. Then, with a complete disregard for strategy, she pushed the button to call back the last number.

It rang once before a woman came on the line.

"What's the matter?" the voice said, breathless and flirty. "You can't live without me for five minutes?"

Ran held the phone to her ear in complete silence.

She recognized the voice as Lee McKeon's wife—the woman Ran offered to kill at least twice a day. McKeon always had some excuse as to why they needed to let her live. It was curious that he'd lied about her phone call. They talked daily. Ran knew that. But he'd given her a traditional Muslim greeting of peace. She must have *"As Saalamed"* him—which was even more of a mystery.

Ran ended the call, turning down the volume so McKeon wouldn't hear it if the woman smelled something off and called him back immediately. When enough time went by, McKeon would just assume he'd accidentally redialed her on the way to the bathroom—if his wife even brought it up.

Ran had just set the phone back on the counter where McKeon had left it when he slid the shower curtain open and stuck his head out.

"Thought I heard you," he said. "I'd hoped you would come and join me."

"Of course." Ran forced a smile as she stepped in beside him. The lukewarm water made her feel like someone was spitting on her. She preferred her showers scalding hot, but she put up with tepid because that was what he liked.

"Here," he said, turning her gently so he could soap her back. She put her hands against the tile wall and braced her feet on the wet tub while he scrubbed. It had always felt good, and often led to them returning to the bed, but now . . . now even his washing felt like a lie.

"We leave shortly after lunch?" she said, knowing the times by heart, but trying to settle her nerves with idle conversation.

"Yes," McKeon said. "We'll be at the Fairmont." He kissed her neck, sending a flush of anger through her belly. "The Secret Service wanted him at the Four Seasons. Prime Minister Nabe will be at the Four Seasons as well, allowing them redundant security."

"There will be an end to this, you know?" she said, both palms still flat on the tile.

"Ah," he said, "but that end will only bring a new beginning. Drake actually believes he's going to ride this out—hiding in some secret bunker while China lobs missiles at the rest of the country." McKeon stood back and wiped the water from his face. "The idiot has no idea what his job entails. China will have no choice but to attack before the US retaliates for his assassination. Congress and the American people will easily see the need to leave the Middle East completely." McKeon resumed his nibbling, taking her earlobe in his teeth. "My guess is that it will all begin to happen before the end of the week."

He could not see it, but Ran's eyes were clenched tight. "You should allow me to kill your wife. I fear she will be a burden to you during the conflict."

"Not quite yet, my dear," McKeon said, too easily for Ran's taste. "When the time is right."

"And what of us then?" Ran said, her eyes still shut. "Are we to 'ride this out' in a secret bunker?"

He held her by both shoulders. "Do not worry about us, my love," he whispered. "All will work out as it must."

Ran shrugged him off, spinning, pressing her face to his chest. He was so much taller it would have been easy for someone to believe he was her superior. In many ways he was. She had never met anyone so intelligent, so driven. It would be all too easy to surrender and give herself to him completely. He gathered her up in his arms and drew her to him, the way he always did. Instead, she thought of seven different ways to kill him before he stepped out of the shower.

Chapter 49

Seattle, 3:55 AM

"She'll do thirty knots," Gruber grunted around a new cigar. He sat behind the wheel of the small Bayliner, his left leg stretched past a thick curtain that hung over the entry to a small cuddy cabin and V-berth in the bow. He'd told them he'd injured the leg in a shoot-out with the RCMP years before and it locked up on him sometimes. Thick smoke swirled in the dark cabin, combining with the ocean chop to make Yaqub feel as if he had swallowed a stone. He wished Gruber would just be quiet, but the man apparently believed it was his duty to explain every aspect of his movement—an odd thing for someone running an illegal operation.

"The trick," the smuggler continued, "is to look like tourists instead of outlaws. If the boat is too slick, too fast, CBP are certain to want to board you. A bunch of Pakis got arrested in BC a while back before they were even able to make the trip. They were buying maps, hanging around, and generally looking suspicious— that's what got them. Fools paid upwards of thirty-five grand each to get to the States and then got themselves picked up on the front porch. Damn shame too. They shouldn't have tried to move when all the agents were in town."

Ehmet slouched on the sofa behind the captain's seat. He spoke without opening his eyes. "What do you mean by that? 'All the agents in town'?"

"I keep tabs on who they send out on detail. I know the staffing pretty well."

"What is a detail?" Yaqub asked.

"The Mexican border is more newsworthy than this one," Jiàn Zǒu said. "It is not uncommon for authorities to take agents from their postings here and move them to the southern border for weeks at a time to augment their numbers."

"Cutting a foot off a board on one end and adding it to the other to make it longer," Ehmet scoffed. "How witless."

"Well," Gruber said around his cigar, "their witlessness is good for us. Around a third of the Anacortes office and a quarter of the Bellingham agents are on detail or out on vacation. We'll sacrifice a boatload of Malaysians and a duffel bag stuffed with BC bud." He tipped his head at Jiàn Zǒu. "Whoever you are, I guess you're important enough to absorb the loss of income from eighteen illegals and write off the arrest of the jockey and his helper. Anyhow, this will tie up every patrol boat in the vicinity while they try to get a piece of the action. Shame about losing that good weed though."

Yaqub took a sip of ginger ale to try to quiet his stomach. "How will the authorities know where to find the boat full of Malaysians?"

"That's the brilliant part." Gruber took out his cigar and waved it like a magic wand. "The CBP port director in Anacortes thinks he has one of my girlfriends on his payroll. The thing is, the government don't pay nearly as well as I do—and like I said, she craves the expensive shit. Anyway, she gives him the information I want him to have—which includes the tip on the Malaysian illegals and the weed. It's a big boat, so they'll turn this into a major operation, give it a fancy code name, and use their record of astounding investigative success to get more money from Congress—while we slip across the border in our little Bayliner fishing boat."

Just as Gruber predicted, there wasn't a patrol boat to be seen. He took them as far as Deception Pass at the north end of Whidbey Island, where two Chinese men in a skiff motored out to meet them.

"Big Uncle's men," Jiàn Zǒu said as the skiff pulled up alongside. It had stopped raining and the sun was just beginning to pink the eastern sky.

"You were going to release the remainder of the funds," Gruber said, spinning his captain's chair around so it faced toward them, away from the console.

"I will." Jiàn Zǒu nodded, reaching into his pocket.

"Nice and slow, now!" Gruber spat.

The curtain to the V-berth behind Gruber suddenly slid open, revealing a young blond woman with a shotgun pointed directly at Jiàn Zǒu's belly.

"Never fails," Gruber said. "This is always the tricky part." He held the cigar between two fingers and used the chewed end to point at the woman with the shotgun. "Remember those expensive girlfriends I was telling you about? Well, this one's my favorite."

"I am merely reaching for my phone," Jiàn Zǒu said. "To make the transfer."

* * *

"We should have killed the bearded fool," Ehmet said fifteen minutes later as they sat in the skiff with Big Uncle's men. Gruber's Bayliner gave a rumbling burble in the water as it motored away back to the north.

"It doesn't matter," Jiàn Zǒu said, turning to Big Uncle's man who sat at the outboard tiller, driving them back to the silver line of gravel that ran between the water and the dark line of old-growth forest. Dressed in olive drab Helly Hansen raincoats and matching sullen frowns, both men looked to be in their late twenties. "We are to take delivery of an important item. Do you know if it has arrived?"

The boat driver nodded, but said nothing.

The endless, mind-numbing uncertainty of the hours since their escape had worn Yaqub down to his last nerve. He just wanted all of this to be over, no matter how it turned out. "Is it in the car?"

The man at the tiller turned his head slightly to stare at him. He spat over the side, then shook his head. "Big Uncle wants to meet you."

Yaqub felt as if he were the edge of a carpet that was coming unraveled at every turn. They were so close, and now this Chinese gangster was going to change the rules.

Ehmet sat at the bow, facing aft, his arms stretched out and running along the gunnels as if he owned the place. "We are in a hurry," he said, peering out through narrowed eyes.

"So is Big Uncle," the boat driver said, eyeing Ehmet as if he saw the latent danger there. "He has a big charity event tonight. We are to bring you by to pick up your item and get some food." He turned to Yaqub, his look of respect falling into a sneer. "Don't worry. You won't be long."

Chapter 50

Seattle

The British Airways flight from Charles de Gaulle touched down just after noon. They had booked the seats at the last minute, which could pose a problem. Quinn knew it was a sure way to be flagged for extra screening, but it couldn't be helped. Song had used a credit card under the name on her passport, assuring Quinn that only her most trusted allies in the Ministry of State Security were privy to that particular identity. Quinn was glad to finally hear the engines wind down and the chime letting everyone onboard know it was okay to get up—even if it meant facing a humorless officer from Customs and Border Protection. Worrying and waiting didn't make it any less dangerous.

They traveled as a couple so Quinn had filled out the single form required for entry into the US. He reminded himself that he was John Martin from Sydney, Australia, in the States on holiday. "Holiday" was one of those words that sounded slightly Australian, no matter who said it.

It took them nearly fifteen minutes to get off the

plane and enter the cattle chute that fed them toward US Immigration.

Song yawned as they walked, slowing some to let a crowd of college-age boys hustle by as if they were in a race to see who would be interrogated first. She leaned in toward Quinn.

"Do you remember how I was your stylist at the hospital in Kashgar?" She kept her voice low as other passengers jostled by.

"The spit bath." Quinn moved his neck from side to side, working to rid himself of the cricks and kinks from the ten-hour flight. "I wondered when you would bring that up."

"What do you mean, you wondered?"

Quinn leaned down to Song's ear, whispering, "I'm a US Marshals' Top Fifteen fugitive. I don't know much about you, but I can tell you're much too skilled to chance facial recognition spotting us as we go through customs. I'm assuming that towelette back in the hospital had some sort of reflective makeup on it."

"Exactly so." Song nodded, apparently pleased that he'd figured it out on his own. "It is sensitive information, so I did not wish to divulge it if possible." She looked away for a moment, as if deciding whether or not to go on. "Facial recognition software is far from perfect, but you are distinctive and, as you said, a wanted man. If you have been listed in any sort of rogues' gallery, it would be a simple matter for such a program to match your passport photograph when it is scanned."

"But your secret chemical towelette took care of that."

"I believe so," Song said. "The software focuses on areas like the cheekbone and the spot between the eyes. Long hair or heavy makeup applied to one side of the face has been shown to defeat the program."

"But a clear reflective makeup is a lot less notice-able," Quinn said, looking at the towelette Song took from her vest pocket. She dabbed it between his eyes and along his cheekbone. Passersby would think she was merely helping her husband with something on his face after the long flight.

"Correct," she said. "It is a clear base, somewhat like sunscreen, that reflects the end of the infrared spectrum barely visible to the human eye. Many FR readers scan this wavelength. As I told you before, your Australian passport is authentic, complete with the biometric chip containing a digitized copy of the photograph I took in the hospital."

"And you put the makeup on me in the same place when I was in the hospital in Kashgar." Quinn rubbed a hand across his whiskers. She'd thought of everything. Theoretically, with the makeup reflecting the same large portion of light that bounced off the skin over his cheek and between his eyes, facial recognition software would not recognize him enough to match with any gallery of fugitives, but a scan of the passport would match a photographic scan of his face taken at screen-ing.

"And you've tested this invisible makeup on pass-port scanners from the United States?"

"Most of them." Song shrugged.

"That's a tall order," Quinn said as they walked along nearing the snaking queue to immigration for non-US citizens.

"Not really." Song gave him an impish wink. "A sur-prising number of your machines are made in China."

They made it through immigration with little more than a "Business or pleasure?" question. The young woman at the customs counter welcomed them to the US and admitted that she'd always wanted to visit Australia, before nodding them through with their luggage.

With a prohibition on cell phone use inside the screening area, Quinn had to wait to call Thibodaux until they'd made it out into the terminal lobby. He walked toward the Gold Streak counter as he punched in the number.

"We're here and secure," Quinn said when Thibodaux picked up.

"Glad to hear it," the big Cajun said.

Quinn took a deep breath, afraid to ask the next question. "How's Ronnie?"

"She's sleeping now. Been through a hell of a lot."

"The guys that had her?" Quinn asked. He'd run through a hundred different scenarios during the flight, none of them good. His jaw clenched so tightly he had to concentrate to keep from cracking a tooth.

"He's taken care of," Jacques said. "She already had one done when we showed up. Anyhow, I'll tell you all about it when I get there. You get your package?"

"I'm going to the counter now," Quinn said. "Thanks for doing that."

"Don't thank me," Thibodaux said. "Kim and Camille needed something to do to work off their jitters anyhow."

"You involved Kim?" Quinn said, loud enough to gain the attention of other passengers in the terminal and draw a quizzical look from Song.

"They were already involved up to their neck bones, *cher*," Thibodaux said. "Long story. We'll all laugh our asses off about it if we don't die in a mushroom cloud. Anyhow, the boss is chompin' at the bit to talk to you. I'll let him know you're on the ground."

Quinn picked up the small duffel he used as a go-bag from the Gold Streak counter and took the escalator up toward the taxi stand in the parking garage. Song lagged a few steps behind him, talking to one of her contacts in frantic Mandarin. He could tell she was checking on any last-minute information about the triad boss known as Big Uncle. Quinn's cell began to ring two minutes after he'd hung up with Jacques.

"We're here," Quinn said, knowing his boss would want to get straight to business. "What have you got?"

"We?" Palmer said.

"Long story." Quinn glanced over his shoulder at Song, who was still locked in the rapid-fire conversation with her local contact—someone Quinn would have loved to identify for future reference. "I'm sure Jacques has already filled you in on the woman who saved my life—and the weapon."

"You're still with her?" Palmer said, stifling a cough. "That's rich."

"Turns out not everyone in that part of the world thinks war is such a hot idea. All indications put her and me on the same side—"

"Until she decides to put a bullet in your ear," Palmer said. "Listen, a source in the IDTF tells me Drake and the Japanese Prime Minister will both arrive in Seattle later this evening. They have a ten a.m. event together tomorrow at the Japanese Cultural and Community Center where Drake is supposed to clarify US support for Japanese sovereignty over the Senkaku Islands. Drake's assassination will provide the perfect first domino that will push us into war."

"Perfect target," Quinn said, half to himself.

"I'm thinking so too," Palmer said. "Scout it out and get back to me. If you can't locate the guys you're after, we've got some serious decisions to make before tomorrow morning." Palmer cleared his throat. Quinn heard the click of a cough drop against his teeth. "It goes without saying that this new friend of yours surely has an agenda very much her own."

"Roger that," Quinn said. The thought crossed his mind at least once every ten minutes. He hung up, checking the time on his Aquaracer. It was just after one. The last forty-eight hours had left him with fifteen stitches to close the wound on his chest, a pulled muscle in his hip, and a painful sprain in his right shoulder—not to mention the aftereffects of the ricin and surgical anesthesia. He was far from in his best shape and his only backup was a Chinese agent—and that wasn't the worst part. He had to figure out a way to save President Hartman Drake, the man behind ninety percent of his woes.

Song caught up to him, phone in one hand, dragging her bag with the other. She bounced on the balls of her feet like a child who couldn't contain important news.

"I have found Big Uncle," she said. "I'm not sure where he is at this precise moment, but he's hosting a formal reception and charity art auction beginning at five this evening."

Quinn filled her in on the pertinent points he'd learned from Palmer as they walked. She shook her head when he was finished.

"This President is more vocal about your animosity toward my country," she said. "But the truth is the United States has always had a problem with China's claim to the Diaoyu Islands." She called the islands by the Chinese name for the disputed rocks rather than Senkaku as the Japanese preferred. "From our point of view, the US has fought us over every inch of ground that has historically been ours."

Quinn sighed. "Look," he said, "there is an endless list of perceived slights, human rights violations, or other misdeeds either one of us could bring up regarding the stand our countries take on given issues. But now is the time to work, not talk. And when I work, I worry about the person who wants to kill me—or kill my friends. I look at his hands. His race, religion, nationality, or political philosophy don't even get a footnote in my brain. Some . . . no, most things are beyond the vagaries of politics—and this is one of them."

Song stood and looked at him, blinking slowly. "Hmm." She shrugged, as if she'd just been baiting him. "I have never heard you say so much at one time. It is enlightening. In any case, we should go and make ourselves more presentable. You are in desperate need of a haircut and I would appreciate a shower. All I packed for us was an assortment of T-shirts and underwear so we should stop somewhere and pick up some more suitable clothes. Big Uncle is a dangerous man with dangerous associates. It is much better that we meet him in a public place like this formal reception."

Quinn closed his eyes and gave a low groan. Not because he was worried about Big Uncle or his dangerous associates. If this was a formal reception, he was going to have to put on a tie.

Chapter 51

Yaqub Feng did not become aware that he stunk until Big Uncle's man behind the counter at a bank of elevators in the lobby of the downtown Seattle high-rise recoiled at his approach.

"The boss is expecting you," the man grunted, scrunching his face in disgust. He was young, maybe twenty-five, and spoke with a directness peculiar to Chinese culture. "The boss is waiting on the nineteenth floor, but you will need to stop on eighteen for a shower and clean clothing. Mrs. Wang will help you find what you need."

"We have no time to bathe," Ehmet scoffed. "We came to get what is ours and move on."

"Suit yourself," the young gatekeeper said. "But you must be nose-blind if you do not smell yourselves. And you should know, the boss once shot a man for farting too close to him."

"We will, of course, make the stop on eighteen first," Jiàn Zǒu said, shouldering his way in front of Ehmet. Yaqub was startled at the sudden abruptness of the skinny snakehead. Ehmet's face fell into a twitchy scowl.

"I can see that you are angry," Jiàn Zǒu said, as they boarded the elevator.

"You won't think it's so funny when I stick a blade in your neck," Ehmet said, leaning against the back corner. "People who speak to me that way do not live long." The walls of the elevator were mirrored and Yaqub squirmed at so many scowling images of his brother

"Just because people are silent does not mean we smell of jasmine." Jiàn Zŏu bounced slightly against his hands that were folded behind him. Yaqub did not think it was a nervous tic, but more of a way to restrain his hands from doing anything rash. "How do you think you smell? The whores in Dubrovnik were too terrified to tell you, but the stink of Dera Ismail Khan does not wash off with a wet cloth. You must learn to trust me, my friend. This is my livelihood."

"I am not your friend," Ehmet spat as the elevator chimed and the doors opened to the bright marble halls of the eighteenth floor. "You are an infidel who has likely served his purpose. It would do you well to re-member that. A livelihood is pointless if you are dead."

A smiling woman who was old enough to be their grandmother met them at the door with a stack of neatly folded white towels. As it turned out, half of the eigh-teenth floor was a gym, complete with rows of treadmills, exercise bikes, and sweating heathen women in obscenely tight clothing. Mrs. Wang ushered them into the men's locker room, surprisingly following them inside, though there were a half dozen other naked Chinese men get-ting ready to work out. Jiàn Zŏu bowed slightly and whispered something to the old woman. She gave a wan smile, then nodded and took her leave.

His brother's dark mood notwithstanding, Yaqub found the hot shower exhilarating. The clean jogging suit felt like silk compared to the rough prison clothing he'd been forced to wear for his endless months of captivity.

Fifteen minutes later, all three stepped out of the dressing room, smelling like shampoo and countertop cologne, to find they were alone in the gym with a man who had to be Big Uncle. The gangster boss had a broad, jowly face, common to well-fed bosses. He wore a charcoal-gray pinstripe suit and an orange silk tie. Not a tall man, he appeared to be plenty strong and the look from his dark eyes filled every corner of the room with an imposing presence. Yaqub found it uncomfortable to meet his eyes directly.

Jiàn Zǒu stepped forward, giving the man in the gray suit a subservient tip of his head. "We are so sorry to keep you waiting, sir."

"My man said you were in a hurry," Big Uncle said, with an apparent ease that belied the fact that he was one of the most powerful crime bosses on the West Coast. "I thought I would meet you here and save you the trouble of coming to me. My standing in the community is quite important to me. I am fairly new to the area, so I wish this first event to be beyond perfect. You understand."

"Thank you for taking the time to meet with us," Jiàn Zǒu said, bobbing his head again as if he was afraid he might anger the other man if he wasn't subservient enough.

"It is no problem," Big Uncle said. As secretive as the triad boss was supposed to be, Yaqub found it interesting that he was so open with three total strangers. "My people are busy making certain tonight's event is up to standards. I am sure they are relieved that I stepped away to give them a few moments of peace."

"We have showered away our filth as you required," Ehmet said, shouldering his way forward to eclipse Jiàn Zǒu. "A certain item was delivered to you. We will require it at once."

Yaqub froze, half expecting Big Uncle to clap his hands as a signal for his men to come in and murder them all for his brother's abrupt behavior. He did not imagine anyone "required" much of anything from a man like Big Uncle.

Instead of having them killed, the triad boss tilted his head to one side, so far that his ear almost touched the padded shoulder of his suit, considering Ehmet for a long moment. Finally, he nodded and indeed clapped his hands. One of his men entered immediately. Instead of carrying a gun to kill them all, he brought in a hard plastic case, approximately a meter and a half long and half a meter tall. It was marked with a red peony blossom on either side, and three strong combination locks kept it closed.

Big Uncle gave a dismissive flick of his hand. "Your package," he said. "You may have it when the agreed-upon amount is wired to my account."

Ehmet snatched the mobile phone from Yaqub's hands and sent a quick text. A confirmation tone came back almost immediately. Big Uncle shot a glance at his man, who made a call. A moment later, the man nodded.

"Very well," Big Uncle said. "Our business is complete. Your item remains sealed, as it was when I received it."

"I should hope so," Ehmet said, drawing a quizzical look from Big Uncle's man as he handed over the case. Ehmet passed it to Yaqub, who found it cumbersome but not too heavy to lift. He estimated it to be less than thirty kilos.

"Thank you, sir," Jiàn Zǒu said. He didn't exactly step in front of Ehmet, but it was enough to earn a hostile glare from the younger Feng brother.

Big Uncle stood, chuckling under his breath. "I find it extremely amusing," he said, looking at Ehmet, "how this one is so angry. He does not seem to understand that your politeness and understanding of decorum is the only reason he is still alive."

Ehmet opened his mouth to speak but Yaqub stepped in, asking some inane question about the box and the weapon.

"Please, my brother," Yaqub whispered, leading Ehmet toward the doorway. "Let us be on our way. We have important work."

"I will be a moment," Jiàn Zǒu said, as they reached the door. It was too late for all three men to turn around without looking foolish, so the brothers continued toward the elevator, with Ehmet fuming at the snakehead's usurpation of his power.

"What is it?" Big Uncle asked as the skinny Chinese man approached.

"I have a favor to ask, sir," Yaqub heard Jiàn Zǒu say, as the door swung began to swing closed. "On a very sensitive matter—"

A moment later, Big Uncle's man followed the Fengs out into the hallway, leaving Jiàn Zǒu in the gym alone with the powerful triad boss.

"What do you supposed they're talking about?" Yaqub said, regretting it as soon as the words escaped his lips.

"I do not care," Ehmet snapped, grabbing the weapon back from his brother. "We are where we need to be and we have what we need to have. There is no need to keep this Chinese fool around any longer."

"He can still assist our escape," Yaqub said.

"There are few things of which I am certain, my brother," Ehmet snorted. "But whatever Allah has in store for our future, I'm sure it does not include escape."

Chapter 52

Quinn lay back on one of the two queen beds, eyes closed, hands on his belly. He was still dressed in the same rugby shirt and jeans, waiting for a turn in the bathroom, but his socks and shoes sat neatly at the foot of the bedside chair, unlaced in case he needed to put them on in a hurry. It was an extremely intimate thing to be barefoot while a woman he hardly knew took a shower in the next room, but he was too exhausted to care. He'd never been able to relax completely on a plane—and considering his recent confrontation with terrorists who were committed to bringing down a commercial airliner with a bomb, that sentiment had only grown worse. These few hours in the hotel before Big Uncle's party was the first time in days he'd been able to lie flat in an actual bed.

As always, inactivity brought thought, and thought brought entire truckloads of worry—over his daughter and Ronnie Garcia and the mission at hand. Working, fighting, just moving from Point A to Point B allowed Quinn to compartmentalize the worry, to attack one problem at a time. He'd heard his father brag to a friend

once that he was one of the hardest workers the elder
Quinn had ever seen. Jericho knew it wasn't true. He
had no particularly strong work ethic. He was just a
coward running from the idleness that brought with it
too much deep thought—and that cowardice had served
him well.

He allowed himself to wallow for a few moments
over concern for seven-year-old Mattie hiding out in
Russia—and Ronnie, recuperating from what must have
been horrific treatment at the hands of the IDTF—all
while he was stuck on the other side of the world, unable
to help either of them. Quinn's conscious mind told
him there was nothing he could do but move forward.
He could almost hear Emiko Miyagi's Yoda-like admonition to "focus on the possible and let the impossible
fade from your mind."

Pushing futile thoughts to the far corners of his brain
for later, he picked up the remote from the table beside
the bed and turned up the volume on the television so he
could hear the local news over the hiss of Song's shower.
A maid began to vacuum out in the hall, so he kicked
up the volume a little more.

A blond woman who looked painfully like Kim
stood in front of a green screen map of the area, fore-
casting rainy weather in Seattle for the next two days.
Quinn closed his eyes again, setting the remote on his
chest, waiting for the news. The torrent of worry began
to flow back in, but he ran to thoughts of the mission at
hand.

The Australian passport that Song had provided had
been secure enough to get him into the country, but he
wanted something that didn't join him to Song at the
hip. The small go-bag he kept stashed in Virginia held
a driver's license and two credit cards under the name
of John Owen. He'd used these to check into the hotel.

Conventional wisdom held that the first name of an alias should be the same as your real one, but a name like Jericho made that problematic. He'd chosen John for nearly all of his false IDs. It was easier to remember under stress.

The John Owen credit cards allowed him to have money of his own instead of mooching off a communist spy—a bad spot to be in, even if they did happen to be working toward the same goal. The go-bag also held five hundred dollars in twenties, a Surefire flashlight, and a ZT folding knife. He'd packed the Riot in his luggage, so he still had that as a tool and close-quarters weapon. He'd not chanced having Jacques send him a gun. He'd been without a pistol of his own since boarding Mandeep's chopper—before that if he didn't count the rusty .45 revolver he'd carried in Pakistan. But guns were like fruit in the circles where he operated, always in season and ready to pick if you knew where to look. He had no doubt there would be plenty of them at Big Uncle's soirée. Hard experience had taught him that awareness and reflexes were much more handy than a sidearm. If you had the former, you could generally get your hands on the latter in a matter of moments if the need arose.

The news anchor on television made small talk with a traffic reporter about the President, Vice President, and Prime Minister Nabe all arriving in separate motorcades later that evening. They talked about how it was bound to clog the already terrible Seattle traffic.

Quinn closed his eyes and heard the water shut off in the bathroom. He couldn't quite get his head wrapped around this Chinese woman. She was extremely intelligent and driven in her job, but the drive seemed that of an automaton. She appeared to be loyal to her country, but her heart was not in her work. No matter Quinn's initial reservations, she'd proven herself extremely tough and more than capable, but tears of regret always seemed just beneath the stony exterior, ready to gush out if given even the tiniest crack.

A cloud of steam rolled through the door when Song came out of the bathroom wearing a white terry-cloth robe from the closet and a matching towel wrapped around her head like a turban. The floppy hotel room slippers did little to add to her image of communist spy and stone-cold killer

"I was thinking," she said, brushing her teeth with a gimme toothbrush from the front desk. "You really need a haircut before we go." She pointed at him with the toothbrush, jutting her jaw to keep the paste in her mouth as she spoke, using the bluntness that the Chinese were so good at. "You are much too shabby to attend a formal event and not quite young enough to carry the unkempt hipster look."

"Especially with you as my date," Quinn said, swinging his legs off the edge of the bed with a low groan. He rubbed his hand through his shaggy head of hair that grew well over his ears. She was right. It was hard to blend in if he looked like he was wearing a mop on his head. "I'll go see if there's a barber in the lobby."

Song disappeared into the bathroom for a moment to spit. Instead of the toothbrush, she held a pair of scissors in her hand when she returned. "I can do it," she said, as bright and bubbly as he'd ever seen her. "Do you really want a stranger next to your throat with a blade right now?"

Quinn took his turn at blunt directness. "I'm not so sure you qualify as an old friend."

Song pulled the desk chair around in front of her, patting the back of it and beckoning him to sit. "Come," she said. "I used to do this for the boys in my university dormitory. It will save us some time and we can arrive at Big Uncle's party early enough to do some reconnaissance." She held the scissors up and snipped at the air. "We'll do it now, before you shower. You should take off your shirt."

Quinn stood. It would save them time. He had no idea where the nearest barber was even located. "I think I'll keep my shirt on."

"Nonsense." She smirked. "Do not be silly. It will keep hair from getting all over everything." She pulled the damp towel off her head. "I'll put this over you if you wish, but I believe I've proven that I can contain myself around your naked torso."

Her eyes flashed over the wounds and scars that covered his chest and ribs as he peeled the shirt over his head—one of them caused by her blade.

"The years have not been kind to me," he said.

"We all have our scars, Mr. Quinn," she said, draping the damp towel around his shoulders. "They are what make us who we are. You are like Odysseus."

"I've been called a lot of things"—Quinn laughed—"but never Odysseus."

"You know the story," she said. "How he was recognized by the scar on his knee he had received from the wild boar as a child."

"Yes," he said. "I'd just never thought of my scars like that."

Her robe brushed against his arm. He could feel the heat of her as she leaned in to begin cutting. Quinn closed his eyes, listening to the scissors as she worked around his ears.

"Do you know any of Big Uncle's associates?" Quinn said, relaxing in spite of the snipping blades so close to his neck.

"There is a man named Lok," she said. "A sort of

bodyguard who acts as what the Italians might call a *consigliere*. His hair is long and pulled back in a pony-tail, so he will be easy to recognize. He spends a lot of time lifting weights and looking at himself in the mirror."

"Curls for the girls." Quinn chuckled.

"I'd say that describes Lok," Song said. "I have never seen him in action, but Big Uncle is a wanted man in several countries with a large reward for his capture. The fact that he remains alive and at large speaks to Lok's abilities. From what I hear he is trained in kung fu and Muay Thai kickboxing." She stopped cutting for a moment. "And, of course, he will be armed."

"Good," Quinn grunted, ready to get on with things. "I need a gun."

"You are so confident," Song laughed. "I suppose that comes from experience."

"Or apathy," Quinn said, only half joking.

"Oh, you care deeply about many things," she said. "Just not your own safety. But I understand. Warriors prepare themselves to die. It is your way."

"Our way," Quinn reminded her.

"I am not prepared to die," Song said, hand flat to her chest. "I am just incredibly brave." She started back in with the scissors. "Anyway, does this not remind you of an American adventure movie? The handsome spy getting a shave from the mystery woman." She laughed the most honest laugh she'd given him since they'd met. "Is that what you're thinking of, Mr. Quinn?"

"To be honest," he said, "I was thinking more of *Sweeney Todd*."

"Who?"

Quinn glanced up, careful not to move his head and chance a nick with the scissors. "*The Demon Barber of*

Fleet Street. It's a play about a barber who cuts people's throats and takes the bodies to a lady who uses them in her meat pies."

Song stopped cutting for a moment. "Well," she said, "I suppose sometimes a haircut is nothing but a haircut."

Finished, she stepped back and nodded to herself. "Extremely passable," she said.

"Thank you for the nothing but a haircut then," he said.

Song sat on the edge of the bed and leaned forward, elbows on her knees, chin in her hands. "Did you know that Mrs. Nabe gave up a career as a classical dancer with the National Ballet Company of Japan?"

"I did not," Quinn said, stopping at the bathroom door, towel in hand.

"Apparently, their twelve-year-old daughter is traveling with them," Song said, brown eyes twitching back and forth with the images on the television. "She is a dancer as well."

As always, the mention of anyone's daughter made Quinn think of Mattie. He sighed, pushing the thoughts away.

Song suddenly sat straight up, looking directly at Quinn, mouth pinched as if she'd eaten something sour. "The Prime Minister's wife abandoned her passion in order to follow her husband."

"Maybe she found another passion," Quinn said.

"Perhaps." Song nodded, unconvinced. "In my country, it would not matter what I gave up," she said. "Few Chinese men would consider me marriageable material."

"That's not true," Quinn said, wishing Ronnie or even Thibodaux were there to rescue him from talk of marriage and relationships.

"No," she said. "It is. In China there are said to be

three genders—men, women, and women with graduate degrees. An educated woman like me who has
spent a decade as a government operative may as well
be another species." She stretched her feet out in front
of her, kicking off one of the slippers. "My grandmother certainly does not approve of what I do. She
thinks I should have quit school while I was yet marriageable and given her a great-grandson. Perhaps if I would
have listened to her, I would still be able to spend time
with the violin instead of dying young working for the
Ministry of State Security."

"Life can play tricks on us," Quinn said, not knowing what else to say.

"My grandmother lectures me on it every time I see
her." Song looked up with a wan smile, shaking her
head at the memory. "She asks me if the people I kill
have toes. Can you imagine such a thing? Then she
says, 'Do you yourself not have toes? People with toes
should not be killing other people who have toes,' as if
such thinking made all the sense in the world." Song
fell back on the bed, staring up at the ceiling.

"That's a well-meaning sentiment," Quinn said
softly. "Until those toes are attached to feet that would
be happy crushing your neck."

"I wish you would speak to my grandmother," Song
said, a catch in her voice as if she was about to cry.
"Go. Have your shower. I will try on my new dress."

Quinn closed the door, happy to step away from the
outpouring of emotion. He felt like he was stuck in this
adventure with a college student who was pretending
to be a spy—acting out the things she'd seen in the
movies. Song had done a good job on the haircut—as
good as possible with his unruly mop. But he didn't
need a barber and certainly didn't need "Love" Song—
some "Unchained Melody" crooning on about tender-

ness and emotion. He needed the Song who had dispatched Anton Scuric without hesitation.

He showered quickly, then scraped away the stubble on his face with a cheap razor from the front desk, before stepping into a new pair of navy blue slacks. He left the bathroom with his white shirt unbuttoned and the French cuffs hanging over his hands. Song turned to face him when he opened the door. She stood facing the wall mirror wearing a loose T-shirt and a pair of skintight spandex shorts that would presumably allow her to fight while wearing the dress. Dark eye makeup lined each eye and bright rouge highlighted her cheeks. It was twice the makeup she normally wore, meant to capture Big Uncle's attention. A deep red lipstick had transformed her from college coed to femme fatale while Quinn had been in the shower. The tiny purple dress lay draped across the foot of the bed shimmering under the room light like the feathers of some exotic bird. Beside it was a thin ripping dagger in a sheath that would wrap around her thigh. Made of a sticky neoprene, the sheath was held in place by a garter that presumably snapped to her spandex short shorts. Ronnie used similar shorts when she wore a dress; they gave her extra support for the holster as well as a touch more modesty during a fight. The neoprene sheath had enough room for a small pistol as well as the blade—in the event that Song was able to find one. Quinn looked at the rig and smiled.

"What?" she said, turning away from the mirror to help him with his cuff links.

"Nothing," Quinn said. He didn't say it, but he was glad "Killer Queen" Song was back.

Chapter 53

Clay Gillette, the sandy-haired lead agent for Lee McKeon's Secret Service detail, used his knuckles to rap on the back window of the black Cadillac. He was noticeably twitchy, casting worried looks toward the woods on the long hill across the highway from the airport. As the official limousine of the Vice President, the Caddy was code-named "Trailbreaker." It was fully armored with steel plating and equipped with exterior microphones, dual batteries, smoke machines, and windows that were nearly two inches thick.

The windows would not roll down, so McKeon pushed open the heavy door.

"You asked to be informed, Mr. Vice President," Gillette said. "Air Force One is wheels-down in two minutes."

"Well." McKeon chuckled. "Half an hour of shaking hands and kissing babies with the reception committee and we should be in position to bring rush hour traffic to a standstill. That should ingratiate us to Seattle locals."

"That's what we're here for, sir," Gillette said, his

face impassive. It was impossible to tell what the man was thinking.

McKeon thanked the agent and pulled the door shut. He looked across the leather seat at Ran, who stared out the window in the other direction. Never a particularly vocal person, she'd grown even more distant in the last two days. In anyone else McKeon would have chalked the behavior up to nerves, but he wasn't sure Ran Kimura was ever nervous about anything.

Beyond the vice presidential motorcade was a second line of marked cars from Seattle PD and the Washington State Patrol. A dozen police motorcycles that were part ceremonial and part intersection-blockers queued up in the front. Three black Cadillac limousines, identical to McKeon's, sat flanked by a half dozen Chevy Suburbans of the same color. The "straphanger" vehicles were used to transport presidential staff and other nonessentials who were not included in the Secret Service protective package. They'd been provided by the Seattle office. The "Beast," as they called the POTUS Cadillac, along with Trailbreaker, and hardened decoys for both limousines had been flown in earlier that day on two Air Force C17s.

McKeon looked out the tinted window, past his contingent of twitchy Secret Service agents, as the blue-and-white 747 seemed to float in slowly from the south. The Air Force colonel at the controls touched down without a bounce. The big bird's engines whined as they pushed her along the taxiway.

Staged vehicles began to move the moment the ramp attendant chocked the 747's wheels. Motorcycles roared past, setting up in the front of the motorcade. A marked Washington State Patrol lead car pulled in behind the bikes with the Beast rolling up next. A suited agent stood with his hand in the air, directing the limo driver to align the rear door perfectly with the end of a red carpet rolled out below the portable air stairs. A Secret Service muscle Suburban bristling with agents with heavy weapons came up next, followed by the decoy limo and several straphanger sedans and other marked police units. McKeon quit bothering to count after he got to fifteen. A rambunctious press gaggle had formed behind a rope barrier on the other side of the limo, away from the plane. Local luminaries, including the governor of Washington, two congressmen, and a handful of generals from Joint Base Lewis-McChord, formed the greeting party. Two Air Force NCOs in Class A uniforms stood at attention at the base of the air stairs.

"Look at all those buffoons," Ran said without bothering to turn around. "Standing around to touch the hand of the nation's biggest idiot."

"It's a much smaller group than it should be." McKeon sighed. "Half the delegation in Washington hates us and the other half are terrified of being implicated in an IDTF investigation. I had to have David Crosby threaten most of these into showing up. All the love and adulation keeps POTUS's mind off of us."

Drake appeared in the open doorway of the aircraft a moment later, dressed like a peacock in a dark suit and flamboyant yellow bow tie.

"Watch him pause as if he is a magazine model," Ran said, her voice dripping with disgust. "And now he turns to flex his puffed chest so the press can have plenty of B-roll. It is pornographic. . . ."

McKeon opened the door and stood by the limo while he waited for Drake to schmooze with the congressmen. The fact that there was not a single female staffer among the military contingent was not lost on McKeon. Word of the President's ruttish behavior had evidently trickled down from the Joint Chiefs, who had to live with it every day. Waving again at the press corps, Drake turned and said something to the nearest Secret Service agent. A moment later, Agent Gillette spoke into the mic on his lapel, then stepped up to McKeon.

"He'd like you to join him in his limo for a moment," Gillette said. "We can drive you up, sir."

"That's all right, Clay," McKeon said. "I'd like to stretch my legs." Ran came around from the other side of the limo and stood beside him.

Five agents formed up in a loose diamond around the pair as they walked the twenty meters between the two limos. Always vigilant, they were more agitated than usual, as if they sensed something bad was going to happen on this trip.

Drake's face twisted into a dark scowl when McKeon sat down in the backseat of the Beast facing him. Ran ducked her head to follow him in and sat to his immediate right.

"Is everything all right, Mr. President?" McKeon said, smiling softly as a detail agent shut the door behind him, giving the three their privacy.

"No, it is not," Drake said. "Hell, the last briefing I got on the plane has half the people in the world thinking I need to be impeached. Every network is carrying this garbage news poll as breaking news." He shook his head, staring off into space the way he did when he was frozen by the stress of his job—which happened more and more every day. "And that doesn't count the large portion of the population who think it would be a good idea if someone assassinated me."

"Nonsense," McKeon said.

"Is it?" Drake said, raising his eyebrow and giving McKeon a probing gaze. "Are you sure you're not one of those people? This event smacks of shoving me out front to take a bullet."

"We've covered this," McKeon said. "The Secret Service has been here for a week locking everything down like a drum. Let's get you through tomorrow, make the announcement supporting Japan's primacy in the East China Sea, and pose for a few photos. You can give the order to move the Fifth Fleet into the Pacific once you're back aboard Air Force One. My father trusted you for a reason. You are pivotal to this plan, my friend."

"Whatever you say." Drake came back on track easily— as he always did when made to feel important. "This has me stressed, that's all. Last I heard, Jericho Quinn was still unaccounted for. That sneaky son of a bitch has already gotten to me once."

"Not yet," McKeon said. He did not mention the fact that Quinn had apparently killed every one of the Albanian hit men Rhanjani had hired in Croatia. "But it is only a matter of time. I have IDTF snipers embedded with the Secret Service Hercules teams. They are on alert for Quinn and any of Palmer's other operatives. You don't have to worry about them, Hartman, believe me. In just a few more hours, you and I will have created a very different world."

"Easy for you to say," Drake said. "You're not joined at the hip with Nabe for three hours tonight watching a bunch of men dance around in tights."

McKeon gave a wan smile, hiding his disgust. "There will be plenty of women in tights at the ballet," he said. "In any case, I believe you will find tonight's performance enjoyable. I took the liberty of arranging a local ballerina from the University of Washington to accompany you. Prime Minister Nabe will have his wife and daughter to accompany him. It is only right that you should have a docent to explain the intricacies of the dance to you."

"Very well," Drake said. "But we're back on the plane first thing tomorrow morning, right after the event."

"Of course, my friend," McKeon said. "Things will work out as they must."

Beside him, Ran stiffened and turned away.

Chapter 54

Song stopped Quinn the moment they got out of the rain, tugging him by the sleeve toward one of the granite columns on the concrete steps outside Big Uncle's office building. She gave him a scolding grimace as she straightened his tie. Her hair shone in the halogen lights of the covered entry, still damp after the short dash from the taxi.

Quinn rolled his eyes, surrendering to her style-police tactics. In truth, he felt as if he was being strangled.

Song stepped back to admire the dark blue suit she'd picked out for him at the Nordstrom just down from the hotel. The jacket and slacks were off-the-rack separates, but with a crisp white shirt, ebony cuff links, and the cursed gray noose of a necktie, he looked as if the entire ensemble had been tailor made. Lightweight Rockport dress shoes felt like sneakers, dressy enough for a Seattle art party with the added benefit of a grippy sole in case he needed to run.

"You clean up to be a handsome man," she said, giving a nod of approval.

"It's the haircut." Quinn grinned, raising an eyebrow at Song's minidress. It was deep purple, the color of a dark moon. "Doesn't matter though. No one is going to notice me with you wearing that little thing."

She ran a hand down the hip of the tight fabric for the benefit of any cameras that might be watching their approach. Big Uncle had apparently met her before, but he would have had many interactions with public officials—most of whom he would have bribed. A simple note from some former MSS contact would be unimpressive to him. It was imperative that they arouse his curiosity without getting themselves thrown out. And that's where the dress came in. Shimmering silk, the cap sleeves, and a choker collar gave a nod to Song's Chinese heritage. Stopping a few inches above her knee, the dress revealed a great deal of leg while leaving plenty to the imagination—not to mention the hidden knife. A half-moon cutout from the nape of her neck to well below her shoulder blades exposed the honey-colored richness of her back.

"I thought you said every girl should have a little black dress," Quinn said, offering his arm to escort her through the door.

"And they should," Song said. "But tonight, I don't want to be every girl. We must stand out and be noticed."

"You've got that covered," Quinn said as they made their way across the expansive marble lobby to a bank of elevators. "You worry about Big Uncle. I'll take care of Lok if he has any heartburn with us."

"Lok is a bad man." Song turned as the elevator chimed and the doors slid open. "Both of them are. But it is good to deal with truly bad men. I find it much easier to make a decision. Don't you think?"

"You sound like my friend Jacques," Quinn said.

"Is that a good thing?"

Quinn smiled. "That, my dear, is outstanding."

The elevator doors slid open to the clatter of cock-tail plates and buzzing chatter. Hit in the face with an overwhelming odor of alcohol, perfume, and hair products, Quinn couldn't help but think of the gashouse in OSI Basic. Big Uncle might be a triad crime boss, but he threw quite a party. Just as Song had predicted, a sea of little black dresses dominated the shoulder-to-shoulder crowd. Paintings, pottery, and ornate handblown glass sculptures of every description lined the walls and took up valuable floor space, begging to be knocked to the floor.

"That's him," Song said, thirty seconds after they'd stepped into the crush of people.

"Lok or his boss?" Quinn scanned the crowd. There were art lovers from various races, but more than half the group was drawn from Seattle's Asian population. Quinn estimated nearly two hundred people were crammed into the open gallery area that resembled the lobby of a bank with smaller, windowed offices around the outer walls.

"Big Uncle," she said. "He is standing behind that long table of glass flowers." She took her glasses out of the tiny beaded clutch she'd bought along with the dress and put them on long enough to scan the crowd.

"You should just wear them all the time," Quinn said. "They flatter you."

"Ha!" She snatched the glasses off her face and used them to point at a small group of men directly in front of Big Uncle. "And there is Lok. I did not see him at first behind that wide woman. He is one of two body-guards within reach of Big Uncle."

Quinn located Lok and his partner quickly. Both men wore expensive-looking suits, larger than usual, the same way Quinn's OSI suits were cut to conceal a weapon—or two. Lok was maybe ten years younger than Quinn—which seemed the case for everyone he fought nowadays—with a puffed chest and thick arms that filled the suit. The second man was even younger with a buzz cut and neatly trimmed goatee. This one's left arm floated away from his side a fraction farther than his right. Quinn guessed he was wearing a shoulder holster under the suit jacket.

"Big Uncle knows me," Song said, tentatively, as if trying to convince herself. "Once he sees I am not here to arrest him, he should tell his guards to stand down."

"That would be nice," Quinn said, though he knew things rarely ever turned out that way for him. "I'll keep an eye on Lok. You focus on the kid with the goatee."

It was not wise to underestimate strong men like this, especially when they were armed. But there was the strength of youth and the strength of knowing what to do in the moment. Quinn still had a relatively good amount of the first and a whole lot of the latter.

He wasn't worried until Song barged forward, shoving her way through the crowd toward the triad boss and his bodyguards as if they owed her money.

Big Uncle glanced up from his chat with a lithe blonde and locked eyes with Song. Almost imperceptibly, he maneuvered to the left, using the woman as a human shield. Lok caught his boss's sudden flutter and threw Quinn a pick-on-someone-your-own-size sneer.

Quinn came up on the balls of his feet, lightening

his center so he could move quickly. Song peeled off, homing in on Goatee. *Good girl*, Quinn thought. At least she'd heard him—or was smart enough to see what needed to be done.

Lok was confident enough in his size and physical prowess that he waited a fraction of a second too long to make his move. Quinn caught a glimpse of a pistol on the left side of the bodyguard's belt, grip facing forward—a cross draw.

Lok's ponytail flipped as he canted his head, sizing up his opponent. Quinn kept coming, picking up speed while calling Lok by name as if they were lifelong friends. He waved, lifting his hand to where it was even with the point of Lok's shoulder. The bodyguard's hand dropped, reaching across his body at belt level, indexing the pistol—but he was too late.

Shielded by the crowd of party guests, Quinn stepped in close. He kept both hands open and his body centered, low in his belly. A wicked right snapped hard against the forearm of Lok's gun hand, disrupting the man's movement but not disabling him. Rolling one hand over the other as if playing a child's game, Quinn followed up with an immediate left, catching Lok hard above the elbow, knocking the arm straight and directing it well away from the sidearm. Another lightning-fast right, left, right combination hammered the bicep as Quinn worked up the arm and stepped across with a powerful right elbow across the bodyguard's jaw. It was over before it had even begun and Quinn caught him as he sagged.

Holding Lok in a bear hug, Quinn glanced over his shoulder to see Song in a chest-to-chest embrace with Goatee. Her body blocked the man from accessing his shoulder holster. She kept her hands low, between them, out of sight. Lips almost brushing the young bodyguard's face, she whispered something in his ear. Quinn remembered the thin ripping dagger hidden in her garter. He could imagine what she was saying.

Big Uncle stepped forward, shaking his head. He patted an unconscious Lok on the shoulder.

"I wish you would not kill my men," he said, deadpan. "I have more, but there are so many people at the party. The fight would be terribly messy."

The triad boss recognized Song as an MSS agent and agreed to meet in a private room at the back of the main exhibit hall. Agile for a man of his age, Big Uncle hopped up to sit on the edge of the wooden desk, letting his feet dangle. He motioned for Quinn and Song to take two of the half dozen soft leather seats along the glass wall. A stunned Lok and Goatee took up a position behind their boss, their egos damaged far more than anything else.

"How can I help my esteemed colleagues with the Ministry of State Security?" Big Uncle asked in Mandarin, ignoring Quinn as if he wasn't even in the room.

Song nodded meekly, then explained that they were looking for the Feng brothers. She was hesitant in the telling as if she did not want to offend such a powerful man and noted apologetically in her explanation that witnesses had overheard the Fengs talking about their connection to the crime boss.

"It would seem to me," Big Uncle said, "that the MSS would be pleased if men such as this spread a little mayhem in the United States."

"That is incorrect," Song said, throwing Quinn a glance he couldn't quite read. "But the Fengs must be arrested before they cause irreparable damage."

"Please understand," Big Uncle said, "a business

such as mine depends on a certain amount of . . . discretion. Even the stupid American would understand that."

"I understand plenty," Quinn said in Mandarin.

"Big Uncle," Song growled, rising from her seat. Her face went from meek to malignant in a flash. This was the same Song who had threatened to cut off Habibullah's balls and Quinn was happy to see her reappearance. "Allow me to be blunt. The MSS has allowed you a great deal of latitude in your business transactions in Europe. If you wish that policy to continue, then you must cooperate."

Big Uncle stared at her for a long moment, then gave a great belly laugh. "I like you," he said. "You are brave. Foolish . . . but very brave."

Song took a step forward, looking amazingly authoritative for someone in a tiny purple dress. "I will require the location of the Fengs—now."

"I will tell you what you need to know." Big Uncle waved her off with a thick hand. "You really are a bright young thing. But I suggest you wear your glasses more. They keep you from squinting."

Ten minutes later, Big Uncle watched the flippant MSS bitch and her American friend hurry toward the elevators. Clenching a beefy fist until it shook, he sent the nearest glass vase crashing against the floor as soon as the elevator door slid shut. Even destroying the five-thousand-dollar vase didn't make him feel any better.

The guests mingling just outside the office peered through the window at the noise, but the look on the crime boss's face told them a broken glass was something they should ignore.

"You let him take your guns?" Big Uncle turned to Lok, cuffing him on the back of the head and sending his ponytail swinging. "Why do I even keep you around?"

"Forgive me, boss," Lok said. He knew better than to make excuses.

Big Uncle folded his arms across his belly, still sitting on the edge of the desk. He raised thick eyebrows and looked from one bodyguard to another. "Well?" he said. "What are you waiting for? The Feng brothers will be waiting to kill these fools. Go and help them. I'll decide what to do with you when you return." He glared at the kid with the goatee. "That is, if that little MSS girl does not beat you up and take your gun again."

Chapter 55

"I don't like this," Quinn said, standing at the top of the Harbor Steps and looking down the broad gray stairs that tumbled from First to Alaska Way, ending across from the waterfront. A low sun peeked under the ragged cloudbank across Puget Sound, casting a pink glow on the wet sidewalks and pavement above, but darkness already gathered under the Alaska Way viaduct at the bottom of the steps. Pockets of aimless youth and a handful of lost tourists moved up and down the broad terraced steps.

Big Uncle had given them the address to an apartment building located below Seattle's lively Pike Place Market. It was a high-rent district for a terrorist flophouse, but the building was supposed to be under construction. There was a better than average chance the triad boss was sending them into a trap, so Quinn and Song ignored his suggested route directly below the market and decided to take the Harbor Steps and approach from what they hoped would be an unexpected route.

Like Quinn, Song had worn stylish but sensible enough

shoes that she'd be able to run in them if the need arose. The tight dress might pose a problem, but that's where the spandex shorts would come in. She stood directly beside Quinn, close enough he could feel her shiver.

"I do not believe Big Uncle would lie to us outright for fear of retaliation by my government," she said. "I don't think he knows we are essentially operating on our own."

"He doesn't have to lie," Quinn said. "He can just tell the Fengs we're coming. He wins either way."

Song's face grew dark, her mouth pinched. "If I find that he has betrayed me, I will kill him myself. I do not care if he has toes."

"Come on," Quinn said, starting down the stairs. "We can worry about Big Uncle later. If we don't locate the Fengs tonight, my boss will have to warn the Secret Service of the threat. They would call off the President's meeting with Prime Minister Nabe tomorrow morning."

"And the Fengs would know we are closing in," Song said, thinking it through. "They would simply readjust their plans to utilize the Black Dragon somewhere we do not expect."

"Yep," Quinn said, already moving down the stairs.

He pulled up short a few steps before the bottom. A steady thump of even traffic pounded down from the Alaska Way viaduct above, echoing off dusty concrete pillars and puzzle-piece stacks of orange construction barriers along a paved jogging trail.

It didn't take long to locate the apartment building, six stories of dark red brick. Sections of eight-foot chain link lapped against concrete Jersey barriers to form a semblance of a security fence around the construction zone. Scaffolding ran up the south wall where the renovation project had been started. At the north end, a dim light flickered in a fifth-floor window, behind dusty panes of cracked glass.

"You think that's them?" Song nodded at the light.

"Maybe," Quinn said. He checked his watch. Jacques and Emiko would land in less than an hour. The first rule of a gunfight was to bring a gun. The second was to bring a bunch of friends with guns, so the wisest course of action would be to watch and wait. A low building that looked like some kind of small warehouse ran off the end of the brick apartments, back to the south. Heavy foliage covered the hillside along the active train tracks, providing a likely spot to set up a hide until reinforcements arrived.

Two homeless men sat hunched on their blankets outside the fence panels. The shopping cart beside them overflowed with plastic bags and other bits of tattered treasure. The hulking shadow of a yellow backhoe loomed above them, heavy arm and bucket drawn up and back, throwing the men in even darker shadows. Both met Quinn's gaze, their dark faces shining with the shellac of open-air life, with no bath for weeks on end. He stared back, sizing them up as threats.

When he was young, Quinn's mother had seen the direction life was taking him and implored him to "be kind," but his father had pulled him aside for a little deeper counsel. While not exactly going against his wife's admonition for kindness, the elder Quinn had explained to both his sons that there were those on whom kindness did not work. "Dig deep," he had said. "Get inside yourself and find that part of you that makes anyone who happens to look in your direction want to do nothing but escape." It was good advice and Quinn had taken it to heart.

"Got a match," the nearest homeless man mumbled

around a dangling hand-rolled cigarette as Quinn walked by with his arm around Song, still playing the part of a vacationing couple.

Quinn had bought a packet of two disposable lighters as soon as they'd arrived at the hotel lobby, in keeping with his habit to carry a knife, a light, and something to make fire with at all times—even if he didn't have a gun. Years of experience in surveillance and investigation had taught him that the homeless were often ignored and overlooked, making them a wealth of information as long as they weren't alienated.

Quinn tossed the guy one of the lighters. "Keep it," he said.

Song laughed softly. "You are an interesting person," she said. "I would have expected you to stare a dagger into him and you decide to be nice."

"I'm not nice." Quinn shrugged. "Just practical. We're operating in their backyard. Best to stay on their good side."

The homeless man waved in thanks and lit the cigarette, blowing a huge plume of smoke into the darkness. A bright beam of laser light pierced the cloud an instant before a red dot tracked across Song's chest.

Quinn dove sideways, pushing her toward the cover of the backhoe. Chips of concrete flew through the air. Metal clanked and sparks flew as bullets from at least one suppressed weapon stitched the side of the machine. The homeless men dove for cover, upending their shopping cart as they scrambled for the nearest concrete column.

Quinn drew the Sig Sauer he'd taken from Lok and did a quick peek around the side of the backhoe's thick boom. More shots pinged off the metal.

"I count two of them," Quinn said, glancing over his shoulder to check on Song. He heard an odd metal squeak, almost a groan, and turned in time to see the shadow of a heavy length of chain arcing directly at him from high on the scaffolding. The blow threw Quinn fifteen feet, flipping him into the air and slamming him into the security fence like a baseball against a backstop. He slid to the ground with a sickening thud, completely still.

Chapter 56

Jacques Thibodaux unfolded his right leg and stretched it into the narrow aisle, trying to regain some semblance of circulation, and resigned himself to the fact that the other leg was just plain doomed. He knew a man of his bulk should really buy two seats, but thankfully Emiko Miyagi had decided to sit beside him. Tough as a leather boot, Miyagi was small enough they didn't fight over the armrest and play dueling shoulders for the entire five-hour flight out of Reagan National.

Thibodaux fished the cell phone out of his pocket as the plane settled in over the runway, turning it on before the tires squawked on the asphalt.

He tried Quinn twice and got nothing.

"The boy's gone dark," he muttered half to himself.

"I will call Palmer-san as soon as we're off the plane," Miyagi said. "You can try him again then."

"I got a bad feeling," Thibodaux said. "If I don't get ahold of him pretty damn soon, I say we head straight to Big Uncle's party and start crackin' heads."

Miyagi turned slowly in her seat and raised a thin black brow. Endowed with what Jacques called "relaxed bitchy face"—at least when it came to their relationship—the Japanese woman was so stoic it was sometimes painful to talk to her. "Crack heads?" she said.

"That's what I'm sayin'," Jacques said.

"For once, Thibodaux-san," Miyagi said, "we are in complete agreement."

Chapter 57

Quinn woke unable to move anything but a back tooth. A throbbing jaw told him he was still alive and with a little effort, he was able to spit out the loose molar. It landed with a *tink* on the porcelain that pressed against his face, mixing with the slurry of water and what appeared to be his blood.

He held his breath, straining to hear over the whoosh of his own pulse that convulsed in his ears. A constant drip tapped at the porcelain and a hollow gurgle came from some kind of drain near his feet. He blinked his eyes, bringing the grime ring of a decrepit bathtub into view, a few inches from his nose. About this same time, he realized his ankles were bound with duct tape and his hands were trussed behind his back. It occurred to him that the gurgling was caused as much by his blood draining away as it was the dripping water.

Quinn caught a bit of conversation over the top of the tub and turned his head to try to get a better angle. The movement brought a fresh gush of blood down his face and a stab of pain that arced from his shoulder blades to the small of his back. He had the fleeting notion that he might have broken his spine, but decided there was nothing he could do about it if he had. This was definitely one of those times his father had warned him about when it was better to fight through the objective and die in the assault than lie around and wait to be killed. Bound and tossed bleeding into a grimy tub— the outcome did not look promising. Quinn had found himself in worse predicaments, but not many.

Straining through the searing pain in his neck, he did a half sit-up to look at his feet. He had little feeling there, but as he suspected, they were bare and wrapped at the ankles with several turns of duct tape. On his back, Quinn lifted his legs and touched the mouth of the ancient faucet with his toe, feeling the years of mineral deposits even through the numbness. It was rough and jagged, crusting the lip of the faucet enough that by hooking his ankles under the spout and pulling toward his head, he was able to cut the tape.

Feet free, he collapsed into the tub from the effort, and tried to make sense of the voices coming from the other room. Some were brassy and scripted and Quinn recognized it as a Chinese-language television drama. The other voices grew more animated and spoke in rapid-fire Chinese.

". . . and you thought it wise to bring them here?" A male voice dripped with derision.

"You forget your place, Jiàn Zǒu," another voice said, also Chinese but with a heavy Turkic accent. The man in charge—this one had to be Ehmet Feng.

"You could not have just killed them and been done with it?"

"What is it to you?" Ehmet said. "We have time. I want to work on this one a little, see what she knows. Go ahead and kill the other one if you want. He's almost dead anyway. I plan to take my time here."

"There are others with us!" It was Song's voice, panting and tightly drawn. "They will arrive at any moment."

Quinn felt his heart race with silly hope. As long as she was alive, there was a chance.

"Ha!" Ehmet's voice dropped so low Quinn could barely hear him. "You have severely misjudged the situation."

"Yaqub Feng!" Song said, her voice frantic. "It is not too late to walk away. You are much too smart—"

Quinn heard a loud slap as someone, presumably Ehmet, shut her up. Song growled, fighting through the pain of the blow.

"Chinese bitch!" Ehmet spat, hitting her again. "My brother and I are one. He will have a turn with the iron when I grow tired of your screams. You would like that, wouldn't you, Yaqub?"

"I . . . suppose . . ."

Quinn heard the hiss of steam. "I think it is ready," Ehmet said.

"You are such a fool," Jiàn Zǒu said, sounding preoccupied, as if he could not be bothered with something as trivial as torture.

Song's pitiful scream filled the room. A second cry followed on the shattered peals of the first, trailing off in a series of breathless sobs as she worked through the pain.

Quinn thought of the poor college student, intent on nothing but the study of her violin, pressed into a life she wanted no part of. He peeked over the lip of the tub to find Song tied to a chair ten feet away, just outside the bathroom, facing the door. The stunted form of Ehmet Feng stood behind her. Quinn had known he was not a large man, but was unprepared for how small the Uyghur actually was. He looked like a child, dwarfed

by the remnants of a dilapidated kitchenette. A line of
sagging cabinets ran along the wall, their doors in various stages of falling off. Quinn noted the loose vinyl tile
that would give him little footing when he did decide to
move.

Someone stood directly to the Uyghur's right, beside an old mattress on the scabby shag carpet. Song
was tied to a high-back chair, her lips and nose battered
and bloody. Strands of matted hair hung down in front
of a swollen face. Her purple dress had been pushed up
to expose her thighs—where the Uyghur had pressed
the hot iron.

Boiling with rage, Quinn bolted upright, twisting in
the tub. Song screamed a third time, panting, begging
Ehmet to stop. Quinn jammed his wrists backwards,
sawing them against the jagged lip of the faucet. He'd
hoped to free his hands, but only managed to flay off a
layer of skin, just nicking the edge of the tape before
Ehmet Feng glanced up from his work and looked directly at him.

Quinn used his chest to clamber over the side of the
tub, then launched himself through the bathroom door.
Hands still taped behind his back, a single thought
pushed him forward—killing Ehmet Feng.

The threshold of the bathroom door blocked all but
a sliver of his view so Quinn had no idea if the men who
belonged to the other two voices had guns or where the
third was even located. He knew he'd find out soon
enough. Blood flowed freely from a wound above his
right eye, blurring his vision but adding to his rage. It
took several drunken steps to get his feet back under
him after the cramped quarters of the bathtub, but he'd
picked up a full head of steam by the time he plowed
into Ehmet Feng.

Stepping deftly around a clumsy swing with the

steam iron, Quinn impacted the snarling Uyghur center chest with the point of his shoulder, effectively using the other man's rib cage as a spring to send him flying backwards. Feng kept a death grip on the iron as he fell and Quinn knew he wouldn't stay down long.

Quinn spun long enough to get a quick assessment of the other two men. Yaqub Feng stood almost within arm's reach, mouth hanging open, pistol still shoved down the front of his jeans. Quinn caught a glimpse of movement across the room. Whoever it was, he was too far away to deal with under the present circumstances. His best course of action was to keep moving, making himself a more difficult target in case the man had a gun and more gumption than Yaqub Feng.

Hands still taped behind his back, Quinn bent at the knees, staying as centered as he could with his head spinning from the wound. Bringing his shoulders down in a low crouch, Quinn threw the full weight of his body against Yaqub's knee, wrenching the joint later-ally with a sickening crunch as cartilage and ligaments stretched and tore. Both men fell hard against the thin mattress, with the Uyghur's demolished knee breaking Quinn's fall.

Quinn sensed Ehmet before he saw him and rolled to escape a wild swing of the heavy iron. Yaqub fum-bled with the pistol, yanking it out of his waistband as if he were scared to touch it. Quinn took advantage of the indecisiveness and sent in a snap kick that launched the gun across the room. He bobbed back, using the in-jured man as a shield when Ehmet brought the steam iron around with a whoosh.

Step-dragging to keep a kneeling and sobbing Yaqub in front of him, Quinn worked to focus Ehmet's attention away from the terrified Song, who still sat bound and helpless in the chair.

One eye on Ehmet, Quinn tried to wipe the blood off his face with a shoulder, bringing another wave of nausea. The Uyghur saw the momentary flutter and pressed his attack.

"Kill him, you fool!" Ehmet screamed at the other man across the room. Quinn heard a door slam, bringing some measure of relief that he didn't have to deal with an extra gunman.

"No!" Song screamed.

Ehmet's face screwed into a ball of rage. He swung again, clobbering his own brother on the point of the chin. It was a glancing blow, but kept Yaqub reeling, still on his knees. Circling quickly so both men now faced him, Quinn sent a low kick with his right leg flying past Yaqub's right ear, putting Ehmet on the run. Instead of trying to connect with the smaller Uyghur, Quinn brought his foot around behind Yaqub's neck in the same motion, striking the Uyghur in the back of the neck just below the skull, driving him into the floor face-first, leaving him motionless on the filthy carpet.

Too dizzy to deliver the follow-up stomp that would have finished the downed Uyghur, Quinn stepped back to regain his footing. Ehmet screamed in rage, rushing him with the iron. Quinn saw the blow coming. He was able to bob out of the direct line, but the point of the iron grabbed the material of his suit jacket and spun him like a drunken dancer. Quinn moved with the blow, corkscrewing to the floor and sweeping the Uyghur's legs out from under him in the process.

Ehmet cursed and scrambled to get away. He flailed with the iron, but the lack of space on the ground robbed him of a backswing and took the power from his blows. Quinn's wound made him nearly impervious to the pain and he ignored the slapping iron, pulling the Uyghur down with the crook of his leg. Being on the ground

gave Quinn the added benefit of not having to worry
about the birds spinning in his head. He could fight
through the nausea if he didn't have to worry about
toppling over.

The tape around his wrists felt looser after the hard
fall and Quinn struggled to pull free as Ehmet continued
to swing the iron. Both men ended up on their backs, with
the Uyghur perpendicular to Quinn. Shrimping toward
him on feet and shoulders, Quinn chopped viciously at
the stunned Uyghur's throat with his heel. His hands
came free of the tape and he was able to trap the flopping steam iron before it struck something vital.

Flexing his fingers to bring the circulation back,
Quinn managed to pry the iron from Ehmet's hand at
the same moment Song let loose a shattered scream.

"Stop him!"

Quinn turned to find Yaqub staggering to his knees,
his hands wrapped around a wooden chair he intended
to use as a weapon.

Quinn swung as he stood, bringing the iron across in
a tight arc with all the torque and backup-mass his exhausted hips and shoulders could muster. He connected
with Yaqub's temple with a resounding *thunk* and sent
him back to the floor for good. Quinn continued with his
swing to impact Ehmet in the jaw, staggering him but not
knocking him out. Instead of chambering for another
swing, Quinn caught him again on the backswing, snapping his head around with a loud crack. A nauseous fury
filled Quinn's belly as he dropped to his knees over the
fallen Uyghur and struck him again and again with the
heavy iron.

"Stop it!" Song panted. "Stop it now. He is getting
away!"

Covered in blood and gore, Quinn let the iron fall to
the floor and stumbled over to her.

"We must hurry." She yanked against her bonds, her voice slurred from her swollen jaw. "Jiàn Zǒu. We have to stop him."

"Jiàn Zǒu?" Quinn stared at her. Hands shaking from adrenaline and fatigue, he cut her free with a knife he took from the dead Uyghur's pocket. Three burns, brands from the point of the iron, blotched the flesh of her left thigh. Angry and swollen, the three-inch triangles were already filling with fluid.

Song sprang to her feet, gritting her teeth as she tugged the hem of her skirt back down over the burns.

"Jiàn Zǒu is a Chinese soldier," she said, already starting for the door. Quinn didn't know if her face had gone pale from the Ehmet's torture or from seeing Jiàn Zǒu. "Please hurry. He must not escape."

Quinn fought the queasiness in his gut and took an extra second to grab the Uyghur's cell phone and scoop up the Glock pistol he'd kicked out of Yaqub's hand. He staggered toward Song, who leaned out the open door, looking for threats up and down the dark hallway.

"In your country you would call him special operations," she said, turning toward the door. "He is exceptionally well trained—and he has the Black Dragon."

Chapter 58

Vice President Lee McKeon sat with Ran, across from a frowning Hartman Drake in the presidential limo's vis-à-vis backseat. McKeon's motorcade had joined the President's and Drake had asked him to ride in the Beast, saying he wanted to talk on the way to the ballet performance. In reality, it was likely because he was frightened of being left alone. The President had hardly said a word since leaving the hotel.

McKeon had expected this behavior. If he'd inherited anything from his father it was his ability to read people—and Hartman Drake was all bow tie and bluster, easily manipulated into following the path of least resistance—so long as it made him look like a rock star. A Tajik by birth, he'd been taken from his family while still a child and raised to follow the path of jihad. Instead, he'd become tempted by the vices of men and was now vastly more interested in fame and power. Such a weakness made him controllable.

McKeon stared past his own reflection, watching rivulets of rainwater crease the tinted ballistic glass.

Dusk had begun to fall outside, earlier because of the rain, but intermittent streetlights illuminated the roadside trees and shrubs of Seattle Center.

They were nearly there.

Yelping sirens announced the arrival of the presidential motorcade as a phalanx of Seattle PD motorcycles led seventeen shining black SUVs and armored limousines under the monorail track above Fifth Avenue. They jumped the small curb onto the wide concrete path beneath the Space Needle and continued south past the Armory food court and a grassy amphitheater to circle the vehicles below a long gray structure along the Fountain Lawn called the Fisher Pavilion.

With both POTUS and the Prime Minister of Japan attending the ballet, security personnel were on high alert. Nabe had brought with him a small number of his own security from the elite *Keibibu Keigoka*, but while a foreign leader was on American soil, the United States Secret Service shouldered the protective responsibility. Each of the Japanese security men had attained the rank of third-degree black belt in either jujitsu or kendo in order to have even applied for the job. They buzzed around their leader like fussy bees, wearing natty suits with a red ties and matching pocket squares. The driver of their follow vehicle—the Secret Service demanded to be the limo driver—wore white gloves as was customary in Japan.

The Secret Service chose the pavilion as a staging area because it was near the Marion Oliver Hall where the Pacific Northwest Ballet was performing and because of the large parking area below the two-story building that overlooked the fountains and park. Teeming with security, the building would provide protection and cover in the event of an attack. The President's motorcade would stage directly outside the performance hall for quick egress in an emergency, but the cavalry of big guns would stage at the pavilion. A virtual army of snipers and lookout agents had already posted all over the complex, covering the Key Bank Arena, the parking garages across Mercer Street to the west, the Sacred Heart church tower to the southeast, and even the Space Needle itself, which had been closed to civilian visitors for the past twelve hours. The Secret Service briefing had noted that careful attention had been given to posting agents at every point around the venue that could give cover to an attacker. Seattle PD would provide a protective ring around the outer perimeter. Secret Service marksmen could lay down intersecting lines of fire at any moment in the unlikely event that someone was able to slip through. The supervisory agents for all three details had assured their charges that every precaution had been taken. The President was safe—and as long as he was safe, everyone was safe.

McKeon glanced across at the witless Drake and smiled serenely. If only they all knew.

It would be good to finally be rid of the idiot. He'd been a necessary evil that Allah had seen fit to place in the right place to assume the US presidency. And now, he had one more task to complete. At least the black tuxedo gave his ridiculous bow tie a home that didn't seem to scream buffoon.

"Tell me again why you're not attending," Drake said, running a finger around his starched collar to get more air.

"It is protocol, Mr. President," McKeon said, greasing the man's already monstrous ego with the title. "Heavy is the crown."

"So they say." Drake stared directly at him. "How can I be sure you haven't ordered one of your private IDTF goons to shoot me in the face?"

Ran threw back her head. "I have begged to kill you a thousand times. If he wanted you dead—"

McKeon squeezed her knee, half thinking she might cut his hand off. She didn't, but at least she stopped talking. The fact that Ran Kimura wanted to kill him was no surprise to Drake. She told him so every other day with her eyes. Words were rare from the intense Japanese woman, but her meaning was generally crystal clear.

"My IDTF goons are your IDTF goons, Mr. President," McKeon said in the verbal equivalent of rolling over and showing his tender white underbelly. "In any case, I need to make sure the venue change you ordered for the event tomorrow is taken care of."

"Very well," Drake grunted. "So long as you and your girlfriend here know who's in charge."

"Believe me, Hartman." McKeon raised both hands and smiled. "After your speech tomorrow, no one in this country will have a doubt as to who is in charge."

"There you go again." Drake shook his head. "I swear you creep me out with that kind of bwahahaha talk."

The motorcade took a right, then an immediate left, a river of black sedans pouring onto the concrete apron between the South Fountain Lawn and the Fisher Pavilion. From above, it looked like a choreographed dance. The Beast came to a controlled stop and a moment later an agent rapped on the President's door. A petite woman with dark hair cut over her ears the way Drake preferred stood beside the agent. David Crosby had done a good job finding this one. She was an accomplished ballerina from the University of Washington who would give the flighty President something to concentrate on during the lengthy performance. Her silver dress was accented with sequins, elegant enough it wouldn't raise any eyebrows from the social elite while still doing the job of raising Drake's blood pressure.

"Your guest for the ballet, Mr. President," the agent said, monotone, as if he'd seen it all before. "She's been thoroughly screened."

"I'm sure that was quite the pleasant undertaking." Drake grinned. His doubts and fears apparently flying from his mind at the arrival of a pretty woman, Drake patted the seat beside him. "Have a seat, my dear. The Vice President and his friend are just leaving."

"Miss Elliot." McKeon nodded, taking Ran by the hand in order to help her out of the limo. She would never exit merely because Drake told her to.

"Make certain to work out those arrangements, Lee," Drake said, flexing his POTUS muscles in front of the girl.

"Of course, Mr. President." McKeon could barely contain his smile. Groveling was easy when he knew the man would be dead before nightfall.

Chapter 59

Quinn pulled up short, stopping in the darkness at the bottom of the stairs to do a quick peek around the edge of the doorway. He trotted through the shadows to peer around the backhoe. The fact that he had no shoes was a problem. It was tough to do much fighting in bare feet, no matter what the super-duper cool ISIS training videos showed.

Evening traffic thumped on the viaduct overhead. Birds chirped and cooed, settling in for the evening in the trees that ran along the hillside that led up to the city. Quinn had hoped to catch a glimpse of Jiàn Zǒu running away, but he'd had too much of a head start. He stuffed the Glock into his waistband and put a hand on Song's shoulder as she came up beside him, intent on rushing past. She had been inconsolable since she'd recognized the man she called Jiàn Zǒu.

"Listen to me," Quinn said, leaning against the rear tire of the backhoe. "Both of us look like we've been mugged. My face is covered in blood, your lips look like someone hit you with a brick, and our shoes are gone. We have to use our heads here. We'll get stopped by the police before we make it a block. We don't know if he went up toward the Market or got picked up by a boat—"

"He went up," a voice said from under the viaduct. "Toward Pike."

Quinn drew the Glock again, scanning the shadows.

"You're the one who gave me the light, aren't you?" the voice spoke again. "Jeez Louise, those boys had it in for you. We thought they was going to murder your ass right here. Scared Burt so bad I think he's halfway to Tacoma by now. . . ."

Quinn relaxed a notch when a homeless man stepped around a concrete pillar. He held a plastic grocery sack in his tobacco-stained hand.

"I found your shoes," the man said, offering the sack to Quinn. "Was gonna sell 'em, but it looks like you still got a need."

Quinn thanked the homeless man, who said his name was Jiggy, and took Song gently by the hand to lead her back toward the apartment. "I have to make a call," he said. "And we need to take a look at those burns."

"The burns will heal." Song was breathing hard, about to hyperventilate. "I fear you do not understand. Jiàn Zǒu is not like the Fengs. He is a professional."

"So are we," Quinn said. "But we're going to need some reinforcements."

Back in the dilapidated apartment, Quinn had Song sit on the sagging couch while he knelt to look at her wounds. It was surreal, even to Quinn, to come back and sit with the bodies of the two men they'd been chasing for what seemed like an eternity. He moved the couch so the Fengs were out of her line of sight, hoping Song could focus on the Chinese-language news program on the television over his shoulder.

Quinn knew time was of the essence, so he used the dead Uyghur's cell phone to call Jacques, holding it against his ear with an aching shoulder while he knelt at her feet. Being engaged like this with someone else made lifting the hem of her dress feel less intimate, and more comfortable for both of them.

Three almost identical brands from the tip of the iron formed the beginnings of a rough circle on the otherwise pale skin of her inner thigh. Ehmet Feng had just been getting started with his torture—having only gotten past the taunting phase when Quinn stopped him. The Uyghur had applied just the tip of the iron, leaving behind small, triangular burns, complete with spots from the steam vents. It was as if he'd been drawing a flower with each nasty burn forming a pink and blistered petal.

Thibodaux answered on the second ring.

"'Allo?" the big Cajun grunted, not recognizing the number.

"Hey," Quinn said, feeling a little light-headed at the sound of his friend's drawl.

There was nothing in the shabby apartment that was even close to sterile, so Quinn did the best he could by ripping away some of the lining of his suit jacket and, after running it under cool tap water, applying it to Song's thigh to bring down the temperature of the wounds. There was little else he could do without first aid supplies, but he knew from harsh experience that small wounds could become big problems if left unattended.

"We're alive." He adjusted the cell phone with his free hand and rolled his neck to try to ease the pain. "That's something, I guess."

Quinn pressed the cool cloth lightly to Song's thigh, as much to keep her sitting as to treat the burn.

"Oo ye yi! *L'ami*," Thibodaux said. "Don't you do me that way. Where you at?"

Quinn gave their location and a rundown of events, including the new information about this Chinese commando, Jiàn Zǒu. He didn't know much, but he gave Jacques what he had.

He left out how badly he was hurt.

Song remained inconsolable, bouncing in her seat and looking toward the door as if she wanted to bolt. She suddenly tensed, moving his hand off her leg, nearly knocking him over as she jumped to her feet, pointing at the television.

"Hang on," Quinn said into the phone. "Something's happening." He turned to see a pretty Chinese reporter standing under an umbrella near the Space Needle. The camera panned away long enough to show a seemingly endless line of black limousines driving onto the concrete pathways of Seattle Center. It was obviously a motorcade.

Quinn listened long enough to get the gist of the story. A familiar knot formed low in his belly. He put the phone on speaker.

"Did you know anything about the President attending some kind of concert with the Japanese Prime Minister?"

"No idea," Thibodaux said. "It wasn't on the schedule this morning. Must have been a last-minute thing."

"It's a ballet," Song said, eyes still glued to the television. "Remember Prime Minister Nabe's wife was a ballerina, as is his daughter. . . ." Her voice trailed off and she turned to look at Quinn. "Jiàn Zǒu will not wait until tomorrow morning. This is the target."

Thibodaux gave a low whistle when he heard the news. "I know POTUS is a shitbird and all, but I think we should make an anonymous call to the Secret Service and get him out of there."

"It won't matter," Quinn said, looking at the glass walls of McCaw Hall. "That place must hold a couple of thousand people—"

"They say three thousand," Song corrected him, slowly shaking her head.

"If we tip our hand, Jiàn Zǒu will just shoot into the building. The US will blame China."

"You said this Jiàn character is a Chinese Army GI Joe or some shit," Thibodaux said. "Sounds to me like the Chinese are the ones behind this."

"Not China," Song said. "General Sun. It is he who wants a war. Jiàn Zǒu was a member of the *Nan Dao* or Southern Broadswords, the Special Forces unit operating in the Guangzhou Military Region. I trained with them for a short time as well. General Sun was the commander of this unit. Perhaps our countries will be at war one day, but this is the work of General Sun. This operation was not ordered by President Chen Min."

"Tough thing to be sure of," Jacques said at the other end of the line.

"I am sure," Song said. "If he'd wanted to kill your President, Chen Min would have sent me."

Quinn nodded at that. "It really makes no difference. If Jiàn Zǒu deploys the Black Dragon, the US will blame China—"

"And the Chinese would feel like they had to shoot first," Jacques finished his thought, "before we unleash a certain hell all over them."

Quinn shot a glance at Song. "Are you okay to move?"

"Of course." She frowned, shaking off his doubts. "I have been burned before."

"You're the only one who can identify Jiàn Zǒu," he said. "I was so busy with the Fengs that I never got a good look at him." He turned back to the phone. "I'm thinking we need to split up. Jacques, you go and rattle branches at Big Uncle's. See what he and his men know. I'm pretty sure he sent us into an ambush with the Feng brothers, so don't go easy on them. Emiko-san, if you—"

"She's gone," Thibodaux cut him off. "We were only about ten blocks away when you called. Crazy woman beat feet as soon as she heard where you are. I expect she'll be crashing through the door any minute now with her badass sword ready to protect her favorite."

Miyagi's voice crackled on the line, conferenced in from the beginning. "I am still listening," she said.

Thibodaux's cringe was audible, even over the phone.

"I am almost there," Miyagi said. "Meet me under the viaduct in five minutes."

More static came over the line.

"Almost there?" Quinn muttered, half to himself. "What are you driving?"

Nothing but static.

"Her broom, likely as not," Jacques offered, thinking she'd hung up.

"Still here, Thibodaux-san," Miyagi said. "It is no wonder you think Jericho is my favorite."

Chapter 60

The throaty *brap* of a Honda CBR sport bike echoed off the concrete pillars of the viaduct five minutes later when Miyagi rode up. She wore a scuffed black helmet, jeans, and a dark blue Helly Hansen rain jacket against the drizzle. She removed the helmet and shook her head to tame her hair before removing a small leather backpack and placing it on the seat of the bike.

"I believe you will require stitches, Quinn-san." She stared at his forehead, but did not ask for an explanation.

"Is it still bleeding?" Quinn asked, dabbing at the tender spot above his eye.

Miyagi shook her head.

"Well," Quinn said. "That'll have to be good enough for now." He looked at the bike. "I'm not even going to ask how you got this."

Miyagi shrugged. "The keys were in it," she said, as she rummaged through her backpack. "And you need transportation to the target site." She brightened, locating what she was looking for, and took out a smartphone and Bluetooth earpiece to match the one she wore in her ear.

"You carry around an extra earpiece?" Quinn couldn't help but smile.

Miyagi handed it over. "What is it you say? *Two is one and one is none*. Like you, I prefer to be prepared."

Quinn took two extra minutes to apply a piece of gauze from Miyagi's wound kit to the burns on the inside of Song's thigh. She demurred at first, saying they had no time—until he showed her the high position of the passenger seat on the Honda, pointing out how her thighs would hit him right at the waist.

"I have an extra pistol if you need it," Miyagi said, hand in her backpack.

Quinn gave Song Yaqub Feng's Glock that he'd tucked under his shirttail. Better to trust a pistol from Miyagi over one he picked up off a dead terrorist. She treated all her weapons as she would a katana—with reverence and care. The extra she'd brought with her was a Kimber Eclipse in 10mm, much like the Ultra she'd presented him when he'd first started working for Palmer. Even better, she had an inside-the-waistband holster so he wouldn't have to worry about losing it in a fight like he had the last few pistols that had come into his possession.

Miyagi frowned as she gave him the weapon, focusing again on his wound. He'd had time to wash his face, but there were no mirrors in the apartment so he'd not been able to see the damage. Her motherly looks and the throbbing headache made him think it was probably a doozy.

Quinn swung a leg over the bike and planted both feet, waiting for Song to climb on behind him.

"Be on your guard," Miyagi said, moving toward the Harbor Steps that would take her back up to Pike Street and downtown. She never said, "Be safe." There was no way to do what they did with any measure of safety.

All they could do was mitigate danger. "From your description of the weapon, Jiàn Zǒu will be able to fire it from some distance away. I will be your eyes and ears at the venue."

"How is she going to get there?" Song asked, settling in gingerly behind Quinn.

Miyagi merely smiled and trotted up the stairs.

The Honda CBR had plenty of power to haul two people, especially if one was as light as Song, but the seating arrangements were a different story. The passenger seat was set several inches higher than the rider's seat, directly over the rear wheel. Quinn had insisted Song wear their only helmet. At every stop she had a tendency to knock him in the back of the head with her face shield and slide forward enough to push his groin against the CBR's fuel tank with sickening regularity.

"Put your hands on the tank," he yelled over his shoulder.

"What?"

He patted the fuel tank with his left hand. "Reach around me and brace yourself right here," he said. "It'll keep you from sliding forward and hurting your burns so much. Not to mention keeping you from knocking me silly. You lean when I lean. Got it?"

"Got it," she said, but Quinn could tell from her voice she was hurting.

Riding more as one now, Quinn rolled on the throttle, feeling the welcome wind. Drizzling raindrops bit at his face and hands, but he didn't care. He was riding toward a problem that needed solving and he'd choose that over a comfortable chair any day.

Her knees up like a jockey, Song drew a round of cat-

calls from a group of sailors heading into the Spaghetti
Factory as he took the corner off Alaska Way onto Broad
Street, rumbling over the train tracks. Quinn jogged
back to his left two blocks up, weaving his way through
the back streets in the general direction of the Space
Needle and Seattle Center. Riding without a helmet on
a stolen bike with a girl in a dress hiked up around her
waist—and looking like he'd just come from the losing
end of a fight—he decided it was best to avoid law enforcement contact.

He rolled in from the west, parking the Honda a
block away from the Key Bank Arena to walk up for a
closer look. The rain had stopped, leaving everything
wet and glowing in the last moments of dusk.

Quinn knew he would be in some Secret Service
sniper's crosshairs if he rode up on a bike. His penchant
for motorcycles was noted in his file. Hartman Drake was
no brilliant tactician, but according to Jacques, McKeon
was running the show, and he was smart enough to put
everyone on alert for anyone on a motorcycle. Approaching on foot, under cover of dusk and with Song
at his side allowed him to blend into the dozens of
other couples walking around the complex hoping to
catch a glimpse of someone famous.

Quinn noted the ambulance and line of black SUVs
parked on the wide sidewalk outside McCaw Hall. And
the second group of identical vehicles formed up on
the circular drive on the other end of a grassy field—
out of the way but within easy reach.

"Your Vice President," Song said, watching the
same group of dark vehicles. "He is there, hoping to
see the attack."

"That would be my guess," Quinn said. "But we'll
have to deal with him later." He watched a steady line

of patrons as they filed into McCaw Hall. Many looked like college students, some even younger. All fit and trim, likely from local ballet companies, Quinn thought. They bunched at the doors, a bouquet of tuxedos and brightly colored evening gowns, waiting their turn to pass through one of three metal detectors operated by uniformed Secret Service officers.

"Looks like the President and Prime Minister are already inside," Quinn said. "Tell me more about Jiàn Zǒu."

"What do you mean?" Song said. "I have told you what I know."

Quinn shook his head. "The Fengs were extremists, very likely ready to die for their cause. What about Jiàn Zǒu? Do the Southern Broadsword Special Forces train for suicide missions?"

"They are true patriots for China," she said. "Our Special Operations units deal primarily with nontraditional security threats we call the 'three forces': terrorism, separatism, and extremism. A suicide mission would be a last resort. From what I have seen of Jiàn Zǒu, he would have a plan for escape."

Quinn veered left toward a large fountain in the middle of the huge green lawn, avoiding two lumbering men in ill-fitting suits he expected were IDTF agents on the prowl. Both were on their phones, oblivious to the fact that one of their prime targets was walking by less than fifty feet away.

"The Black Dragon," Quinn said as he and Song walked toward the fountain, facing the concert hall. "Tell me about the guidance system."

"Much like your American Javelin," she said, wincing at the pain from her burns. Quinn stopped walking, drawing her in close by his side as if they were having a romantic moment by the fountain. "The launcher is simply aimed like a gun. Once an IR image of the target is uploaded to the missile's memory, the shooter may, as you say, fire and forget. And, he could shoot it from virtually anywhere within the two-mile range."

"Not quite anywhere," Quinn said. He stood back from Song as if to take a photo with his phone, giving him the chance to have a prolonged look at the venue without drawing too much attention. "He has to be in a place to see what he's shooting at."

Quinn made a slow turn, noting the buildings that blocked any direct view to McCaw Hall: the Key Bank Arena, Seattle Repertory Theater, and the Cornish Playhouse to the west, the Fisher Pavilion and the Seattle Science Center to the south, and the Armory to the east. He considered the Space Needle. At over six hundred feet high, it would make the perfect spot from which to shoot nearly anywhere in the area. But an undetected escape past the legion of Secret Service personnel would be next to impossible—even if he'd had time to get there before them—which he had not.

That left the area to the north. Quinn looked at a campus map on a wooden sign near the fountain. There was a parking garage across from McCaw Hall, on Mercer Street. Raised parking made for a good sniper hide, but this one was close enough to be crawling with Secret Service agents. The Fengs might have shot from nearby, but if Jiàn Zǒu was a professional, he'd utilize the two-mile standoff the weapon system provided.

That left Queen Anne Hill. Several radio towers, big-money mansions, and the lights to what looked like a large set of condos rose up through a wide gap in the buildings, directly to the north. Any number of places would make a perfect firing position.

"Sorry to put you through this, but we need to go for

another ride." Quinn returned the phone to his pocket, nodding toward the hill. "He'll be somewhere up there."

"How do you know?" Song asked, grimacing around the pain.

"Because that's where I would be," Quinn said.

Chapter 61

McKeon leaned against the leather headrest and closed his eyes. It was only a matter of minutes now until his father's plan would finally come to fruition. In the span of a breath, the course of the world would change irrevocably, ridding the Middle East of the American pests and ushering in a caliphate that could sweep across Europe unimpeded. There were only last-minute details that he would have to clear up. Not the least of which was the Japanese woman sitting next to him. McKeon's wife knew about her, of course. Ran Kimura was a necessary, and, though he did not go into detail with his wife, an exquisite evil. He would not likely have made it this far without her protection. But his wife was a good Muslim woman, devoted enough to allow him the latitude to accomplish what his father had begun—and devout enough to follow him through Hell.

"And what of tomorrow?" Ran asked, running her fingers over his knee, as if she were reading his mind.

"Tomorrow?" he asked, trying to gain time. A consummate politician, he was rarely caught flatfooted with a question. "Tomorrow, Hartman Drake will be nothing but a greasy blot of memory and I will be President of a nation at war."

"Of course, my love." Her fingers worked their way up his thigh. "I know all that. But what of your wife? What of me?"

McKeon forced a chuckle. "My wife is still in Oregon. We will have plenty to keep us busy, my dear."

"Do you know the last words you spoke to Drake?"

McKeon shook his head. "I really don't remember." Something about the way Ran looked at him made his blood run cold. He was suddenly taken back to the night they'd first met, when she stood over him naked, killing sword in hand.

"I remember them clearly," she said, withdrawing her hand. "You said 'things will work out as they must,' the same thing you said to me when I asked about your wife."

Ran leaned back against the seat, letting her head fall sideways so she was looking him directly in the eye from just inches away. "And how must they work out, my love? Tell me now, for I fear your life depends on your answer."

McKeon fumbled in his pocket for the key fob panic button, hoping to activate it before Ran knew what he'd done. The privacy screen was up between the front and the backseats—and the agents were used to a certain amount of noise when Ran accompanied him. If he banged on the partition, she'd kill him before anyone had a chance to respond.

"Looking for this," Ran said, opening her hand to reveal the panic button. Her lips turned down in a stoic frown. "I suppose that is all the answer I needed."

"Please," McKeon said, casting his eyes around the backseat for some avenue of escape, something he might say to change her mind.

"Please?" Ran said, her eyes closing to narrow black lines. Her head still lolled against the seat, but that only made her all the more terrifying. "I thought a man of your talent would come up with something better than that."

Chapter 62

Back on the Honda, Quinn headed west, giving Seattle Center and the attendant security a wide berth. He cut back to the north on Third Avenue, working his way up the hill by feel, using his senses as much as his intellect. Human beings tended to follow natural lines of drift and there was a very good chance that if he just looked for what he considered the perfect spot for a sniper to hide, Jiàn Zǒu would be somewhere nearby.

The trouble was any one of a dozen locations would make a good firing location. There were multistory mansions, at least three wooded parks, and a half dozen businesses on Galer Street that would all do the trick. Song sat behind him, arms around his waist, both hands pressed flat on the gas tank in front of him. He was sure she was in terrible pain, but she said nothing.

He had both Miyagi and Thibodaux conferenced in so he could hear them on the Bluetooth earpiece.

"You getting anything, Jacques?" he asked, hoping Big Uncle would have provided some clue to narrow down his choices.

"Working on it," Thibodaux grunted. "Big Uncle has barricaded his shitty little self in the back room and his man Lok is awfully hardheaded."

"All the patrons appear to be inside the event hall."
Miyagi's voice came into his ear as clearly as if she
were sitting on the bike behind him. "The Secret Service agents with the vehicles look like they are settling
in for the long haul."

"You're too close if you can see that," Quinn said.

"I'm on top of the theater next door. It gives me the
perfect vantage point to be your eyes and ears."

"That's inside the blast radius, Emiko," Jacques cut
in, sounding as if he was still in the middle of thrashing
someone. "Too close."

"He's right," Quinn said, riding past an ice cream
parlor, a glassblowing studio, and a bike shop, any of
which could have been the ideal sniper hide for a shot
with the Black Dragon. "You're in grave danger if we
don't manage to stop Jiàn Zǒu."

"Thank you for your concern," she said. "Both of
you. But we are all in grave danger if you do not stop
Jiàn Zǒu."

"Copy that," Quinn said. The aftermath of the fight
and the initial adrenaline dump of pursuit left him feeling muddleheaded and doomed to fail. "Tell me what
you got, Jacques."

"You mean besides the unconscious dude with a
ponytail and his fat ass boss I had to drag through a
mile of broken glass—"

Quinn let off the throttle and grabbed a handful of
front brake, feeling Song pile up behind him as she
was thrown into his back by the rapid stop. She gave a
stifled whimper as the back wheel hopped up a hair in
a modified *stoppie*. Quinn planted his foot and poured
on the gas, throwing the Honda into a controlled 180 to
head back the way they'd come.

"Get ready to go," he said over his shoulder to Song.
"He's at the glass shop."

Chapter 63

Ran's blade struck quickly, entering Lee McKeon's neck below his ear, nicking his spinal cord and rendering him unable to move—or speak above a choked whisper. The eyes that he'd used so often to entrance her flew open, twitching as if he wanted desperately to close them but could not. She'd missed any major arteries and only a thin trickle of blood wept down the side of his neck, soaking into the white collar of his shirt.

"Whaaaa?" A hoarse croak escaped his gaping mouth.

"I am sorry, my love," Ran said, withdrawing the blade and wiping it on the leg of his slacks. "You always imagined you would die in a glorious jihad, but instead you were killed by your Japanese whore." Her voice grew tense and she fought back a tear. "I was incredibly foolish, letting you under my skin like the black ink of my tattoo. You will not feel this," she said, drawing a long, whip-like blade from the belt of her dress. "I wish it were otherwise, but paralysis is the only way I could be certain you would not cry out." She gave a flick of her hand so the blade clipped his aorta, just below the stomach. She kept the wound small, containing everything, including the copious amounts of blood that now flooded his gut. "As you are so fond of saying, things will work out as they must."

Ran said good-bye to the dead man as she opened the door, going so far as to throw him a flirtatious wink the Secret Service had come to expect. She nodded to the two agents posted near the front of the armored limo. Neither of them noticed the small droplets of blood on the dark blue dress she'd worn for that very reason. She'd have plenty of time to disappear into the crowd before they even knew their traitorous boss was dead. By then, they would never find her.

Flat on her belly, Emiko Miyagi watched as agents rushed to encircle a black limousine parked at the base of Fisher Pavilion. She was perfectly hidden on top of the Cornish Playhouse adjacent to McCaw Hall, watching events unfold five stories beneath her.

"Something's happening," she whispered into her earpiece.

"You see him?" Quinn said.

"No," Miyagi said. "I believe it is something to do with the Vice President." She worked her way around an air-conditioning unit, giving her an unobstructed view of the pavilion, but exposing herself to anyone who happened to be scanning the rooftop.

"I'm heading your way," Thibodaux said. "In the meantime, I respectfully suggest you get your ass out of there."

Chapter 64

Quinn killed the Honda's engine a block away from the three-story redbrick building that housed the glass shop and gallery. Considering all the ornate hand-blown glass at Big Uncle's charity event, he should have realized this was the place the moment he'd ridden by.

Quinn planted his feet and let Song slip off behind him. The evening hour and a fresh drizzle had chased any pedestrians away and they had the street to themselves. He padded up to the edge of the building with Song right behind him. The inside of her leg was smeared in blood—a consequence of her burns rubbing against his belt as she took the many turns and bumps on the back of the bike. She seemed to do better back on the ground and moved quickly, assuring him she was in fighting shape as he did a quick peek into the alley that ran alongside the shop.

It was clear, so he moved up next to the front window, Kimber in hand.

"Watch my back," he said as he inched his way up on the window to have a look without alerting anyone inside.

"I count three Asian males," he whispered, as much

for Jacques and Emiko's benefit as Song's. "Three furnaces up and running."

Had this been an earlier time, when he'd had more control and moles hadn't infiltrated the government, Win Palmer would not have hesitated to call in an airstrike on the shop, obliterating the building and the threat. As it was, Quinn had no high-tech equipment or sophisticated drones to rely on. If Jiàn Zǒu was to be stopped, it was up to him and a pretty Chinese spy who could barely walk.

One of the three men removed a long metal tube from the nearest furnace, spinning an orange glob of molten glass the size of a cantaloupe on one end. He extended the tube out in front of him, blowing on one end as he spun it expertly in his hands. A second man followed suit, retrieving a similar glowing orb from the neighboring furnace. This one worked with a partner assisting him as he blew into the pipe and spun the liquid glass into a squirming orange ball. Pumpkin-sized spheres and huge blossoms of flowering glass hung like an inverted garden from the shop ceiling and lined row after row of shelves. A wooden counter, meant to provide a safe place from which patrons could watch the artisans at their work, divided the furnace floor from the main showroom.

Formulating a plan of attack, Quinn caught a glimpse of movement beyond the counter at the base of what looked like a set of stairs. He motioned Song forward, nodding to the back of the shop. "Is that him?"

The sudden tension in Song's body answered his question. Jiàn Zǒu walked out into the shop, talking on the phone as he watched the three men work their glass. He was a slight man, well-muscled and, as Quinn suspected he would, moved with the military bearing of a man who knew what he was doing. He pressed a cell phone to his ear, nodding, listening intently to whoever was on the other end. A moment later, he snapped to attention, the way someone ingrained with military protocol would act if he was just given a direct order from a superior officer, even over the phone. He'd surely just been given the green light to shoot.

Instead of walking toward the stairs as Quinn suspected he would, Jiàn Zǒu stepped to the wooden counter, checking out the window as if he expected someone might be following him. Quinn tried to take a step back and get out of his line of sight, but with Song tucked in tightly behind him, there was nowhere for him to go.

Chapter 65

The IDTF sniper seated on top of Key Bank Arena panned his scope across the top of the Cornish Playhouse and caught a glimpse of movement. He called out the target over the radio.

"Hercules CP, this is Nest 4. I have a visual on the Playhouse roof. Asian female, dressed in black. We have anyone up there?"

The command post asked him to stand by and there was a long pause on the radio—as he expected there would be. The entire campus below him had erupted into a frenzied circus with the flashing lights of emergency vehicles running in every conceivable direction, providing cover over the escape of the fleeing black snake that was the VP's motorcade.

The sniper had memorized the position of every Secret Service countersniper and lookout unit and had been given orders to dump anyone not on that list—but he wasn't about to get jammed up by shooting some Secret Service darling who wandered into the wrong spot.

After what seemed like forever, he got the answer he was looking for. "Nest 4, Hercules CP. She's not ours.

Green light on the target. Repeat. Nest 4, you are green to go."

Verbal orders, logged and heard by many over the radio, relieved him of that worry—giving him the CYA he needed to pull the trigger. The playhouse was supposed to be clear of anyone, and yet there she was, a dark female, possibly Asian, peering through a set of binoculars from the shadows behind an air-conditioning unit.

Using the laser on the side of his night vision scope he ranged the target at 211 meters. He chuckled to himself, careful not to lose sight of the woman. Anything under 300 meters was point-blank range for his .300 Winchester Magnum. One of the handful of consummate professionals in the IDTF, the sniper didn't rely solely on the laser. He knew a normal air-conditioning unit was approximately five feet tall. This one filled up eight mil-dots on the crosshairs of his scope. He did the math in his head and confirmed that the laser rangefinder was correct. At that range, no adjustment to his scope was necessary. He was high enough off the ground that the suppressed shot was not likely to even be noticed by any of the agents below, especially when scrambling around in code black on the VP. Pulling the stock in tight against his shoulder with his off hand, the sniper slipped the pad of his finger over the trigger and let the crosshairs of his scope settle on the Asian woman's ear. He took a deep breath and slowly began to release it, settling his body into the shot. This was almost too easy. A whisper of wind shattered his concentration, like the flutter of a bird on the roof behind him.

Ran Kimura buried her blade in the sniper's neck. She flicked it back and forth as she shoved the rifle sideways in the event of any involuntary convulsions of his trigger finger. He collapsed facedown without ever even knowing she was there.

Ran shoved his body sideways, taking up a position behind the scope. She made it her habit to carry a cloned Secret Service radio and had heard him call out the target and description. It had taken her precious seconds to make it to the top of the Key Bank roof and she'd had to kill two agents on the way up.

Settling in, she slid her finger over the trigger and took a deep breath. "Hello, Mother," she whispered as the crosshairs settled over Emiko Miyagi's face. "How nice of you to drop by." She swung the rifle a hair to the left and pulled the trigger, sending a 180-grain bullet singing off the brick a scant foot in front of Miyagi. "That is much better," Ran said to herself, watching her mother duck behind the air conditioner. "How will we ever get to know one another if you get yourself shot?"

Ran moved quickly, sliding along the slanted roof to disappear into the darkness behind the glowing red sign of the Key Arena. She had no doubt that she would see her mother again, or that she would be the one to kill her. It would not be soon—but when it happened, she would not hide behind a riflescope from a great distance away. It would eye to eye and heart to heart.

Chapter 66

Quinn bolted past the window as Jiàn Zǒu sent two rounds crashing through the glass. Song returned fire, forcing the other man to duck behind one of the heavy glass furnaces long enough for Quinn to boot the door. The action sent a wave of pain up his already injured hip, but luckily the frame separated under the first kick. Stumbling forward, Quinn sent a round downrange, keeping Jiàn Zǒu's head down so Song could make it in past the fatal funnel of the demolished door. Two of the Asian men working the furnace floor had their hands full with the balls of molten glass. The third stepped behind a wooden partition to reappear an instant later with what looked like an M4 carbine. He sprayed a volley of fire into the shop, sending shards of shattered glass flying in every direction. Quinn and Song dove for a line of tall Oriental vases that would provide some semblance of concealment if not actual protective cover. Vases and glass shelves alike exploded behind them as the shooter tracked their movements with the rifle.

Quinn came sliding to a stop behind a leather sofa at the far end of the shop, likely meant for tired husbands to rest their feet while their spouses continued to shop. Song looked up from where she lay beside him, both eyes locked in a grim stare.

"Go left," he whispered. She nodded, rolling away and laying down a line of fire. Quinn rolled to his right, putting two .45 rounds in the chest of the rifleman. The crash of glass and a sharp cry told him Song's rounds had found their way into one of the glassblowers.

The rifle began to bark again as Jiàn Zǒu sprayed the ceiling with lead. Razor-sharp shards began to rain down, causing both Quinn and Song to shield their faces to keep from being blinded. Exposed skin, clothing, and even their hair were covered in tiny blades they couldn't brush away without being cut. Deadly icicles, remnants of the broken flowers, swayed on thin wires above, threatening to slice anyone to pieces who happened to be walking under them when they fell.

When the shooting paused, Quinn caught a glimpse of the second glassblower working his way around the wooden counter, carrying his metal tube tipped with molten glass like a spear.

"I will take care of this one," Song said. "Jiàn Zǒu ran up the stairs. You must stop him."

Song rolled away from the heavy sofa, advancing on the man with the hot glass as she shot into the wooden partition.

Quinn ran for the stairs, Kimber up and ready to shoot as soon as he had a sight picture. Jiàn Zǒu sent two shots down the stairwell but Quinn could tell they were unaimed and meant only to slow Quinn's advance so he could arm the Black Dragon. At this point, it mattered little if he even hit his intended target. If a Chinese weapon was fired anywhere near the President, it would be enough to cause a war.

Quinn made it up the stairs in two bounds, knowing

he would be a bullet sponge before he got Jiàn Zǒu in his sights. But the commando had overestimated Quinn's aversion to gunfire, expecting him to come creeping up the stairs. A look of genuine surprise crossed his face when Quinn rushed into the room.

Surprised or not, he had time to raise his pistol and fire, striking Quinn in the right shoulder. The shock of the bullet's impact sent the Kimber flying from Quinn's hand as surely as if it had been slapped away. Instead of slowing, Quinn plowed straight ahead, impacting the Southern Sword commando with the full weight of his body. Both men fell to the floor, Quinn's left hand shoving the barrel of the other man's pistol out of the way as he pulled the trigger again, inches from Quinn's ear.

The concussion sent a shower of lights through Quinn's brain. Ambient noise was replaced by a piercing whine in his ears. His right arm nearly useless, Quinn struck out with a flurry of knees and his good elbow, biting, kicking, and head butting in his best impression of the cartoon Tasmanian Devil.

Thankfully, the sudden outburst of energy knocked Jiàn Zǒu's pistol away in the struggle, but the wiry man seemed able to soak up any beating Quinn was able to dish out.

Growling a string of Chinese curses, he sent a volley of his own punches into Quinn's face and ribs. Quinn rolled away as best he could, but with a broken right wing, there was little he could do to block the man's powerful left hooks. Momentarily stunned, Quinn felt himself being dragged along the floor by the collar. Jiàn Zǒu meant to throw him down the stairs.

Song's pitiful scream drifted up from the floor below. Instead of tensing, Quinn let his body go limp as if he'd given up. It allowed his exhausted muscles a split second to regroup and made it more difficult for Jiàn Zǒu to drag him.

"*Ben dan!*" He barked in Mandarin. "Stupid fool." "It is over."

Still relaxed, Quinn felt Jiàn Zǒu lift, ready to toss him down the wooden stairs.

"Go to hell," the Chinese commando spat.

Quinn twisted like a cat over a bathtub as Jiàn Zǒu tried to let him go. His left arm shot around the man's waist. Arching his back, Quinn pushed off the wall with both feet, spinning the startled commando and sweeping his knees. With his energy already moving in the direction of the stairs to throw Quinn, Jiàn Zǒu teetered forward, with nothing left to stop his fall. Quinn helped him on his way, slamming the man's face into the steps and riding him all the way to the bottom in a short but bumpy trip.

Quinn rolled away as soon as they rattled to a stop. Jiàn moaned, staggering to his feet. Song crouched at the base in the middle of the furnace room. Quinn could tell she was hurt, but things were moving too quickly for him to be sure how badly.

Growling, Jiàn Zǒu kicked Quinn aside and began to limp toward the stairs. Song shrieked, throwing herself at him, trying to drag him back, but he just shook her off. She looked at Quinn, beckoning him to his feet with her eyes. She said something, but Quinn could hear nothing but the constant ringing in his ears. Then her eyes flashed toward the long metal tube that protruded from the glowing orange opening of the nearest furnace.

Seeing that he understood, Song flung herself at Jiàn Zǒu again, just as he reached the base of the stairs. She sank her teeth into his ear as Quinn yanked the heavy tube from the furnace. Stumbling forward, he planted the business end in the center of Jiàn Zŏu's chest. The commando twisted, screaming as he tried in vain to use Song as a shield. His shriek was cut short as the fist-size ball of 2,500-degree glass vaporized his lungs and shattered his spine. The sickening odor of roasted flesh filled the air in an instant. He was dead before he hit the ground.

Song flinched in pain as Quinn dragged her away from the sizzling corpse. For the first time, he noticed her injuries. Her left shoe was blackened and charred, presumably in her fight with the second glassblower. Closer inspection showed a piece of hot glass the size of a quarter had burned its way through the top of her foot, between the bones and out the sole of her shoe. The pain must have been unbearable and Quinn found himself getting queasy at the thought of it.

"Call in," she said. "Let them know we are good." She pulled herself sideways, toward an overturned wooden bench, her back to Quinn now.

"I will," Quinn said. "Let's get you flat on your back before you go into shock."

She coughed when he rolled her over, wincing at the slightest movement.

Quinn took a bottle of water from the workbench and poured it over her foot in an attempt to bring down the temperature. He put his fingers to her neck, checking her pulse, fearing that she was falling into shock. It was then that he saw she'd retrieved the Glock that must have fallen behind the wooden bench during her fight.

She raised it with a feeble hand.

"There is still the matter of the Black Dragon," she

groaned, her breath coming in rapid gasps. "I cannot allow it to fall into American hands."

Quinn shook his head. "Song—"

"At least tell them I made an attempt." She let the pistol fall with a long sigh. "I cannot shoot you, Jericho Quinn. You have toes."

Chapter 67

Consistent with protocols after a security breach, the Secret Service should have whisked Hartman Drake away from the concert hall as soon as they realized the Vice President had been assassinated. The lead agent for his detail informed him of the death, as agents formed a protective barrier around him. Instead of ushering him straight out to the Beast, they took him into the back offices that had been designated by Advance as a safe room in the event of a shelter-in-place emergency.

His back to the wall and surrounded by machine-gun-wielding agents, Drake began to sweat profusely. He suddenly found it impossible to breathe and all but tore the bow tie from around his neck.

"What's going on?" he demanded of the young agent standing inside the door. "It's been over an hour. Why aren't we moving?"

"I'm not sure, Mr. President," the agent said, eyes focused on the door.

"Is the Vice President really dead?" Drake shuddered at the thought. No matter how much he despised the man, going forward without him seemed impossible.

"I'm not sure, Mr. President," the agent said, as if it was the only phrase he knew. Then he put a hand to his ear, nodding at some radio traffic. He looked at Drake. "Please stand by to move, Mr. President. They're bringing up your limo now."

The short move from Seattle Center to Boeing Field and Air Force One should have taken ten minutes, especially with a Seattle Police escort. For some reason, the Secret Service seemed to be taking their own sweet time. Alone in the backseat of his limo, Drake pounded on the partition.

"Why are we taking so long?" he asked as the tinted glass screen lowered with an electronic whir. A different agent turned to look back at him from the front passenger seat. It was Jack Blackmore, the Special Agent in Charge of President Chris Clark's protective detail. "What's happened? Where is my detail?"

Blackmore smiled, the crow's feet around his dark eyes adding to the rugged, outdoorsy look Drake had always found off-putting. "We believe your detail was compromised, Mr. President. Not to worry though. We're almost there. You'll be wheels up in five minutes."

"Thank you," Drake said. Things were happening much too fast for him to make sense of them. He relaxed a notch when they turned through the secure gate at Boeing Field and pulled up alongside Air Force One.

Drake very nearly threw up when he stepped on board. He would have fled the plane had not the steward shut the boarding door behind him.

Waiting in the executive seating area just inside the door sat Winfield Palmer, Chairman of the Joint Chiefs Admiral Ricks, Secretary of Defense Andrew Filson,

former Secretary of State Melissa Ryan, and Virginia
Ross, former director of the CIA.

"Admiral," Drake coughed, trying to still the spinning in his head. "These people are fugitives . . . Secretary
Filson, I'm appointing you acting Attorney General and
ordering you to place them under arrest. . . ." His gaze shot
around the plane, falling on the form of another man
seated three seats back with his head down. Drake's
legs buckled when he realized it was Jericho Quinn—
bruised and bandaged but very much alive. The reality
of his situation came crashing down around him with a
suddenness that made it hard to breathe, let alone keep
his feet.

"Have a seat, Hartman," Win Palmer said.

"I am the President—"

Palmer shook his head. "We're way beyond that," he
whispered.

Drake's eyes locked on Quinn, who had not moved
from his seat. "Keep him away from me. . . ." He turned
to the admiral. "What is this? A coup?"

"Think of it more as career advice," Andrew Filson
said. "Something for you to think about when your acting term is expired."

"Even in the capacity as acting President," Melissa
Ryan said, "you can still nominate an acting Vice President. The senate would have to approve, but under
present circumstances I believe they'll be glad if anyone wants the job."

"Who?" Drake glared at Palmer. "Am I supposed to
nominate you?"

Palmer shook his head. "No," he said. "I prefer to
work outside the bounds of that office. I'd say we kill
you now, but neither the Speaker of the House nor Senate President Pro Tem want the gig—and Lord knows
we don't want your Secretary of State filling your

shoes. Admiral Ricks, on the other hand, would make a
fine choice. He will take over as acting president upon
your resignation and withdrawal from public life, calling for a special election so the people will actually
have a chance to vote for the leader of the free world.
You had a good run, Drake. Got a little booty in the
Oval Office and got to play big man for a few months
while your VP tried to get us into a war. But it's over.
It's really your call how you go out. And, I have to say,
at this point, your choices are limited."

Epilogue

Two weeks later

The muggy DC weather caused Quinn's suit to stick to his skin as he exited onto the West Wing portico with Ronnie Garcia by his side and nodded to the uniformed Secret Service officer. Hot as it was, the air smelled of roses and freshly cut grass.

The Black Dragon was safely ensconced in a Pentagon lab. The Chinese hadn't liked it, but at least they had not threatened a war. Sources in the Middle Kingdom said that General Sun had found himself in prison shortly after Song had called in to report.

Like the East German Stasi, the IDTF found itself disbanded in a single day. The FBI had already started investigations on senior leadership and many of the younger agents were all too happy to flip and testify against their bosses.

Grateful to be alive and breathing the humid air, Quinn used his left hand to peel away the necktie that Palmer had forced him to wear to the meeting in the Oval Office. His right arm was in a sling.

Senator Gorski had used her clout with the select committee on intelligence to pave the way for Win Palmer to be named as acting National Security Advisor. The position ordinarily didn't need senate approval, but under the game of musical chairs that had become the presidency it seemed prudent to get some consensus from somewhere.

A free man for the first time in months, Quinn pitched the tie into the bed of a shiny black GMC pickup, hoping it would blow out when they reached the Beltway and got up to speed. He opened the door for Garcia and helped her up on the running board with his good arm. A patchwork of sutures hashtagged her cheeks and upper lip. Both eyes were ringed in black like she was wearing a bandit mask. She still couldn't lift either arm much above her waist. Though she wouldn't be doing pull-ups any time soon, her doctor said the chances of regaining full use of her arms were outstanding.

"Well ain't this something?" Jacques Thibodaux said as he walked out behind them, wearing his wife, Camille, like a second skin at his side. He'd shattered his fist on Big Uncle's jaw and his hand was now enveloped in a white cast up to the forearm. "I guess my brave little woman is the onliest one well enough to drive us into the sunset."

"I'm not sure I can ever thank you enough," Ronnie said to Camille from the backseat as she climbed in beside her husband. She didn't mention Kim, who had been cleared to fly and was already in Russia preparing to bring Mattie back to Alaska—where Jericho and Ronnie would meet them.

"Jacques has told me stories." Camille grinned. "I just tried to imagine what you would do." She gave an embarrassed laugh, situating herself behind the wheel.

"I can't believe the President just resigned from public life."

"Well, sugar," Jacques said, "you been through enough to know he didn't exactly resign. He and the guy who held Ronnie prisoner are spending a little quality time together in a black-site prison of their own while we see how much information they actually know."

"What about the Chinese girl?" Camille said, turning to look at Jericho over her shoulder. "Have I been through enough to know about her too?"

Quinn chuckled, though it hurt his ribs. He still found it difficult to take a deep breath without grimacing. "As a matter of fact, she called this morning from the hospital in Beijing. They had to take a good portion of her foot because of the burn, but she doesn't seem too upset about it." Quinn smiled inside himself at the thought of the brave Chinese spy. "I guess the Ministry of State Security feels their agents need to have two good feet. She's been given an early retirement to focus on her music."

Thibodaux half twisted in the seat, peering over his broad shoulder with his good eye. "Where we gonna go now, *l'ami*?"

"I don't know about you," Ronnie said. "But this being wounded stuff makes me hungry. How about RT's?"

Thibodaux slapped the back of his seat at the mention of this favorite Cajun restaurant off Mt Vernon Avenue. "Now you're talkin'," he said. "Puttin' the brakes on the Muslim Caliphate does work up an appetite."

"This is all just like some action movie," Camille said, waiting for the Secret Service to open the gate that would take them past the bollards on the closed portion of Pennsylvania Avenue. She glanced in the rearview mirror, smiling to finally play a bigger role in this part of her husband's life. "I heard someone on the news say Hollywood is tired of Islamic terrorists," she said.

Jericho rested a hand in Ronnie Garcia's lap and they exchanged a knowing glance. "So am I," he said. "So am I."

ACKNOWLEDGMENTS

In tactical training we are ever practicing to "shoot, move, and communicate." I hope my books carry forward that same sentiment.

As usual, I've taken a bit of literary license with the small details, in an effort to tell a fast story without giving the bad guys too much real stuff without making them work for it. It is, for instance, a little more difficult to waltz into Seattle with a load of terrorists in your boat than I make it out to be, thanks in no small part to the good folks at Customs and Border Protection. That said, the border is a big place, and they can't be everywhere.

I had a great deal of help in researching all the shooting, moving, and communicating. Aaron Gough provided insight into the Springfield Armory XDs, a pistol I don't currently own. Ty Cunningham, my friend and jujitsu instructor, walked with me through the fight scenes, exploring the dynamics of real-time, nose-to-nose violence.

Thanks to Ben for all the help with Mandarin and to Dan for letting me use him as a sounding board.

Skipper Steve Arlow helped immensely by allowing me to spend a few days aboard his 65-foot boat in Southeast Alaska, exploring and imagining the possibilities.

Mike, Lori, Ray, Ryan, and Doug down at Northern Knives in Anchorage provided much entertainment as we discussed various blades and techniques. Scott Ireton remains a friend and valuable bike expert, as do Andy and Troy at the BMW shop in Salt Lake.

I consider myself a horseman, but I had my friend, Jill Marshall (who also happens to be an expert *pistolera*) check my ideas for the *buzkashi* match, utilizing her expertise in dressage and other equine matters.

Earlier this year I bought a little Bond Arms derringer, thinking it would be perfect for Ronnie Garcia to carry. I didn't know how right I was. I need to give a big thanks to Gordon Bond and my new friends at Bond Arms for the factory tour and in-depth discussion about the Snake Slayer.

My friend Dan Cooper continues to inspire me with tales of his motorcycle trips through Central Asia. I really want to be like him when I grow up.

My agent, Robin Rue, her assistant, Beth Miller, and my editor, Gary Goldstein—and all the folks at Kensington—are some of the best people I've ever met, in or out of the publishing business.

As always, thanks to my sweet wife, Victoria, who deserves all the credit and none of the blame.